ASLEEP

Book I of III

Wendy Raven McNair

Scribbler & Sketcher

ISBN-10: 1442125241
EAN-13: 9781442125247

For my daughter KJ and all girls like her
past, present, and future.

ASLEEP

Book I of III

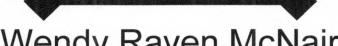

Wendy Raven McNair

CONTENTS

1 ~ FIRST DAY OF SCHOOL

Many times I've been asleep with the distinct impression that someone has just called my name. One instant I'm floating in emptiness, the black void of nothing, and the next, my ears pursue in what direction the suggestion of my name has retreated, vainly searching to locate the source. But I am alone.

I was perfectly still, eyes closed, pondering the change I sensed. The cause of the difference eluded me. The house was quiet and there were no breakfast aromas. The absence of the scent of freshly ground coffee in particular, indicated nobody was up yet. After a few minutes I gave up my mental pursuits and rolled out of bed to trudge to the restroom, feeling completely worn out.

My older twin sisters had a Jack and Jill set up, sharing a restroom that separated their bedrooms toward the back of the house. When we were younger, the twins occupied one of those bedrooms and the other one was mine. When our parents remodeled, adding a master bedroom to the downstairs, one of the twins took my room and I inherited my parent's old upstairs bedroom. That's how I came to have a larger room than my sisters with its own restroom even though I'm the youngest in my family.

I silently performed my morning rituals while mentally contemplating yet another first day of school. When I was done, I inspected my face in the mirror. My dark brown complexion didn't conceal the fresh blemish that had sprouted during the night. I rubbed some acne ointment on the tiny defect. My small afro was working a nice halo effect, gleaming from the conditioner I'd quickly combed through my damp hair. Satisfied with what I saw, I turned away from the mirror before the critical voices in my head could get started which inevitably happened whenever I lingered too long in the mirror.

I stepped into a pair of faded jeans and pulled on a soft emerald blouse with bell sleeves. I could hear people moving around downstairs and a familiar coffee aroma was now wafting upstairs as I crossed over to my desk for my shoes and backpack. My feet wiggled into my shoes while I glanced out the window which had a view of the front yard. A moving truck was parked just up the street and I hesitated in an attempt to catch a glimpse of the new neighbors. My vision was partially blocked by the large marigold and Georgia pine trees but it was evident nobody was out.

I looked over my room thinking I should straighten up some. So I quickly picked up some dirty clothes and tossed them in the hamper, wiped down my restroom, organized some of the clutter on top of my dresser and righted a photograph of my mom holding me when I was a newborn. I surveyed my room one final time before heading downstairs, realizing no matter how hard I tried I would always have the messiest room in our home. Everybody else in my family was a neat freak. Somehow, I'd missed out on that particular gene.

"Mornin' Super Girl."

I cringed at my too familiar nick name earned through my devotion to playing superhero characters way past the age of acceptable behavior. Kylie, in baggy shorts and an over sized T-shirt, sat at the table in the breakfast nook, grinning at me. Her shoulder length dark hair was messily pulled back in an elastic band. Even in her morning disarray she still looked amazing. I considered her the nice twin so I decided to ignore her annoying greeting.

I dropped my backpack next to an empty chair and leaned over to give my dad, who was also seated at the table, a peck on the cheek.

He grunted, "Mornin' String Bean," without looking up from the Atlanta Journal Constitution. His nickname for me, referring to my thin lanky physique, was more acceptable than Kylie's but still irritating.

"There's a moving truck out front," I announced, aware my mom would be pleased to know the house across the street was finally going to be occupied by legitimate tenants. She twisted around from the stove to offer me her cheek and I dutifully pecked it.

"I know. I'll walk over and introduce myself later. I haven't seen anybody out there yet." She cracked an egg into a hot pan that already contained turkey sausages and the sizzling sound rose sharply.

I took a plate off the shelf and placed a slice of bread on it and filled a cup with apple juice from the pantry then turned back to the stove. Mom was waiting and slid the contents of the pan onto my bread and I plopped another slice on top. I was thinking it was great to have them home for breakfast. Usually they would be at work before I woke up but they each took a week off to help the twins prepare to move for their first year of college.

"How're you feeling this morning," mom asked with heavy concern, and just that quickly my warm feelings vanished at the hint of being babied.

"Fine," I said, trying not to show too much attitude. I believed the several inches I had above her in height entitled me to more adult treatment.

I thanked her for the egg and sausage and sat at the table across from my sister.

"I thought I heard you last night...," mom began worrying over me but she was cut off.

"Adeee-sah!" Kylie said my name with disapproving emphasis. "You're a sophomore now, at least make an effort."

I knew she was referring to the fact that I wasn't wearing any makeup but I feigned ignorance. She twisted her beautiful face at me not fooled at all.

"Okay, Adisa, it's time to stop trying to be the son dad will never have. Seriously, you need to get over the grubby girl thing and start embracing your feminine side."

Her words stung and I reconsidered whether she was the nice twin after all as I tried to think of a cutting retort.

"Leave your sister alone. She's fine just the way she is," dad recited in his subdued baritone as he turned the page to his newspaper and absentmindedly rubbed his shoulder. He picked up his coffee and brought it to his lips without even looking.

I was still trying to think of a comeback when I noticed the white sheet of paper Kylie was tapping in agitation. I wondered if it might be why she was actually up before noon when she didn't have to be.

"What's that?" I asked, curious in spite of myself.

She paused in consideration, then flipped the paper over, shoved it across to me and sighed. "Since we won't be there to look after you at Talbot this year, I thought maybe this would help."

The drawing, as usual, was absolutely flawless. Written across the bottom in a dramatic flair of her pen was 'Awesome Adisa's Avenging Angel.'

My eyes went back to the image above the words. Light curving strokes detailed the avenging angel's magnificent wings as they protectively swept forward enclosing me, the damsel in distress. Kylie had perfectly captured my likeness with a few clean strokes, even making me look pretty. However, I couldn't help feeling a twinge of disappointment.

Kylie, catching my expression, laughed out loud. "You wish I'd made you the superhero, don't you!?"

I shoved the drawing into my backpack, embarrassed at being so easily read, then started on my sandwich.

Family conversation drifted around me but I didn't listen. I eased into one of my favorite past times, daydreaming. My dad claims I daydream a lot because I don't dream when I sleep so my mind tries to make up for it during the day.

My brain lazily sifted through a few of my favorite stored imaginings, featuring me in the starring role of superhero. Of course, I kept the details of these daydreams strictly to myself, having learned on several painfully humiliating occasions that it was better for me to do so at my advanced age.

My thoughts were drawn to a vague image hovering in the recesses of my consciousness. The change I sensed when I first awakened suddenly revealed fully formed in my mind.

"I had a dream last night," I blurted out.

My mom, sister, and even my dad looked at me in disbelief because they were well aware that I'd never had a dream in my whole life.

"Well don't keep us in suspense," my dad encouraged, folding his paper aside.

I frowned trying to wrestle the details from my hazy memories. "I was in a field...," I began tentatively.

Mom rushed in, defensively, "Oh Adisa! We've told you that story over a hundred times so you were just daydreaming again.

You were only a toddler when we accidentally left you out in that field and…,"

"I know mom but it wasn't a daydream. I was sleeping and in my dream I was in a dark field and… I wasn't alone," I hesitated. "There was a little boy there and…," I trailed off.

The expression on their faces prevented me from adding the details of the boy's beautiful copper colored skin and how he held my hand and sang to me so I wouldn't be afraid.

If I felt like the freak of the family before, due to my lifelong superhero complex and inability to dream, this certainly wasn't going to help. I realized too late that announcing I'd had my first dream ever and the topic was about what they considered the most traumatic incident in my life, wasn't a smart move to make if I wanted to make it out of the house without drama. So, I decided I'd said enough and promptly shut up.

When I didn't offer up any more information, my dad sighed and exchanged a look with my mom who began to fidget nervously.

"There was no little boy in that field with you," she stated quietly. "There was nobody with you at all except for the good Lord watching over you," she finished under her breath and her bottom lip trembled.

I felt bad for bringing it up, they obviously felt guilty about it, so I tried to lighten things. "You're probably right, I'm just repeating stories I've heard before. I'm an idiot for bringing it up. Forget I mentioned it."

Stupid! Stupid! Stupid! I thought, watching my parents' concerned expressions. But nobody commented any further. After awhile, to my relief, normal morning conversation resumed. And the memory of my dream receded.

Packed suitcases and boxes cluttered the family room floor, evidence of Kelly and Kylie's imminent departure for college. This knowledge failed to thrill me like I thought it would.

I liked my sisters well enough but it's amazing what it does to a girl's self esteem to be so ordinary in the midst of so much beauty. I had eagerly been counting down the years, months, weeks until they left home only to discover now, with only a few days before that greatly anticipated event, that maybe having them around wasn't so bad after all.

Down the hall and out onto our porch, I could feel Georgia's early morning warmth. I descended the porch stairs and crossed the street to the sidewalk that ran along only one side of the road.

The moving truck was finally showing signs of activity with side doors opened wide revealing some of its contents. I spotted a massive head board but I didn't have time to be nosy so I turned in the opposite direction, toward school.

On one side of the road, there was an empty lot and on the other, a thickly wooded expanse of land that extended from behind our home and stretched down the road all the way to my school. Leafy ropes of kudzu vines draped themselves around the trees, piling up so thick in some places that it created giant green sculptures that often took the shape of familiar objects.

I enjoyed guessing what these gigantic natural artworks resembled as much as some people enjoyed guessing what cloud formations resembled. The massive green shapes seemed solid and immobile until the right breeze caught it and sent the whole figure flouncing and swaying in weightless wonder.

The woods had always fueled my imagination, fascinated by its promise of unexplored adventures while at the same time apprehensive of its impenetrable tangle of overgrowth. I often wondered what mysterious creatures peered from its depths to watch me pass.

The walk to school was about a mile and didn't take long. I ran the route regularly over the summer to use my school's outdoor track for exercise. Soon, I could see the faded blue buildings of Talbot Academy in the distance.

Talbot was one of those non-traditional high schools in which class lines were blurred. Upper and lower classmen sometimes shared the same class because placement was determined by interests or test scores rather than age. My greatest fear when I started as a freshman the previous year was that I might actually end up sharing a class with my sisters. Thankfully that hadn't occurred.

Usually, people, upon discovering my kinship to the twins, would inevitably begin comparing us. The first comment would register shock over how different our coloring was, my deep mahogany skin standing out in contrast to their lighter balsa skin tones.

Then it would move on to the fact that I was two full inches taller than my sisters even though I was three years younger than they were. It would go on and on with me cringing inside, feeling like I was part of some crazy aptitude test measuring visual intelligence by requiring participants to identify which sister was not like the rest.

Talbot's staff was given the freedom to conduct their classes anyway they saw fit as long as the students performed well on state tests. So we were plied with a variety of unconventional lessons and teaching styles throughout the year and a competitive spirit was cultivated in the student body as a whole. Talbot also allowed some students to forego some classes if they found a suitable internship that added value to the learning experience. Pretty advanced for high school.

I finally made it to campus and cut across the parking lot, heading for homeroom. I knew where it was because it was the same as it was the year before and would be the same for the duration of my education at Talbot. Just like its name 'homeroom' implied, it was the *home* you returned to every year even though all your other classes changed rooms based on your new schedule. Homerooms were assigned based on a student's last name so my class was filled with surnames starting with S.

I said hi to people I recognized as I made my way over to one of the few friends I'd managed to overcome my shyness with and forge a true bond of friendship. Probably because it was established when we were very young and I hadn't completely retreated into my protective angry shell yet. Avery's creamy complexion and dark mass of curls, confirming his biracial heritage, was a welcome sight. I sat next to him.

"How was your summer?" he asked then quickly followed with, "Have the twins left for Bartlett yet?"

I made a face but then thought it was at least nice of him to ask about my summer before sniffing out news on my sisters.

"My summer was fine, thanks for asking. And the twins haven't left yet. My parents are going to convoy them there this Friday."

Avery frowned, not quite understanding.

"They have a lot of stuff to transport so they're taking both cars to haul it all. Plus, my mom gave Kelly her car as a graduation gift so my parents will leave that car there and come back in my dad's car," I clarified.

"You're not going with them?" he asked, with mild shock.

"Nope," I beamed, unable to contain my excitement over being left home alone for the very first time in my life, even though it was just for one night.

"I can't believe you're skipping out on the opportunity to spend time with the twins on a college campus," he said in disbelief.

Of course, being a guy that would be his fantasy. Mine, was of an empty house all to myself where I could do whatever I wanted without getting overruled. But I wasn't up for explaining so I just shrugged my shoulders.

"Oh yeah, and I think a family of giants are taking up residence in the house across the street from us. Now my mom can stop worrying about addicts breaking in and turning it into a crack house," I added.

"New neighbors, interesting. Have you met them yet?"

"No but I'm sure mom will be over there trying to stuff them with her cooking before the week is out," I replied.

He told me about his summer travels. His parents had money and they usually went away to exotic places over the summer. This time, they had gone to Africa. I swallowed my jealousy and told him how happy I was for him after he briefly shared some of his adventures.

The bell rang and morning announcements started. Each of the classrooms at Talbot had closed-circuit TV which the student audio visual club used to give the announcements. The AVC was an inept group but they made up in determination what they lacked in skill. Mr. Preston, the principal, was giving a welcome and his frame completely filled the whole TV screen. He reminded me more of a linebacker than a principal. Somebody adjusted the zoom, briefly cutting off Mr. Preston's head, then reversed it so he was perfectly centered on the screen.

My homeroom teacher, Mr. Dunley, stated locker assignments would be given out later in the week and had a student pass out class schedules while the announcements droned on. I compared my schedule to Avery's. We had second period gym and last period math together.

I wasn't crazy about gym but it was mandatory every semester and last year's track and field assignments weren't so bad. I enjoyed the running so much, I continued it on my own over the summer. Besides, I knew we wouldn't have to change into our gym clothes since it was early release day and we wouldn't have time. As for math, I absolutely adored it.

The announcements ended with a reminder that this was an early release day, each class would have shortened hours, basically giving everybody a brief introduction to class schedules and sorting out syllabus expectations before beginning the full class hours and instructions the following day. Homeroom was always short, lasting long enough to take attendance, give the announcements and pass out any pertinent school information so the bell rang shortly after the announcements ended.

"See you in gym. Time to go learn some colorful language," Avery said. At Talbot, English classes were referred to as Language Arts. Avery's jokes were hit or miss. That was a miss.

I rolled my eyes, embarrassed for him.

"By the way, I like your new do," he threw over his shoulder, indicating my hair, and hurried off to his first class. I smiled in appreciation as I left the room.

I was excited about my computer class. Over the summer, Kylie had shown me some interesting things on her MacBook Pro, her graduation present. Her plans to major in graphic design, made getting a laptop computer a priority over getting a car and she was just as thrilled with her gift as Kelly was with her car.

The computer room had a bank of computers lined along one very long table against a back wall and groups of four computers on two smaller tables facing each other spread around the middle of the room. I picked a computer in a group of four not wanting to face a wall for the whole semester while working on my assignments. The two computers across from me were soon taken while the one next to me was ignored. I eagerly turned on my computer and waited for it to warm up as I watched students file into the class.

"Please do not turn your computers on until I instruct you to do so," Ms. Fulton stated without turning from the wipe board she was writing on.

I sighed, thinking it's going to be *that* kind of class as I turned the computer off. Patience was not part of my skill set and the idea of being forced to slowly plod through exercises with the whole class when, thanks to Kylie, I had the ability to zip through the basics and start tackling more complex assignments, did not appeal to me.

More students slowly filled the room but the seat next to me remained empty. I wasn't surprised. My social ineptitude was another one of my flaws the twins teased me about. I did not possess their charm and wit to make and keep friends with ease, another gene trait I missed out on. More often than not, I sat alone.

I was glumly watching the last stragglers come into class when *he* stepped through the door. The noisy conversations that filled the room dropped noticeably, so much so that even Ms. Fulton turned from the wipe board to see what was going on.

He paused just inside the door for a moment, but not like he was unsure of himself. Quite the opposite, he carried himself with a confidence unusual for someone so young but without the cockiness some exceptionally good-looking people had.

His incredibly handsome face was expressionless as he surveyed the classroom. His eyes briefly locked with mine and the foolish thought that he was looking for me flashed through my mind. Obviously wishful thinking on my part because then his vacant eyes passed over me as he searched for an empty seat.

There weren't very many left but there were a couple of open spots near him. I watched, transfixed as he started toward them. He paused, deciding which to take, then my breath caught in my throat as he passed them and continued down the aisle toward me.

My heart, which apparently had stopped beating when he first stepped through the door, suddenly launched back into action as he got closer. Its commotion increased with each step that brought him nearer to my table until I thought surely everybody in the room could hear it pounding. I was confused and shocked by my reaction because I'd never reacted to a boy in that way.

He pulled out the chair next to me and sat down, his back rigid, without saying a word. As soon as he was seated, the noise volume of the class went back up, higher than it was originally. I could hear the excited voices of girls near my table and for once thought it was warranted.

His shoulders were wide with well-formed muscles evident beneath the nice cut of his clothes. His skin was an indescribable shade that stood out in startling contrast to his white shirt. His hands rested on his blue jean clad thighs, palms down as he sat staring forward with his unbelievably erect back. Tightly curled black hair covered his head and tapered to soft waves at his neck. I couldn't see a single flaw. He was perfect, a work of art.

Suddenly he turned and met my gaze with a distant look that was void of emotion and I realized I was staring at him. I quickly averted my eyes, embarrassed to be caught acting like the star struck girls I normally scorned. At that moment, I regretted not having some of their flirtatious talent to attract him with. I hated myself for having that thought.

What was wrong with me? Had I suddenly become as insane as all the other girls around me? As my sisters?

My hands were on the table and I realized they were actually trembling so I shoved them under the table onto my lap. Out of the corner of my eye I saw him turn back to looking straight ahead.

The bell rang and Ms. Fulton started talking but I didn't hear anything she said. I was too intensely aware of everything the new boy was doing, which was absolutely nothing but it captured my total attention anyway. I stole a quick side glance at him. He sat so still it seemed as if he wasn't breathing. His steady gaze followed Ms. Fulton as she moved about the class. After awhile, my racing heart managed to return closer to its normal rhythm.

Ms. Fulton instructed us to take notes, stating that the information she was giving us today would be the basics we would need to succeed in her class. She called roll as we took out our notebooks.

I lifted my backpack onto my lap and rummaged for pen and paper. I pulled out Kylie's drawing and was momentarily distracted from my preoccupation with the gorgeous boy sitting only inches from me.

The Avenging Angel's wings embraced me protectively. A profusion of delicate feathers defensively hid most of my body but my face was fully revealed, unlike the angel's. Only his glaring eyes peered above the plumes from around me to ward off danger.

I smiled at my protector, making a mental note to thank my sister since I'd still been too mad at her at the time to do so. I placed the drawing on my desk and pulled out my notebook. I sensed my seat companion looking at the drawing. I worked up the nerve to steal a quick look at him and found him calmly checking me out.

Seeing an excuse to speak to him, I impulsively offered in a voice barely a whisper, "My sister drew it for me. He's supposed to protect me now that she's not here to...," My voice trailed off weakly at the end as I watched him turn away without even a glimmer of interest in his eyes. *Maybe he didn't hear me* I thought hopefully but I didn't have the confidence to try again.

"Micah Alexander," Ms. Fulton called.

"Present," he responded, his smooth boy's tenor startling my heart back into its racket.

Ms. Fulton looked at him and even she seemed a bit disconcerted by his presence.

Thrilled with the knowledge of his name, my mind chanted Micah over and over, playing with this new toy as Ms. Fulton continued to call roll. Micah Alexander, what a perfect name for the mystery boy. *Adisa Alexander*, I tried out, recalling how Kelly repeatedly joined her name to Beverly's in a variety of combinations when they first started dating.

I certainly didn't plan on marrying Micah. But I got a strange rush thinking of our names joined together, my mind thoroughly entertained by the silly immature game. *Adisa Alexander... Adisa Summers-Alexander...*

"Adisa Summers... Adisa Summers!"

"Here!" I answered in a rush, realizing the teacher was calling my name. I glanced at Micah. The mention of my name didn't

seem to have the same effect on him as his name had on me.
Neither his posture nor his expression had changed.

Ms. Fulton completed calling roll and quickly went over some
computer basics before the bell rang. I gathered my things and
headed out the door before Micah. I left, feeling upset. I tried to
convince myself it was due to the fact that we never even turned
on the computers and not because Micah Alexander hadn't said a
single word to me.

When I entered the gym, I saw Avery standing near Liz but
not talking to her. I breathed a sigh of relief at the sight of him.

During our freshman year, Avery had a crush on Liz but never
worked up the courage to approach her and it appeared this was
going to be a repeat of the previous year. I remembered teasing
him about liking strawberries and he would blush knowing I was
referring to red headed Liz. It got to the point that just mentioning
strawberries turned him crimson.

I walked over and stood in the space between them, nodding a
greeting to Liz and punching Avery while jerking my thumb at Liz
but so she couldn't see. Avery quickly shook his head no, with
panic in his eyes.

I sighed in frustration.

"Be my partner," Avery said to me low and in a rush.

"What?"

"Just say yes," he pleaded.

"Okay, yes. Now tell me what I'm agreeing to."

"He's making us dance this year," he said, nodding his head
in the direction of the coach.

"No!" I gasped, unprepared for this unconventional class
twist. What happened to track and field?

I looked at Mr. Winton disapprovingly. At Talbot, we didn't
refer to the coaches as coach. All teachers were either Mr. or Ms.
regardless of any other titles they possessed.

"Girls stay on this side, boys go to the other end," Mr. Winton
commanded and Avery wasn't able to tell me more.

Liz tugged on my sleeve. "I almost didn't recognize you with
your new hairstyle. It's nice. How was your summer?" I noticed
she was staring at my hair but clasped her hands together as if she
was resisting the urge to touch it.

She had grown her own hair out and her glasses were missing. Poor Avery, she was even prettier this year than last.

"Thanks. It was all right. How was yours? I see you're missing your glasses," I responded.

"My vision miraculously self-corrected," she enthused, looking flushed that I'd noticed. "It freaked me out at first and my dad couldn't believe it but the doctor confirmed it. The best part was when my brothers threw a fit because their favorite summer entertainment of hiding my glasses and watching me stumble around like an idiot looking for them was ruined."

"Well, you look great."

"Thanks, Adisa."

"All right everybody," Mr. Winton began, "I'm going to do this quickly because I want you all to pair up and get in a couple of turns around the floor before the bell. The gentleman makes the request, 'May I have this dance' and the lady responds, 'Yes, thank you.' And then they dance. Simple.

Today we're just jumping in and getting our feet wet. Formal dance instruction starts tomorrow and we'll cover a variety of Latin styles this semester. I'll take roll while you're dancing so gentleman, please begin."

Somebody started the dance music and all the boys, dazed by Mr. Winton's abrupt instructions, started hesitantly toward the girls, except for Avery; he was striding confidently in my direction.

I was a little overwhelmed with how quickly things were moving, but grateful, that Avery was going to be my partner; no agonizing over who would pick me or whether I'd get picked at all.

Liz's green eyes stared across the gym in apprehension. "I hate this," she said under her breath.

"Avery said he'd be my partner," I said, so selfishly immersed in my immunity from impending humiliation I didn't think to pity her. Avery was one of the few boys at Talbot who had actually caught up to and passed me in height. And probably the only boy on the planet I would actually feel comfortable dancing with so closely.

As he came forward, I beamed my appreciation and he smiled back. But just as he was about to pass by Liz to get to me, her hand suddenly shot out and snagged his arm.

"Avery, pick me, please," she said, urgently.

Avery's eyes lit up like Christmas and he just nodded his head without making the request. Liz gave me an apologetic smile and they were off and dancing, leaving me with my jaw on the floor. Traitors!

I swallowed the lump in my throat as I scanned the remaining line of prospects.

I heard a nervous laugh on my other side and turned to see Lucia standing next to me. I looked at her long wavy hair and large dark eyes. She had nothing to be nervous about.

I watched the wall of boys advancing and tried to adopt a posture of nonchalance. Several couples were already dancing and I saw Mr. Winton walking amongst them with his roll book. Fran and Dee, best friends usually joined at the hip, danced next to each other, talking while ignoring their partners.

Then I spotted Avery and Liz, laughing and dancing across the floor quite well together. I tried to crush them with the force of my glare but they weren't paying any attention to me.

"Who is that?" Lucia's awed lilting accent interrupted my thoughts. I turned, scanning the line of boys again to see who she was referring to. The second I spotted him I knew Micah was the subject in question. My heart skipped a beat, a fierce possessiveness taking hold.

"I don't know," I heard Sonjia answer from the other side of Lucia. "But he is fine!"

Sonjia was a member of my church but we weren't particularly close. Not everybody who sits on a pew can be considered a saint and Sonjia was definitely missing the charitable nature Christians were supposed to strive for.

When we were younger, before I got my first perm, Sonjia made fun of me for not having good hair like my sisters. When I told my mom, she said everybody had good hair—hair the good Lord rooted in each and every head. However, not long after that, mom brought a perm kit home and spread the thick white viscous contents on my hair. I returned to church the following Sunday overjoyed my hair was now just like my sisters' and I shook my bone straight tresses all up in Sonjia's face.

Micah and a number of other boys were headed our way and they all had their eyes glued on Lucia as the prize. They certainly weren't racing for me or Sonjia, the female versions of Laurel and Hardy, physically not comically.

The boys were moving fast but not running because nobody wanted to appear that desperate. Micah was in the lead but Justin was a close second and I could see the distress in his eyes as he contemplated how to out maneuver Micah. Justin looked frantic while Micah seemed quite calm, easily maintaining his lead position. It was comical watching the boys jostle for position and Justin seemed to seriously consider shoving Micah aside.

As they neared, I looked at Lucia and could clearly tell who she wanted to win and fortunately for her, he was in the lead. I was somewhat surprised, however, because I thought she and Justin had started dating during our freshman year. Then I took another look at Micah's stunning features and had to concede, I'd make an exception for him myself.

I took a step to the side to avoid being trampled and bumped into someone. I looked up surprised it was Micah. I had inadvertently stepped right into his path.

"Sorry," I mumbled embarrassed and took a step back to get out of his way. He followed, stepping forward with his hand extended.

"May I have this dance?" His voice was as mesmerizing as his face even though neither held a hint of feeling. I blinked in confusion.

I saw Justin triumphantly step past Micah, deliver his request to Lucia and grab her arm, practically dragging her onto the gym floor without waiting for her reply. She gave Micah a disappointed look as she was being towed away. The other boys looked equally dissatisfied as they turned to seek out alternate partners.

Micah was waiting patiently. I tried to collect my thoughts as I stared at his flawless skin, still unable to describe its radiant color. I forced my mind to recall the appropriate response to his request and finally managed, "Yes."

I gave him my hand and felt myself tremble at his touch. I thought I saw something flash in Micah's blank gaze but it was so brief I couldn't be sure as his glazed over eyes now calmly observed me. His face retained its emotionless composure as he drew me into his arms. It was my first time being so close to a boy and I worried he might hear my heart's wildly irregular beat.

I tried to calm my nerves and sort out my jumbled thoughts but his arms were urging me along in a dance that my feet refused to cooperate in. I struggled to get them under control.

I had to look up to see Micah's eyes because he was actually taller than I was. They were a gentle brown and even though we were close together, they maintained a distance in them. I stepped right onto his foot.

"Oops! Sorry. I'm so clumsy," I exclaimed, nervously.

He paused but showed no other reaction. We started again and he subtly adjusted his movement to make it easier for me. I was so distracted by our touching I managed only three steps before coming down hard on his foot again.

My hand clutched at the firm muscle of his shoulder to prevent myself from falling into him and I could feel the strength in his hands as they steadied me.

"Sorry! I'm such an idiot," I muttered, seriously upset with myself.

I trembled like a leaf in a strong wind, dying inside because I knew he could feel it. Apparently he didn't have similar qualms because he was as steady as a rock.

Again we tried. I moved awkwardly in his arms trying to stay away from his toes but eventually, I got them again.

"P- p- please, I really... really ap- pologize," I stuttered.

I glanced into his beautiful hazel eyes and they were devoid of any compassion, they were completely empty. We started again with me practically stumbling around the floor because I was afraid to move at all. But no matter how carefully I moved, I ended up on his toes.

We continued that way, dancing a few steps, me getting his toes and then apologizing and berating myself. Through it all, he maintained a detached air and I was amazed he didn't appear upset in the least over the abuse his feet were suffering.

When the music stopped, mercifully ending our painful ordeal, I quickly stepped away from him, so ashamed I couldn't even look at him.

"I completely understand if you don't want to be my partner next time," I admitted, giving him an easy out before he had a chance to reject me first.

Why couldn't Mr. Winton teach us track and field like he did last year, I thought miserably.

Mr. Winton came by with his roll book. "No you can't change. All partner assignments are final," he was saying to the previous couple as he approached us.

If I hadn't been so stressed out, I might have found it funny how standing next to Micah made Mr. Winton look like a small angry child. I was at least two heads taller than Mr. Winton myself.

I looked at the couple he was speaking to and they both looked highly upset with each other and with Mr. Winton's decision as well. I felt a twinge of dread.

Mr. Winton addressed us. "Okay, Adisa and this is...,"

"Micah," I supplied without thinking and then immediately wanted to take it back. I didn't want Micah to think I was obsessing over him, knowing his name before he even introduced himself to me.

"Micah...," Mr. Winton repeated, his pause indicating he was waiting for a last name.

I clamped my mouth shut, refusing to humiliate myself further by supplying it even though I knew perfectly well what it was.

"Alexander," Micah's voice rumbled evenly, raising goose bumps on my arms. I self consciously tried to rub them away, feeling foolish.

Mr. Winton searched and found the name on his roll.

"This is your first time here at Talbot?" he asked.

"Yes."

"And you're a junior, correct?"

"Yes."

"Welcome to Talbot, Micah. I'm sure you'll do well in this class. I noticed you had a very nice frame for your partner while you were dancing."

Mr. Winton said all this while noting our names on a sheet of paper attached to the clipboard beneath the roll sheet. Then he informed us we would be partners for the semester before moving on to the next couple.

In an instant, I realized two things at once. First, Mr. Winton hadn't complimented nor offered a single word of encouragement to me regarding my dancing. And second, Micah would be forced to endure my assaults on his toes for an entire semester whether he liked it or not. As the bell rang, I couldn't get out fast enough.

Later in the day, Liz and Avery found me at lunch time even though the cafeteria was crowded.

"Who was that you were dancing with?" Liz asked enthusiastically, jostling the crowd for a position in line next to me.

"Micah," I said offhand, determined to keep all of my answers equally brief, hoping she would lose interest. Besides, I was still a little hurt because she stole Avery but I was too proud to mention it.

I noticed Avery was giving extra attention to his lunch selections. Either he was trying to avoid hearing Liz gush over another guy or he was too chicken to face me after his backstabbing move in gym.

We found a table and I steeled myself for Liz's onslaught, thinking our lunch time wasn't very long so she wouldn't have time to do too much damage. But I wasn't going down without a fight.

"What makes Mr. Winton think he can go from teaching track and field to teaching Latin dances!?" I said roughly, trying to redirect the topic.

"Micah is absolutely gorgeous," Liz declared, undeterred. "You did say his name was Micah, right?"

"Yeah," I answered dismissively before continuing my rant against Mr. Winton. "I mean, what qualifications does he have to teach any kind of dancing?"

"Maybe he does it in his spare time and just wanted something different this year," Avery offered helpfully. I suspected he was trying to make up for abandoning me for Liz on the gym floor but I appreciated his input anyway.

"Don't you think he's gorgeous, Adisa?" Liz asked without missing a beat.

"Who?" I stalled for time, taking a bite of my chicken patty.

"Micah, of course," she said impatiently. "Don't you think he's good looking?"

"I guess," I said, noncommittally.

Liz gasped. "Are you kidding!? Did you get a look at him? Avery, you saw him. Tell her how good looking he is," Liz demanded, as a couple of her friends, Fran and Dee, joined us.

Avery, a comedian at heart couldn't resist now that he had an audience. "Girl, he was fine!" he said giving his over the top sistah impersonation. "I'm telling you, I couldn't tear my eyes off of him and didn't want to either."

Liz giggled but refused to be distracted. "What did he say to you?" she asked me.

I frowned, picking over my lunch as it slowly dawned on me that outside of the formal request for a dance, Micah hadn't said a single word to me. I felt irritation start to wind its way uncomfortably through my thoughts. Why would a stranger apparently seek me out and then say nothing to me? Twice in one day! And what was up with his attitude or, more accurately, the absence of it?

"What did he say?" Liz repeated when I failed to give her an answer.

I shrugged and mumbled that I couldn't remember, unable to admit that he had said nothing, probably due to my horrific dancing.

Liz turned to her two friends for support. I got the distinct feeling that the three of them had already discussed the situation in depth as I recalled both Fran and Dee were also in Mr. Winton's class.

"Can you believe her?" Liz asked them.

"No!" Fran volunteered emphatically.

"Two words, Frances," Dee insisted, "total recall."

"That's what I'm trying to say, Delaney Rose," Fran agreed. "There's not a single solitary syllable that particular individual could utter in my presence that would ever escape my memory." She spoke in a serious tone while holding up her finger for emphasis. It was odd how they participated in the conversation but only addressed each other.

Avery and I exchanged a look and I knew that at some point in the near future, he would imitate their mannerisms so accurately, I'd be in tears laughing.

"Total recall," Dee repeated, confirming that Fran's words explained and revealed the meaning of her words in their totality.

They continued to speak in this fashion for the duration of lunch. Dee would say a few words, as abbreviated as their names, Fran and Dee. And then Fran would concur, elaborating at length. Then Dee would repeat her few words, confirming Fran's interpretation. I would've found it highly entertaining if I hadn't been busy deflecting Liz's Micah questions.

"Adisa, I can't believe you don't remember what he said to you," she continued. "I think he's interested in you. He walked right up to you and asked you! Like he knew you or something."

Her emphasis on you implied 'with Luscious Lucia standing right next to you' but Liz was at least kind enough not to go all the way there.

"I don't think he's interested in me. I know it sounds weird," I tried to clarify, "but it was like he was dancing with an object, not a person. I don't know how to explain it."

"But he picked you Adisa. That has to mean something," she pressed her point.

I was beginning to chafe under the stress she kept putting on *you*, which was sounding more and more like *repulsive beast*, and Avery picked up on it and came to my defense.

"Ease up Liz. She says it's no big deal."

"But he picked her Avery, out of all the other girls. If nothing else, the fact that he went out of his way to pick her is significant."

"Well, you picked me. Is there something significant in that?" he asked.

Liz became flustered and fortunately for me, other students came and sat down and the conversation finally shifted to less embarrassing topics. I smiled in gratitude at Avery and he gave me a wink.

The conversations droned on around me but I was only half attentive. Avery mentioned to Liz that he got his driver's license at the end of summer break and now his dad had him delivering for one of their restaurants.

"Frances, check out Miss Thang," Dee said while critically inspecting my head. "Nice hairstyle."

"I hear you, Delaney Rose. The whole crinkly, curly, coily Afro-centric, letting your natural beauty shine for all the world to see, is fab-u-lous. I'm talking Mickey D's ba-da ba ba-dah, I'm lovin' it!" Fran elaborated.

"Exactly," Dee affirmed. "Nice hairstyle."

"Thank you," I said as I self consciously stroked my small curls. The two girls hadn't addressed me directly but I felt obligated to acknowledge their compliment.

They were soon caught up in a group discussion at our table and I didn't have time to tell them how I acquired my extreme change of hairstyle, going from long straight hair like the twins' to my short chic afro.

My mind drifted back to the fight with my sisters that brought on my drastic transformation. Two weeks of summer break had already passed and I was still locked out of their busy social schedules. They were always with their friends or double dating or locked up in each other's room discussing their friends, dates, and college plans.

It was odd. As much as I fought with my sisters, I still wanted to hang out with them, especially when I had nothing else to do over a long boring summer. I couldn't even go anywhere beyond walking distance unless one of them took me because at fifteen, even if I had access to a car, I couldn't drive it by myself.

So I started asking for some of their time and then I started whining, then demanding and finally threatening. But they were eighteen and threats of telling mom and dad just didn't work like it used to. So, I resorted to begging.

"Please, Kylie, please take me with you," I pleaded, appealing to her as the nicer twin. We were in the incredibly well organized Jack and Jill restroom and she was trying to put a necklace on that had a clasp that was difficult to manipulate.

"Adisa, I am not about to take my little sister on a date with me."

"But you and Kelly double date all the time!" I cried, incredulous.

"Fine. You dig up a date and we'll all go out together."

I was stung by her cruelty. She knew I had never been on a date before; there wasn't a long line of guys waiting outside our home to ask *me* out. Besides, it was dad's rule that his girls didn't date until they were sixteen. I suddenly had an idea and had to swallow my pride to ask, but I was desperate.

"Could you find a date for me?" I pleaded. "And then we could go out together because it wouldn't be like I was going out on a date alone with a boy. It would be a group of friends going to the movies or something."

"Why don't you call up some of your own friends?" she suggested in irritation still struggling with the clasp.

"I don't have any friends."

"What about Avery?"

"His birthday's not until the end of summer so he's not old enough to drive yet. Besides they always travel during the summer so Avery's probably gone anyway."

She got her clasp to hook just as the doorbell rang. Her date no doubt. I waited for her answer. She looked at me then and I must have looked pretty pitiful because she promised to borrow Kelly's car and take me to the movies the following Saturday.

However, the following Saturday, Kelly decided she wanted to go to Lake Lanier with a group of their friends and they needed her car for transportation. There was no room for me but even if there had been, I knew Kelly wouldn't want me hanging around their friends.

Kylie looked at me like her hands were tied. Since it was Kelly's car and mom and dad had taken their's out of town for the weekend and MARTA didn't extend out to our neighborhood, we didn't have transportation to the movies. So Kylie figured, since she couldn't take me to the movies, she might as well go with her friends to Lake Lanier.

I pointed out that she could stay home with me and she rolled her eyes, completely losing patience with me.

When they left with their friends, I locked myself in my room. The heat of my anger and frustration was a physical discomfort that sought release. What was the use of having sisters if they didn't even want to be around me? It would've been better if I'd been born an only child. At least then I wouldn't have the added insult of having siblings who rejected me in addition to being alone.

I picked up my mom's black and white photograph. She was so happy and beautiful with her short curly hair framing her face. She had my baby face pressed against hers and my miniature afro made me look like a tiny replica of her.

Kylie and Kelly looked more like her than I did, particularly since they all had the same balsa skin coloring. The only time I thought I looked like my mom was in that photograph. I wanted to recapture the feelings I saw there, feelings of belonging.

In a flash of temper, the idea came to me. Impulsively, I rummaged through my drawer until I found a pair of scissors and took them along with the photograph into my restroom. I balanced the picture on a stand next to the mirror so I could see it while I worked and then I began to cut.

My straight black hair fell just below my shoulders. I lifted a section and cut without thinking and felt a thrill go through my stomach as I lifted the detached hair away from my head and dropped it into the small basket at my feet. I lifted another section and then another, working my way around my whole head. I kept glancing at the photograph for guidance but what I was seeing in the photograph was not reflected in the mirror.

I started to panic, just a little, but continued cutting, thinking it would get better. I stopped to assess how bad the damage was and it was pretty awful. The problem was that my hair was not curling. Short straight spikes stuck out all over my head.

I turned the sink water on and bent over it to wet my hair, thinking that would help it curl. After dousing my head with water several times, I grabbed a towel and blotted my hair. It didn't help. Now I had short messy spikes and matted hair all over my head.

I eventually gave up and stayed in my room moping for the rest of the night.

When I woke up the next morning, it looked even worse. I crawled back into bed. Mom and dad hadn't returned from their weekend get away and the twins didn't stir until lunch time. I heard them go down together.

Much later it was Kylie, concerned that I might be sick, who came searching for me. After several initial refusals, I unlocked my bedroom door. She actually screamed when she saw me, her hand flying to her mouth, her eyes wide with disbelief.

I heard Kelly's alarmed footsteps on the stairs, moving faster than I'd ever heard before. Mercifully, at least she didn't scream.

But then, she laughed. She laughed so hard she fell against the wall and slid to the floor. I stood there enduring it. And she laughed on and on. She held her sides and would laugh to the end of her breath, then struggle to drag in another breath around laughs still fighting to get out, and then laugh out loud some more. Her hysterical fit created moments of silent convulsions. Tears streamed down her face as she shook her head from side to side. She crawled just inside my doorway for a closer look too weak to stand, and still she laughed.

To her credit, Kylie looked sincerely sorry for me but even she couldn't stop a smile from twitching at the corners of her mouth. And Kelly in the background, still laughing.

Tired of listening to Kelly's racket, Kylie turned and half pushed, half rolled her twin out my door and then locked it. And on the other side of the door, still she laughed. I heard her gasping to catch her breath and when she had caught sufficient air, she was off laughing again.

Kylie was beside me now, tentatively touching my hair and reassuring me that it could be fixed.

I came close to actually crying. If mom was around, she would've said I was feeling good and sorry for myself.

I could hear Kelly's voice outside the locked door, struggling to say something around her laughing. "She looks... She looks... like a... a chicken head," she wailed and started laughing all over again.

I snatched a pillow off my bed and angrily flung it at the door. And still she laughed.

"Why Adisa?" Kylie asked.

"Because I'm a big idiot!" I declared, holding out the photograph of me and mom.

Kylie looked at the picture and then looked at me and I could see she understood.

After that, she helped me cut a little off the ends of my hair every couple of weeks, giving my naturally curly hair a chance to grow in a little at a time before losing all of my chemically straightened hair.

During the process, Kelly suggested I scalp myself and go bald, completely re-growing my hair from scratch. I actually considered it but wasn't brave enough to go without any hair at all, preferring to hang on to the butchered patches I had until enough new growth came in.

Days later, when I finally grudgingly forgave her, Kelly stood in my restroom, scrutinizing the picture of me and mom while Kylie carefully clipped the ends of my hair.

"Funny, I don't ever remember mom wearing her hair natural," she observed.

I must admit, after all the drama, things did get better. Dad had signed the twins up for a self-defense class in preparation for going away to college. He said he wanted his girls to know how to defend themselves against fools who couldn't grasp the concept 'no means no.' They took me with them and my favorite offensive move was the kick. The important thing was to commit and kick through your opponent with your heel.

Also, Kylie spent more time with me going to the movies, shopping, and working out with me. She preferred going to the gym but actually ran with me through the neighborhood a few times because she knew I enjoyed outdoor workouts better. She let me watch her while she created computer art on her new laptop and even showed me how to create basic web pages. When she tried to make up my face just to 'see what I looked like,' I had to draw the line.

Even Kelly took me out a few times in her car to an empty parking lot and gave me driving lessons and she regularly drove me downtown to volunteer at the Atlanta Children's Shelter for the rest of the summer. And most shocking, she set me up on a double date with her, her boyfriend Beverly and one of Beverly's friends, telling dad it wasn't a real date, just a group of friends going to the movies.

Big mistake!

We had a huge fight after it was over. She declared she would never double date with me again because I embarrassed her, treating Beverly's friend like he was diseased. And I told her that was fine with me because I didn't plan on ever making a fool of myself over a boy like she did. Then for emphasis, I made loud kissing noises with my tongue.

She called me an immature lunatic and I told her watching her and Beverly together made me throw up a little in my mouth. It wasn't completely true but I was mad.

She called me a big baby and I said her boyfriend's name was stupid and that he looked about as much like a 'Beverly' as the Incredible Hulk did. I regretted mentioning the Hulk because that's all she needed to start in on me and superheroes. And due to years of experience, she was really good at cutting me down using that particular subject.

Though she stayed mad at me for several days afterwards, she did continue to take me downtown regularly to volunteer with the children and I grudgingly showed my appreciation by accepting her rides. Truthfully, being with the kids was the brightest time of my whole miserable summer.

Mom and dad liked my new hairstyle once Kylie finished nursing it back to health. At first dad grumbled about women cutting their hair but then he came around. I couldn't help wondering at the sadness mom tried but failed to conceal when she first saw my new haircut. But I determined it was because she worried over my persistent outbursts of temper.

The shrill piercing ring of the bell brought me out of my reflections. Lunch was over already. My fingers nervously stroked my curls again, before I rose with the others to clear away the lunch scraps and head to class.

I didn't see Micah again until my last class. I sat at the front because it was my favorite subject, math. Avery and Liz soon joined me.

I was instantly aware when Micah entered the classroom. It was a repeat of my computer class. He stepped through the door and conversations altered in volume as he paused just inside, surveying the room with his vacant eyes. I began to think that his detached appearance concealed a keen sense of awareness. It was as if he was taking in the information of his surroundings before making a decision.

A quiet air of confidence emanated from him as he moved to take a seat. The desks beside me were taken but the one behind me was empty and that's the one he selected.

I sat staring at my desk, intensely aware of his presence directly behind me, desperately hoping Liz wouldn't start up again.

Ms. Gator quickly called roll and started class with a competition reviewing math from the previous year. She randomly called two students to the board on either side of a make shift partition that blocked their view of each other's answers and gave them math problems until one got the incorrect answer. Then another challenger took the place of the loser and the competition continued until one of them failed and another challenger was sent up.

When Ms. Gator finally got around to calling me, Makena, the math wiz, had been standing at the board through several challengers.

I took my place at the board thinking at best, I could tie her until the bell rang. I didn't believe she would miss any of the math problems.

We went through the first two problems and as I predicted we both got them correct. The third problem involved approximating the surface area of a figure. When Ms. Gator said time was up and we had to stop writing, I stepped back to look around the partition and saw that my answer didn't match Makena's. *Better luck next time* I consoled myself just before Ms. Gator announced that my answer was correct, to my complete astonishment.

I saw Makena checking her work against mine and then she smiled in concession before returning to her seat. Ms. Gator called Avery up and he took Makena's vacant spot.

I could hear Avery writing with quick sure strokes through the next problems and thought that maybe we would close out class with a tie. Then Ms. Gator gave us a discrete probability problem involving the multiple roll of a dice and I heard Avery's hesitant marks and constant erasures on the other side of the partition.

As I confidently began solving the problem, I recalled how I tried in vain to help Avery last year with this particular math concept. Suddenly, I was aware that Avery was standing directly in front of Liz as he worked on the equation. I could almost see the red rising on the back of his neck as he struggled to recall how to solve the problem. Then I thought of how he'd come to my defense during lunch when Liz was badgering me and how happy he looked when he was dancing with her in gym. They also came to lunch and to math class together I reminded myself.

For the first time, they were hanging out together instead of just in a group and even though it was only for a couple of minutes between classes, I knew it took a lot of courage on Avery's part. For all his bravado, he could be pretty shy about things like that. Maybe this wasn't going to be a repeat of the previous year after all. Maybe I could make some small contribution to ensure that it wouldn't be.

I wasn't a fan of dumbing down but I was willing to take one for the team if it meant helping Avery. I stared at my answer, knowing it was correct. My back was to the class, blocking my work. Nobody would ever know. I picked up the eraser and wiped out my answer and wrote a number that was off by one.

When Ms. Gator announced that Avery was correct I looked around the partition, in disbelief. To my chagrin, I saw immediately that he did have the correct answer. Avery's expression was almost as shocked as mine but it was clear he was quite proud of his achievement. I was happy for him but regretted my impulsive and unnecessary submission. We could have ended class in a tie.

It wasn't until I met the emotionless gaze of Micah as I returned to my seat that I realized my actions had resigned me to the very fate I thought I was saving Avery from. I was highly annoyed with myself as I sat down. Thankfully the bell rang before my replacement even reached the board.

Everything was a blur until I found myself crossing the school's parking lot to head home. I was so consumed with berating myself, I was barely aware of my surroundings.

I didn't even notice the black jeep until I was practically standing on top of it. Micah was behind the wheel, his glazed over eyes observing me.

"What do you want?" I asked in a nasty tone.

"Do you need a ride?" his perfect voice asked.

Completely unnerved by the day's roller coaster ride, I snapped, "I can't accept rides from strangers!" My rudeness made me feel childish.

But Micah looked thoroughly unmoved by my outburst. "We're not strangers. I danced with you in gym," he insensitively pointed out. Surely he had enough sense to know I didn't want to be reminded of *that* embarrassing performance. Was he laughing at me behind those empty eyes?

I could feel my mouth working but only stunned silence came out. My anger was rising and the rage wanted to come out.

"You intentionally missed that last math problem," he continued, catching me completely off guard. "You shouldn't diminish yourself to get Avery to like you."

What!? I was insulted he actually believed I played dumb to get a guy to like me. I was trying to help a friend by not embarrassing him in front of the girl he liked, not snare him for myself. How did Micah know I intentionally missed that problem anyway?

"What is your problem? Who are you? Why are you acting so… so…," but I couldn't describe how he was acting. The words were crowded out of my mind by a temper I barely had under control. "Look, I can't even deal with this right now so leave me alone. I'm going home!" I said, on the verge of completely losing it.

I knew I was probably over reacting but I was so disturbed by Micah's unsettling affect on me, I wasn't thinking rationally. My legs were shaking as I hurried across the street to the sidewalk that would take me home. I took deep breaths of air trying to distract myself by concentrating on the faint scent of pine as I passed the woods.

Micah's jeep drove by and I glimpsed his perfect posture and forward gaze. A flash of his dazzling skin filled my thoughts for a moment. I suddenly realized in the midst of my raging emotions, that I actually could describe its indescribable color.

It was copper.

2 ~ THE DINNER PARTY

The pile of clutter in the family room had grown since this morning, encroaching and covering the orderly space like a living growing indoor mountain. The house was full of the delicious aromas of mom's cooking. I wanted to hurry upstairs to my room but the Summers ladies wanted to hear about my first day back at Talbot and I was obliged to entertain their interests until they were satisfied.

I briefly gave the boring details of my day, carefully avoiding the subject of Micah.

"Kelly, we should go back some day this week to say bye to our old teachers," Kylie suggested.

We were all standing in the kitchen watching mom sample dishes while dad moved in and out through the patio door, tending to the grill out back. Even with the air conditioner blasting, the kitchen was overly warm.

"Why? We already said bye to everybody when we graduated," Kelly said offhand.

"I know but it would be a nice gesture. Don't you want to see everybody one last time before we leave?"

"No," Kelly bluntly stated.

"You always have to be so difficult," Kylie accused before giving up.

Dad walked in holding his barbecue mop, a large serving fork with a towel wrapped around the prongs, dripping with his secret barbecue sauce over a bowl full of the same.

"The meat's just about ready Opal. I finished mopping on my sauce and I'll pull the meat off the pit soon so it won't dry out," he said.

"I hope you don't plan on serving that spicy version of your sauce tonight," mom warned before adding, "I don't know why you insist on smoking meat during the hottest part of the day. It's a wonder you haven't fallen out from heat stroke."

"It's better than you burning the oven all day heating up the whole house." He started rummaging through the cabinets.

"What are you looking for now Frederick?" mom asked.

"I'm trying to find a pan to put the meat in when it's done."

"I already set one on the counter for you over there," she said, shaking her kitchen towel in the general direction.

Dad spotted the large roasting pan and smiled. "Perfect. Thanks."

Mom used her kitchen towel to pull a peach cobbler out of the oven.

"Anything special happening for dinner," I asked, realizing the preparations were a little more elaborate than usual.

"Your mother invited the new neighbors over," dad said, as he filled a glass with cold water from the refrigerator.

Mom glanced at him as he took a long satisfying drink and a flaw in her dinner plans suddenly dawned on her. "I forgot about drinks."

"I'll go pick some up," Kelly offered. "But I need money."

"Okay. Would you please bring me my purse. It should be on my bed. We'll need some ice cream too," mom added.

"Can I go with?" I asked, thinking I could escape any further conversation. I wasn't thrilled with the idea of having dinner with strangers when all I wanted to do was hide out in my room and torture myself by replaying the day's events in excruciating detail.

"Sure, come with," Kelly consented.

"Me too," Kylie volunteered.

When we went out to the car, Kylie automatically took the front passenger seat next to Kelly. For once I didn't mind, preferring the solitude of the back seat. I actually didn't have to worry about conversation with Kelly even if I had sat up front with her. Kylie and Beverly were the only people she spoke more than two words to without having her arm twisted.

I stayed in my room after we got back, planning on hiding out until dinner time but I soon became restless. I quickly changed into some shorts and a T-shirt then slipped on my running shoes.

"Mom, I'm going running at the school," I called to her from the hallway.

"Okay but get back well before dinner. I don't want you coming through the door smelling like a billy goat with our guests sitting in here."

"Okay."

As I headed for the front door, I heard Kelly griping, "Leave it to Disa to runaway when there's work to be done."

"You shouldn't complain against your sister so much," mom's voice censured.

"Mom, you baby her too much. She could at least clean the hallway floors while we're in here cooking and that family room is a wreck. Not to mention..."

I closed the door firmly behind me, not quite slamming it. I glanced up the road at our new neighbors' home. The moving truck was still there. I started speed walking in the opposite direction, warming up on my way to the track.

When I arrived, the campus appeared deserted except for a few cars in the parking lot. I had the track all to myself. Talbot didn't participate in intramural sports so I knew I wouldn't have to worry about competing with team practices for the track. Any student interested in athletics had to get what they could from the mandatory gym classes or their own personal pursuits outside of school.

I briefly stretched my leg and back muscles and then hit the track at a slow jog and worked my way up to a real run. I went around the track three times before I started to really relax into a comfortable stride. My breathing was easy and it felt great feeling my muscles expand and contract, effortlessly propelling me forward. I remembered when I first ran around the track last year for gym class, I couldn't even run one full lap around. Now, I felt like I could go on forever.

As I went round and round, I thought about Micah. Never in my life had I been so stressed over a single individual. Why was I so deeply affected by this boy? I'd seen good looking guys before but I'd never reacted like this.

I thought of my sisters and how they would have handled the situation. A whole lot better than I had, I concluded. Sure they would've lost it but they would have done so in private. In front of the guy, they would be confidently flirtatious, subtly drawing him in until he was snared in their web. I smiled at the image in my mind. I had to admit, they really were skilled.

Suddenly I wanted to kick myself for all those years of missed opportunities, I could have been learning at the twin feet of experts under my own roof. Instead, I'd squandered my chance, mocking and criticizing their actions in spite of their great success. Now who was laughing? I had absolutely no idea how to approach a boy like Micah.

But why would I want to, I thought defensively. Sure he was incredibly handsome but his behavior was bizarre. And at times, he even seemed rude. As I listed his faults, I knew I was just being the fox crying sour grapes. But I didn't care. My newly awakened emotions scared me and I stubbornly tried to hold onto the safety of the old scornful Adisa.

I eventually determined that thinking about Micah wasn't resolving anything so, with some difficulty, I tried to put him out of my mind.

I thought of Avery and Liz, wondering if they might actually start dating this semester. I smiled thinking this would be his first real girlfriend if things worked out. Even though he was my friend and I planned on helping him as much as I could, I was still going to mercilessly tease him. I knew he would do the same for me some day.

I checked the time and was surprised at how long I'd been out. I finished my lap and headed home. When I got back to the house, I saw Beverly's car in our driveway. That boy loved to eat.

As I entered our front door, I saw somebody had already cleaned the hallway floors so I slipped off my shoes before entering and then carefully tiptoed across the wood floors to the stairs. As I passed the family room, I noticed somebody had attempted to straighten things up in there as well but it was a hopeless cause. I didn't see anybody but I could hear activity in various parts of the house.

I went straight to my room to shower and change and didn't even consider going down again until it was almost time for dinner. My run had increased my appetite and I was really starting to get hungry when I headed downstairs. The table was colorfully set and mom had her alternative jazz music playing softly in the background.

Kelly and Kylie must have been upstairs in their room because I heard only mom, dad, and Beverly at the back of the house in the kitchen when the doorbell rang. I turned in resignation to answer it. I pulled the door closed to the cluttered family room as I passed by, thinking mom would be mortified if our guests saw that mess. Then I felt a little guilty for not joining in to help out earlier. I defensively concluded it was Kelly and Kylie's college junk so why should I have to straighten up after them? Not only were they practically emptying our home of its contents, in addition they were going on shopping sprees hunting for bargain priced necessities to add to their growing pile.

I mentally composed my greeting as I opened the front door, words of welcome on the tip of my tongue... then stood in stunned silence. Cool distant hazel eyes stared at me from a flawless copper face.

I could hear mom, dad, and Beverly coming up behind me and I sensed there were other people standing on the porch but all I could see was Micah.

"Adisa, where are your manners?" mom exclaimed, moving me to the side so her guests could enter. "Please come in."

I managed to slide behind the door somewhat as they all filed in, wiping their feet on our welcome mat before stepping onto our gleaming wood floors, Micah and a boy about eight followed by two adults.

Kelly and Kylie came down to join the introductions. Mom did the honors for our side since she was the one who extended the invitation.

"I'm Opal Summers of course, and this is my husband Frederick. These are my twins Kelly and Kylie and this is Beverly, a friend of the family. Now ... where is... she was just here. Oh there she is. This is the baby, Adisa."

I cringed but somehow managed a smile as I came from behind the shelter of the front door, closing it before turning to face our guests. If I hadn't been so stunned by Micah's presence, I would have found it funny that mom still couldn't bring herself to call Beverly, Kelly's boyfriend in dad's presence.

The woman spoke up for her group. "I'm Harriet Alexander and this is my husband George and these are our sons Micah and Jason." Her hands gracefully indicated each member of her family as she introduced them, lightly touching her husband and then coming to rest on her youngest son. I noted that Mrs. Alexander was sensitive enough not to refer to Jason as the baby even though he was much closer to being one than I was.

"I'm sorry we didn't bring anything. We've been so busy with the move," Mrs. Alexander apologized.

"I told you not to worry about that," mom gently reminded her.

I stood back observing as everybody exchanged comfortable greetings. Mr. Alexander had his arm casually draped around his wife's waist while Jason squeezed in the middle wrapping his arms around each of his parents' legs.

The Alexander family as a whole was very striking. They all were different shades of copper with Mr. and Mrs. Alexander being respectively the lighter and darker extremes of the color while their sons were a different mix of the two. Micah just happened to be the shade I found the most appealing of them all. But something was out of sync with this perfect family though I couldn't quite put my finger on it. The thought nagged at me all evening.

My family was being their naturally charming selves. Even Kelly managed to come across as welcoming. I was the only one shyly standing aside, unable to think of anything to say.

We all moved further down the hall, mom leading the way, apologizing for the house being so hot and assuring them things would cool off quickly since she recently turned the oven off which had been keeping the food warm.

Waving dismissively at the family room door as we passed, she declared it a disaster area. "Our older girls are packing for their first year of college," she explained proudly.

Mr. and Mrs. Alexander directed words of approval and encouragement toward the twins and asked what college they planned on attending.

Kylie answered. "Bartlett. It's a small private college that's only a few hours from here. We didn't want to go too far from home."

"Did you girls consider Spelman?" Mrs. Alexander asked, referring to the historically black women's college near downtown Atlanta.

"They considered it," mom replied. "But I think it was too close to home."

The enigmatic look my sisters exchanged implied there was plenty of truth to mom's words.

"Since we're all concerned about it being a school night, let's go ahead and get started," Mom suggested. She pointed out the spacious guest restroom for some to wash up there and took the rest on into the kitchen to wash up in the double sinks. Mom was a stickler about cleanliness particularly when it came to handling food.

"The table is already set but we need to fill the serving dishes and take them to the dining room table," she instructed. Pretty soon everybody was washed up and busily pitching in to help.

Dad pulled the large roasting pan out of the oven and set it on the counter. I helped him transfer the contents onto a large serving platter.

Mom and Kelly were busy filling a variety of serving dishes with savory food and then passing them on to waiting hands. Kylie accepted a dish first and led the way into the dining room to place her dish and the others followed her lead.

Mom was a social genius. She could have easily had everything set up before the Alexander's arrived but she always intentionally left some task undone so that she could invite her guests to help. The activity put everybody at ease and gave them a sense of contributing. The good mood encouraged easy conversation and laughter, fostering a relaxed atmosphere for the gathering.

Through it all I was intensely aware of Micah, nervous that he would mention our dancing in gym class but he hadn't said a word about it. He only spoke when someone asked him a question and then he would give a polite though brief response.

I couldn't stop stressing over Micah, my dance partner, actually being in my home. Even Avery, my closest friend ever, had never been to my home. I suddenly thought, what would dad think if he knew how closely I'd danced with Micah just earlier today. I didn't think he would survive it.

I avoided Micah as much as I could in the confines of the kitchen. My stomach was so nervous, I miserably thought of all the delicious food I wouldn't be able to eat even though I was practically starving.

In no time at all everything was ready and it was time to be seated. As the last dish was placed on the table, I started worrying about the seating arrangements. I was scared to death that I would end up next to Micah, dreading him holding my trembling hand in front of my family during grace. To avoid this, I eased around the table away from him.

Mom and dad naturally settled at opposite ends of the table telling everybody to sit where they liked. Mr. Alexander settled next to dad and Mrs. Alexander sat next to mom with Jason next to her. I slid in next to Jason, remembering how much I enjoyed my time with the children at the shelter over the summer.

Jason appeared a little older than the kids at the shelter but I was sure he'd be the easiest member of the Alexander family for me to talk to. Kylie sat next to me since Kelly had abandoned her to sit with Beverly. That put Kylie next to dad. Opposite Kylie was Mr. Alexander and pulling out the chair next to him was Micah, which, to my horror, put him directly opposite me. Beverly sat next to him and of course Kelly sat beside Beverly placing her next to mom and opposite Ms. Alexander.

I consoled myself with the thought that at least I wouldn't have to hold Micah's hand while we blessed the food but for some reason, the thought of not holding his hand was more of a disappointment than a relief. As we joined hands to say grace, I couldn't help remembering how Micah's hand had felt in mine while we were dancing. I pushed the thought away as I took Jason's hand in mine and Kylie's in my other one.

After dad finished grace, mom, and Kelly were up filling everybody's drink order. Mom had conveniently filled two serving dishes of each item, ensuring that everybody had easy access to all that was offered. Dad's platter of meat was at the center of the table loaded up with enough to make passing it around out of the question. People out of reach would have to send their plate down to get their requests filled.

Dad explained that he had smoked some chicken, beef links, and beef ribs. I knew that even though dad was partial to pork ribs, he didn't smoke any so as not to offend our guests in case they abstained. Dad also proudly pointed out the serving bowls that contained his secret barbecue sauce. He cautioned that the sauce in the red bowl was spicy and suggested the sauce in the white bowl for those who were not as adventurous, claiming only real men should attempt the red bowl.

Mr. Alexander immediately took the challenge, asking for the red bowl to be passed to him while he sent his plate down for ribs from the platter. The sauce was passed along with a chorus of spirited uh-ohhhs from my family.

Dad sent his plate down and I put a chicken breast and link on it as instructed before sending it back to him.

Kelly filled Mr. Alexander's glass and then dad's and continued to work her way around the table while mom started at the other end.

Mr. Alexander liberally spread some sauce on his ribs and then passed the bowl to dad's patiently waiting hands. I saw mom give dad a look but he either didn't see it or ignored it as he poured the spicy sauce over his chicken and links. He cut a chunk of link and speared it with his fork then held it up and looked at Mr. Alexander who was waiting with a rib ready. They both took a mouth full and began chewing.

You could hear a pin drop. Our eyes went from one man to the other. Almost immediately, Mr. Alexander shifted from leaning to the side to sitting straighter and a few nervous laughs spilled over from us in response. The two men stared at each other while they continued to chew. Suddenly Mr. Alexander grabbed up his glass and we all started but then he slowly smiled and placed it back on the table and we started cracking up because he'd psyched us out.

We continued to watch the men but it was noisy now as we encouraged one or the other and guessed who would break first. When both men had finished the first bite, they prepared to take a second. The suspense was killing us. They both took another mouth full and watched each other chew.

Mom and Kelly sat down, having finished serving drinks to everybody. Mom watched awhile and then finally said, "Okay Frederick, that's enough. The object of a dinner party is to feed our guests not hurt them."

"Ahhh mom," Kylie said, laughing. "It's so exciting."

"George won't be able to taste the food if he burns all his taste buds off," mom insisted.

Dad raised an eyebrow at Mr. Alexander and he seemed to get the message. Both men reached for their glasses at the same time, slowly lifted to their lips, paused and then drank at the same time. We all broke out in applause thoroughly entertained.

"Whew!" Mr. Alexander loudly exhaled in relief, his eyes watering. "That burns real good."

Dad laughed and wiped his own eyes with his napkin. "Nobody has ever lasted that long," he said in admiration.

Everybody was busy talking as they went back to serving themselves and passing dishes around. Mrs. Alexander helped Jason make his selections. I saw Beverly pull two ribs off the platter and send them back to mom then proceed to load his plate up as if we would refuse him a second go around. I couldn't help smiling.

Kylie passed a salad bowl to me. There was chopped lettuce, broccoli, onions, and tomatoes with boiled eggs sliced diagonally and placed as a garnish around the sides for those who liked eggs in their salad. After serving myself I passed the bowl along. I added a serving spoon full of steaming brown rice to my plate and waited for the pinto beans.

While waiting, I glanced across at Micah and saw he was busy filling his plate as well. I suppressed a smile as I watched him take a sample of barbecue sauce from the red bowl. I began to relax a little.

The beans finally made their way to me. They sat in a rich broth seasoned with a smoked turkey leg instead of mom's usual ham hock. I saw bits of onion and chopped peppers mixed in and the steamy aroma made my mouth water.

The collard greens were next. They had also been flavored with a smoked turkey leg and slowly simmered and seasoned to perfection. I added a barbecued chicken thigh next to them and reached for the white bowl of secret sauce, keeping well clear of the red bowl. I didn't have a death wish.

I took a square of hot buttermilk cornbread and slathered it with butter. By the time I got around to the yams, there was hardly any room left on my plate. The bright orange yams were glazed in brown sugar and butter and were so sweet it was like a dessert.

Thinking of dessert, I reminded myself to save room for the peach cobbler and chocolate cake.

My track run had increased my appetite and everything was going so well that I was able to eat in spite of Micah sitting directly across from me. I was starting to actually enjoy myself as I listened to the different conversations around the table.

"Jason, you can't just eat the yams. Try some of the meat and greens," I heard Mrs. Alexander say.

"But I like the yams," he responded, his fork poised to scoop up more.

"I know honey, but this is your second serving and you haven't touched anything else."

I noticed he was wearing a Power Boy T-shirt and smiled in recognition. It was one of my favorite super characters.

I heard Mr. Alexander politely trying to pry the recipe to the spicy secret barbecue sauce out of dad. I doubted he would be successful. Dad had never even shared it with us. I think it had something to do with the combination of exotic peppers he used and some ingredient that enhanced their potency.

Beverly was telling mom that he was sorry he wouldn't be able to help Kelly and Kylie move into their dorm but he was headed out of state for school in a couple of days. I could tell by Kelly's face that she wasn't happy about Beverly leaving and I felt sorry for her.

"You doing okay?"

I turned to see Kylie looking at me.

"Sure, I'm fine. Why?"

"You're even more quiet than usual," she explained.

"I'm just too busy eating to do much talking."

"Oh, I see," she said looking at my half empty plate. "How in the world do you eat so much and stay so skinny?"

I knew she was trying to tease me but I treated her question seriously just to annoy her. "Well, today was an early release day at school so lunch was way earlier than usual and I didn't eat much anyway. I haven't had anything to eat since then plus I went running at the track...,"

"Kelly... no Kylie, right?" Mr. Alexander interrupted, looking across at Kylie. She nodded her head.

"What are you and your sister majoring in?"

"I'm in graphic design and Kelly's in business," she answered.

"Oh that's great. So you're the artist and your sister will manage all the money to keep it in the family," he suggested lightly.

Kylie smiled. "Something like that. Kelly and I are identical twins and I believe when we split she took the left brain and I took the right. So I'm more creative and she's definitely more business oriented."

"What about you, Adisa?" Mr. Alexander asked, drawing me into the conversation.

My fork, loaded with food, hovered between my mouth and my plate. I reluctantly put it down. "I'm still in high school."

"I know, I hear you're at Talbot with Micah," he admitted and my heart skipped a beat. Had Micah told them about my atrocious dancing?

I glanced at Micah. He was quietly eating his meal as if he hadn't heard a thing. *Well it's nice to know he's not a robot* I thought distractedly, watching him eat real food.

When I realized Mr. Alexander was waiting for a response, I smiled shyly at him, unsure of what to say since he hadn't asked a question.

"So have you given any thought to what you might like to study when you graduate high school?" he asked kindly. I got the impression he was truly interested and not just being polite.

"I really haven't thought about it much. I still have two years of high school after this one so I haven't decided yet." I desperately wanted his attention taken off of me so that I could get back to my meal but he persisted.

"Micah is part of FLEET. That's the Future Law Enforcers Elite Team. Talbot allows him to substitute some of his classes there with this training program. Does that sound like something you may be interested in?"

I'd heard of FLEET before, a teen organization considered next to impossible to get into. In fact I didn't know of anybody personally who had ever gotten in. Nobody at Talbot belonged even though many applied each year.

Some disillusioned applicants even referred to the members as kiddie cops, baby fuzz, or piglets who ran around half the time playing cops and robbers then spent the other half filling out a multitude of reports about their experiences. But they were just being haters.

The fact that Micah was part of FLEET was impressive. I didn't think I had the credentials to be accepted, better students than I was had tried and failed. I felt put on the spot and squirmed in discomfort not wanting to admit my deficiencies would probably keep me out. I sensed that Mrs. Alexander was listening intently, awaiting my answer as well. My suspicions were confirmed when she interjected.

"George, you can't expect her to have her whole life planned out at fifteen," she gently reprimanded. "She must feel like she's being given the third degree. I'm afraid being a part of law enforcement causes my husband to forget how to talk to civilians."

"I just like to keep our youth involved with constructive activities. It gives them focus and direction, keeps them out of trouble," Mr. Alexander said defensively, visibly retreating but he didn't seem happy about it.

"You're a policeman?" I asked, feigning interest to smooth things over.

Mr. Alexander shook his head. "Not exactly. I'm part of a special unit that has different responsibilities from patrolmen. My department sometimes work on national issues in conjunction with the military."

"You mean Dobbins Air Force?" I asked.

"Yes, we work with them along with other military units."

I found it interesting that a local police department was working so closely with the military but before I could pursue the subject further, Kelly interjected.

"I know what Adisa wants to be when she grows up," she announced. I realized the whole table was listening in on our conversation now. I felt uneasy.

I heard Kylie give a knowing laugh on the other side of me and my anxiety increased.

"*Super Girl,*" Kelly said softly in a singsong voice. I saw mom smiling indulgently. She thought it was cute. I was mortified, desperately hoping my sisters wouldn't go too far with Micah sitting right across from me.

They launched into the Crank That song by Soulja Boy that was so popular on the Internet, replacing the word superman with super girl and in unison started making the arm cranking gestures that went along with the song. I tried to smile as if it wasn't killing me inside.

I suspected this was only the beginning. They were about to really start in on me. I silently pleaded with them to no avail.

I looked at Micah in desperation. How much of my life's humiliation would he be witness to? First my dancing and now my freakish superhero past.

"Adisa wants to save the world," Kelly began in earnest. "She wants to be a superhero."

I saw Mr. and Mrs. Alexander exchange curious looks.

"It's true," Kylie confirmed next to me. "For most kids, Christmas is their favorite holiday but not for Adisa. Halloween was always her favorite because she got to dress up like superheroes."

The Alexanders were smiling and looking at me strangely. I tried to eat but discovered I had completely lost my appetite.

"Oh, remember when we used to put towels on our head to play fancy ladies?" Kelly recalled.

Kylie was nodding emphatically. "Yeah, you'd always try to get the longest towel no matter what color it was because you wanted the longest hair."

"And you always wanted the black towel because you wanted realistic looking hair. Well, Adisa, instead of putting the towel on her head, would drape it around her shoulders like a cape and pretend to rescue us," Kelly beamed in delight.

There was laughter around the table at the mental image of me rushing about trying to save my sisters.

"The funny thing is, Adisa was a little taller than we were by then and she could actually pick us up, just barely. One time she picked Kelly up and dropped her and Kelly hit her head so hard, a knot the size of an egg swelled up right in the middle of her forehead."

I stared down at my plate with a fake smile plastered on my face. How did such a warm beautiful evening turn into a nightmare so quickly? I pushed my food around in agitation, my fork scraping in protest against my plate. The food didn't look quite as appetizing as it had only moments before.

Kylie excitedly added, "Me and Kelly would be in front of the mirror, pretending to put on our makeup, swinging our towel hair, waiting for Adisa to come save us. It was too much fun. Sometimes she would try to pick us both up at the same time and she nearly could. It was crazy."

"Remember that day she insisted on wearing her Superman costume to school and dad was going to let her but mom found out and stopped her?" Kelly was laughing so hard her words were barely intelligible.

"Oh I remember that," dad smiled as if it was one of his fondest memories.

Kelly continued, "Mom made her change but Adisa kept her superman panties on and was showing the kids at school. That's the most popular she's ever been with the boys. It's been down hill ever since."

Dad's appalled, "What!?" only served to increase the volume of laughter, it reverberated from all sides of me.

"Superman panties are for boys not girls," Jason stated. "I mean not panties. It's underwear," he laughed correcting himself.

"You're right," Kelly confirmed. "Mom couldn't find little girl superhero panties so Adisa bugged her to death for some boys underwear and mom finally gave in. She didn't know Adisa would be so proud she'd go to school and model them for her whole class."

I looked across at Micah and realized, he was the only one at the table besides me not laughing. He had the same wooden emotionless posture he had maintained through the entire evening, through the entire time I had known him. I realized that he hadn't even laughed during our dads' spicy barbecue sauce competition.

"Oh, Oh! What about the time she went berserk?" Kylie asked.

"Which one?" Kelly frowned thinking.

"When we told her only boys were superheroes so she said she wasn't a girl."

"Oh, yeah. We held her down pretending to put make up on her because we said girls had to be pretty. She went crazy, screaming she didn't want to be pretty because she was a boy." Kelly paused, remembering. "Even mama couldn't calm her down. We had to just let her scream until she wore herself out."

Micah was watching me from across the table and for an instant, I thought I saw something flicker in his eyes but it was gone in an instant. I searched his eyes but it wasn't there.

I lowered my gaze back to my plate thinking surely they were almost done. There couldn't be too much more to tell that was as embarrassing as what they had already revealed.

Suddenly a distinctly masculine voice stated, "I've always found a woman of action more admirable than a woman who spends her time fussing over her image in a mirror, waiting for others to take action on her behalf."

Mr. Alexander's head jerked around to his son. He appeared to be as stunned as I was.

All laughter immediately died down. I stared at Micah's unchanged expression. Had I not recognized his voice, I would have thought somebody else must have spoken.

Kelly, her pride wounded, was quick to respond. "Hello! They're not mutually exclusive. Kylie and I have managed to do a little fussing in the mirror in addition to graduating high school with honors and getting accepted into college. And I'm sure you'll find out soon enough that it's not easy to get A's at Talbot but we managed and qualified for the Hope scholarship along with several other academic awards. So don't worry, we're not waiting for anybody to 'take action' on our behalf. We're taking it for ourselves."

Kelly didn't work her neck like some girls did when they got upset. She pinned Micah with a cold stare as she sat deadly still.

Beverly, seated in between them, placed his hand on her shoulder and it surprised me as usual that the simple gesture calmed her. The stiffness visibly left her body as if his touch had drained it from her. I knew from personal experience how hard it was to quiet passions once they were raised and I couldn't help admiring their connection.

Micah appeared completely unfazed. He was still quietly observing me. "I agree with you Kelly. You can have both. Wouldn't you agree that despite her previous resistance, Adisa has managed to look beautiful in addition to achieving academic excellence?"

I couldn't believe my ears. A boy dared to call me beautiful in the presence of my dad, in his home, under his roof, at his very table, eating his food and in particular his secret barbecue sauce! I knew in my dad's mind, Micah had practically proposed marriage. And how did Micah know I was excellent academically? It was too much.

I stole a peek at my dad, grateful that Mr. Alexander was sitting between him and Micah. I didn't want the boy to be harmed for defending me.

Before Kelly could respond, Kylie smoothly filled in. "Of course we're aware our sister is beautiful and I'm glad you recognize it as well. But a lot of kids like us don't see it. They only seem to admire a more stereotypical type of beauty."

How did my 'beauty' become the subject of dinner conversation? I was not liking it, not one bit!

"With all due respect Kylie," Micah asserted, still staring at me with his distant eyes, "your peers must be blind."

I could've fainted, my shock was so great. Micah hadn't volunteered a single word all evening without direct prompting and now, suddenly he was speaking up in my defense.

Mr. Alexander pointedly referred to the woods in back of our home, asking if there were walking trails. It was an awkward attempt to change the subject but it worked. Dad commented that it was completely wild, adding that he had attempted to explore it a few times but found it rough going.

Gradually smaller conversations broke out around the table and things returned to normal but the mood had been ruined for me and all I wanted was the seclusion of my bedroom. The only thing that kept the evening from being a total loss, was Micah's defense of me. But even that was marred by the persistent thought that he knows. Now he knows what a freak I am.

"I'm sorry for his behavior. He had a rough first day at his new school," I overheard Mrs. Alexander explaining to mom.

"I'm not going back to that school. Those kids are mean," Jason said emphatically.

"What did they do that was so mean?" mom asked, her voice full of real concern as if he was her own child.

"They called me dumb and said I'm too big for first grade and I'm supposed to be in second grade."

I'd thought he was in second or third grade myself. But I should have known better particularly after all the insults I'd endured regarding my height.

"He's only six and he's big for his age," Mrs. Alexander was explaining and continued to talk about him to my mom as if he couldn't hear her. I guess she was like every other parent after all.

Jason, distressed over his mom discussing him so openly, began twisting around in his chair and nearly knocked his drink over. He started pulling on her to break up her conversation and refused to sit still when she told him to do so.

He began talking loudly about wanting more yams and when Mrs. Alexander refused his request, encouraging him to try some of the chicken, he wrapped his fingers around the meaty part of the drumstick on his plate and squeezed until the juicy sauce slowly flowed between his fingers.

Mrs. Alexander scooted her chair back, reaching for Jason so she could take him to wash the greasy mess off his hands but he refused, hanging onto his chair in resistance.

I quickly intervened before Mrs. Alexander lost her temper. "You know I have some Power Boy soap that will clean that toxic waste off your hands."

Jason looked up at me in surprise, still clutching the chair.

"But you can't use it unless you know the secret Power Boy oath," I added.

He said nothing.

I realized I would have to make it more enticing for him. "Of course afterwards, you would get to see Power Boy in person. I have him upstairs... in a box... in my closet."

Jason's eyes widened in disbelief.

I saw Mrs. Alexander suppress a smile.

"Think about it," I suggested with disinterest. I turned back to my food and attempted to eat but I couldn't enjoy it. I still had no appetite and desperately hoped the boy would take the bait so I would have an excuse to leave the table.

I glimpsed him studying his hand in consideration.

After awhile I heard him say, "Okay."

I turned to him and waited.

He looked at me puzzled.

I sighed, faking impatience. "First I need the oath," I said in a way that implied I doubted he knew it and I was wasting my time dealing with him.

He quickly and confidently recited the oath.

I pretended surprised disappointment, then resignation. "Fine. Follow me. And don't touch anything."

He unwound his arms from the chair, careful not to touch it with his sticky fingers.

"Are you sure?" Mrs. Alexander asked me as Jason stood to follow. "He can be a handful once he gets going."

"No problem," I assured her.

As I headed for the stairs, I heard mom explaining to her how I'd volunteered over the summer to work with children his age. I chanced a quick glance at Micah before I rounded the corner out of view. He was still staring at me.

Jason stood solemnly in front of my sink. He suspiciously eyed the bottle of regular pump soap sitting on my counter. I explained to him it was just a decoy. I opened a cabinet and pulled out a large colorful bottle with a wrap-around picture of Power Boy, poised to throw a flaming power rock.

"Wow!" he said grinning from ear to ear.

I smiled, pleased that I could impress a six year old.

He admired the bottle before pumping enough of the thick blue gel to wash his hands for a week. He rinsed and washed them again. He lifted his fingers to his nose and sniffed then gave a satisfied smile.

He gave his hands a final rinse and I tossed a clean towel to him. I returned the Power Boy bottle to the cabinet and put the used towel in the hamper after Jason was through drying his hands.

I walked out the restroom and pretended to head back toward the stairs.

"Uh wait," he called.

I turned, looking confused, almost laughing when I saw the serious expression on his face. It sort of reminded me of Micah. "What is it?"

"Uhmmm... Power Boy?"

"Yeah, what about him?"

He fidgeted and I almost gave in. I'm a pushover.

"You said I could see him after."

"After what?"

"After I got rid of the toxic waste."

"Oh yeah. About that... he really isn't much to look at," I hedged.

"I don't care."

"He's only about yea-big," I indicated a small size with my hands. "And he's not even real."

"That's okay."

"You don't really want to see him," I said and turned to go. I was wicked.

"I'm not leaving!" he insisted. He planted himself in the middle of my room, refusing to be cheated.

I studied him carefully. "Oh all right," I relented.

We walked over to my walk-in closet and I reached over head to pull a chain. Light flooded my closet. I reached up on a high shelf and took down a box that had a clear plastic front.

Power Boy stared out at me. I held the box possessively for a moment before passing it to Jason. He took the box reverently and it was really hard not to laugh out loud. I had an inkling of why my sisters took such pleasure in teasing me.

He turned the box over and over in his hands but he didn't open it.

I decided to give him another shock.

I quickly snatched the box from him.

"No...," he started and then his eyes nearly popped out of his head as I opened it and withdrew the superhero.

Power Boy was a limited edition, an almost impossible to find collector's item. Many collectors never opened boxes, keeping their figures sealed so they would retain and even increase their monetary value.

I believed superheroes were made to be played with not just looked at. All of my boxes were opened.

I handed Power Boy to Jason and I thought he was going to burst.

I followed him as he walked slowly out of the closet and sat on the floor with his back against my bed. I sat down next to him and watched him turn the figure over and over in his hands.

"I bet if the kids at school saw this they wouldn't call me dumb," he finally said.

I felt a real pang of alarm.

"Power Boy has never left my home since he came to live here," I said, hoping to squash his asking before he attempted. "Besides, you're not dumb."

"How do you know," he challenged.

"Because my mom has never invited a dummy into her home," I stated with self-assurance.

"There's a first time for everything."

I tried to change the subject. "Why were you only eating yams?"

He shrugged his shoulders. "Everything else was nasty."

"You didn't even taste anything else," I accused.

He started moving the figure's parts to see how they worked. I still had the box and pulled the accessories out.

"Here, you put a power rock in his hand like this," I said demonstrating because it was a little tricky.

Jason pulled it away before I could finish so that he could do it himself. He fumbled a bit but then discovered how to do it.

"See, you are smart," I pointed out. "You figured that out all by yourself. The first time I tried I had to ask my sisters to help and they still don't know how to do it. It took me a long time before I found out how to do it myself."

He looked unconvinced as he drew the figure's arm back and released it. The power rock flew pretty far across the room. He scrambled after it and brought it back.

"You don't have to go chasing just that single one. There's more," I said dumping a small pile of power rocks beside him.

We sat as he launched every single rock in a row, one right after the other. Then he went and collected them all and sat beside me again.

"I did try that green stuff," he said.

It took me a moment to realize he had returned to our earlier subject and was referring to the collard greens. Kids jump around off topic a lot. You have to be alert to keep up with them.

"Did you like it?" I asked.

He shook his head in disgust.

I shrugged. "I guess it's an acquired taste. It's all relative."

He frowned, concentrating. "That green stuff is your relative?" he asked looking at me, sure I was fooling him this time.

"Not that kind of relative. Relative, like in comparison. For instance, I wasn't crazy about peas. But after tasting some brussel sprouts, peas were like chocolate chips in comparison. In fact, now I consider peas the chocolate chips of vegetables."

He seemed pleased with that idea. "I like peas," he affirmed.

Seeking to further clarify what relative was, I decided to use numbers. I was always looking for an excuse to use math.

"Another way to explain relative is... say you have five dollars, that would be pretty nice, right?"

"That would be great. I only get a dollar for allowance."

"Well say you have your five dollars and you're all excited until you see your friend and she has a twenty."

"I don't have any girl friends!" he protested, indignant at the suggestion.

"Fine," I relented. "Your friend is a boy and he has a twenty. How would you feel about your five then."

He shook is head screwing up his face in dissatisfaction.

"Yeah," I agreed. "Five is fine until somebody else has a twenty and then it's not so great. So you see, how you think about the five is relative because it changes based on how you feel. Do you understand?"

"I think so."

"Suppose you took your five and found a friend who only had one dollar," I suggested. "How would you feel then?"

"This friend can be a girl this time," he offered.

"Why?" I eyed him suspiciously. "Because she doesn't have more money than you?"

He smiled sheepishly. Men, they're all the same.

"Whatever! She's a girl and she only has one dollar, wouldn't you feel great again?"

He frowned again in concentration. "No...," he said slowly. "Then she would feel bad like I did when my other friend had a twenty."

I paused in surprise.

"Well, what would you do about that?" I asked, curious.

He shrugged.

"Here," I said sliding five power rocks in front of Power Boy. "This is your five and this...," I said quickly returning to my closet and retrieving an Enviro Girl figure, "is her one. What would you do to make her feel better?" I placed Enviro Girl in front of him with a single power rock.

He ignored it at first then he took his five power rocks in one hand and her one in the other. Then he pooled them together on the rug in front of him.

"I'd share my money with her," he finally answered.

"Well, that's all well and good while you're together but suppose you had to leave, how would you share then?"

He considered my question and then placed one small power rock by Power Boy and then the next by Enviro Girl. Then he put another one by Power Boy and the next with Enviro Girl. He continued until there were two equal piles of power rocks beside each figure.

I felt a tingling deep down inside. Math excites me.

"That's great Jason. You'd have three and she'd have three."

He smiled at my approval.

"I have one last question for you. How many of your power rocks did you have to share with her to make her feel better?"

"You mean money," he corrected. Kids were such sticklers to the reality of their fantasy.

"Yeah, money," I agreed.

He looked at the pile in front of Enviro Girl and slid one power rock away and then another, leaving only one beside the figure. He held up the two power rocks in his hand.

"Genius," I declared.

He glowed at the high compliment.

"Listen to me," I said seriously, facing Jason.

He put everything aside sensing this was important.

"You are not dumb. In fact, you are the exact opposite of dumb."

I could see he didn't really believe me so I pressed ahead.

"Jason, you just did addition, subtraction, and division. Now it's been a long time since I was in first grade, but I'm sure they weren't doing division."

"I did division?"

"Yes."

"When?" he sounded upset that he had missed it.

"When you divided your pile equally between Enviro Girl and Power Boy."

He frowned. I was beginning to find that frown very adorable. "Is that why they call it division, because you divide it?" he asked.

"Yeah, I guess so," I laughed.

He laughed too, pleased with his discovery.

"But seriously," I continued. "The most important thing you showed me was your ability to learn from your experience. When you said you wouldn't feel great because your friend with only one dollar would feel bad like you did when your other friend had the twenty... Jason, I wish I could explain to you how special that is."

He just stared at me. I could tell it wasn't quite registering.

"Okay, just promise me one thing, Jason. Promise you won't let those kids make you think you're dumb. You're smart and some day you'll do great things so don't let those kids tear you down. All right?"

He nodded but it was obvious he was just humoring me.

I sighed. "We better go back down. We don't want to miss out on dessert."

Jason helped me straighten up before we went back downstairs. I could tell he wanted to hang onto Power Boy but I wasn't ready to let him go.

The Alexanders were getting ready to leave when we rejoined them. They were thanking everybody for a wonderful time and collecting their generously packed bags of extra food, compliments of mom.

"This'll be easier on you Harriet with your home still unsettled. You have my number. Call if you need anything," mom said as we all walked outside together. It was dark out but the street lights supplied sufficient brightness. I noticed Beverly's car was missing and realized he must have left while I was upstairs with Jason. I sat on our porch swing, listening to the drawn out farewells as I absentmindedly rocked myself back and forth.

We watched from our porch as the Alexanders finally walked up the road back to their new home. Watching the retreating figures, I suddenly realized what was out of sync that had been nagging me all evening.

The rest of Micah's family behaved nothing like him. They were normal. Then I realized something else. They all touched each other, except for Micah. I watched as Jason swung happily from the hand of each of his parents, their fluid motions working in unison to lift him as his feet kicked out wildly so he could go even higher. Micah followed behind, his posture rigid. He was the last to walk through their door.

I didn't realize I'd stopped swinging until I got up to head back inside. Like Micah, I was the last one in.

"Toxic waste?" dad cringed as I entered the kitchen. "Did you have to refer to my chicken as toxic waste?"

Kelly and Kylie smiled at the expression on his face.

"Dad, kids like drama. You know your chicken is the best," I consoled.

Mom came into the kitchen with several plates and headed for the sink.

"Mom, you and dad have been busy all day. Go to bed. Me, Ky, and Disa can clean up," Kelly said, taking the dishes from her.

"I have school tomorrow...," I began weakly, and Kelly glared at me. I looked at mom and dad, ready to plead my case to them. I was surprised at how tired they looked, especially dad. I remembered I'd done nothing to help prepare for our guests.

"Kelly's right mom," I said. "We can clean up."

With a little more encouraging, they finally went to bed, leaving the mess to us.

After they were gone, Kelly came up behind me and flicked a dish towel at me. "I do believe you are starting to grow up a little Baby Girl. We'll make a woman out of you yet."

I started to protest but after the Super Girl beating I'd received at the dinner table, I decided Baby Girl wasn't so bad.

I was so tired by the time we finished cleaning up, I barely had the strength to change into my pajamas. It seemed like the longest day of my life had finally come to an end. As soon as my head hit the pillow I fell asleep without torturing myself with one single replay of the day's excruciating events.

3 ~ *CHASED BY AN ANGEL*

One major benefit of the inability to dream, is missing out on nightmares. Unfortunately I no longer enjoyed that luxury because on the second night in a row, I had a dream. A very bad dream.

I bolted up in bed awake, heart racing breathing loud and Kylie was sitting on the side of my bed.

"Shhh, Adisa, you'll wake mom and dad," she whispered.

She had considerately turned on the light in my restroom because the full glare of my bedroom ceiling light would have startled me.

I could clearly see her face in the soft light.

"You were having a nightmare. You're okay now," she said reassuringly.

I grabbed her hand to make sure she was real and held on so she wouldn't disappear.

"You're shaking," she squeezed my hands back. "Are you okay?"

I looked around quickly for more assurance that I was back in the safety of my room. The dream had seemed so real.

My backpack was still on my desk where I'd left it the day before and I could see my clock radio on the night stand with the time glowing at me. My mom's photo still smiled at me from my dresser.

"Adisa, are you all right?" Kylie's voice was clearly worried.

I finally nodded and took a deep breath to calm myself. I smiled at her tentatively and she smiled back.

I was reminded of how she would give me that same smile when I was much younger. I would cry at night sometimes, scared to be alone in my room but too scared to leave my bed. She would come padding barefoot through the Jack and Jill restroom that separated our rooms at the time, take my hand and lead me back to the room she shared with Kelly.

"Get that baby out of here!" Kelly would grumpily demand, plugging her ears, clearly upset I'd disturbed her sleep.

But Kylie would ignore her, giving me a flashlight to hold while she drew pictures to entertain me and keep me quiet until I fell back to sleep.

"That's a record for you. Two nights in a row," she marveled now, still holding my hands.

I nodded in agreement, looking around again just in case.

"What were you dreaming?"

I shuddered involuntarily.

"Hey it's okay. You're safe now." She squeezed my hands again.

"Can I come sleep with you?" I blurted out.

"You're a little too old for that don't you think?"

I quickly shook my head no and she laughed quietly.

"Girl, scoot over," she said, releasing my hands.

I quickly complied and she settled in next to me. We lay quietly in the dark for awhile, facing each other.

"So are you going to tell me about your dream? You don't have to but I think it might not seem so scary if you did."

She waited, while I collected my thoughts.

"We were out in the backyard," I began. "You, me, and Kelly were in that little kiddie inflatable pool we used to have and we were splashing and laughing. Dad and mom were sitting in lawn chairs beside the pool. I felt so happy and it seemed so real."

I paused, remembering how the warmth of the sun felt even though the woods shaded our backyard. I could still feel the strong sense of love and belonging I felt in the dream.

I continued. "We were playing in the water and suddenly Kelly went under like something had pulled her down. You know, like in that movie Jaws? She was gone that quick. You were crawling around feeling under the water for her. I was too scared to help, thinking that whatever got her would get me too.

I looked at mom and dad but it was like they didn't even see what was going on. I called them but they didn't hear me. When I looked back, you were struggling to keep your head above the water. It had you too and was pulling you under. I could see the fear in your eyes. I reached for you but you wouldn't take my hand. You didn't say anything but I knew you didn't want to pull me down with you, then you were gone.

I looked at mom and dad again but their chairs were empty and I saw them walking into the woods. I called but they didn't look back and then they were gone.

I was in the water alone now but then I knew that thing was behind me, waiting for me to turn around and see it. I didn't turn around because I was scared it would get me. So I sat like that for a long time, not looking back, thinking if I didn't see it then it wouldn't get me. I just sat, staring at the woods for a long time. Then I slowly got out of the water thinking that if I was real quiet it would leave me alone.

I tried to get to the woods because I knew I would be safe with mom and dad. Just when I was about to reach them, I heard that thing behind me about to tear me apart and I woke up."

Kylie waited to make sure I was finished. "Wow. I got goose bumps just listening to that. I can't imagine what it was like for you to experience it. But it's not real, Disa."

"It seemed real. I don't like dreaming. It's just like you're awake all the time."

"It's not always like that. Sometimes you even know you're dreaming while it's going on."

"Kylie, why do you think I've started dreaming now? Do you think there's something wrong with me?" I asked worried.

"No. You've probably been dreaming all along. Maybe the only difference now is that you're starting to remember some of them."

"I don't think I dreamed before. I used to just float in nothingness. Now, it's like my mind doesn't stop working. I can't shut it off. It wears me out. I don't see how you people have put up with dreaming all this time. No wonder you wake up so tired."

"Uhmmm," Kelly sighed her amusement. She was starting to get drowsy.

"You know, now that I think about it, I never used to be tired after I would wake up but I was practically dragging yesterday morning after my first dream. I bet I'll be tired when it's time to get up for school. What do you think?"

"Maybe," she mumbled.

"Kylie thanks for my angel picture," I remembered.

"Uh-huh," she hummed.

"You have bad dreams too sometimes don't you?" I asked trying to keep her talking.

It was awhile before she drowsily whispered, "Sometimes."

"Tell me about them," I said, willing to listen to horror stories just so she'd stay awake with me.

But she never did. I considered turning the restroom light out but I was too scared to put my feet down on the floor. I knew it was childish.

I daydreamed about Micah until I drifted back to sleep and found it very comforting. When I woke again, Kylie was gone and the sun was shining behind my curtains. Another day of school. I was very tired as I trudged to the restroom to perform my morning duties.

Only mom was up when I went down for breakfast and I was disappointed she wasn't sleeping in because I wanted to have peach cobbler for breakfast since I didn't get any dessert the night before. I got a bowl of cereal without milk instead. Mom cut up some fruit then quickly sautéed strips of chicken while boiling some grits then scrambled some eggs. She placed it all in front of me with a side of buttered toast.

It was another warm morning as I headed to school. The moving truck was gone and I recognized Micah's jeep still in their driveway so I knew he hadn't left for school yet. It really didn't surprise me that he drove to school even though it was only about a mile down the road. If I had a car and a license I would drive to school too.

I was looking forward to seeing Micah, pleased that I had three classes with him, computer, gym, and math. Then I remembered how the twins had humiliated me. Then I recalled how he had defended me. Then I thought of dancing with him in gym and felt completely conflicted. School hadn't even started yet and I was already back on that emotional roller coaster.

"Oh!" I said startled.

Micah was standing by a tree on the wooded side of the street. He looked magnificent as if he had stepped straight out of a movie. He had on a dark blue shirt and jeans and he looked incredible in them.

"I thought you were still at home," I said then realized it sounded like I was keeping tabs on him or something.

"Is something wrong with your jeep?" I asked.

"No." Even that brief response was the perfect pitch that gave me flutters in my stomach.

I waited for him to explain why he was walking today when he was driving the day before. When he didn't, I asked. "Why are you walking?"

"I wanted to."

I fleetingly wondered if he'd been waiting for me and then rejected the idea. I felt ridiculous trying to have a conversation with him while we were on opposite sides of the street but he made no move to join me on the sidewalk, which was the logical choice since there was no sidewalk on his side.

"Did you enjoy yourself at dinner last night?" I asked. Personally I had mixed feelings about it.

"Yes."

He was driving me crazy! Why couldn't he talk in a complete paragraph? I was happy to hear that he had a good time though. I fidgeted trying to think of something to ask him so I could hear more of his fascinating voice.

I gripped my backpack straps in determination and hurried across the street before I changed my mind. He watched me with his beautiful distant eyes without comment. When I stood in front of him I had to tilt my head slightly to see his face.

I was breathless. He was insanely attractive. His full lips were sculpted perfection and he had a gently chiseled jaw that I wanted to trace with my fingers.

I turned away forgetting what I was going to say, my thoughts confusing me. He waited patiently. He was so self-possessed it was unnerving. I turned back to him when I remembered what I was going to say.

"I just wanted to thank you for defending me yesterday. I really appreciate it." I was overwhelmed by my conflicting emotions and felt vulnerable having crossed the street to mention my humiliation to him.

He didn't respond, simply looked at me as he would a lamp post, a bush, or a stop sign. How could a boy defend a girl like he did one night and then act as if she didn't exist the next day? "Well, that's all I wanted to say." I felt foolish. I crossed back over to the sidewalk and headed for school. My footsteps and the buzzing, chirping, and rustling of nature were the only things I heard.

I looked back expecting to see Micah still standing by the tree but he was walking along, on his side of the street, silently keeping pace with me. I frowned in confusion. He was seriously starting to annoy me and as I finally made it to campus I wondered if he was more than a little mental.

"Seriously Adisa, it was down right criminal what you were doing to that man's toes," Avery teased when I made it to homeroom.

"Shut up! I'm surprised you could stand looking past Liz long enough to see anybody else was around."

I was relieved Avery was joking with me. When I first sat down, he seemed reserved. When I discovered he thought I was mad because of the way I'd rushed out of class after I missed the last math problem, I quickly set him straight. He said he thought it was suspicious that I'd missed the problem when I was the one who taught him how to apply that concept in the first place.

He offered to share his prize for being the last one standing at the board since I had been acting on his behalf. But I declined, insisting he had earned it. With the misunderstanding cleared up, we quickly slipped back into our easy friendship.

"I hope he's wearing steel-toed shoes today," Avery continued and I cringed.

"Was it really that bad?" I asked, distressed.

"You should know. You were there."

"I know but I was hoping it didn't look as bad as it felt," I said fishing for reassurance.

"Let me put it like this, I believe this may be the first class you don't make an A in here at Talbot," he predicted.

"That bad?"

"Don't worry. It'll be a good character building experience for you. Give you something to overcome."

"Please, please stop," I begged.

"Okay, I'll stop," he mercifully relented.

We watched the TV announcements for a while.

"Guess what," I said.

"What?"

"He's my new neighbor."

"Who?" he asked, looking confused.

I gave him a pointed look.

"No!" he exclaimed with dawning understanding.

"Yes."

"Him?"

"Yes."

"No! This is too good. You can't write this kind of stuff. How'd you find out?" he asked, thoroughly amused.

"Yesterday, my mom invited the new neighbors to dinner. When it was dinner time, I opened the door and guess who was standing there?"

"No!" Avery laughed. I joined him. It was good to have somebody to laugh with over the whole ridiculous situation. It took the sting out of it, a little.

"So how...what... do you...," he couldn't figure out what to ask.

"I know," I said. "I completely understand. The whole time I was scared to death he'd mention our dancing but he never did. Which reminds me, now I have to dance with him for the whole semester. It's a weird mess and it's driving me crazy. He's in my next class too and ...,"

The bell rang.

"Great," I groaned. "Guess I'll see you in gym."

"Well, there's always a chance that you injured him so severely he won't be there," Avery couldn't resist a final jab.

I rolled my eyes in frustration. "He's perfectly fine. He practically walked me to school."

"Really?" His shocked expression was hilarious.

I left without explaining.

I was relieved to see that Micah wasn't in the computer class when I arrived. I chose to sit at a different group of four computers, thinking it was only the second day of class and we hadn't even turned the computers on the first day so surely nobody was too attached at this early stage.

I remembered Ms. Fulton's restrictions from the previous day and left my computer off, silently praying that somebody, anybody would sit next to me before Micah got there. *I hate roller coasters,* I thought as I silently nursed my bruised ego from the morning's fresh humiliation.

A girl walked over and I smiled at her in expectation, remembering Kylie once told me I should smile more, it made me more approachable. The girl frowned in irritation and walked away. I realized it was probably her seat I had taken.

I was aware the moment he walked through the door. I saw him turn toward where we were sitting the day before then he stopped. My heart was pounding. I concentrated hard on twisting and untangling my fingers together. I heard the chair next to me pull out and he sat down without saying a word.

I felt flush with anger. Why was he doing this to me? Was he trying to drive me insane? I glared at him not caring if he saw. He looked at me with his distant eyes. His face was so heartbreakingly beautiful with its incredible glowing copper. I couldn't bear it. I was the first to look away.

After the bell rang, Ms. Fulton stated that where we sat was our team. She had to divide the long table with the bank of computers into groups of four then she passed out markers and stacks of poster board paper cut down into large rectangles. We were going to have a competitive group pop quiz to see how much we already knew about the Internet before starting our computer lessons. Talbot was big on competition.

There was only one boy across from Micah and me. He came around to our side of the table so we could confer as a team and I scooted closer to Micah to make more room for him.

I inadvertently brushed against Micah's arm and nearly jumped ten feet. Micah didn't move at all. It was small comfort that whatever aversion he had to talking to me did not cause him to recoil from my touch. Then I thought, if it didn't bother him, I wouldn't let it bother me. So I let my arm fall naturally but didn't dare look at Micah. It brushed up against his and I immediately felt warm tingling sensations. I tried to ignore it.

Ms. Fulton asked the first question and the boy, Jody, crowded in so the other teams couldn't hear our discussion. I felt him press against my arm and marveled that I felt nothing while my other arm, barely touching Micah was electrified.

"The World Wide Web," Jody said, and we all agreed that's what the letters www stood for. He took the marker and wrote our answer on a rectangle of poster board.

When Ms. Fulton called for the class to reveal their answers, he held ours up and cards went up for the other groups as well. Ms. Fulton noted points for the groups who answered correctly.

"That was an easy one," she said. "This one is a little harder. What does html stand for?"

Jody leaned in, shaking his head that he had no idea.

"Hypertext Markup Language," I supplied.

"You're sure?" he asked.

"She's correct," Micah confirmed, the rumble of his voice setting off a dizzying mental thrill that gave me an incredible buzz.

I was convinced I was in some kind of teen Hell for contemptuously mocking my sisters on numerous occasions when they were acting ridiculous over some boy. But this punishment was excessive compared to my crime.

Jody wrote down my answer and on the reveal, we were awarded more points.

Ms. Fulton continued. "This one's True or False: You have to have Internet access to create web pages."

Jody wrote true without even consulting us.

"That's actually false," I corrected.

He leaned forward to look past me at Micah for confirmation and my irritation flared but I firmly kept my gaze down.

"I'm sure we can trust Adisa. So when she gives an answer, just write it down," Micah said.

I would have fallen off my chair when he said my name if I hadn't been wedged between the two of them. My head was spinning. He said two whole sentences. Two whole sentences and my name. And, incredibly, defended me yet again.

Jody ripped up his answer then wrote false on a new card and again, we received points.

Ms. Fulton explained, "All you really need to simply *create* web pages is a computer and a text editor. You don't need to be connected to the Internet until you're ready to upload the web pages you've created."

The questions got progressively harder. By the time Ms. Fulton was asking us to write sample code to place text and images on a web page, I was the only one giving the correct answers.

At the end of class, our team was declared the winner and I made a mental note to thank Kylie for her summer web training. Ms. Fulton gave our team certificates to eat at some restaurant and I put mine away without even looking at it.

"I hope we at least get to turn the computers on tomorrow," Jody grumbled after Ms. Fulton was out of hearing range then returned to his side of the table, waiting to be dismissed.

I had to admit, it was strange that after two days in a computer class, we hadn't even signed on for a password yet.

After the bell, students began filing out the door but I took my time hoping Micah would leave first. I was dreading gym and wanted to put it off as long as possible. But Micah was waiting, not even making a pretense of collecting his things. I suddenly realized that I was normally the first one to leave our classes, usually in a state of turmoil, running from some embarrassing incident either involving him or he had been witness to.

When I realized he wasn't going to budge until I did, I left.

Mr. Winton gave us the option of dressing for gym or not. He did suggest that we wear clothing that would not inhibit our dance movements and warned that if our dress did interfere with our dancing, he would start requiring we wear the usual gym attire.

The thought of dancing around with Micah in nothing but shorts and tank top so rattled me I felt lightheaded. I was a very conservative dresser and the image of being so close to him without the barrier of that extra material was unnerving.

Mr. Winton gave us a brief overview of Latin dance and said the style we would begin with was Jive because it was a fun energetic dance. He also informed us that he would always introduce each new style we learned by performing it himself.

To demonstrate the Jive, he had recruited Ms. Becket, an administrator from the front office. I was surprised because she was a full figured woman who I rarely saw standing or expressing emotion, particularly not the joyous energy Mr. Winton claimed the Jive required. I doubted she would have much energy to pull off any style of dance that exerted her.

The music started and the couple transformed before my eyes. Tiny Mr. Winton seemed to pull himself up several inches taller and Ms. Becket's expression spread into a radiantly beautiful smile.

They began bouncing lightly in unison, crisscrossing their legs and delivering sharp well placed kicks between and to the side of each other's legs, moving across the floor as if there was no such thing as gravity. The dance was energetic and their feet appeared to move lightning fast.

I watched in awe as they smoothly crossed the floor at incredible speed. They made it look so easy and effortless as they made pass after pass.

It's hard to impress high school students so when the dance came to an end and everybody in the gym was applauding and cheering in amazement, both Mr. Winton and Ms. Becket looked a little overwhelmed.

I looked at Micah with dread. He was the only one besides me not applauding, his arms rigid at his sides. Sure, I was sometimes mad at Micah but I certainly didn't want to maim him. Especially not now since he had two times defended me. I could barely follow him around the dance floor walking, how was I going to pull it off spinning and kicking at him?

Micah's face, as usual, didn't betray a hint of emotion. Not one flicker of alarm for his legs.

When the applause died down, Mr. Winton and Ms. Becket demonstrated the proper hold and other basic dance techniques. Afterwards we had to demonstrate the same as he came around adjusting us.

Micah put out his hand for me without hesitation and I mumbled under my breath, "You are one brave bizarre boy."

His eyes seemed to come alive for a moment but when I looked more closely I determined it must have been a trick of the light. My heart was as active as ever as Micah held me in his arms.

When we were done walking through the basic steps, Mr. Winton started the music. I tried my level best not to but I tore Micah's legs up anyway. They were hard as rocks and I sometimes hurt my own foot when it slammed into him. Not once did he cry out or even flinch.

So now, not only was I stomping on his toes, I was inflicting vicious blows to his shins as well. Of course I offered up my apologies and berated myself to no end but that didn't save his legs.

Not once did he kick me. His kicks and flicks, as Mr. Winton called them, were always perfectly placed outside or between my legs where they were supposed to be. He held me gently but firmly, guiding me with the utmost care around the floor.

When Mr. Winton came by to observe us, I saw him visibly flinch as I delivered one particularly violent blow. He offered advice and readjusted me, positioning me with his hands but he did not, as I'd seen him do with other couples, step in and dance with me himself. *Smart man*, I thought resentfully. When he was done correcting me, he walked away without saying a word to Micah but his eyes clearly extended his sympathies.

I was nearly in tears at the end of class as I offered Micah my final apologies then rushed out.

At lunch I couldn't eat anything. I sat with Avery, Liz, and a few other regulars.

"Cheese and rice, Adisa! I would hate to see what his legs looked like after you got finished with…," Avery was saying but I didn't hear the rest.

I had run into the hall, ducking outside, hoping nobody would follow me then burst into tears when I was sure I was alone.

I sat on the ground secluded by trees away from the building. Tears silently streamed down my face as I contemplated my situation. There was no way I could continue. My nerves were stretched to the limit and I knew it would start affecting my studies if I didn't do something about it.

After awhile, I was able to calm myself and even smiled at Avery's use of cheese and rice to avoid the blasphemy of Jesus Christ.

Voices drifted through the trees to me and I recognized Lucia's lilting accent and Justin's voice. His words surprised me because they were low and menacing.

"I told you I don't like you wearing that. Do you want other guys looking at you?" he hissed.

"Justin please, you're hurting... ow!" Lucia's voice was strained.

"I'm sorry. I didn't mean to hurt you," Justin's voice was pleading now. "If you just didn't wear that kind of stuff, everything would be fine. If you only knew what the guys say about you... It drives me crazy. I love you so much."

"Okay Justin. I won't wear this again since it upsets you. I can wear the black one you bought for my birthday," she offered.

"No! That's for when we're alone."

"Okay. How about the yellow one with the large flower print?"

"Yeah that's okay," he consented. "So, I'll see you after school?" he asked.

"Justin I told you my mother's sick and she needs... ow that hurts," Lucia's voice was in real pain now.

Justin ground out angrily, "Just for a few minutes, Lucia. I swear...,"

"Lucia," I said stepping from behind the trees. "Mr. Preston sent me to get you. He said he was coming to get you himself if I didn't hurry back with you. Your mom called and I think it's pretty serious."

I spoke with an authority I didn't feel in the least. And used the name of our physically imposing Principal, hoping his image would loosen the grip that I saw Justin's large hand had on Lucia's fragile looking arm.

I went right up to Lucia and took the arm Justin did not have and started pulling her after me. For a moment, I thought Justin was going to play tug of war with her. I heard the bell ring.

"Mr. Preston's coming. We'd better hurry," I said forcefully.

Students were out, changing to their next class.

Lucia tried to twist her arm out of Justin's grip and he reluctantly released her.

"I'd better come too," He said.

"NO! Mr. Preston said just Lucia. Besides you'll be late for class."

Lucia let me rush her along, distress etched on her face. When we were a safe distance away, I assured her everything was okay and there was no call from her mom. After a brief moment of relief, she got angry at me for lying.

When I told her why I did it, she got angrier and told me to mind my own business and stay out of hers. Then she stormed off, leaving me in a crowd of students.

When it was time for my math class, for the first time ever in my life, I seriously considered skipping, not wanting to face Micah. It took every ounce of courage I had to walk into that classroom. Avery and Liz looked worried and I apologized for being a drama queen and running out of the cafeteria. Avery looked really sorry for teasing me.

Micah came in and took his seat behind me. I didn't hear anything the teacher said because I was thoroughly consumed with concentrating on the prickly feeling on the back of my neck due to Micah's presence.

When I walked home, he was there on his side of the street. We didn't say a word.

I considered talking to my sisters about my dilemma but they were immersed in the last minute details of their college departure.

At school the next day, I listened to Avery speak glowingly of Liz. They were really growing close and it appeared it was thanks to me. Out of their mutual concern for me, they were beginning to form a close bond. I told Avery I was glad to help out.

In computer class, we were finally able to turn our computers on and I kept my head buried in my monitor. I typed up an anonymous letter to the counselor and printed it out along with our class exercise. I turned in the assignment but kept the note. On my way to gym, I made sure nobody was paying attention then I slipped it in the counselor's office box. I felt like a snitch.

When I got to gym, I noticed Lucia was leaning against the wall. Justin was nowhere to be seen. Halfway through class, when

I saw the counselor come and pull Lucia out of class, I felt guilty. Micah continued to endure my abuse of his toes and legs in silence. I had stopped apologizing and berating myself. If he didn't seem to care, why should I?

Justin didn't show up until Friday. He was now assigned to dance with Sonjia but his eyes followed Lucia around the floor.

I noticed Avery and Liz were dancing kind of stiffly and was surprised. Their Jive didn't have the same spring it usually had. Something was wrong.

After class I tried to catch up to Avery but he was out the door quicker than I'd ever gone and Liz avoided me. Neither one was around for lunch so I sat with the rest of the students who usually shared our table.

I overheard one of the girls spreading a nasty rumor about Avery and Liz and before I knew it, I'd lost my temper.

"That's a lie!" I said, my raised voice silencing the chatter at our table and a couple others.

Sonjia, the girl passing on the vicious gossip looked at me, startled at being challenged.

"I heard them with my own ears, Adisa." She sounded so confident, for a moment I felt a little unsure of myself.

"Then you miss-heard," I quickly recovered. "You shouldn't go around listening in on other people's business anyway," I retorted, deciding until I heard it from my friends, I wasn't going to believe it.

Sonjia got right up in my face and I felt intimidated. She was a big girl and I could imagine the damage she could inflict on my skinny behind.

I tried to stare her down and was surprised at how beautiful she actually was. Her full dark face had a soft dreamy quality about it that I'd never noticed before. Probably because her nasty attitude usually twisted her face into an unattractive expression.

"You're one to talk," she said, her voice emotionless. "Lucia told me you were hiding out, listening to her and Justin and then you told a bunch of lies on them. Now they can't be together and they're both miserable and it's all your fault."

Her vacant eyes and matter of fact statement dumped all the blame on me. But I was too stunned by her words to respond. Why would Lucia do that? I went out on a limb to save her and now she's mad at me and wants to be with that idiot who was hurting her.

I glared at Sonjia and considered making fun of her stupid name. She claimed it was actually 'son jee ah' instead of 'son ya' like it should have been pronounced. I'd heard some of the kids tease her about her size and about how dark she was as well as the ignorant way she pronounced her name and I considered adding my insults to theirs.

But all the fight left me and I didn't have anything left to say to her as I seriously began to worry about my friends.

In math class Avery and Liz came in separately. I waited until they were both seated.

"Where were you guys at lunch today?" I asked trying to mask my anger and hurt.

Liz couldn't even look at me and I could see color start to rise in her cheeks.

"I had stuff to do," Avery said, glancing at me.

"Are you sure you two love birds weren't off somewhere together?" I persisted.

Liz looked at me then. She must have heard the anger in my voice. My eyes were furious. She turned bright red and looked away.

"Is it true?" I asked, my voice low but full of anger.

Her eyes came back up and pleaded with me and I could see tears shining in them. "Adisa please, not here."

"Just tell me if it's true or not because if it is I don't have anything else to say to you for the rest of my life."

"You don't... understand. It's...It's... complicated," she stuttered.

"Is it true you won't date Avery because his mother is black? Yes or no!" I demanded.

"Don't do this Adisa," Avery leaned toward me. He put his hand on my arm. "We'll talk about it later. It's not her fault."

I snatched my arm away. What was wrong with everybody? First Lucia and now Avery! They stared evil people right in the face, let them do and say bad things to them, and they still wanted to be with them, defend them.

At that moment, Micah walked through the door and all the pent up rage I had for Liz, Justin, Lucia, and now even Avery spilled onto him. He was just as bad as the rest with his weird rude ways. I hated him too.

Class started and I didn't say anything to anybody and nobody spoke to me.

After class, I hid out in the girls' restroom, not wanting to see Micah walking home on his side of the street. I swear, if I saw his vacant eyes and rigid posture one more time I would snap!

I refused to cry while I waited and thought about my family. They would be on the road by now, headed for Bartlett. Dad said they were pulling out at lunch time to get there before rush hour traffic. Suddenly I wished more than anything that I'd gone with them. I wasn't looking forward to going home to an empty house after the day I was having. I stopped thinking about them when tears seriously started to threaten.

I thought of Avery and it wasn't much better. He was almost like family. I thought of the pain I saw in his eyes then I thought of Liz with disgust. I thought she was our friend. How could she do something so mean and hateful. And Avery, I knew he was a nice guy but this was ridiculous. How could he defend her?

I tried to push Avery out of my thoughts as a new idea tried to creep inside my mind. I tried not to face it but it had me cornered in that restroom stall. Maybe I was afraid that deep down inside, maybe I was just like them because even with his rude behavior, I was still attracted to Micah. And if that was true, if I was just like them...

I opened the stall door, hoisting my overloaded backpack onto my shoulders. Talbot piled homework on us even on the weekends. There was nobody out in the hall as I headed out.

I was so wrapped up in my thoughts that I almost didn't see him at first. He was further ahead in the shade of the trees but he was looking the other way so he didn't see me. He was waiting there, rigid and still as ever. I wondered if he was waiting for me.

On impulse, I crossed the street and dove into the woods. I'd had enough! I stomped deeper into the dense greenery looking for a short cut to my backyard. If the road that wound around to my home was about a mile then it had to be an even shorter distance through the woods. I was athletic. I had run the neighborhood and school track all summer and I'd run the school track every afternoon this week. I felt pretty confident that I could make it to my back door without ever having to see Micah's ridiculous beautiful face.

I walked around hanging kudzu and stepped over fallen trees with roots pulling up the earth to expose the red Georgia clay. I headed in the general direction of my home. I imagined Micah standing in the shade of those trees all night, waiting. And still being there the next morning. But the next morning was Saturday and there was no school. So I imagined him still standing there through the weekend. I wondered if he would actually register surprise when he saw me heading out for school Monday morning. I smiled to myself at the image of him with some actual emotion plastered across his face and some of my anger faded.

I couldn't see the street from the depths of the woods and I was insulated from the sounds of cars on the road. The tangle of overgrowth wasn't too hard to navigate but it definitely was a bit more challenging than the sidewalk.

I was walking through a clearing when I first sensed I was being followed. I felt exposed as the sun burned down on me so I hurried to the safety of the shade on the other side. As I stepped between the trees, I thought about crouching down and waiting to see who or what was following me but then thought I'd rather try to put as much distance between us as possible.

I pushed forward looking back every now and then but the trees behind me blocked my view. What was that old saying? I can't see the forest for the trees.

I kept moving faster and faster because it sounded like whatever was following me was getting closer. My mind flashed on the nightmare I had a few nights back. The thing in the pool that pulled my sisters under.

I started running as I distinctly heard something now crashing through the woods behind me. My heart was racing as I blindly stumbled over the uneven ground filled with nature's debris.

I bounced wildly off of trees that I wasn't quick enough to step around and at one point it felt as if something yanked me back violently before releasing me. I felt lighter afterwards as I sped ahead, panicked beyond reason. I felt like I was running up an incline but wasn't sure as my eyes frantically searched for openings in the dense foliage.

Suddenly I was falling and thin branches pulled at me. A pile of vines and leaves cushioned my long drop. I scrambled to my feet and continued to push forward not knowing which way I was heading now, just trying to get away from whatever was behind me. It felt like I was swimming in a sea of green and my feet felt wet. I wondered how that happened but I didn't stop to find out.

I couldn't hear anything behind me anymore but I kept going, wanting to get as far away from it as I possibly could. I was starting to wear out and I was berating myself for my rash decision to cut through the woods in the first place when I slammed into something that stepped directly into my path.

I instinctively veered to the side away from it and saw two arms reaching for me. I jerked away and fell backwards and started scrambling back and away, too scared to focus clearly on what I was trying to get away from.

It fell on top of me, pinning my wrists to the ground beside my head, the grip was loose enough so as not to hurt my wrists but closed enough so I couldn't pull my hands free. I struggled, but whatever was on top of me was inhumanly immovable. I was blinded with fear and increased my efforts.

Then it spoke. "Stop. You're hurting yourself."

As soon as I heard his voice, void of emotion, all my fear frustration and anger boiled over and I wildly yanked my arms down trying to free them. But it was like they were being held by stone shackles that didn't budge at all.

"Be still and I'll let you go," the emotionless voice said.

But I couldn't stop myself now, I was beyond mad. It was like the rages I used to experience when I was a child. They would take hold of me and I couldn't control them. All I could do was let it run its course. I twisted my arms until they hurt, not caring, straining to break free.

Suddenly I sensed a change, like a barrier between us had been removed and he felt close, unbearably close. In the same instant, I heard him let out a deep groan and I wondered if I had actually managed to hurt him somehow.

He continued to restrain my arms as I fought but it was different now. I could feel the warmth of his hands and the smooth texture of his skin as he held onto my wrists. And it was more of an effort for him to subdue me. Now he kept shifting as he struggled to keep me restrained.

"Adisa, *please!*" he gasped and it was his anguish filled plea that finally pierced my frenzied mind. Hearing emotion in his voice was like Beverly's hand on Kelly's shoulder. I was stunned into stillness.

I stared up into his face, finally able to focus. The first thing I saw was a pair of eyes. They were no longer vacant. They were filled with emotion, overflowing. Not distant anymore, instead very present. I could feel his breath on my face. I felt him trembling as he released me and moved to the side.

He kept his hands raised as if to show me he meant me no harm but strangely enough, my fear and rage were completely gone, replaced by a cautious curiosity.

"Please... just give me a minute," his voice rasped. Talking seemed to be an effort for him.

I stared at him in fascination. He was trembling and I could tell he was trying hard to control it. I had the impression that if he didn't think I would run off the second he turned his back, he would have turned away to hide his internal struggle from me.

He shuddered and his eyes showed a vulnerability that made me want to reach out and reassure him. But I resisted and just lay still.

We stayed like that for a long time as he slowly gained control of himself, his hands floating in the space between us as if to hold me in place without actually touching me.

I studied him. Now that my emotions were under control, I could see him clearly. He was still incredibly attractive but now he appeared more human, which made him even more appealing. His hazel eyes were filled with such raw emotion it made me feel self conscious to see him so exposed.

His skin was glowing and I could actually see a fine mist of perspiration on his forehead. I couldn't recall ever seeing him sweat before and Georgia had been extremely hot.

I was even impressed by his breathing. His whole body moved with it. I recalled the many times I'd sat right next to him, even dancing the exhausting Jive with him, and he appeared not to be breathing at all, ever.

I was amazed by everything about him.

When he finally had control of himself the first thing he asked was if I was okay.

I nodded and relief swiftly filled his eyes. I gasped at the immediate response. I couldn't believe he cared that deeply.

He slowly lowered his hands as if he wanted to be careful not to make any sudden movements around me.

"What were you doing?" His eyes filled with so much confusion, it hurt to look at them.

"I was... trying to... get home," I finally choked out.

"Why didn't you use the sidewalk like you usually do?" His anxiety was so genuine I actually felt guilty.

"Because you were there," I answered, too overwhelmed to lie.

"Me?" he said in surprise and it was a wonder to see that emotion appear in his anxious eyes. Then they filled with confusion again and I was getting lightheaded watching the intense changes play across his dazzling features.

"You were trying to get away from me?"

I nodded, my eyes still glued to his face, curiously waiting to see what emotion my response would bring to his eyes this time. It was guilt and it twisted my heart with regret to know I had caused it.

"I frighten you? Oh, I... I'm sorry... I didn't know," he stammered.

His apology took me by surprise and his halted speech was the first time I'd ever heard him speak in an imperfect way.

His eyes quickly inspected me as if to make sure I wasn't hurt. Then he carefully reached out to me. "Let me help you sit up."

He gently took me by the shoulders and helped me straighten up. Then he slowly slid his hands down my arms, over my elbows and with the utmost care, cradled my wrists in each of his hands.

"You are hurt," he said. The pain I saw in his eyes registered more than the pain in my wrists.

I felt a light rubbing sensation over my wrists and, with much difficulty, I forced my eyes away from his face to see what he was doing.

He drew his thumbs slowly, back and forth across the bruises and scrapes on my wrists. I was surprised to see them.

"You shouldn't run through unfamiliar areas like that. You could have been seriously hurt," he said, concern edging his voice.

The force of his gentle reprimand took me by surprise and I defensively yanked my wrists out of his hands and blurted out, "Well I didn't know who you were or why you were chasing me or what you wanted. For all I knew you could've been... some kind of...," but the memory of my fear washed over me and my voice faltered.

His eyes filled with horror then anguish. "I would never... I couldn't...I wouldn't even think of..." I could see the heat of his emotions burning in his eyes as his jaw clinched.

"We'd better go," he finally said helping me up, and the remorse in his voice sent a pang through me so sharp I trembled as I stood. He kept his hands on my arms to steady me and where they touched, my skin tingled.

When I was sure I wouldn't fall down, I took a self conscious step back and he let his hands fall away. Suddenly I was aware that I was in the middle of nowhere, alone with a boy and my dad's disapproving face filled my mind. Guilt and sorrow filled my eyes with tears.

Micah reached up as if ready to wipe them away if I couldn't hold them back and I abruptly turned away, ashamed he had seen. He started walking around as if he was looking for something. I saw him stop and bend down to pick something up.

He came back over to me with several dark green leaves bearing a distinct pattern. He crushed them, releasing a pleasant aroma and squeezed a creamy white substance out then reached for my wrists.

I pulled back. "Hey, that might be poison ivy or...," I started to protest but stopped, dazzled by a small smile dancing around the corners of his mouth. I'd never seen *that* before. He looked positively angelic.

"They're not poisonous. It's just a little trick I picked up in Africa. It's an antibiotic and it'll draw the soreness out and help heal your scratches but it only works on minor ones like these," he said.

He gently rubbed the milky material onto my wounds as he explained to me. It immediately cooled and soothed the stinging marks.

"Better?" he asked and I realized he thought I was emotionally on edge due to the pain of my wrists, unaware that I was missing my family, surely at Bartlett by now.

I nodded, too choked up to speak.

He kept rubbing until the creamy substance was completely absorbed into my skin.

I was staring intently at his face so it took me awhile before I realized he was still rubbing even though the cream had long disappeared, a curious bewildered look of wonder in his eyes. It was as if he just discovered the sense of touch and was now starved for it. I moved away blushing, glad for my dark coloring which I was sure hid it from his inquisitive eyes.

An image of Liz's crimson blush flashed in my mind and I felt a twinge of sympathy for her. It must be awful to have your own body betray your emotions when you'd rather keep them hidden. Then I remembered why she had blushed and some of my old anger returned.

"Did I upset you?" Micah asked, his eyes searching my face.

I shook my head, not wanting to talk about it. It was still too raw. I looked around to see which way to start back and didn't have a clue. I turned around trying to pick out a familiar path but all around us looked impenetrable and foreign to me.

Micah walked over to a curtain of vines and lifted them aside then extended his other hand to help me through. I took it and stepped over the tangle of brush at my feet and he followed me letting the vines fall behind him.

He released my hand as we walked across a fairly level patch of land but took it again to help me over fallen branches and any other obstacles. Soon, he was helping me so often, he just kept my hand in his.

We walked without saying a word and I became aware, as he was picking out our best route, that he was absently tracing circular patterns on the back of my hand with his thumb.

I tried to ignore it but fiery sensations crowded out all other feelings until that was all I was focused on.

We crossed a small trickling stream that I didn't remember passing before but then I thought of my wet feet and figured that was how it happened.

Soon we came to a giant fallen tree. It was enormous. I definitely didn't remember this. I saw a large pile of dead leaves and vines piled high against its sides and thought back to my fall. How did I get to the top of there in order to fall down here? It seemed impossible.

Micah looked at each end of the tree and neither end looked negotiable. He took a hold of a sturdy vine hanging down from high above the fallen tree and released my hand to test his weight on it.

Then he turned back and pulled me close to him. Before I knew what was up, I was sitting sideways on his lap as he scaled the side of the tree, using the vine to hoist us up as his feet walked up the side of the solid trunk. I leaned heavily against his chest, feeling his heart beat, my feet dangling as the ground receded behind him.

My face fell against his neck, his body gently rocking me as I felt his legs working up the tree beneath me. He smelled incredible. I resisted the urge to press a kiss against his skin, thinking I shouldn't try to take advantage of a boy attempting to rescue me.

We made it to the top and he eased me onto my feet, releasing the vine before reclaiming my hand. A long stretch of earth was built up against the tree on the other side and I vaguely remembered running up an incline. That's how I'd gotten to the top before my fall.

We walked to the bottom of the incline and Micah paused to pick something up that was snagged on a tall bush. It was my backpack. I hadn't even realized I didn't have it. The bush must have grabbed it right off my back, relieving me of my burden. That's why I felt lighter afterwards.

"I've got it," Micah said holding the backpack away from me when I reached for it. I felt guilty. In addition to dealing with my demented behavior, he now felt obligated to carry my heavy books.

We walked a little further and Micah used his backpack hand to hold back a final curtain of vines. Still holding hands, we stepped through together.

Somehow we had bypassed the clearing where I remembered first suspecting that something was following me. We stepped out where I remembered he was standing before I stupidly went running into the woods.

His backpack was hidden by a bush and he scooped it up, adding it to the one he already carried. He seemed completely oblivious to the fact that now he effortlessly carried two heavy backpacks in one hand.

I was self conscious holding his hand now that we were out of the concealing woods. I was only fifteen, still not old enough to date according to my father's timetable, and even if I had been old enough, I knew dad still would not have approved.

But my hand felt so secure and familiar in Micah's and I thought of spending the night all alone in my empty house, my family gone, and I wasn't ready to let go yet.

We started walking toward my house, staying on his side of the street. Suddenly his silence was unbearable. It reminded me too much of when his eyes were always vacant, before our magical moment in the woods.

I searched his eyes. He smiled at me. They were still filled with emotions. I smiled back shyly.

"Don't you ever just make small talk?" I finally asked.

"No," he said softly.

We walked on in silence, my disappointment heavy as my mind went blank and I couldn't think of a single witty thing to impress him.

"Uh...Nice weather we're having," he mused and I looked at him, mildly jolted by his comment. He actually made a little joke. I didn't want to patronize him by telling him good job so I reciprocated with some small talk of my own.

"How about those Braves?" I asked.

He smiled and glanced up the road. "I got a great deal on my house because of the housing slump," he countered. He was obviously new at this.

"These high gas prices are killing me," I said.

He looked at me, humor shining in his eyes. "You don't even drive. That one should've been mine."

I thought my heart would burst out of my chest. I couldn't believe we were actually having a conversation, even an inane one.

"Tough. It's mine," I said, a little breathless.

"Okay." He thought for a moment. "Do you think the drought will last much longer?" he asked.

We were at the bottom of my porch stairs. I looked at the driveway and through the garage window, both cars were gone. I hesitated, not ready to face the empty house.

I wanted to ask Micah about the change I sensed in him but I was afraid if I did, he'd change back into that distant stranger again. I wanted to keep this new sensitive Micah, whose eyes filled with his emotions. The one I could talk to and feel as if he cared about me.

I wanted to say all this to him and more but I didn't have the nerve. Instead, I asked a weak, "Come here often?"

He looked down at me, his beautiful expressive eyes bright with his feelings, "I'd like to."

My jaw fell open. It was like coming out of the coldest arctic winter into a hot tropical summer. I nervously faced him, feeling completely out of my depths.

"I'll need my backpack now, please," my voice quavered.

He held my gaze for a moment longer before giving my hand a small squeeze then reluctantly releasing it. He separated my backpack from his and handed it to me. I thanked him and started up the porch stairs. I turned around at the top and was startled to find he was right behind me. How could I not hear him following me so closely?

"Oh, I... uhm... No boys allowed without... adult supervision," I stumbled.

"Oh, yes. Your parents took your sisters to Bartlett," he said.

I felt miserable.

He stepped back down off the stairs. "Are you here by yourself all weekend?" he asked and my heart raced at the concern that filled his eyes. Why did my heart race when he showed concern but when my parents did I only felt irritation?

I nodded in answer to his question.

"My parents left our number when we came to dinner last Monday," he said.

For some reason, I was surprised he remembered that dinner. It seemed like ages ago. He was so different now. It was hard to believe that just earlier today at school he had been that same wooden individual that sat in my home, eating dinner with my family. Now, a completely different person stood before me.

"Mom stuck it on the refrigerator," I said, conveniently leaving out that I could recite it to him from memory then and there.

"Well if you need anything, call. Promise me?"

I looked down at him thinking of Nettie's line in The Color Purple, 'Nothing but death can keep me from it.'

But I said out loud, "Promise you."

I turned and unlocked my door then turned back to him.

"Thanks. I had a really nice time," I said.

He just smiled his beautiful smile and looked at me quizzically.

It wasn't until I was inside with the door locked that I remembered we hadn't been out on a date. I'd been running through the woods away from him and now I just told him I had a nice time!

Stupid! Stupid! Stupid! No wonder he was looking at me like I was a fool because I was acting just like one.

I ran to the window to peek out at him. He stood at the bottom of the stairs for a while dangling his backpack from his hand. Then he turned toward his house looking relaxed as he casually swung his backpack.

The closer he got to his house, the stiffer he appeared. The backpack stopped swinging, and he put his arms through the straps and hefted it onto his back. By the time he got to his driveway, his arms were rigid at his sides and I saw no trace of the caring boy who's eyes filled with his emotions.

A shiver passed through me as I walked upstairs. When I got to my room I dropped my backpack on my desk and thought about starting on my homework. Then I thought about getting a snack but I wasn't hungry.

I walked down the hall to the twin's rooms. They were quiet and empty, stripped down to nearly nothing.

I went down to mom and dad's room and curled up on their oversized bed. It made me feel small. I thought about calling Micah and sat up smiling, reaching for the phone on the night table. Then I remembered how he looked by the time he reached his house and decided it would be best not to appear too desperate.

I wandered into my parents' restroom. It was more modern than the one I had upstairs because it had been added during the remodel. The tub was oversized and spotless. I thought guiltily of the ring that was in mine, left from the bath I'd taken last night after my evening run at the track. I decided to go and clean it.

As I passed by the vanity mirror, I stopped and stared at my reflection, trying to see what Micah saw. Average eyes, nose, and mouth. Nice curly afro. A few facial blemishes but nothing too out of control.

I started comparing myself to my sisters like I normally did and realized Micah hadn't expressed any kind of interest in them when he came for dinner. Even Avery had a minor crush on them, his silliness going into overdrive the few times he'd been in their presence at Talbot.

I thought of my time with Micah in the woods. I had experienced the lowest of lows and the highest of highs in such a short period of time. It was dizzying. First wild terror that something was chasing me and then pure elation when I discovered how much Micah cared about me.

My moment of manic rage scared me as it always did because during those times, I felt I was capable of anything. I'd proven I was even capable of hurting myself, regardless of the consequences.

That reminded me of my wrists and how surprised I was when I saw the dark bruises and scratches that covered them. I absentmindedly rubbed my thumb across my wrist, remembering the sensations I felt when Micah did it. Then I thought of something I hadn't considered in the midst of all the tumultuous events. In the woods, how did Micah start off so far behind me, practically catch up to me, and then suddenly appear way ahead of me?

The phone rang and I nearly jumped through the ceiling. I ran and snatched up the cordless beside the bed then wandered back into the restroom to look for some ointment to put on my wrists.

"Hello?" I said, remembering that mom also gave our number to Micah's mom. Could it be that he had decided to call me?

"Hey, baby. How're you enjoying your new found independence?"

"Mom!" I shouted, overjoyed. "You guys made it there okay?"

"No, not yet," she said.

I was surprised. If they left at lunchtime, then they should have gotten there by now.

"What happened?" I asked, distracted opening the medicine cabinet and reading the labels. I opened a bottle of antiseptic, to clean my scratches in case I had a bad reaction to whatever it was Micah had pulled from the wild and rubbed on me.

"Well, we got a much later start than we planned. So late in fact that we're still in town and…,"

I didn't hear anything else mom was saying because I was staring at both my wrists and couldn't find any trace of the scratches nor the bruising. I turned them over and over but there was nothing there.

"What?" I finally said into the phone, realizing mom was still talking.

"I said, we only left the house about an hour ago and stopped off and spent a fortune gassing up both cars. Then the girls had to stop at the store for some things and dad got mad because they didn't do it before we were all packed up and on the road.

Anyway, long story short. Dad discovered he left his wallet with his driver's license at the house and I don't have my glasses so we're heading back to pick them up."

"Kylie can drive your car," I suggested, regaining my senses. I must have been mistaken about the bruises and scratches. Maybe it was just a trick of the dim light that penetrated the gloom of the woods.

"We thought of that but we're coming back tomorrow. I still won't have my glasses and your dad still won't have his license. Who's going to drive the car then?"

"Oh," I said understanding the dilemma.

"Listen, we're going to be there in a few minutes. Could you grab dad's wallet off the dresser and meet us in the driveway. He's already in a bad mood and I don't want him to get more aggravated. You know it's not good for him to get all worked up."

"Okay, mom," I said, replacing the antiseptic and closing the medicine cabinet. Then I walked over to the dresser to pick up dad's wallet. "It'll be ready for you when you get here. Do you want your glasses too?"

"Yes, I'd better, just in case I have to drive. Thanks, Disa. See you soon."

After I got off the phone with mom, a bubble of an idea occurred to me. I grabbed mom's glasses in addition to dad's wallet and ran upstairs to pack. Apparently, God sometimes answers wishes as well as prayers.

I tossed my overnight bag onto the backseat and then squeezed in beside it. Kelly and Kylie's stuff was piled up taking up a lot of the space. Mom and dad exchanged one of their looks but didn't say anything to me about hopping in the car with a packed bag.

I passed the wallet and glasses to mom who was in the front passenger seat.

We pulled out of the driveway and drove by Micah's house. He was standing on his porch looking like a fashion mannequin. The only thing that moved on him was his head as it turned to follow our car.

I twisted around to see him through the car's rear window as we sped up the road. When I turned back around to settle in for the long ride, I saw dad watching me in the rearview mirror.

To distract him, I asked, "Where's Kelly and Kylie?"

"We left them at the store. It's on the way to Bartlett so we'll swing by and they'll join us," mom answered. Then she added, "If they had cell phones, we could call and check on them."

Dad didn't respond even though he must have known the comment was directed at him. He refused to give any of us girls cell phones fearing boys would have additional access to us beyond his control. Mom, however, was willing to take that risk in exchange for having more access to us herself. Mom was a worrier.

I looked out the window, watching the passing scenery.

"So what do you think of that Alexander boy?" dad asked.

I froze. "Who, Jason?"

"No. The other one. The one who goes to school with you."

Dad was more observant than I gave him credit for.

"Oh, Micah. He's okay," I gave the understatement of the millennium. "He really doesn't talk to me that much. In fact, he ignores me most of the time."

It was the truth but it was intentionally misleading. I didn't feel good about it but I believed it was necessary.

We drove in silence but I caught dad looking at me in the rearview mirror occasionally, as if he was trying to figure out what

I was thinking. I couldn't daydream about Micah under that kind of scrutiny.

I decided to ride with the twins. I didn't want to endure dad's suspicious looks all the way to Bartlett.

When dad pulled into the store's parking lot, I hopped out to ask Kelly if I could ride with them.

"Super Girl! Did you fly all the way here?" she asked, looking genuinely pleased to see me.

"Ha! Ha! Very funny," I said but I didn't let that stop me from asking for a ride.

She grumbled and griped the whole time she was rearranging stuff so there would be room for me in the backseat of her car. But I don't think she really minded all that much even though she was being mean about it. Habit I guess.

I settled in and we were all on our way to Bartlett. I adjusted my seatbelt so I could lie down on the backseat, putting some of the clutter on the floor to make more room for me. It felt great to be with my family and I was glad to have escaped the empty house. I wondered what I ever saw in staying home alone all by myself.

I briefly considered consulting my sisters on Micah but I was scared they would tease me. I thought of how gentle he'd been in the woods and how his eyes filled with his emotions. Why wasn't he always like that? If he was always like that, things would be so much easier for me.

I heard the radio come on and pretty soon, I heard the twins singing along. It was an Alicia Keys song I hadn't heard before. I liked it.

"What's the name of this song?" I asked lifting up on my elbow.

"Diary," Kylie answered and then continued to sing along with Kelly.

I lay back down and listened to it all the way through. When I heard Alicia's voice sing the next song I knew it must be a CD.

"Hey, replay Diary," I called out.

There was no response from up front, they just kept singing along with the song that was playing.

"Pleeeeease!"

"Just needed to hear the magic word," Kelly said in response to my whining and in an instant, I heard the familiar beat of Diary start again.

Alicia was singing about keeping the secrets of her boyfriend like the pages of a diary. I listened to it all the way through, trying to commit the words to memory.

When it ended, I wanted to ask Kelly to repeat it again but I didn't want to push my luck. Fortunately for me, one of the twins decided they wanted to hear it again because I heard it repeating. This time I sang with my sisters. We made good harmony from years of singing in the church choir. My whole family loved music.

I sang the song with feeling thinking of Micah. The song perfectly expressed my feelings toward him. There had to be a reason he was acting so strangely and I didn't think he would share it with me if I just asked him directly. What was his secret? I had to find out. But first I had to get close to him. I would need my sisters for that. But how could I get their help without the teasing?

As the song came to an end Kelly said, "Dang, Disa! You were feeling that weren't you?"

I took a deep breath. "A little," I admitted, and waited for the fallout.

Kylie peered over her seat at me. I gave her a shy little smile.

Her beautiful face broke into a big happy grin. "I think we have a makeover project, Kel!" she said, looking at Kelly.

Kelly tried to look at me but my head was behind the driver's seat and we were on the highway so she couldn't twist around far enough to see.

"Sit up, Disa. Let me see you," she commanded, taking one hand off the steering wheel and flapping it behind her seat to try and flush me out.

"No!" I protested, giggling.

"I think you may be right. She's ready," she said. "I guess you were right about Micah at our dinner party too, Ky. Girl, you have a gift for reading people, truly. I admit, he was great on the eyes but he seemed kind of dull to me."

I froze, amazed as usual at how perceptive my sisters could be sometimes. Then I waited for the hellish teasing to begin, deciding it was the price I'd pay to get what I wanted.

Kylie started chanting, "Go Di-sa, Go Di-sa, Go Di-sa, Go Di-sa."
Kelly joined in and they were doing body rolls and snapping their fingers and switching up the words but keeping the same beat. "Go Di-sa, She's rea-dy, Go Di-sa, She's rea-dy."

I couldn't help smiling as it morphed and transformed to, "A di-sa, Is rea-dy, A di-sa, Is rea-dy."

I couldn't resist and started dancing while still stretched out on the seat, letting my arms float up in the air, snapping my fingers to the beat, "Oh yes-ah, I'm rea-dy, Oh yes-ah, I'm rea-dy."

We were rocking that car down the highway and I felt confident that with my sisters' help, everything was going to work out the way I wanted.

Kelly suddenly slowed down and I heard her say, "Oh, no. I think I got them riled."

I lifted up to see. "Who?" I asked, expecting to see a cop car. I saw dad's car driving alongside Kelly's and he was giving her a stern look.

"We'll have to party later girls. I don't think dad appreciates the way we were rocking the car," Kelly said.

Kylie waved at them, flashing her beautiful contrite smile and soon dad fell back in line behind us again.

I stretched out on the back seat again and my thoughts turned back to Micah. I almost felt sorry for him. He wouldn't know what hit him. I'd felt a little intimidated by him due to my own inexperience but I was about to rectify that and turn the tables on him.

I was giving myself over to two experts. I was leaving Atlanta a naïve wide-eyed novice and I would return secure in the knowledge gleaned from seasoned professionals.

It was much later, long after the chanting had abruptly ended, that I remembered my other problem, Liz and Avery. I didn't think my sisters could help me with that one and it was still way too painful for me to talk about anyway.

We arrived at Bartlett during the rush hour but the town was so small that traffic was negligible. We parked at Kelly and Kylie's dorm and after they went in and got their room assignment and key, we started hauling their stuff up to their room.

Mom stayed in the room to start arranging things and we went back down for a second load. After that, dad was pretty winded so he stayed with mom while my sisters and I finished unloading everything.

The Resident Assistant for their dorm floor dropped by to welcome them and assured mom and dad she would keep them in line. I doubted this girl, a student herself, would be able to do that when mom and dad, two full grown adults had barely managed it.

After the RA left, we took mom and dad to their hotel to get checked in and afterwards, we all drove to a restaurant just off campus and had dinner. Mom and dad were maxed out after that and we left them at their hotel.

I was excited because I was going to stay in the dorm with my sisters. We walked around campus exploring and discovered there was a dance every Friday night at the Student Union and the first one of the new school year was tonight.

The flyer bearing the information looked homemade and I thought Kylie could have done a much better job. It said 'Bartlett Mixer: Come get acquainted with your fellow students' in an unimpressive script. A silhouette of a dancing couple and a small group gathered in conversation was stuck in the corner of it. The who, what, when, where, and why was hardly legible. But my curiosity was piqued. What was a college party like? I'd never even been to a high school party yet.

Kelly and Kylie exchanged one of their enigmatic looks. Sometimes they acted so much like mom and dad it wasn't even funny.

They told me exploring time was over, we had work to do. When we got back to their dorm room they turned on some music and got to work right away.

> Adisa you have dark skin so wear light colors, it shows it off better.
> Your legs are amazing, they go on forever.
> Your eyes are your best feature. Look at those lashes. They're ridiculously long.
> Your eyebrows are out of control. I'll have to pluck them to give you a nice arch.

Okay, seriously, you have got to start shaving. This wild woman thing is getting old. I have a razor you can use.

Don't sit like that. Slouching wrecks your posture.

Don't look down, you have nothing to be ashamed of.

Make eye contact, just long enough to mentally say 'I see you and I acknowledge you' and then look away. That way you avoid the psycho stare but you're not showing disinterest by looking away too fast.

And smile, Disa. You have a beautiful smile.

You have pouty lips just like mom's. You both have that full bottom lip.

Adisa, always decide what you will and won't do before going on a date, that way it's easier to stop when you see that line is about to be crossed.

Do you know how to tell if a guy is serious about you? Ask him to buy some feminine products for you. A little complaining is to be expected but if he flat out refuses, dump him! He's a child or an idiot and you don't want to waste your time on either.

Oh, turn the music up. That's my song. You know Disa, you can use music to set a mood to snuggle up to instead of dancing.

Your hair is perfect. It's really growing out now so for variety, you may want to start wearing different headbands, scarves, and little decorative combs. I have a couple of combs you can wear tonight.

I can't believe you never got your ears pierced. You claim you want to be a superhero but you're scared of a little needle.

Disa, guys can be funny about money. Some
think they own you if they so much as buy you
a stick of gum and some are too stingy to even
part with that. Find a guy with a generous
heart but always be prepared to pay your own
way.

When it comes to makeup, less is more until
you know what you're doing.

Oh, here. You can wear this tonight. It's
perfect for showing off your figure.

Your feet are too big to wear our shoes and
the pair you have, completely unacceptable.
Kylie, take the keys to the car. There was a
shoe store at that little strip mall by the
restaurant we ate at.

I was like raw material in their capable hands.

When Kylie got back she dropped a pair of shoes in my lap
that were absolutely adorable. Then she went to work on my
eyebrows.

"Cheese and rice!" I exclaimed, squeezing Kelly's hands as
Kylie mercilessly plucked me. For some reason, my sisters thought
it was all too hilarious.

After Kylie was done, she spun me around so I could see. It
wasn't half bad. Then she started on my make-up with Kelly
supervising closely. They actually started to disagree.

"I want to give her a smoky eye," Kylie said.

"What's a smoky eye?" Kelly asked, sounding unsure.

"Just a little smoke on the eyes," Kylie assured.

"Ky, don't give her raccoon eyes," Kelly sounded critical.

"Just a little smoke on the eyes," Kylie repeated, sounding
irritated.

When she finished, I had to admit, my eyes were smoking.

As we walked from the dorm to the Student Union, for the
first time ever, I felt just as beautiful as my sisters.

We walked three abreast, me in the middle, laughing and
talking, my head swimming with all the advice they'd given me. I

was even glad to be a little taller than they were. It made me feel older, like I was a college student too.

I felt nervous excitement as we entered the Student Union. It was dark outside and light was pouring out of the building reflecting off the couples as they came and went or just milled around in the courtyard. We could hear the music before we entered. It was loud dance music with a strong beat.

For an instant, I felt my insides seize up, thinking of my Jive with Micah. But when we entered, I was so distracted by the sights and sounds startling my senses, I forgot all about the Jive.

There was a bar in one corner and a large dance floor surrounded by overcrowded tables. The noise was unbelievable.

Suddenly it went dark and colorful rays from spotlights mounted in the ceiling reflected off the crowd. The noise formed by the music and people made conversation almost impossible.

The crowd pushed in on us and I was glad to have my sisters flanking me for protection. I was feeling just a little bit intimidated.

I started focusing on some of the faces in the crowd as my sisters expertly guided me through. Girls would check us out with disinterest but the boys were another matter. I should say women and men, because though they were students, they looked way more mature than the kids at Talbot.

All the tables looked taken. Kylie spotted one with a lone occupant sitting near a wall and headed for it. At least two different groups approached the guy and were turned away before we got to him. There were exactly three empty chairs he was attempting to hang onto.

"Are these taken," Kylie beamed at him but he was looking the other way.

"Yes they…," he turned, sounding irritated then saw Kylie's dazzling smile and his whole demeanor changed. Now that's what I wanted to learn how to do. She needed to give me some pointers on that.

He stuttered. "I was…uh supposed to be meeting my… some friends but they're late."

Impossible as it sounds, Kylie turned up the wattage on her smile. "Would it be okay if me and my sisters sit here until they come? We promise we'll leave as soon as they do. Plus you get the added bonus of not having people continually bugging you about these seats."

"Hey, that sounds more than reasonable to me," he said, looking more confident and pulling out the chair closest to him. "Have a seat."

Kylie took the seat without hesitation, thanking him profusely. I noticed he'd left his arm along the back of her chair. I considered knocking it off, knowing he was trying to touch Kylie on the sly but she didn't seem to mind.

As Kelly and I pulled out our own chairs, I couldn't help thinking to myself, the nice twin scored a hit.

I saw the guy lean toward Kylie and ask if we'd like some drinks.

"No thank you, we're fine for now," she answered for all of us.

"By the way, I'm Fabian," he said, using his free hand to shake Kylie's.

"Nice to meet you Fabian. I'm Kylie and these are my sisters Adisa and Kelly."

Fabian's hand lingered on Kylie's before releasing to briefly shake ours as well. He was looking back and forth from Kylie to Kelly. "Are you two twins?"

Oh what a genius, I thought sarcastically then reprimanded myself, thinking that kind of attitude was why I was in this situation to begin with.

Kylie answered in the affirmative, still flashing her pearly whites and I smiled as if he was just too clever, remembering what she told me about being approachable.

While Kylie and Fabian were talking, a guy came up to Kelly and whispered in her ear. She turned and whispered her reply in his. He looked disappointed at first but then started smiling as she finished.

"Okay, I'm going to hold you to that," he said before leaving.

These two were lethal. Two hits and our seats weren't even warm yet.

Kelly smiled at my wide eyed admiration.

"You doing okay?" she asked.

I nodded.

"I told him I'd dance with him later. I want to make sure you get settled first," she reassured me.

I appreciated it more than she could know but I had to ask. "Don't you think Beverly will be jealous of you dancing with another guy?"

She shrugged. "It's just dancing. Besides, I don't slow dance with anybody but Bev."

The song smoothly transitioned into another dance tune with a driving beat.

Kylie turned to me, raising her voice to be heard above the noise. "Adisa, are you ready?"

My eyes widened in alarm. "Ready for what?"

"To put into practice what you've learned."

My mind went blank.

"Start looking around at the guys at tables and standing around. Not the ones who obviously have dates already. If there's one you like, give him the 'I acknowledge you' look and then look away. Don't forget to smile. Oh and preferably, try to pick one who looks like he wants to dance." She made it sound so easy.

I started scanning the crowd. At first they all seemed alike to me but then I started noticing things like one guy was standing with his arms folded, frowning, and feet apart, not very inviting. Another was casually bobbing his head to the beat, scanning the dance floor, possible but he wasn't looking my way. There was a guy with a drink in his hand, bobbing and weaving doing some kind of wild weird dance by himself, absolutely not, way too scary.

I saw one nicely dressed guy with a boyish face, standing against the wall, who was a possibility and he was looking directly at me. I quickly looked away. Oh! I forgot both the 'I acknowledge you' and the smile. But it was too late now.

After awhile, I chanced another look in his direction and he was still looking at me. What surprised me about him, was that he was looking at me, not my sisters. I managed a quick 'Iacknowledgeyou' and looked away, my heart racing with my success, then realized I still forgot to smile.

He was at my side in under a minute. I was shocked. I could feel his breath on my ear as he asked me to dance.

I looked at Kelly for guidance. She lifted an eyebrow as if to say, it's your choice.

I nodded and he stepped back to give me room to stand.

I stood up and we were on the same eye level. He seemed a little surprised by this but not unpleasantly so. We stood there, me waiting for him to go first, when I realized he was being a gentleman and trying to let me go first.

Seeing my hesitation, he took my hand and led the way. I looked back at my sisters to reassure myself and they were watching me with pride in their eyes.

As we weaved our way through the crowd to the dance floor, I started to get nervous, remembering I would actually have to dance. I chided myself for not asking the twins for a quick dance lesson before we left the dorm.

We stepped onto the dance floor and he guided me to the center of the pulsing throng. We were in a sea of bobbing gyrating bodies. He released my hand and started bobbing with the rest. He had nice rhythm. I started doing what he was doing and was relieved to find that dancing separately was a lot easier than dancing in somebody's arms.

He smiled at me and I returned the smile.

"You look really nice," he said, leaning in close to be heard and I felt a flush of warmth over a stranger boldly telling me I looked nice. Then it dawned on me. I was actually dancing with a college boy! I stumbled at the realization.

He caught my elbow.

"Are you all right?" he asked and I nodded.

"It is pretty crowded up here. Are you okay with that?"

I nodded again.

"By the way, my name's Avery. What's yours?"

I nearly fell over hearing my friend's name for this stranger. I immediately liked him. I shoved down the negative thoughts dogging me concerning my Atlanta Avery, and concentrated on the positive.

"Adisa," I answered, smiling at him. His eyes moved to my mouth.

"So you can talk," he noted and I giggled, feeling foolish.

"You have a beautiful smile, Adisa," he said and I thanked him. He was certainly generous with the compliments. But I wasn't complaining.

We danced through several songs and I would occasionally glance over to where I'd left my sisters. Sometimes they were seated there and other times they were on the dance floor with various partners.

Sometimes, all three of us would end up dancing side by side. And that was the most fun.

Finally, when a slow song came on and couples began embracing in a more intimate dance, Avery and I left the dance floor. I was thinking of Kelly's words and Avery's toes.

It wasn't as crowded as when we first came. There were a couple of empty tables. Avery picked one and pulled out a chair for me. I sat down.

"Your stamina is incredible, girl," he said, looking relaxed.

I laughed. "I run a lot."

"Really?"

I nodded.

"Who're you running from?"

I was about to clarify when I saw a twinkle in his eye. I laughed again. He was just like the Avery back home except not as tall and a lot darker.

My sisters miraculously appeared at our table and sat down.

"Avery, these are my sisters Kelly and Kylie. This is Avery," I introduced everybody.

Avery waved acknowledgement from his side of the table, not even taking the opportunity to shake their hands as an excuse to touch them. I admired his restraint.

"You two watching out for baby sis here?" he asked.

They folded their arms in unison and nodded. Every now and then they did quirky twin stuff like that.

Avery laughed. "I ain't mad atcha' but FYI, she's safe with me."

They laughed and said, "Yeah, right!" I could tell they liked him too.

"So are you two freshmen? I've never seen you on campus."

"Yes," Kelly answered. "We just got here today."

"Well, welcome Kylie and Kelly," he said pointing at the wrong one as he said each name. They corrected him.

"So exactly how old are you?" he asked abruptly, catching me by surprise.

"Fifteen."

"Oh, no," he said laughing and revealing perfectly straight gleaming white teeth. "That's some serious jailbait."

"It's not jail you'd have to worry about," Kelly said, giving him a serious look."

"My bad. I meant no disrespect, Kelly. Seriously."

I noticed him looking at a group of guys by the doors. "Would you ladies excuse me for a moment, please? I'll be right back. Do you need anything before I go?"

Kelly and Kylie said no thank you. I was a little disappointed because I was starting to get thirsty.

As soon as he left, Kylie leaned over to me. "Did you want to practice on him?"

"Practice what?" I asked.

"Kissing."

"What?" I gasped.

"It's just a kiss Disa and me and Kelly are right here."

"He called me jailbait," I hedged.

"You don't go to jail for kissing," Kylie replied.

I wasn't so sure. Just then Avery came back and slid into his seat.

I stared at his lips. He looked at me puzzled and I quickly stood up and excused myself to the ladies room. Kelly was up and following me.

When we found it, I turned on the water, wet a paper towel and held it to my face. The place was uncomfortably warm and the cool compress made me feel a lot better.

Kelly checked her hair and twisted around to make sure her outfit was still okay.

"Come on," I said and we headed back out.

Avery and Kylie were still seated, looking off bored. I sat down.

"You ladies sure you don't want anything to drink?" Avery offered again.

"Sure, thanks. I'll help you carry them," Kelly said.

Avery stood to walk her to the bar.

"Sodas, right?" she said to me and Kylie and we nodded.

I watched her and Avery at the bar. Avery placed the orders and then they were talking, their heads leaning close. Avery turned and caught my eye then winked at me.

Soon the drinks were ready and Kelly carried them to our table while Avery stayed to pay.

When she arrived, she passed them out and said. "Adisa, never let a guy you don't know handle your drinks. Always keep your eye on your drink."

I nodded and thirstily began drinking.

Avery came back and took his seat. He didn't have a drink. Suddenly I felt bad like we were using him or something.

"How much do we owe you?" I asked.

My sisters looked at me like I had lost my mind. I felt stupid especially since I didn't have a dime on me.

Avery looked at me and smiled. "How sweet," he said. "It was my pleasure, Adisa. Just sitting here with you three beautiful ladies has made me the envy of every man in here and that's payment enough."

He was so smooth and self-confident. It suddenly dawned on me.

"You're a player." The words fell out of my mouth as soon as I thought them.

Kelly and Kylie looked like they wanted to strangle me.

Avery laughed and then leaned over and said in a silky voice clearly heard around the table, "Would you like to play with me, Adisa?"

I started choking on my drink. Avery laughed along with Kelly and Kylie while he smacked me on my back.

I didn't think it was the least bit funny.

Avery danced with each of us for the rest of the evening and Kelly and Kylie also danced with other guys but I was too shy to do another 'I acknowledge you,' so I just sat out when Avery wasn't available to dance.

At one point when I was dancing and laughing at Avery's jokes, I thought I saw a flash of copper out of the corner of my eye. When I looked, it was gone.

At the end of the evening, I found myself standing off with Avery while my sisters talked with a couple of new friends, all the while carefully keeping an eye on me.

"So did you have a good time, Adisa?" Avery asked.

"Yes, thank you."

I started fidgeting as he stood staring at me so openly.

"I hope you'll follow your sisters here when you're done with high school. I'll be waiting for you."

I looked at him in surprise to see if he was teasing me but he looked serious. "Won't you have graduated by then?"

Avery laughed and said, "That's the plan but I may be in a masters program here."

He was a nice looking guy and seemed pretty decent. It made sense to practice but I didn't like the idea of using him even if Kylie said guys wanted to be used like that.

Avery cocked his head to the side, looking at me as if he was trying to figure me out. I thought it would be nice to know what I was doing before I tried anything on Micah. And Avery seemed like the perfect guy to practice on. Being a player, I figured he must be an expert at kissing.

He shifted, bringing him closer to me. I liked Avery well enough but I knew I didn't want to kiss but one boy, and Avery wasn't him.

Avery came closer and tilted his head, moving in more. I impulsively stuck out my hand, nearly striking his face. I tried to keep my hand steady but I didn't completely stop the tremor. He looked at it surprised, then smiled and slowly shook it.

I smiled in relief. "Thank you. I had a lot of fun."

He took my hand between both of his and leaned in close to whisper, "Anytime you want to practice, Adisa, look me up."

My eyes grew wide in surprise. How did he know!?

"Kelly!" I shouted, glaring at her after we left the Student Union and were walking back to the dorms. "That wasn't funny. I saw you talking to him at the bar. You told him!"

"Don't look over here," she said. "It wasn't me."

I looked at Kylie, stunned. "Kylie?"

"Don't be a baby about it, Adisa. I was just trying to help. When you went to the ladies room, I explained the situation and he was more than willing," she claimed.

I stomped ahead wanting to be alone. Kelly and Kylie walked a few feet behind, laughing and talking, discussing the boys they'd danced with.

The next day, I played Mancala with dad while mom went with the twins on yet another shopping spree before we headed back to Atlanta.

Deflated looking marbles were divided liberally in the two rows of scooped out spaces on the wooden board. It was a game that originated in Africa that dad had recently discovered. He said it used to be played with rocks and shallow holes dug in the ground. Dad liked interesting bits of trivia like that.

I liked the game because it involved some math logic. Dad had more deflated marbles at the end of the board than I did, indicating he was winning.

"You and your sisters do anything interesting last night, String Bean?" he asked a little too casual.

I was becoming aware that dad's idle-interest posturing masked a keenly aware mind that knew a whole lot more than he let on.

I stared at him suspiciously and he broke.

I huge grin spread across his face. "I heard Kelly and Kylie talking to your mom before they headed out. There's nothing to be ashamed of baby. I'm proud of you. At fifteen, sometimes I think you have more sense than both of your sisters put together."

I'd heard them too, whispering about how mom and dad had nothing to worry about because I was too scared to kiss that guy and how I nearly put his eye out trying to shake his hand while he was trying to plant one on me.

I wondered if it would wipe the grin off dad's face if he knew I didn't kiss that guy because I was saving my lips for Micah.

I caught up to him and won that game of Mancala. Then I beat him again before mom came back interrupting another game that I was well on my way to smoking him on.

"What's the matter, hon?" mom asked, seeing the confused look on dad's face. He just shook his head.

I smiled packing away the game pieces. Dad didn't know I'd been letting him win most of the games in the past. I'm very good at math.

The trip back was uneventful and I was glad to be home again even though it felt weird without Kelly and Kylie.

Mom and dad rested awhile before they started getting dressed for a church function. Dad was opening the family room blinds, letting the sun in and asked me if I wanted to come with them. Since I had already missed the Junior Choir rehearsal that had been scheduled earlier in the day while we were still on the road, I declined claiming I was too tired.

Dad grumbled something about me not being too tired to go dancing all night after I'd spent all day in school and then hours on the road to Bartlett.

I felt duly reprimanded but stuck to my decision.

They said they were going to go and check on mom's mother after church so they would be later than usual.

Mom started asking me about what I wanted to eat and I chafed at being babied and went upstairs to start on my homework.

Later, mom came upstairs to check on me again before they headed out and asked what I wanted to eat.

"Mom, I'll fix something if I get hungry."

"Disa baby, I don't mean to be negative but when it comes to cooking, you know you fall a little short in that category."

"Mom!"

"I could whip you up an omelet real quick before we go. You really need to eat more, you're so thin, baby."

"I'm not hungry," I insisted.

"What's this?" she said picking something up that had fallen out of my backpack. "Looks like a restaurant coupon."

"Oh yeah," I said without looking up, busy working on some math problems. "I won that in my computer class."

"I'll order this since it's free. I'll leave this coupon on the counter by the door with some tip money."

"Okay, but have them deliver it later. I'm really not hungry right now."

I was still tackling homework long after my parents had left when I remembered the outfit Kylie had given me. It was a two piece white short set she said would make me look irresistible.

I decided to take a break and try it on. I had to admit it didn't look bad but I felt self conscious because it hugged curves I didn't know I had in ways I wasn't used to. I was more comfortable in baggier clothes.

I checked out my arched brow. Kylie had done a great job. I looked at my eyelashes. They *were* pretty long. Funny, I'd never noticed that before.

Suddenly I heard something creak downstairs and was reminded that I was in the house alone. I saw it was dark outside.

I peeked out of my bedroom, down the stairs, straining to hear, wishing Kelly and Kylie or mom and dad were here. I didn't hear anything but went to my closet and took out an oversized sword just in case. It was a store prop from a fire sale of superhero paraphernalia. It wasn't real but it looked real enough and I figured it could probably scare somebody off who didn't want to get close enough to find out if it was real or not.

I tiptoed downstairs, listening to the wind outside and the bushes scraping against the house. It was really creepy.

A piercing ring sent the sword flying out of my hands. It was the doorbell.

"Who is it?" I called out in a strained voice.

"Delivery."

The voice sounded familiar. I saw a coupon with a few dollars on the counter and remembered mom said she would order food for me.

I hurried to open the door.

"Avery!" I said, surprised.

"Adisa?" he said, sounding just as surprised as I did. His pale face seemed to float against the dark background.

I suddenly felt self conscious thinking of the quarrel we parted on. I stood awkwardly holding the door and neither of us could think of anything to say.

Avery finally spoke up. "Somebody called in a delivery."

"Oh, that was my mom. I didn't realize it was your restaurant. I didn't know you delivered."

"Yeah. My dad has me learning the business from the bottom up."

We stood in strained silence again, not knowing how to get back to our easy friendship after the school blow up we'd had, or rather, I'd had at him.

"You look great," he said.

"Thanks... Oh, let me get your tip and coupon," I said and walked over to the counter to get it.

When I turned back around, Avery had stepped inside and closed the door behind him. I started to say no boys allowed but it was Avery and I missed him and I didn't want to make the rift between us bigger. Plus, I was still a little spooked about being in the house alone.

"So this is the Summers' mansion," he said and I smiled, glad to hear his old joking nature again.

It was nice of him to say. I knew he had a real mansion. He had pointed it out to me once when we went on a fieldtrip and the bus took us right by it.

"Not bad. Sweet wood floors," he proclaimed, walking in further.

"Here's your coupon and tip," I said holding them out to him.

He took them then walked into the family room and placed the extremely large pizza on the coffee table.

"You guys must be pretty hungry tonight," he said.

I groaned. "No. I'm home alone. It's my mom. When it comes to food she's out of control. She's always trying to stuff people."

There was awkward silence again.

"Look Adisa," "Avery," we both started at the same time. Then we laughed.

"You first," I said, still not sure of what I wanted to say.

"Okay. Adisa, I'm sorry about last Friday. You were so upset and I didn't know what to do. I actually tried to call you after school but I just got your machine. Did you get my messages?"

"No. We just got back from Bartlett today and I don't think anybody checked it yet."

"Well, it says that I'm sorry and I hoped to talk to you so we could clear things up and... and... I can't believe I'm standing in your house talking to you. Did you call my restaurant on purpose to get me here to talk?"

"No," I assured him. "My mom was bugging me about getting food before they left for church and she found that coupon I won in computer class, which I never would've won if Kylie hadn't showed me how to create web pages over the summer. And I never even looked at it when Ms. Fulton gave it to me." I stopped, thinking I was starting to ramble.

"Well, I don't have any more deliveries right now. Do you want to hang out and talk?" he asked.

I looked at the time. Mom and dad wouldn't be back for at least another couple hours and Avery and I wouldn't have any private time at school to talk so I said okay.

"Would you like some pizza?" I asked.

"I'd love some, thank you. I hear it comes from a pretty good restaurant."

"Oh, really? I hear it sucks," I said, as I headed to the kitchen for plates.

"Ouch! This isn't going to be fun is it?" he called after me.

I returned with plates and two flavored waters, carefully holding his by the top to avoid touching the chilled sides since his came from the refrigerator. I'd retrieved mine from the pantry so it was room temperature just the way I liked it. We sat on the sofa and started eating in silence.

"This is good," I conceded.

"Glad you like it. I made it myself."

I pretended to gag and spit it back on my plate.

"Adisa! I was just kidding."

"So was I," I said laughing and after awhile he did too.

"You are so gross," he said.

"Yeah, well, you bring out the worst in me. So let's get started. Explain yourself."

He was looking at me like he was trying to figure out the right words to use.

"Just spit it out Avery. You have to be gone before my mom and dad get back."

"Oh. Long story short, I asked Liz out. She said she would love to go but her dad didn't approve of interracial dating," he said in a hurry.

"She told you straight out like that?"

"She's a very honest person."

"She could have lied and said thanks but no, I already like somebody else or anything instead of making you feel like dirt."

"Why? It's not her fault her dad's a bigot."

I thought about it, Avery's logic working on my nerves.

"She really said she would've liked to?" I asked.

"She said, and I quote 'I would LOVE to go.' My emphasis on love," he admitted with a sad little smile.

My heart was breaking for him. "Avery, I'm so sorry. I didn't mean to make things worse for you."

"No, you were your usual explosively delightful self."

I started laughing. "Shut up. I hate you."

"I hate you too."

We looked at each other.

"So what are you going to do?" I asked.

"The same as I did last year. Worship her from afar."

He was trying to cover it with jokes but I could tell he still really liked her and was hurting because of it. I tried to imagine what I would do if Micah and I were in that situation.

"But you have to dance with her, Avery," I reminded him.

"I know. Isn't it just awful?" he said crinkling his nose in disgust, but not sounding like he really thought so at all.

I laughed. "You're a glutton for punishment."

"When it comes to suffering, Avery is just code for avarice."

"What can I do to help," I offered in earnest.

"Just be your regular self, passionately defending me. Just go easy on her. She's hurting too. Okay?"

"For you, I'll try."

I picked up another slice of pizza. "Would you like some more of this nasty pizza?" I offered.

"Why sure. I thought you'd never ask."

We ate in comfortable silence, glad to have repaired our rift.

"So how are the twins doing?" he asked after awhile.

"They're still twins."

"How unusual," he said, matching my sarcasm.

I smiled. "Guess what," I said.

"What."

"I went to a college dance with the twins and danced all night with a college boy named Avery!"

"You little liar," he accused, grinning at me in disbelief.

"No seriously. It was so bizarre. I was all nervous but when he said his name was Avery... I felt so at home with him."

"I knew you'd have a great time with the twins at college. Who wouldn't?" He paused. "Wait a minute. Let me get this straight. So while I was here all heartbroken, trying to call you up so I could cry on your shoulder, you were at Bartlett, getting your freak on?"

"I was not getting anybody's freak on! I was dancing," I objected.

"This Avery guy at Bartlett, tell me, did he still have all ten of his toes when you left?"

"Avery! I can't believe you went there."

"Oh I went there baby. I went there with bells on."

I frowned in confusion. "What does that mean?"

"I don't know," he admitted.

"I think the pizza is making you delirious," I suggested.

"Maybe you're right."

We sat.

"Adisa?"

"Yeah?"

"Would you do me a colossal favor?"

"What?" I asked.

"About this Liz thing..."

"What about it?" I was instantly concerned.

"Would you... kiss away the pain?"

"What?"

"Just one of your sweet chocolate kisses and I'll forget all about her."

"Avery! What are you... No! Stop!.. No tickling!" But it was too late. His fingers had found the sensitive spots on my sides which my top was barely covering. I started laughing and wriggling around, trying to get away from him.

"Please, Adisa. Just one little kiss from you and I'll stop craving strawberries forever."

He was puckering his lips in exaggeration, looking completely ridiculous.

"Stop Avery. You know… twins tortured me… like this."

"No. I won't stop until I get my chocolate," he declared, clearly enjoying my suffering.

His face had been right over mine the whole time and if he really wanted a kiss he could have taken one. But he was my friend and didn't take advantage.

We were both laughing now as I futilely struggled to get away from his fingers.

I gasped. "Please Avery. Please stop. You're killing me."

No sooner had the words left my mouth than Avery disappeared off of me in a stunning flash. I sat up in dazed confusion and saw him pinned against the wall by a pair of copper hands.

I stood up shakily from the sofa.

"Micah! What are you doing?" I asked, in shocked disbelief.

I ran over and tried to pry Micah's hands off of Avery. But they were like stone.

Avery looked stunned and not a little scared. Micah actually had him lifted off the floor, holding him in place.

I looked at Micah's face. It showed no emotion.

"Micah!" I screamed. "Let him go!"

He looked at me. "He was attacking you."

"I was not!" Avery squealed, indignant.

"He wasn't Micah. He was teasing. Let him go," I pleaded. "I'm fine."

Micah released him and Avery dropped to the floor and almost fell down.

I helped him straighten up.

"Are you okay, Avery?" I asked.

"Fine. You need to tell your boyfriend they have medication for people like him. He should look into it."

"Avery I'm sorry," I said. "Micah, apologize."

He said nothing.

"Avery, we're really very sorry. Are you sure you're okay?" I asked.

"I'm fine. I gotta' go."

"Did you want to take some pizza with you?" I asked, trying to smooth things over.

He looked at me like I was deranged. "I'll let you in on a little secret. Where I'm going, they have tons of that stuff lying around so no thanks."

"Oh, sorry. I think I was channeling my mom."

"Bye, Adisa," he said in exasperation and glared at Micah as he left.

I followed him to the door, trying to make amends but he didn't say anything else, just got in his car and left.

I stormed back to the family room entrance. "What is your problem?"

"I thought he was attacking you," Micah calmly stated.

"What gave you that stupid idea?"

He walked over to the family room blinds that were wide open facing the street.

"Oh," I said, slowly comprehending. From outside the window, I guess it could've looked like an attack.

I watched Micah close the blinds and then he walked over to me.

"Wait a minute. How did you get in here?" I asked, suspiciously.

"The door was unlocked."

"I never forget to lock the door."

"It was unlocked," he repeated.

Then I remembered Avery had come in and closed the door. I guess he didn't lock it.

I stood staring at Micah feeling at a loss for words. He looked exactly as I remembered, visually stunning.

"Close the door," he said and I realized I'd left the front door wide open.

I was about to close it, then I remembered. "No boys allowed," I said automatically, holding it open for him.

"Oh really? So you're telling me Avery is a girl or are your parents invisible?"

He said this without expressing any emotion but I sensed he was angry.

"Micah, if you're here when my parents get home, my dad will kill you and then he'll kill me," I pleaded, exaggerating only a little.

"I'll leave before they come in."

I hated deceiving my parents and very rarely did, unlike the twins, but I had already broken the 'no boys' rule with Avery. Once more wasn't going to make it that much worse. Plus I figured Micah was okay because if he didn't attack me in the middle of the woods where there were no witnesses, why would he attack me in my home when Avery could identify him. When I thought of how scary it was earlier when I was alone, my resolve completely crumbled.

I looked outside once more and then closed the door against the darkness and locked it.

Micah stood watching me with his vacant eyes.

"You can sit down if you like," I said, walking over to the sofa to take a seat.

He sat down in his usual manner, wooden posture, both palms down on his thighs.

I was highly sensitive to his presence and couldn't think of anything to say and he certainly wasn't volunteering anything.

My eyes fell on the pizza.

"Would you like some pizza?"

"No."

"Would you like a drink?"

"No."

We sat in silence. It was not the comfortable silence I had shared with Avery only moments before. I wondered how I could get the sensitive Micah whose eyes filled with his emotions to come out.

I fidgeted.

"What were you doing out there anyway?" I asked.

"Watching you."

My eyes flew to his face. "Why?"

He didn't answer.

I thought of the times I'd passed by homes lit up inside while it was dark outside, my eyes drawn to the interior. If I was that nosy about strangers, how much more fascinated would I be if I actually knew the people who lived inside. I was the one who stupidly forgot to close the blinds. Leaving them open like that was practically an invitation to all outside to gawk at my private life.

I impulsively stood up to clear away the pizza box and suddenly remembered I was wearing Kylie's outfit. I hurried to the kitchen and dropped the box on the counter. I turned to the pantry to get a drink. Then remembered I had flavored water in the family room.

When I turned back around I bumped into something solid.

"What?... Micah! Cough, clear your throat, hum... do something to let a girl know you're behind her. Don't just sneak up on people."

He stepped back.

"What do you want from me Micah?" I asked.

Silence.

I was feeling defeated. Then I remembered, I had been trained. I was no longer the novice. I had some arsenal. I tried to remember what Kelly and Kylie had taught me and my mind went blank.

Then I thought, music for mood... not just dancing.

"Would you like to listen to some music?" I asked.

"Yes. Nina Simone."

I was delighted he actually had a preference and one I recognized. I headed back to the family room and popped in the requested CD. Nina started singing about wanting a little sugar in her bowl.

I heard a throat clear.

I turned and Micah was standing there, his eyes looking at me from far away. How on earth did he move so silently?

"Thanks for the warning," I smiled.

"You're welcome," he said, solemn.

For some reason I thought that was funny. The width of his shoulders was doing strange things to my concentration.

"May I have this dance?" Micah asked, extending his hand.

"No! No!" I said alarmed, thinking of our Jive. "This isn't for dancing. It's for listening."

"Why? I like dancing with you."

At first I thought he was kidding. But when he stood there seriously waiting for an explanation, I looked at him as if he had lost his mind.

"Forget it," I said, turning the music off.

"Why?"

I thought of all my sisters' hard work and how wrong everything was going. I couldn't even remember anything in his presence. All their efforts were wasted. He was just too distracting. I was starting to feel like the inept klutz he knew so well instead of the polished protégé of seasoned professionals.

"You're a great dancer and I'm not," I finally admitted.

"I like the way you dance."

"Well I don't!" I snapped, wishing he would drop it.

When he continued to stare at me with his empty eyes, my confidence completely left me. I felt beyond defeated.

"Micah… it's embarrassing," I finally revealed, unable to meet his steady gaze. I actually felt on the verge of tears and turned away from him. I'd really feel stupid if he saw me crying.

"Wait," he said and I distinctly felt the air vibrate though both of us were standing perfectly still. I turned around. The invisible barrier was gone and he felt close. This time there were only small tremors but he got them under control pretty quickly. I heard him take in a deep breath, saw his chest rise and fall with it.

His eyes were full.

I wondered fleetingly if he was some kind of modern day Jekyll and Hyde.

"There you are," I said. "Welcome back."

He smiled at me and I was grinning back at him like an idiot.

"Before I forget, I just want to let you know, I like this Micah better than the other one."

He looked confused. "What do you mean?"

"The other one, the robot, is a little scary."

"I'm the same person."

"No, you're not."

The width of his shoulders before had been pretty distracting, now the width of his shoulders coupled with the rise and fall of his chest just about pushed me over the edge.

"May I have this dance?" he repeated, hand extended.

Oh no, he still wanted to dance!

I shook my head emphatically.

"Please, I think I can help," he assured me.

It had been easy to turn down the rigid Micah but this one with his eyes filling with the desire to share something with me that he enjoyed... It wasn't easy. I couldn't do it.

"Okay," I relented. "Two minutes of trying and if I'm not enjoying myself, we stop."

The happiness shining in his eyes was breathtaking. I sent up a silent little prayer. *Please, please let this work. I so do not want to disappoint this boy.*

I let him take me into his arms and shivered involuntarily. I heard him catch his breath.

I was as stiff as he had been moments before, my eyes tightly shut, anticipating disaster. Then he pulled me close and I heard his voice, tense in my ear, "Just follow my lead and my body will let you know where I'm going."

We didn't do the Jive, thank everlasting goodness. First he just started swaying and surprisingly, my body followed and then we graduated to making slow turns hardly lifting our feet at all, then we moved to actual steps. I was keeping up! I didn't step on a single toe. I was impressed with myself. It was just like he said, somehow his body was cueing me where to go.

It took me awhile before I realized there was no music and I was completely relaxed. We continued to dance around the family room in silence but I didn't feel the least bit silly.

"Why didn't you do this before?" I asked.

"I didn't think it was necessary."

"You liked the way I was dancing before?"

"Yes."

"Why?" I asked incredulous.

"I got to hold you."

I was going crazy inside but pressed on.

"Didn't I hurt you with all that kicking?"

He smiled. "No."

I felt him draw his thumb across my wrist as he lifted it and looked it over carefully. Then he inspected my other wrist as well.

I gathered my courage and tried the direct approach. "Micah, why do you act so differently, rigid, sometimes?"

His eyes clouded and I got scared the distant Micah would return.

"You don't have to answer. I was just wondering," I quickly amended.

"It's a kind of... concentration," he finally said.

Encouraged by his response, I pushed forward a little more.

"Why do you have to concentrate so hard? Why can't you be like this all the time?" I ventured.

He struggled for an answer. Finally he said, "Protection."

I pushed a little more. "Protection from what?"

His heart beat so hard I could feel it through his body and my heart beat in unison with his.

I decided to try a different approach.

"I learned a song yesterday that I'd like to sing for you," I said.

He looked at me in such wondrous surprise, I had to look down from the intensity of his eyes.

"You did?" he asked and I felt him tracing the familiar pattern on my palm.

"Yes," I shyly said into his shoulder.

"Go ahead," he encouraged. "Sing."

"Like this?" I indicated us dancing around with no music.

"Why not? I don't want to stop holding you and I want to hear your song."

What boy talks like that I wondered as I tried to collect my thoughts to sing the song.

After awhile, I began singing Alicia Keys' Diary. I started off hesitantly at first but slowly started to sing with more assurance as Micah adjusted our dance to the tempo of my song.

When I was done I said, "I just want you to know that when you're ready to tell your secret, you can trust me." I couldn't look at his eyes. They burned me. We were pressed close together, barely moving.

I heard a car pull into our driveway as the light from the headlights shone through the blinds and I could hear the garage door opening.

"They're back!" I said panicked, breaking the spell.

I felt Micah's hands on my face, holding it steady, as he urgently peered into my eyes.

"Adisa?"

His voice cut through my panic and I focused on him.

"The Nina Simone CD you were playing?"

I looked at him confused, but nodded.

"Listen to Lilac Wine. Okay?"

"Kay," I agreed dazed by his blazing eyes.

Then he was gone out the back.

The garage noise stopped and after awhile, I heard the car pull inside. I stood in place trembling, trying to pull myself together in time to face my parents. Then I heard the garage door closing. The whole time I never moved from my spot.

Mom came in through the door to the garage.

"Oh, you're still up," she said as she closed and locked the door behind her.

I looked at her puzzled. "Where's dad?"

"He went around back. He thought he saw something...,"

I was already at the back patio door, sliding it open and stepping out onto the patio.

Dad stood in the middle of our yard, looking up into the sky.

My eyes frantically searched the dark gloom of our back yard for any sign of Micah. There wasn't a trace.

Dad walked onto the patio and we walked back inside together.

I was so greatly appreciative to God's grace that I silently promised him no more boys in the house without adult supervision then added I'd go to church tomorrow morning with my parents and I meant it! I was going to protect the sanctity of my dad's house.

"Did you see anything?" mom asked as we entered the kitchen.

Dad shook his head no but looked uncertain. He went straight for the pizza box on the counter.

"Frederick no! Not at this late hour," mom exclaimed. Then spying the leftover contents of the box after dad opened it, she exclaimed, "Goodness Adisa. I guess you had more of an appetite than you thought."

I swallowed hard and tried to look innocent.

Dad took a slice and headed for the family room, not even bothering to heat it up. "What's this?" he asked, picking something up off the floor then waving it in the air.

I recognized it.

"Um… that's my Ancient Singing Saracen Sword."

"Huh," he grunted but said nothing more. I heard him working the answering machine.

"How's Gran?" I asked mom.

"She's doing okay. She knew who I was this time." I saw her eyes glisten.

I went and put my arms around her.

After awhile I heard dad call from the family room, "Disa, there's a message from Avery for you. It sounds pretty urgent."

I waited until after my shower to go down and retrieve the Simone CD. I took it along with the jacket cover up to my room and pulled out my portable CD player, slipped the CD in and, consulting the jacket, cued up Lilac Wine.

I lay in bed, listening to the haunting melodies, confused by the words yet touched in a place deep inside. When it got to the part about lilac wine being sweet and heady like her love, I hugged myself as the achingly beautiful words swirled around me.

As the song drew to a close, I smiled in wonder. Was it true? Was he ready?

I pushed the loop button on my CD player so I could listen to Micah's song, singing to me all night. I had the strangest most beautiful dreams.

5 ~ CHANGE OF HEART

I awakened Monday morning with a smile on my face. My dreams had been awash in vivid colors, splashing light in the crevices, swirling away the lurking shadows. Lilac Wine had suffused my very being in its intoxicating words and rhythms. I stretched languidly. Today I would see Micah and according to his song, he was ready.

I stayed in bed awhile, hugging my knees tight to my chest, giddy thrills flowed through me as I thought of the possibilities. When I finally got up to start my day, I felt an unsteady headiness that was surprisingly pleasant.

I flashed through my morning routine, skipping breakfast, then rushed down my porch steps and hurried along the sidewalk, briefly noting Micah's jeep was in his driveway. When I arrived at the tree Micah usually waited at, there was nobody there. I quickly scanned the area but no one was out.

I waited awhile, indecisive. Then I headed toward Talbot.

A cloud drifted over the sun and I thought how appropriate. I kept looking back to see if Micah was running late but he was never there.

"How's your boyfriend?" Avery asked in homeroom.

I looked at him in frustration. "If you saw somebody attacking Liz, what would you do?"

"I wasn't attacking you," he grumbled.

After that, he wasn't very talkative which was good because I probably wouldn't have paid much attention as distracted as I was.

As soon as I heard the bell for first period I was out the door for my computer class. Micah wasn't there. I sat at my computer with my eyes glued to the door but he never came.

I walked to gym, clinging to shreds of hope. He wasn't there either. I had to sit on the bleachers, my stomach growling from lack of food, and watch my fellow classmates Jive around the floor. Mr. Winton mentioned we would be starting Rumba in a few weeks and I wondered what fresh Hell that would be.

I spotted Liz and Avery. They weren't looking at each other but they were moving together a little better.

I kept checking the gym entrance, just in case.

Liz and Avery showed up at lunch, separately. Liz sat several seats down and across from me and Avery.

He said to me under his breath, "She still thinks you're mad at her."

"I am," I said, looking away from where she was seated.

"Why? I thought we determined it wasn't her fault."

"It's really hard for me to separate, Avery," I admitted stiffly.

"Well could you try?"

I was getting a little upset. "If it was me, I'd fight for you."

"Everybody is not like you Adisa," he rationalized.

There was a long pause and Avery never looked away from my face even though I refused to look at his.

"Fine," I capitulated. "I'll make it my top priority."

Avery was satisfied. He trusted that even though I said it sarcastically, I would make a real attempt. I wasn't as confident as he was.

Micah wasn't in math class and I was really worried. Where was he? Was he sick or skipping because he changed his mind? I hated not knowing. I mentally debated whether or not it would be better to have bad news rather than no news at all.

I watched the clock until math was over, holding out one last hope. But he wasn't there, waiting to walk me home.

As I crossed my yard to the porch, I kept my eyes glued on the Alexanders' house. Micah's jeep was still in the driveway. I stood on my porch looking at it, considering whether or not to go over. But my home training required I not drop by without calling first.

I went inside and opened all of the front blinds so I would have a good view of Micah's house. I saw no activity as I got myself a snack and a drink.

The phone rang and I nearly leaped across the whole room to get it. It was mom checking on me.

"I bet you're missing Kelly and Kylie?" she said

And strangely enough I was. I just didn't realize it until she said it. We spoke a little while longer before hanging up.

After I got off the phone with her, I went upstairs to start my homework. I opened the curtains and blinds over my desk, giving me a view of Micah's house.

I put Lilac Wine on and started doing my homework. I saw absolutely no activity out front. As I finished my homework, I had an idea.

I went down to the kitchen and dialed the number by heart, quickly before I lost my nerve. I listened to the automated voice while planning what I would say after the beep.

"Hi, this is Adisa Summers and I was calling to see if Micah needed the homework assignments for today. I could bring them over if he needs them. Please give me a call if he does."

I left our number, even though I knew mom had already given it to them, just in case.

I turned on the TV trying not to think about Micah. I thought of Kelly and Kylie at Bartlett and mentally debated whether or not to call them. They were probably out, busy living their college lives to the fullest.

The phone rang and again, I nearly broke my neck trying to get to it in a hurry. It was Kylie calling to say she and Kelly were set. They had their schedules straightened out and scholarship money deposited. She and Kelly had opened checking accounts at the bank branch on campus.

She said all the students would be given email accounts and she would email that to us.

I asked where Kelly was and she passed the phone to her. Kelly asked what I was doing and I said watching TV. She said I needed to pick up some more of the slack at home now that she and Kylie were away. I told her I already had a mom so she could quit it. I got off the phone soon after that.

Mom and dad eventually made it home, looking tired and mom started on dinner. I headed upstairs to mope but then decided to stay and help.

"Mom, do you know if the Alexanders are traveling?"

"Not that I know of why?"

"Micah wasn't in school today and it seems like nobody's home. I called and offered to take homework assignments over."

"That was nice of you. How was your day at school?"

"All right."

Dinner was quiet without Kelly and Kylie's chatter.

"Oh, I forgot to tell you, Kelly and Kylie called. They're all settled in. They even have checking accounts and they're going to send us their student email addresses."

"That's great," dad said then rubbed his shoulder. "Adisa, my old football injury is acting up. Can you take care of it after dinner?"

"Sure dad."

Dad's shoulder sometimes gave him problems and it seemed I was the only one who new how to massage it just right to keep the pain at bay for more than a few days in a row.

I helped mom clean up the kitchen and then went to their bedroom. Dad was seated on the foot of the bed, shirtless, with his ointment and a towel.

I took them, tossing the towel onto my shoulder and began working the ointment into his left shoulder. I noticed his body seemed to be slumping more than usual and there were more gray hairs scattered across his chest and back than I remembered.

Mom came in and lay across the bed, appearing thoroughly exhausted. I didn't remember my parents looking so old. Had Kelly and Kylie's departure aged them prematurely or had I simply not been paying attention?

Dad thanked me and I put the ointment away and headed to the door, wiping my hands on the towel. I turned and asked if they needed me to do anything else for them before I left and they both looked shocked. I was a little insulted. I wasn't that bad. Well, maybe I was, just a little.

They said no and I went to my room. I looked out my window but still no activity. I went to my restroom, tossed the towel in the hamper, and used the Power Boy soap to wash the residual ointment off my hands. I smiled remembering the toxic waste incident. I really hadn't been kidding when I told Jason the regular pump soap displayed on my sink was a decoy.

My sisters would sometimes come to use my restroom when the other occupied theirs and they didn't have time to wait. I didn't want the flak over my superhero soap, hence the decoy. But now they were gone.

I put the decoy in the cabinet and proudly displayed Power Boy.

I started to return the Simone CD but then decided to keep it one more night.

It was very late, and all the lights in our house were out when I heard a car pull into the driveway across the street. Lilac Wine was still looping softly in the background. I got out of bed and went to the window and saw a car parked next to Micah's jeep.

I saw three people get out and one reach back in and pull out what I believed to be a sleeping Jason. I recognized Micah's rigid posture standing alone and I breathed a sigh of relief. They all moved to the porch with Micah in back.

Mrs. Alexander unlocked the door then stepped in holding it for Mr. Alexander who was carrying Jason. They disappeared into the house. Micah remained on the porch facing the door, his back to me.

I quickly fumbled with the light next to my desk, knowing he couldn't see me without light. My room instantly lit up. Micah was still facing his door.

I leaned over my desk and touched the window pane, resisting the urge to throw it open and call to him because I didn't want to wake the whole neighborhood at that hour. I willed him to turn around.

He did.

He stood staring up at my window. I waved but he did not return it. I crawled on top of my desk and put my forehead on the cool glass.

He continued to stare. Then he turned just his head as if somebody inside his house called to him. He looked back at me for a moment, turned then disappeared inside.

I couldn't get out of the house fast enough the next day. I was early and knew he probably wouldn't be there but I planned on waiting.

When I got to the tree he was there and I was so pleased I could have done flips. I was about to cross the street when a police car pulled in between us and came to a rest alongside Micah.

I realized it was Mr. Alexander and decided to cross anyway. Just as I was stepping off the curb, he turned and looked at me. He lowered the front passenger window, leaned over and said, a little unkindly, "Adisa, I need to talk to my son alone. Do you mind going on to school?"

I could have died on the spot of embarrassment. I looked at Micah and he looked back with a blank stare.

I backed back onto the curb with a mumbled apology and headed to Talbot. I looked back several times but they remained the same until I was out of sight.

Avery noticed my agitation in homeroom. I told him about Micah's mysterious absence and Mr. Alexander's rude behavior. Avery didn't see anything out of the ordinary.

"Avery, do you notice anything unusual about Micah?" I asked tentatively.

"Besides his tendency to break into your house and beat up your guests?"

"Never mind," I said.

"Sorry," he managed to sound contrite. "Like what?"

"Like the way he acts, doesn't talk much... his posture," I listed.

"He is stiff and mute but those aren't criminal offenses, just nerd tendencies."

I gave him a withering look.

When the bell rang for first period, for some reason I was more frightened than eager to go.

He was there. I took the seat next to him. He didn't look at me.

"Hi, Micah," I said

"Hello, Adisa," he returned, still not looking at me.

"I missed you yesterday," I said, encouraged he was at least speaking to me but he didn't respond this time.

"I phoned you too."

Still no response.

"Is everything okay, Micah?"

"I'm okay."

"Then why won't you look at me?" I accused.

He looked at me briefly then, with vacant eyes, and then turned away. I had no more courage for conversation after that.

In gym I was nervous about dancing with him. But he held me gently but firmly, guiding me with the utmost care around the floor as usual. And we actually were dancing the Jive better. This gave me the courage to attempt conversation again during a break.

"Micah, I want to ask you a question but I don't want you to get mad."

He looked at me from a distance. "Okay."

"May I speak to the other Micah for a minute please?"

There was a brief pause.

"I think it's better if I stay like this," he finally said.

"Why?" I knew I sounded like a petulant child. But I couldn't help it. I needed the sensitive Micah who would actually have a conversation with me.

He didn't respond.

I was quiet for awhile lost in my own morose thoughts. Then I thought defiantly, *Fine, I'll say to the robot what I wanted to say to the sensitive Micah.* After all, he did say they were the same person.

"I listened to Lilac Wine like you asked me to."

Something definitely flickered in his eyes, a passion that died down to sadness and then disappeared back into his vacant stare.

I pressed on. "It was beautiful but I didn't understand the words. Would you explain them to me? Why did you want me to listen to that song?"

His perfect mouth opened as if about to say something but then closed.

So I continued, "I thought that maybe it meant you were ready for your love." I was so nervous it was barely a whisper.

"Adisa, my father knows I was at your house Saturday and he doesn't approve."

The blood drained from my face. Micah's father knew I'd had a boy at my house with no adult supervision! I wanted to die. What must he think of me? No wonder he was so abrupt with me earlier in the morning. What if he told my dad?

"Oh," I croaked. Micah must have gotten in trouble and now he changed his mind about being ready.

Before we could say anything else, the break was over and we were back to the Jive and it was too hard to talk with all the bouncing and kicking and spinning.

Then class was over and he was gone.

After math, he was on his side of the road walking home with me.

I crossed the street and planted myself in front of him. I figured his father couldn't think any worse of me now.

"Micah, my birthday is coming up and I'd like you to come to my party and kiss me." I said it all in such a rush my mind was spinning.

The sensitive Micah appeared so fast I nearly fell over. I had to take a step back.

His hazel eyes, full of confusion and shock, stared at me for a moment before he asked, "Why?"

"It'll be my sweet sixteen and I've never been kissed," I said, transfixed by his stunning features.

Then he looked at my lips and I thought I'd die of embarrassment, wondering if they looked all chapped and undesirable.

He didn't answer as he continued to stare at my lips. I was totally flustered so I began rambling. "It's a rule in the Summers household that the girls don't date until they're sixteen which I think is ridiculous because age is just a number and doesn't truly define maturity. It's just a state of mind. I mean there're some fourteen year olds who are more mature than some eighteen year olds. I know it may not be the standard but there are some cases I'm sure. And anyway it's just that I'll be sixteen and I'll be old enough to date and... I'd like you to be there." I finally ran out of words.

I hoped he would pick up on the point that since I was old enough to date that meant he could ask me out. I knew I was being a glutton for punishment for wanting this inconstant boy to ask me out but there was something special about him, I just knew it.

Internal conflict was apparent on his face before he finally said, "Okay, I'll kiss you on your birthday."

To say that the clouds parted and the sun appeared and the birds sang would've been an understatement.

Micah's eyes went vacant and I hurried back to my side of the street.

When I got home, I called my mom and asked her if it would be okay for me to have a real birthday party this year.

"I thought you hated parties?"

"But this is special mom. It's sweet sixteen," I pleaded.

She relented and after I hung up, I was bouncing off the walls.

I called Kelly and Kylie's dorm room but there was no answer. They were probably still in class. I left a message.

I was full of so much nervous energy I couldn't concentrate on homework, not even math.

I called Avery and invited him, telling him that the details hadn't been worked out yet.

After his initial shock, he said, "It's about time."

I'd been to a few of his birthday parties usually held at amusement parks or 'party land' type establishments and he used to berate me for not having parties saying I was missing out on a great American tradition.

When he asked me to invite Liz, I was feeling so generous, still on a high because of Micah's yes, I actually agreed.

Then I called the twins again but they still weren't in. I didn't leave another message.

I suddenly had an idea and washed my hands first, knowing what a stickler mom was about cleanliness before handling food. Then I checked the refrigerator, shuddering as the frosty air prickled my skin.

I pulled out a whole chicken, some onions and bell peppers. Then got the rice out and opened the freezer, using a towel to take out some frozen spinach.

After I got all that started, I called mom again and asked for the recipe to homemade cornbread.

"Why?" she asked suspiciously.

"I'm making dinner."

"Oh, Disa no! That's all right baby. I'll take care of it when I get there."

"Mom, I need to help out more. You work hard all day, you don't need to come home and have to hang over a hot stove all evening."

"Disa, I don't mind. I love to cook."

"It's too late, I've already started dinner and now all I need...,"

"You have! What are you making?" She actually sounded alarmed.

"Chicken, spinach, and rice," I said.

"Oh. That's not too difficult," she conceded.

"So may I have the cornbread recipe now?"

She gave me the recipe and I hung up and got started on it.

When mom and dad got home that evening they found me in the kitchen, on the verge of tears. Mom was surprised to find that the chicken, spinach, and rice dish wasn't three separate dishes but one big single dish. She looked at the slimy grainy sloppy mess in dismay.

"It's all right, Disa. You tried your best," she said and then sent dad out to get some take-out.

When he got back I had calmed down and we used the cornbread I'd made, which actually turned out pretty decent, to complement the take-out.

Dad made a big show of saying how delicious the cornbread tasted and I appreciated it.

Even mom, when dad had left to get the takeout, sent me to wash my face so I'd feel better. When I came back down there was no sign of the offending chicken, spinach, and rice dish and I appreciated that too.

After I was ready for bed, I went down to thank them for being so great about the whole thing. I overheard them talking.

"What I don't understand," mom was saying, "is how she got the chicken and rice raw but the spinach burnt."

I heard dad chuckle. "Our Adisa is a special talent."

"Oh Frederick, you need to quit it," she laughed.

I waited a few moments and then bounced into their bedroom and hopped right in the middle of them on their bed.

I put an arm around each and planted a big kiss on each cheek and then said, "I want to thank you two for not making me feel bad about dinner. I really tried hard to make it something special for you and the fact that you didn't say a single negative thing about it makes me feel so much better. But then, I know you two would never say anything hurtful about me because that would just completely crush me."

When I saw them exchange guilty looks over my head, I knew my work was done. So I said good night and I bounced out of bed and up the stairs to daydream about Micah.

I put Lilac Wine on loop and promised myself for real that I would return it the next morning.

My birthday preparations were on such short notice that party rental space was all booked up so mom planned to have it at our house. Kylie and Kelly finally called, surprised I was having a real party with guests and everything instead of just our usual small family gathering.

Kylie immediately agreed to design my invitations and send them to me so I could pass them out at school. My sisters wouldn't be able to make it to my party because it was on a school day but they promised to do something with me over their next break.

I had fun planning the menu for my party with mom.

"You sure you don't want that chicken, spinach, and rice dish?" she asked cutting her eyes at me while trying to suppress a smile.

"Mom!" But even I had to laugh.

When the package of invitations arrived, I tore into it. I gasped out loud they were so beautiful. On the front cover it said 'You're Invited…' in the most beautiful cursive script and beneath it was a minimalist pen and ink sketch of me in profile. On the inside it said '…to join the celebration' in a toned down version of the cover script. Then it gave the details of who, what, when, where, and why.

At the bottom it said 'Come have a Super time with a Super girl.' I smiled. Kylie had put it just right so it wouldn't embarrass me. Then I saw she had added the part I requested. 'In lieu of gifts, please submit a donation to the Atlanta Children's Shelter.'

The inside was filled with beautiful swirls and abstract shapes. I took the invitations to my room to start filling in the names of my guests.

The next day on the way to school, I crossed over to give Micah his invitation. Ever since the sensitive Micah appeared so quickly after I asked him for a birthday kiss, I'd been working on a theory. If I said something shocking to robot Micah would sensitive Micah pop out involuntarily?

While Micah calmly put the invitation away, I gathered my courage to test my theory and asked timidly, "Do you remember what you promised me for my birthday?"

His eyes didn't even flicker as he said, "Yes."

I wasn't brave enough to say anything more daring at that time. *I'll just have to keep on trying*, I thought as I crossed back to the sidewalk.

I gave Avery his in homeroom. He opened it and whistled. "That girl sure is talented."

I waited until lunchtime to pass out the rest of my invitations. I gave Liz hers before we sat at the table with our usual group.

After giving it to her I had a flare of temper and said, "Are you sure your dad will let you go? I am black you know."

When I saw her flinch I immediately regretted my rash words.

"It only extends to dating. I'll be there. Thanks for inviting me," she said, her head down.

Her honesty and politeness put my rude words to shame and I guiltily hurried off to pass out the rest of my invitations. I gave one to all the people I usually sat with at lunch including Fran and Dee, and even Sonjia who glanced at it and then dismissively tossed it on the table.

I couldn't blame her. I had publicly called her a liar. I imagine I probably would've held a grudge too if it was me.

As I walked away, I heard her saying she wasn't going to my lame party because she would be too busy with her own. And then she extended a verbal invitation to the same people I had just handed out invitations to.

It galled me to think I actually shared a birthday with Sonjia. I wondered who's party they would choose to attend. Probably Sonjia's. I decided I didn't care because I was going through the whole charade of a party just for Micah and his attendance was the only one that truly mattered.

I had one more person to give an invitation to but I didn't find her until it was almost time for lunch to be over. She was talking to two girls and I wanted to wait until she was alone but they weren't budging. So I gathered my courage and went over to her.

"Hi, Lucia. I wanted to give you an invitation to my birthday party." I held it out to her, fully expecting her to slap it out of my hand.

But she didn't. She took it. Encouraged that she had been more gracious than Sonjia, I offered, "It's against my better judgment, but I'll invite Justin if you want me to."

She looked at me curiously.

"I didn't mean to make trouble. I was just trying to help," I explained.

She smiled and then said, "That's okay, Adisa. You were right. Justin and I are no good together."

She had such a pained expression on her face, it made me wonder if something really bad had happened between them to finally convince her. But due to my home training, I was way too polite to ask her.

"I'll consider this," she said gracefully waving my invitation in the air. "Thanks."

School was very easy for me now. Leading up to my birthday, I didn't see sensitive Micah again except for one fleeting moment. But I didn't mind the robot. We were actually much improved in dance. The week the Rumba was introduced, Mr. Winton once again recruited Ms. Becket.

He explained it was a slow dance with brief bursts of speed done with controlled fluidity. The music started and once again the couple transformed. Mr. Winton grew several inches taller again. But this time, instead of a radiantly beautiful smile, a look of longing and desire spread across Ms. Becket's face. Her desire for Mr. Winton was so blatant, I felt embarrassed for her. Then I saw the same expression was on Mr. Winton's face as well. I felt like a voyeur, eavesdropping on a very private moment.

Then I saw the way they were dancing together and my eyes nearly popped out of my head. They moved around each other with twisting hips and slow stretching undulations, their movements so suggestive it was barely legal. Since when was such behavior allowed on school grounds? I wanted to look away but couldn't.

Then there was the way Mr. Winton was dragging his hands down Ms. Becket's arms and up her legs and switching her hips around. Mercy!

When the dance was over there was stunned silence. Then slowly the applause rose until it was deafening and the boys were even whistling and whooping. Ms. Becket was blushing profusely.

When the noise died down, Mr. Winton spoke of the basic moves and holds that were involved and demonstrated them and then it was our turn.

I swallowed hard before turning to face Micah and for once, I was glad to have the robot for a dance partner. I didn't want to think of what sensitive Micah's eyes would have been full of.

Dancing the Rumba was like going back to the first day of the Jive except without the kicking. I was stiff and unsure and as usual Micah was flawless.

At one point I glimpsed Avery and Liz awkwardly performing the mechanics of the dance, hesitantly touching each other. They were both bright red. Thank the Heavens for dark pigment!

T he day of my birthday I was awakened by Alicia Keys singing Superwoman. I sat up looking around confused, wondering if I was still dreaming. Then I spied twin grins peeking around the corner of my bedroom door.

They came!

I was so happy I didn't even get mad at them for their Superwoman joke. I just stood up in my bed and started dancing, bobbing my head, and singing the words to the beat of the music.

My sisters came through the door laughing.

"Mom, Adisa's jumping on the bed!" Kylie called but I didn't care. Alicia was singing to me about being Superwoman, I was invincible. Besides, I knew Kylie was bluffing, mom and dad were long gone by now.

"Girl, you better get down before mom gets up here," Kelly said laughing.

Pretty soon Kylie couldn't resist and joined me on the bed and then I saw mom and dad by Kelly and realized they must have decided to take the day off.

Kelly, not wanting to be left out, joined me and Kylie on the bed and we were all three singing and dancing on my bed. It was just like when we were little kids.

Mom disappeared, claiming she had to get this on film.

Dad went in my restroom and brought out three towels.

"Oh give me the black one dad, please, please, please," Kylie said reaching out both hands for it.

He tossed it to her then he tossed one to me and the longest one to Kelly.

Kelly had a beach towel and when she put it on the long way, it went all the way to her heels.

Kylie put hers on and tucked the corners behind her ears and it reminded me of Egyptian headdress.

Mine was blue and of course I put it around my shoulders and we all kept right on singing, dancing, and posing.

When mom got back, she could hardly hold the camcorder still because she was laughing so hard.

Dad stood in the doorway smiling at us.

Then I remembered seeing America's Best Dance Crew, and a group called Super Cr3w won the competition so I started throwing their S sign up with my hands whenever Alicia sang about an S on her chest. My sisters soon joined me in throwing up the sign.

I was giddy, I'd finally brought my sisters over to the side of truth and justice.

When the bed broke, we all screamed and I banged my head on the headboard. But the only thing that hurt was our sides from all the laughing.

After getting ready for school, I came downstairs and was shocked to find streamers and balloons and all kinds of decorations in the dining room and family room. Both rooms looked completely transformed. I was amazed.

"When did you guys do this?" I asked.

"We got in late last night and wanted to surprise you. I thought for sure we'd wake you but you sleep like the dead Disa," Kylie said.

"Thanks," I said, thinking the word was not enough to express what I was feeling. I couldn't believe the twins went through all that trouble just to surprise me.

When I passed by Micah's tree, he was there. We headed for Talbot, he on his side of the street and me on mine. Occasionally I would peek over at him remembering his promise and my heart would start beating so fast, I had to look away.

In homeroom, Avery teased, "Sixteen years old today. You hardly look a day over fifteen."

I made a face at him then reminded him I wouldn't be in gym or math because of my Science class fieldtrip. We were going to Lake Lanier to check out the lowered water level due to the drought. None of my friends were in my Science class so I'd be doing the loner thing but I wanted to see the drought effects so I was okay with it.

I reminded Avery not to be late for my party and he said he wouldn't miss it for the world because it was going to be the social event of the year.

In computer class I told Micah about my fieldtrip and reminded him to be on time for my party. His emotionless voice confirmed he would be there.

Randomly, I still attempted to shock the sensitive Micah out by saying wild things but I hadn't been successful. The robot would either calmly answer or ignore me, giving not the slightest sign of emotion.

When class started and we were working on our web pages, I suddenly had an idea.

"Micah you do know, of course, that this being my first kiss, there is absolutely no tongue."

I was instantly rewarded with a fleeting image of the sensitive Micah, his eyes filled with alarm. Success!

I burst out laughing and Ms. Fulton actually reprimanded me but I didn't even care.

After computer class, I filed onto the yellow school bus, that would transport us to Lake Lanier, with my science classmates.

When we arrived, we could see, even from the bus, the ravages the drought had inflicted along the banks. A muddy ring, starting at the water's edge transformed into dried mud as it extended back up the bank several feet, encircled the entire lake.

Some piers were no longer anywhere near the water at all. We saw a large beached boat. Apparently somebody had failed to come out and properly store it on dry land or move it further out into deeper water while it was still buoyed by higher water levels. Now it leaned on its side wedged in dry mud, caking its sides.

We divided into small groups and were given a questionnaire that required us to list the ravages we saw. We spread out along the bank working on our assignment. I was distracted trying to determine a math equation to figure out how many cubic feet of water the lake was down by since it was about twelve feet below full pool.

I was standing off by myself, contemplating the problem, thinking I would need the surface area of the lake for my calculations, when my periphery vision picked up a large yellow object moving toward the water. I instinctively knew something was wrong.

I looked at the object, it was the bus and the something wrong was that there was no road so why was it moving toward the water. Then I clearly saw through the open door that there was no driver and then some random trivia my dad must have told me about buses automatically being braked when the bus doors were open made me wonder why the bus was moving at all with the door wide open.

Then to my surprise, I saw the terrified confused face of one of my fellow classmates in one of the windows near the back of the bus. And I didn't even realize I had started running until I pulled myself onto the bus through the open door.

The bus was gaining in speed as I landed inside on the stairs, bumping my shins. I was thinking I needed to get to the brakes as an image of my summer driving lessons with Kelly flashed in my mind. Staring beneath the steering wheel from my vantage point on the bus floor, I couldn't tell which was the brake.

I tried to pull myself up and found it difficult but I did manage to get to my feet. My classmate, a boy whose name I knew but couldn't remember, stepped into the aisle at the back of the bus, his face looked panic-stricken. I turned to look out the front window and saw, to my horror, we were closer to the water than I thought with the bus steadily increasing in speed. I turned, trying to brace myself before the impact but the bus slammed forcefully into the water's resistance, flinging me back into the windshield, violently banging the back of my head.

The next thing I remembered was cold water pouring in through the still open doors while I was on the floor in a twisted heap with the boy. I shuddered violently, completely drenched. I couldn't stand cold water. I quickly disentangled us, noting the sliding movement of the bus. It seemed to be turning onto its side, tilting to the lake floor.

The bus door I'd come through was blocked by a wall of water forcing its way in and the pressure prevented our exit. I instinctively headed along the aisle toward the back of the bus, staying in the safety of the large air pocket. My mind registered the emergency exit there as I pulled the dazed boy after me.

As we made our way along the aisle, water gushed through several open windows and the water around our knees was slanting along the left side of us, indicating the bus was still turning over onto that side. We struggled forward leaning to the opposite side and forward because the back of the bus was higher than the front.

It was difficult negotiating the tilted aisle and gushing water with the throbbing pain in my head and getting to the emergency doors with the boy seemed to take forever. Thankfully windows at the very back of the bus were closed, keeping out the deluge that was pouring through the front windows.

Somehow I got the emergency door open and was attempting to fall out with the boy when the bus lurched throwing me back against the bus seats. I tumbled over the top of them my momentum forcing me against the side of the bus tilting toward the lake floor. I knew the boy had fallen clear but the emergency door had slammed shut behind him. How would I get it open again?

I struggled to get back up and discovered my foot had somehow wedged itself in between the side of the bus and one of the seats. I was dizzy but frantically yanked at my leg trying to free my foot. The water level was at my chest inside the bus but it completely covered the outside of the closed window. I knew the water would rise inside, enveloping my air pocket and I'd be completely immersed.

My leg, back, and head hurt and my movements were becoming lethargic as my strength diminished but I continued to struggle. I had several thoughts as the bus dragged me deeper into the dark watery depths.

I couldn't believe I was going to die on my birthday
I would miss my own birthday party
I would miss Micah's kiss
My family would be heartbroken
Exactly how painful was it to drown

My leg was still anchored as my body floated, my arms awkwardly pumping to keep my head above murky water. I was wearing out fast. I threw my head back, fighting to hold my face in the dwindling air pocket. I felt so alone and scared. I wanted my mom and dad. I cried out. Just as the darkness enveloped me, I sensed I was not alone and wondered if it was an angel.

I felt my weight being supported from beneath me, an arm cradled me while a hand worked to free my leg. I screamed in pain when the pressure was too much and was choked by a splash of water. The hand immediately released my leg still trapped by the seat. Then I heard the groan of protesting metal ripping apart. And my foot was finally free. The last thing I remembered before giving myself over to the comforting darkness was Micah's face.

Everything ached. I wondered why mom was crying, the sound seemed far away. I struggled toward it to reassure her but waves of dizziness submerged me and the effort hurt too much. I could hear people moving around me and things were being done to my body. I wanted to yell as sharp pain shot through me but I couldn't. So I silently endured the torture. I tried to make sense of what was going on but grew more confused. I let the darkness drag me back down.

The bright lights hurt my eyes so I kept them shut. Dad was there telling me everything would be okay, I'd be home in a couple days. I wanted to ask him how my party was but the pain was too great. It felt as if I'd been beaten all over my body. I groaned in agony. Then I felt a prick and soon the pain went away and I slept.

Mom was sitting beside my bed with a bowl of soup, humming and feeding me. I became indignant.

"Mom, I'm not a baby I can feed myself."

"Okay," she said transferring the bowl to a tray and placing it in front of me.

I started feeding myself but for some reason it wasn't as easy as it should have been and I really had to concentrate hard to get the spoon to my mouth. The soup was one of my favorites, chicken and vegetables.

"How's she doing?" I heard dad's voice from my doorway.

"She's fussy again today. One minute she's talking to me and everything seems normal and the next, it's as if she doesn't even know what's going on," mom spoke in a low voice like she didn't want me to hear.

"I can hear you," I accused, not appreciative of being talked about. There was something important I was supposed to do but I couldn't remember what it was.

"Sorry baby," mom said and took away the soup when I couldn't eat anymore.

"I'll be back at work tomorrow. Are you sure you'll be able to handle it," I heard her saying as she moved out of my room.

"We'll be fine," dad said.

I slept.

The morning sun was peeping around my curtains. Dad came in with a tray of food and set it on my dresser.

"You're awake," he said smiling.

Something wasn't right. I frowned trying to remember. I saw my clock beside my bed.

"Dad I'm late for school," I said, quickly lifting my head but dizziness engulfed me and I immediately lay back again. My body was aching all over and my head and ankle were throbbing.

"No school until you're all better," dad said. "Did you want me to feed you or do you want to do it yourself?"

"Why are you and mom treating me like a baby?" I asked confused. "Of course I'll do it myself."

Dad helped me straighten up then propped the tray in front of me. "Adisa, you were in an accident. Don't you remember?"

I looked at him in disbelief. "I was? What kind of accident?"

"You were on a school bus and it went into Lake Lanier."

"Really?"

I wondered if dad was trying to play a trick on me like when I was little and he'd return from some business trip and give Kelly and Kylie a gift and claim he'd forgotten about me. But I knew he hadn't and I would search his pockets and check his hands behind his back until I found my present.

The sensation of cold water and the flash of a panic-stricken face emerged behind my closed eyelids. A name came to me.

"Is Kenneth Williams okay?" I asked.

"He's fine, thanks to you," dad reassured.

"Me?"

"Yes. You saved him Adisa. Don't you remember?"

I frowned in concentration trying to wrestle the memory from my uncooperative brain. My headache went full blown with the effort.

Seeing my discomfort, Dad picked up two small capsules from the tray. "Take this. It should help. But then you need to eat so you won't get nauseous."

I also had to take a large white pill three times a day that tasted so foul I was convinced it not only burned off any lake infection I might have contracted, but also any disease with the misfortune of invading my body for the next fifty years.

I took the medicine. My hands trembled as I lifted the cup of water to my lips. I felt so weak. Something kept nagging me. Something I couldn't remember.

My tray had toast, oatmeal, and chicken sausage. I began eating.

"Where's mom?" I asked after a few bites.

"She went back to work. She was here with you your first few days back home," he said

"Back home? Where was I before then?"

"You were in the hospital."

My eyes widened in surprise. "The hospital!"

"Yes." His eyes were grim with the memory. "When they first brought you in, you were banged all up to Hell and back. Why would you intentionally jump on...,"

I suddenly felt an urge and started to squirm. "Dad, I gotta' go. Can you take the tray out of the way, please," I interrupted.

"What?" he said in surprise.

"I have to use the restroom," I said urgently.

He moved the tray and I pulled the covers aside, struggling to get up. He assisted me. When we made it to the restroom door, he continued to help me inside. I had on my two piece pajamas. When he asked if I was ready and then averted his eyes as he made a move to pull my bottoms down, I stiffened in defiance.

"Dad! I can do it," I said indignant. This baby stuff was going too far.

"I've helped you before. Don't you remember? It must be the memory loss the doctors told us about."

"Well, thank goodness for memory loss," I said crossly. "Apparently it has its advantages."

Dad laughed then and the worry lines left his face. "You really are back this time aren't you, Disa? Okay. I'll leave you to it. But hold onto the sides right here to support yourself. I'll leave the door open so if you need help, call me. I'll be right outside the door."

He carefully released me, making sure I was steady before he left.

With some fumbling and struggle I was able to take care of myself and even made it to the sink, leaning heavily against it as I tried to turn on the water. Dad came behind me and did it for me. I leaned back into him for support as I washed my hands and was reminded of a time when I was smaller, in similar poses. He'd be behind a chair I was standing on or he'd lift me up to reach the sink so I could wash my hands.

I looked in the mirror over the sink and barely recognized the bruised scraped swollen face reflected as my own.

When I was done washing, Dad helped me back into bed. I was worn out and felt drowsy, drifting off to sleep when I suddenly remembered what I'd forgotten.

"Dad where's Micah?"

"I imagine he's at school. He's been by here every morning and after school asking about you."

"I want to see him."

"It's too soon, Disa. When you're up and around, you can see him then," he said.

"I want to see him now!" I said, getting upset at the thought of having to wait to see him. Who knew how long it would take for me to be up and around.

"Disa…," but then he saw the look on my face and relented. "Okay. If he comes by after school today I'll let him up for a few minutes but that's all. You need to rest."

I settled back then and quickly fell asleep, exhausted by my ordeal.

Dad roused me for lunch but I didn't have much of an appetite. I took another bitter white pill. I talked to mom on the cordless phone and she was relieved I was sounding better. She kept telling me she loved me and would see me when she got home.

After I was done, dad offered to call the twins. I said they were probably still in class. Dad dialed anyway and I was surprised he got a hold of them. Apparently after the bus accident, dad bought cell phones for them. How that made sense, I don't know. I was talking to them on some kind of three-way because I could hear their voices on top of each other cutting each other off.

They teased me about finally being a real hero and how next time I should try not to get killed in the process. It didn't seem real to me because I couldn't remember much about it. They said they were sorry they weren't with me but dad made them return to school after I got out of the hospital. They even told me they loved me before we got off the phone which made me feel weird because we didn't usually talk like that.

All the excitement of the phone calls put me right back to sleep.

When I opened my eyes, he was there, seated in a chair next to my bed, back straight, palms down on his thighs.

For a moment, I thought I was dreaming because I knew full well dad did not allow boys upstairs at all. It was as if the upstairs was the tower in which he kept his three maiden daughters safe from the crowd of unacceptable suitors, forever banished below. The crowd was for my sisters, I only had one suitor. Could he be the first that dad had ever invited up the stairs?

"What are you doing here?" I asked.

"Watching you."

And for some reason, his words were very familiar.

Micah's eyes moved from my face to something on my bed. I looked to see what it was, it was my hand.

I smiled in spite of the stiff pull of skin around my scratches. "You want to hold it don't you? Go ahead."

"Your dad has been very vigilant," his emotionless voice informed.

"How so?" I asked but the next moment I heard a creak on the stairs and dad was walking in with a single folded towel.

He gave Micah a pointed look before going into my restroom and putting the towel away. And another pointed look as he left.

After he was gone Micah said, "That's the third one he's put away."

I laughed then stopped short because it hurt. I looked at Micah and he hadn't changed his posture. I pulled back my cover and placed my hand at the edge of the bed near him and then put the cover over it and smiled at him. I figured, I was sixteen now, old enough to date so certainly old enough to hold a hand. If dad couldn't take it I would just have to shield him from the distress.

Micah scooted his chair closer, adding to the visual barrier. Then I watched his hand slip under my covers and felt it find my hand. A shock passed between us and I looked up to see if he felt it too. I was surprised to find his eyes were now full of anxiety, pain, relief and something else that went straight to my heart.

We sat that way for a long time, holding hands, staring at each other. He had a sad broken smile and I could hear his uneven breathing catch ever so often. I felt him tracing familiar patterns on my hand and his copper skin glowed in the light streaming through my window.

There was another telltale creak on the stairs and Micah smoothly withdrew his hand and returned it palm down on his thigh. His eyes went blank and his breathing appeared to stop.

Dad came in with another single folded towel and gave Micah a sharp look before disappearing into my restroom.

When he came out he cleared his throat. "Micah, it's time to go. Adisa needs her rest."

Micah stood without objection and my anger flared. "Why, because you've run out of towels?"

Dad had the grace to look guilty but didn't respond.

Micah returned his chair to my desk then said to me, "It was nice visiting you. I'll come back soon."

He left after that and when dad came back up I told him I wanted to see Micah whenever he came to visit.

"Have you been fooling around with that boy?" dad demanded.

Appalled by his accusation, I fumed, "No, unfortunately. You'll be happy to know that I've never even been kissed." And for some inexplicable reason, this caused me to burst out crying.

Dad, surprised by my outburst, came and sat on my bed, awkwardly patting my shoulder, concerned about hurting me.

"It's okay, Adisa. I'm sorry. But he's been here everyday, morning and after school, asking after you, even though we told him we'd let him know when you could see visitors. Still, he comes with apologies for disturbing us and asking how you're doing."

"Dad, he's my friend, he's concerned about me. If I'm old enough to date now, surely I'm old enough to have a visitor without you hovering and acting hostile. Look at me. What can I do in this condition?"

My unexpected tears softened him. "Fine he can visit you. And I'll allow him up here only because you can't get around yet. But the door stays open."

After that, Micah came everyday after school and once on weekends. Dad restrained himself, patrolling us only once per visit and Micah and I were able to secretly hold hands longer under my covers.

He brought assignments for me to catch up on and didn't get bored watching me work. When I oh so casually asked him who his new dance partner was in gym and he said the bleachers, I didn't even try to hide how pleased I was to hear it.

My favorite poet was Maya Angelou and Micah surprised me one day by reading Phenomenal Woman to me, claiming he thought I was pretty phenomenal. He read it well and it was interesting to hear his male voice claim he was a phenomenal woman and it gave me an idea.

I asked him to read it in a woman's voice. At first he resisted but then relented, delivering far more than I expected. I didn't know he could be so funny. I was laughing uncontrollably when he acted out the swing of his waist and ride of his breasts, his voice an interesting feminine falsetto.

When I eagerly requested, "Again! Again!" he protested, claiming maybe another time. He did read other poems to me. He had a real feel for the way poetry should be read. I could've listened to his extraordinary voice all day simply reciting the phone book.

The twins came to visit on the weekend and it was crazy having them fuss over me as much as mom and dad. Kylie was dating Fabian, the guy we met at the dance who'd been saving seats for his friends. Kelly said Beverly was in the process of transferring to Bartlett because they couldn't stand being apart.

I asked about Avery, the college boy I'd danced with, and they said he was very well known around campus and belonged to a lot of organizations at Bartlett. They saw him occasionally but didn't get to spend time with him because he was always so busy.

They'd seen him just before coming home and he'd asked about me. He sounded really concerned when he found out I'd been in an accident and sent his well wishes, claiming he was going to send me a card or something and they exchanged addresses.

Dad allowed Micah only three hours on the weekend and everybody tried to stay out of the way except for dad who still performed his single patrol.

Avery came to visit and he had a get well card from Liz. I congratulated him for being only the second boy privileged enough to see my bedroom in person. After teasing that only I, the consummate drama queen, would be bold enough to celebrate my sweet sixteenth at the bottom of a lake, he expressed real concern. I reassured him I was doing better and would be back at Talbot as soon as the doctors gave me the green light.

Then he cheered me up with his jokes and gossip from our lunch group and said how everybody wished I'd get better soon. He became distracted when he spotted the flowers on my desk.

"Oh yeah, I got your flowers yesterday. Thanks," I said as he went to take a closer look. "Kylie judges how deeply a guy feels about her based on the size of the bouquet. I didn't realize your feelings ran so deep," I joked.

"I didn't send any flowers," he asserted.

"But the card is signed Avery," I said confused. Then I remembered the college boy. "Oh, they must be from the boy at Bartlett I danced with. The twins said he would send something but I thought it would be just a get well card."

Avery read the card, replaced it, and then looked at me puzzled. I quickly changed the subject, embarrassed when I realized the note on the card should have clued me in to which

Avery had sent them. That bump on my head must have been worse than I thought.

Micah came the next day and noticed the flowers as well. He read the card out loud.

> Adisa,
> Thinking of you... be well.
> Avery
> PS: I'm still available for Practice!

"Is this the Avery at Bartlett, with your sisters?" he asked, a frown creasing his brow.

"Yes," I said and quickly changed the subject.

It wasn't until long after he'd left that I wondered how Micah knew about the Avery at Bartlett. Had I told him and the trauma to my head caused me to forget?

The next day I received a large arrangement of Sterling roses. The card said...

> Adisa,
> Forgive me for being late.
> I wish you a long beautiful life with no more thorns.
> Micah

I kept his flowers right next to my bed. The pale lavender gray petals and the absence of thorns made them unusual, like Micah.

One day Micah's family came with him and I noticed it was the robot that accompanied them, not the sensitive Micah who had been entertaining me with his visits since my accident. I decided not to comment.

Kenneth, the boy on the bus with me, sent a thank you and a get well card from him and his family. My teachers sent cards as well, including Mr. Preston our principal. I also received cards and gifts from anonymous well wishers.

I received thank you cards from the children's shelter for donations that I never sent. They didn't specify the amounts donated but since I hadn't given anything except my time, I knew it must have been a clerical error. My mom had to remind me of my birthday request. My guests apparently made donations as suggested in my party invitations even though my party never took place.

Pastor Douglas Johnson, known as Pastor DJ to our congregation, visited and told me I was on the church's prayer list and with all those members troubling God on my behalf, he expected me to be singing with the choir again real soon.

It was all very overwhelming.

My doctor said I was finally well enough to return to school. So the following Sunday, my family and I attended church services, my first time back since the accident. The congregation was warm in welcoming me back and even gave me a standing ovation when Pastor DJ, acknowledged me from the pulpit.

After church, my family had a meeting in preparation for my return to school. I had a plan for getting back into shape and I knew I might get resistance from dad so I recruited Kelly and Kylie as my backup. They planned on driving back to Bartlett as soon as our family meeting was over so I knew I had to use my reinforcements wisely.

Dad had received the suggestion of Micah driving me to and from school pretty well. By some miracle, I hadn't broken any bones in the accident but I had sustained deep bruising all over my body and a couple lacerations that required stitches. My ankle had been severely sprained and I was still on crutches. So transportation to and from school was a necessity.

"Dad, I want to start walking to get back in shape," I announced, finally broaching the subject I expected would draw dad's strong disapproval.

"That's fine. Your mom and I will be able to help you when we get off work," he reassured.

"It'll be easier if Micah helps me after school," I countered, bracing for his objection. He did not disappoint.

"We don't need to burden that boy unnecessarily. It's enough he'll be driving you to and from school."

"He wants to help. It was his idea," I said.

"Adisa, you are not old enough to date…,"

"Dad, it's not a date and I'm sixteen. So I am old enough to date or did you change that rule just now so I can't?"

"No, you're right," he backpedaled. "Micah can help you walk in the neighborhood once on the weekend. And your mom and I will help you during the week."

Kylie jumped in. "Why can't Micah help her during the week? He's already available and it's easier for him to help right after school."

"Yeah dad," Kelly said joining her. "You and mom will be tired from working all day anyway. Plus you used to let boys drive me and Kylie to after school activities during school nights."

Then, to my surprise, mom waded in. "Frederick, that boy has been nothing but a blessing since Adisa was hurt. He's helped her keep up in school and has lifted her mood all during her recovery. Plus you shouldn't strain yourself after working all day. It makes sense to let the boy help."

It didn't take long with all of us working on him for dad to capitulate but he wasn't thrilled about it. I thanked my sisters as they headed back out to Bartlett and they told me to let them know how things turned out.

Micah drove his jeep into our driveway the next day. Mom had stayed home to assist him on my first day back. He was actually given permission to come upstairs in the morning and help me down until I didn't need the crutches anymore.

However, he could not assist me up at the end of the day. I'd have to stay downstairs until mom and dad got back if I couldn't make it up on my own. Dad's excuse was that if something happened after Micah took me upstairs and left, I'd be stuck up there without any help back down. I knew the real reason was he wanted Micah in my bedroom as little as possible. But I didn't argue.

When Micah entered my room behind mom, I was seated at my desk.

"Hi," I said feeling shy but thrilled with my good fortune to be hurt just enough to need Micah's assistance.

"Hello," he responded in a formal tone.

Mom suggested Micah wait at the bottom of the stairs with my crutches and backpack, to observe how she assisted me first. He watched while mom let me lean on her and the banister as I came down.

"That's how I help her down," she said when we reached the bottom. "If you know a better safer way, that's fine too."

She disappeared to get my breakfast sandwich. We were running late for my first day back.

As soon as she was gone, a smile spread into Micah's eyes and he indicated the crutches as he said, "Let's take these babies out and see how well they maneuver."

I giggled, taking the crutches.

Mom came back and we headed for the front door.

She watched Micah help me down the porch stairs.

"You sure you know how to use the garage keypad?" she asked him as he helped me settle into his jeep.

She was referring to the keypad mounted outside the automatic garage door which opened with the proper punch code. Micah was to use this to gain access to the garage and my parents would leave the inner door from the garage into the house unlocked. Dad didn't want to give out a key to the house nor leave one sitting around outside. In addition, Micah would only have access to the garage and could only enter the house if somebody left the inner door unlocked for him.

"Mom, you went over it with him at least ten times. I'm sure he's got it," I said becoming impatient with her hovering.

"Well okay, I guess that's everything. Oh, here're sandwiches for you both since you guys are running late. Now, you have our numbers incase anything goes wrong?" she asked.

"Yes mom," I said, resisting the urge to say we were late because she had used up all the time going over the code with Micah again and again.

"Got your cell phone?"

"Yes mom."

She gave me a kiss and thanked Micah then said she'd see us after school.

As Micah started the jeep and backed out of the driveway, I felt like the luckiest girl in the world. Then I saw his father watching from their yard. The displeased look on his face annoyed me, diminishing my good mood.

If anybody had a right to be displeased it was me. I was the one who tried and failed to get a kiss from his son. Instead, I ended up sucking down half of the already drought ravaged Lake Lanier and getting banged up so badly I was unrecognizable.

Mr. Alexander didn't have anything to worry about concerning me. I was going to be on my best behavior. I didn't want a repeat performance or something worse to happen if I dared to tempt fate again.

When we arrived at school, instead of assisting me out of the jeep, Micah simply lifted me out. My heart fluttered over the strength I felt in his arms and I was suddenly reminded of when he scaled the tree in the woods with me on his lap.

I felt self conscious as he effortlessly carried me to a nearby bench. I sat, trying to calm my racing emotions, while he retrieved my backpack and crutches.

A small crowd gathered as we made our way to my homeroom, me on crutches fielding questions and Micah close by carrying my backpack.

When we reached my room, Micah helped me get settled and then told me he'd be back to help me to my next class after the bell rang so to wait for him.

Avery, who'd been watching, said he would help me and Micah didn't have to bother. Then they started going back and forth about which one would help me so I interrupted.

"Avery, Micah is in my first and second period classes so it makes sense for him to help me. When Micah leaves for FLEET, you can help me to the rest of my classes."

They both agreed it made sense and Micah left for his homeroom.

After he was gone Avery said, "You look a whole lot better than you did when I came to visit."

"Why thank you Avery. Leave it to you to always make a girl feel…,"

"You know what I mean," he interjected.

I did know what he meant. My face had pretty much returned to normal and my hair was no longer a misshapen pile flattened against my head. It was actually combed and styled.

The announcements came on but I wasn't paying too much attention until I heard my name.

"Talbot's own she-ro has returned," the student announcer was saying. "As you know, Adisa Summers is credited with saving the life of fellow student Kenneth Williams during a school trip to Lake Lanier. We have a video clip."

The video clip immediately leaped into view. It looked like footage from somebody's personal video camera. There I was, running alongside the bus, leaping in through the open door. And then the bus was in the water, sinking fast, the back end tipping up and out of the water as the bus slowly rolled onto its side.

It was almost completely immersed when suddenly the backdoor flung open, and I stood their supporting Kenneth, struggling to shove him forward. The bus lurched and Kenneth was thrown free while I disappeared back inside and the door slammed shut. The bus sank beneath the water.

The student announcer returned. "Many thought that was the end of Adisa but that was only the beginning of a miracle. Fortunately moments later, a professional TV crew captured these images."

Another video clip popped up and Mayor Shirley Franklin's solemn image appeared speaking but there was no sound. It cut back to the student announcer who was heatedly berating somebody off camera.

Then the student announcer, trying to look more composed, said, "We apologize for that technical difficulty. We have the appropriate clip now."

Channel 2 Action News' Monica Kaufman, no, it's Monica Pearson now, was giving an intro to a clip, stating the bizarre footage could not be explained. Then it cut to the footage.

People along the bank were staring at a spot in the water where the bus had disappeared. The lake was calm now. Kenneth had been safely helped to shore by onlookers and sat on the side, wrapped in a picnic blanket, staring out at the water along with everyone else.

Suddenly, the still water became turbulent and the back end of the bus was backing out of... no... appeared to be rising out of the water and stopped when the emergency door broke the surface.

At first everybody was frozen in shock. Then as if one, they surged forward, opening the emergency door, revealing a girl, me! passed out, curled up in the fetal position on the back of the last seat. They pulled me out and then the bus sank again.

The student announcer reappeared. "Later, after the bus was salvaged from the lake and a forensic investigation was conducted on the wreckage, it revealed one of the seats had been ripped from the flooring it was welded to.

Investigators had no explanation for this stating that the crash into the lake should not have caused it. At this point, we haven't heard anything further regarding this mystery.

Now that we are all caught up, let's talk to our own she-ro, Adisa Summers, to see what she has to say about these bizarre events."

Suddenly, my homeroom door opened, and students carrying camera equipment and one carrying a microphone and clipboard came through the door.

It was a live interview for the morning announcements!

"I can't believe I got ambushed like that on my first day back," I complained to Micah as he accompanied me to our first period class. He was the one who had successfully escorted me out of homeroom, smoothly extricating me from a situation I couldn't escape on my own due to my impaired condition. The interviewing student hadn't wanted to give up her scoop so easily. Even the professional news networks hadn't interviewed me, due to my overly protective parents.

"I mean, why didn't anybody interview Kenneth?" I continued.

"They did. The day after the accident, he was in class and they surprised him too. He wasn't lit very well so it was just a talking silhouette but the caption identified him."

"Oh," I said, smiling. The AVC strikes again.

We entered our computer class and took our seats.

"It was really strange seeing myself on TV like that. The footage from the lake… I didn't realize how close I'd come to dying." I shuddered at the thought.

I didn't have much memory of the accident and the doctors said there was no way to know for sure if those memories would fully come back to me.

In gym class, I expected to sit out on the bleachers but Micah insisted we dance. I told him fine but he would have to do the dancing for the both of us because I didn't think I could manage the Rumba on crutches.

Micah took my crutches and placed them aside while I stood supporting my weight on my good leg.

"You stand still. I'll do all the work," he said before the music started.

He took me in his arms and swayed slowly in a way that didn't require me to move my legs at all. Then he began to Rumba around me, dragging his hands down my arms and up my sides, giving me giggling fits because it tickled. I tried to control them but they would burst out after building up for awhile. Micah moved expertly around me looking like a professional dancer while I behaved like a giggling fool.

After class, Micah went to FLEET as usual and Avery helped me to the rest of my classes and lunch.

I was pretty popular during lunch. Many students came over to my table to talk about the accident. I felt bad not having any gory details for them due to my memory loss. Kenneth came over and thanked me personally for helping him. Even Sonjia warmed to me some, saying she thought it was crazy brave of me to jump on a runaway bus.

When Avery took me to math, Micah was already there. It took a whole lifetime and a half for that class to finally end. Micah helped me out to his jeep and we were off.

We were back in my driveway much too soon and mom was coming out onto the porch asking how everything went.

"It was great. Not a single problem," I told her triumphantly.

When Micah picked me up out of the jeep instead of assisting me, I blushed, but mom didn't say anything. I knew that wouldn't have been the case had dad been standing there.

Micah placed me carefully next to the jeep, for support, and retrieved my crutches. We all headed inside.

"Micah did you want to practice that code again?" mom couldn't resist.

"Mom!"

"Okay fine," she conceded.

When I was settled on the sofa next to Micah, mom went to fix us a snack.

She returned with a tray of sandwiches cut into triangles, the way I liked them. They were made of deli meats, cheese, lettuce, tomato, pickles, mustard, and mayonnaise. She also brought drinks, chips, fruit, and homemade chocolate fudge cookies, apologizing for the homemade soup that was still cooking and wouldn't be ready for consumption until late that night.

"Mom, really, this is plenty. Thanks," I said.

"Well I know how much you love soup, baby, and I can't believe I forgot to get it started in time."

While she set things out on the coffee table, she was explaining, "Now Micah, you know when I'm not here, once you two are inside the house, you only have fifteen minutes to get Adisa settled before you have to leave. I'm sorry but my husband is adamant about that."

It was embarrassing. I didn't know why Micah didn't just walk out and not look back. He was a saint to put up with all the restrictions.

He stayed long enough to finish the snack mom had prepared, politely answering her questions.

After he left mom said, "He really seems like a nice boy. A bit stiff though."

The next morning, mom and dad came to my room to say goodbye before they left for work. It was still dark outside.

"Are you sure you'll be okay with just cereal for breakfast?" mom asked, leaning over my bed to kiss me.

"I'm sure," I reassured her.

Dad kissed me too. "Remember those spots I told you to go for if this guy tries anything funny. And don't forget that defensive stuff you learned over the summer with your sisters."

"Dad, he's not going to try anything," I said, trying not to giggle at the image of me attacking Micah the way dad suggested.

Even though he felt somewhat secure in the knowledge that Micah's dad was part of law enforcement and Micah himself was in FLEET, dad couldn't help worrying about his baby girl.

I was ready and seated at my desk window when I saw Micah walk out to his jeep and drive it into our driveway. After a few moments, I heard our garage door opening then heard it again as it closed. I thought for a few harrowing moments what if dad accidentally forgot to unlock the inner door or worse intentionally forgot.

Then I heard the door open. I didn't hear Micah's footsteps on our wood floors and wondered what had stopped him. Whatever it was, it was taking awhile. But then he suddenly appeared in my doorway and I remembered how quietly he moved. I didn't even hear the telltale creaky step on the stairs. The warmth in his eyes, indicated it was the sensitive Micah as I had hoped.

I was very aware that a boy was in my room with me and there was no adult supervision in the house. But this did not go against my promise to God since dad had approved it.

I wondered briefly why Mr. Alexander hadn't objected to our arrangement, since he'd seemed upset when I had Micah over without adult supervision before. Then I figured he probably thought with me being in the condition I was in, there was no way anything could be going on. I was just thankful he hadn't told my parents about that previous incident, further proof of God's grace.

Micah carried me downstairs and I was astonished at how easy it appeared to be for him. He sat me at the kitchen counter and quickly prepared breakfast for me. It was a pleasant surprise because I was hungry for more than just a bowl of dry cereal.

He cooked and served grits, eggs, chicken sausage, toast, fruit, yogurt, and milk. The spread reminded me of one of mom's feasts. And he cleaned up the whole kitchen afterwards while I ate.

The boy had hidden talents!

When I asked why he wasn't eating, he said he'd already had breakfast at home. But when I made a sandwich of my egg, sausage, and toast, then held it out to him, he took a big bite, his eyes never leaving my face. For some reason, that sent the butterflies in my stomach to fluttering.

He went back up for my backpack and crutches, carrying them out to the jeep before coming back for me.

"Micah, you don't have to carry me so much. I mean it's nice but I can use my crutches," I said.

He said okay but lifted and carried me out the front door anyway. As I tried to lock the front door from his arms, I tried to suppress a laugh at how ridiculous it all seemed.

After the door was locked, we left. I noted, surprisingly, that Micah had been in the house for only fourteen minutes. Incredibly talented! And to think, dad hadn't even thought to set a time limit for Micah's morning stay in the house but Micah managed to keep it within fifteen minutes anyway.

This was our normal routine until I no longer needed my crutches and simply met Micah outside on my porch. Dad immediately changed the security code to the garage key pad and reinstated the old rules. No boys without adult supervision and when boys did come to visit they were not allowed upstairs at all.

I noticed Micah was becoming more reserved in his physical contact with me as my health improved and he no longer had to carry me. I wondered if it was due in part to his father's constant observation of us.

Often, on the way to or from school, Mr. Alexander happened to pass us, sometimes in his own personal car and at other times in his squad car. I could feel the change in Micah when Mr. Alexander was present. It was as if the sensitive Micah deserted me, leaving the robot in his place until his father was out of view.

Over time, our physical contact, even casually brushing past each other, was practically nonexistent. The few times we touched were when we danced or when he helped me negotiate some obstacle, immediately releasing me once I was past.

Even though Micah was carefully restricting our contact, he remained considerate and kind to me. I often wondered how long I would have to wait until he finally confided his secret in me.

My ankle was finally well enough for me to start working out again so Micah and I started walking around the neighborhood, slowly increasing our distance everyday until we reached Talbot. We started back walking to and from school after that and I missed being chauffeured in his jeep.

When I was walking pretty well, I decided I would prefer to walk Kennesaw Mountain rather than pound around the school track like I used to before the bus accident. Micah had been regaling me with the benefits and beauty of mountain walking.

When I asked dad for permission to move our walks there, he flat out said no. But to my surprise, mom spoke up on Micah's behalf. Unknown to us, Micah had gained an ally in mom and what a persuasive ally she was, particularly when it came to my dad.

"Frederick, why are you giving these kids such a hard time? You didn't even put Kylie and Kelly through what you're doing to them, and you probably should have knowing those two.

Now, Micah has been nothing but sweetness. Caring, polite, and helpful. He wouldn't even take the money you offered him for driving Adisa to and from school."

I was shocked to hear this part. Micah never told me my dad had offered him money.

I rubbed my eyes, still a little drowsy. I had dozed off on the sofa but was roused by my parents' exchange which came from the kitchen.

"But that's exactly the problem. He didn't take the money so what is he after?" dad asked pointedly.

"Are you really that cynical? You mistake a young boy's devotion for something so base. Have you seen them together?" Then mom's voice turned flirty. "You know, he reminds me of you. All proud and stiff but still shy and sensitive."

"Oh, Opal. Go on away from here with that sweet talk."

But I could hear a smile in dad's voice. In a flash of insight, I wondered if that was where the twins got it from.

The following week, Micah and I were in his jeep headed to Kennesaw Mountain. We were allowed to go twice a week after school. I'd never been before so I was looking forward to the trip though the thought of actually climbing a mountain was just a little intimidating.

I saw the tree covered mountain in the distance as we got closer with its smaller companion attached to it, Big Kennesaw and Little Kennesaw.

Micah pulled into the small parking lot and quickly found a spot. There was a Civil War Museum at the base of Big Kennesaw but we bypassed it and went straight for the hiking path.

I was feeling apprehensive, wondering if it was a good idea after all. Micah, noting my negative attitude, made a deal with me not to quit until we made it to the top, no matter how long it took, even if he had to carry me on his back.

"We can take the paved road, it wraps around the mountain to the top, or we can take the hiking trail which is about a mile through the woods. It's a shorter more direct route but steeper," Micah informed.

I chose the path through the woods.

As we entered the shadowy depths, I was reminded of that day long ago when he chased me through the woods near my home and I first discovered the sensitive Micah. I couldn't believe now I was walking Kennesaw Mountain with him at my side.

It felt secluded on the path except when other hikers passed us from either direction. I couldn't move very fast so we were passed often by people coming up behind us.

The mountain woods had a different kind of beauty from the one behind my home, less alien and more manageable due to manmade alterations, making the path more accessible and easier to negotiate. The giant green leafy sculptures created by the profusion of kudzu vines were missing and I imagined they simply up and walked away, annoyed by the numerous nature loving trespassers invading their mountain.

There were signs along the way cautioning visitors to remain on the designated path. I was drawn to the wild mysteries hidden from view and my active imagination deduced the signs were a ruse to prevent the human interlopers from harassing the shy leaf-swaddled giants further by pursuing them into the woodsy depths.

We started up the first incline, passing a sign cautioning hikers to stick to the authorized path to avoid erosion, and it was relatively steep for me. I had to rest at the very first bench before continuing up. I sat, my feet barely able to touch the ground, amazed at how out of shape I was. From my vantage point, I could just see the bottom of the incline where we started and realized we hadn't come very far. I could feel doubt creeping in.

I did some stretches so I wouldn't hurt too much after it was all over, then we started off again. We rounded a bend and in the distance I saw a split-rail fence. When we reached it, Micah pointed out how the path, now wide enough for a car, went toward the paved road on the left and in the opposite direction it went further into the woods. We went right, sticking to the route that would keep us in the woods.

The path turned sharply back on itself. It widened out even more and was pretty level for a stretch, making it easier going for a bit and I felt my confidence return. Then the path twisted taking us straight up the mountain and things got ugly as I really started to exert myself. The path narrowed and for most of the way up felt steep, even though it didn't look very severe.

I slowed down to practically a stand still, sometimes stopping even before reaching a bench to rest on. Micah was patient and didn't complain about me holding him up but he didn't sit during our rests.

"This can't be much of a workout for you with me stopping every few feet," I suggested during one of our numerous breaks.

"We're in no hurry. The longer you take, the more time we spend together."

His comment confused me. Though he remained physically distant, he would make unexpected comments that implied he liked me more than just a little, at least it sounded like that to me. If he was attracted to me, why was he intentionally avoiding contact with me?

"It was stupid of me to think I could do this," I grumbled, feeling frustrated.

For the first time during our hike up the mountain, Micah sat next to me. But, I noted, not close enough to actually touch me.

"From now on, every time you say something negative about yourself, you immediately have to say two positive things," he stated, surprising me.

"Why?"

"You're way too hard on yourself. I've never heard anybody put themselves down like you do," he asserted.

Where did that come from!?

"I don't put myself down," I said defensively.

"Then why is your vocabulary filled with words like clumsy, klutz, deranged, fool, crazy, idiot, and your all time favorite stupid? Would you ever say those things about anybody other than yourself?"

"Yes, and I have. My sisters," I declared, highly irritated.

His laughter was so unexpected and profoundly beautiful that it cut the tension between us and I felt myself relax for the first time since starting up the mountain.

"Is this your idea of a pep talk? Because if it is, it isn't working. You're depressing me," I said, still stung by the truth I sensed in his words.

"You tear yourself down. I believe you're tougher on yourself than the twins are and I'm sure they've criticized you enough for several lifetimes. It's a wonder you have any self-esteem at all."

I thought about that for awhile before responding.

"I know my sisters seem harsh but they really do care about me. It wasn't easy living with me and my superhero fixation, especially when we were in public. Kids are cruel. Kylie was my comforter, she would wipe my tears and hug me to make me feel better. But Kelly, she was my defender, she'd fight them no matter how big they were. Nobody wanted to fight Kelly. She fights dirty."

Micah was smiling at me and I was trying very hard not to stare at his mouth. I remembered the summer mom sent me to a couple of foreign language immersion camps before enrolling me at Talbot. I learned how to say mouth in Spanish and French and was now distracted as I tried to recall the actual words.

"It's nice you're defending your sisters but you're still putting yourself down. I'm sure you're no more difficult to live with than they are."

"I guess so," I conceded, thinking 'boca' was the Spanish word for mouth but still trying to remember the French word. "We're just weird like that. We fight each other to the death but can't stand it when somebody else has something negative to say about our family."

We sat contemplating each other.

"Bouche," I sighed in remembrance.

"What? Did you say bouche?" Micah's question didn't register at first and then, seeing the amused gleam in his eyes, I realized I had said the French word for mouth out loud.

"Bush! Bush. I think I saw something run into that bush. We'd better go or we'll still be crawling around this mountain in the dark." I jumped up and headed up the path with a renewed surge of energy.

Fortunately Micah didn't object. However, he did hold me to the 'two positives for every single negative' thing. To his credit, he did help me out.

When I called myself a klutz for tripping over a tree root and the only positive thing I came up with was that I had great reflexes for breaking my fall with my hands instead of my face, he said I had a beautiful face well worth saving. I nearly tripped and fell again when he said that.

When I called myself a weakling for having to stop so many times and my required positive was how considerate I was to drag my body off to the side of the trail so I wouldn't impede the traffic of elderly and toddlers charging up the hill past me, he said my body was a gorgeous distraction.

His comments were so disconcerting I really started making an effort not to say anything negative just to avoid the head trip. That's when I realized, I really did say a lot of negative things about myself. I wasn't aware of just how excessive it was until that moment.

We rounded a bend and saw stairs with a single rusted hand rail along one side. I dragged myself up the handrail, holding on to steady myself on the broken paved path then stopped to rest before tackling the stairs.

"We're almost at the top," Micah encouraged.

This spurred me on and I ascended the final steps and saw a small parking lot.

"We made it!" I said, feeling elated, glad the climb was over. "I can't believe I climbed to the top of a mountain!"

I turned to Micah and the expression on his face stopped me before I started a full blown celebration.

"What's wrong?" I asked, a sneaking suspicion creeping over me as I spotted a taller set of stairs ascending on the far side of the parking lot.

"Well, we're not quite there yet. But almost. We have to go up those stairs and one last incline to the top."

"No! I can't climb another step!" My disappointment was sharp.

"Come on, Adisa. We can rest awhile first. There's a great view over there and we can read about the battle for Atlanta until you're ready to continue."

We started walking toward a shiny metal railing with a plaque attached to it but tree brush blocked most of the view beyond it. I plopped down on a wooden bench as we passed. It had a low back and I nearly lost my balance. I really was exhausted and hot and my ankle had a dull ache.

Micah kept walking and stopped when he reached the plaque. I remained where I was, alternately battling to control my temper and feeling sorry for myself. Climbing a mountain is hard. I seriously considered breaking my promise to make it to the top.

"My ankle is really throbbing you know," I testily called out to Micah.

He looked at me. "Come over and see this," he said.

I folded my arms in defiance, not budging. What a jerk! He dragged me up a mountain knowing I had a bum ankle and not once had he touched me to offer any assistance. He could at least help me. Why didn't he touch me? My ankle wasn't hurting all that much but he didn't know that.

"We didn't even bring any water and I'm dying of thirst," I grumbled.

Now that was partly true. But it wasn't Micah's fault. I should've thought to bring some. I was just so used to working out near home and I'd never carried water on my runs because I could always duck into my house or into Talbot. There were no water fountains on the mountain.

Micah was still looking at the view, ignoring me as I pouted on the bench. I sensed that if it was a battle of wills, as stubborn as I was, I would still probably lose if I pitted myself against him.

I got up and walked over to him and gasped as what he was looking at came into view. The land beyond the railing was wild vegetation that dropped off dramatically. And beyond that, trees spread out for as far as I could see, disappearing into the hazy horizon. I felt my cranky mood lift, feeling small and insignificant in the presence of such magnificence.

It took me awhile before I turned my attention to the plaque. It was titled Atlanta – Prize of War. It gave a brief overview of the battle for Atlanta and included a land map pointing out a few sites such as Stone Mountain, Chattahoochee River, and Atlanta.

"Let's go," I said when I was done reading. I headed for the taller set of stairs up the mountain.

"How's your ankle?" Micah asked, clearly disturbed by the way I refused to put all my weight on my sore leg.

Feeling somewhat placated, I guiltily admitted, "It's not that bad."

As we headed for the stairs together, still not touching, I realized my anger toward him was probably due to my bruised vanity that he hadn't even tried to accidentally brush up against me. Here he was, doing me this incredible favor and I repaid him by giving him attitude. I felt contrite.

The stairs were killer but I made it. We took the final incline at a snail's pace, passing a couple of Civil War cannons. Those people must have really wanted to hang onto their slaves something fierce, to climb this wretched mountain and fight over them.

When we finally made it to the top, I wearily noted the time. It took us well over an hour. There was another plaque titled The Fall of Atlanta, an ironic contrast placed at the summit of the mountain. Another spectacular view was spread out around us.

Micah tried to point out Stone Mountain in the distance but it was too smoggy for me to see it so I doubted that he could.

Micah tapped a marker in the ground with his foot, indicating the highest point of the mountain and said many people touched it, ensuring they had officially made it to the top. He also showed me a large boulder which was the unofficial highest point. People actually stood on it so they felt they truly stood at the tallest point of the mountain.

I touched the marker but didn't feel strong enough to stand on the boulder so I simply touched it as well. So officially and unofficially, I made it to the top. I felt an incredible wave of pride at my accomplishment and wanted to hug Micah but didn't have the nerve. I didn't even have the energy to jump around in celebration. We simply stood together in silence, enjoying the view.

We took our time descending, retracing our steps past the cannons and plaques and benches.

When we mercifully made it back to the bottom, I was completely worn out. My thighs were actually twitching from the exertion, my calves were on fire, and my ankle was really throbbing now. But I didn't tell Micah any of this. I was elated. I had climbed my first mountain!

We ducked inside the museum and I nearly drained the water fountain. Micah purchased drinks from the vending machine for the ride home.

As we rode back, I was lost in thought, planning my whole mountain workout routine. Mr. Alexander was on their porch watching as Micah pulled into my driveway.

Wasn't there any crime in the whole of Atlanta that required his attention? For a law officer, he seemed more interested in social rule transgressors rather than criminal law breakers. When I turned to say goodbye to Micah, it was the robot who returned my farewell.

I went inside to soak in a hot bath and contemplate my feat. I would set time goals so that I would get faster going up the mountain. Hiking a mile in over an hour, even if it was uphill, seemed like a ridiculously long time to me. I remembered the constant stream of people passing us on the mountain, and vowed

I was going to do more of the passing. I was determined not to merely achieve my pre-bus crash physical condition but to exceed it.

"I, Adisa Summers, climbed a mountain today!" I announced with pride when my parents came home.

They were truly impressed.

"It took me forever but I made it to the top because, before we started up, Micah made us promise we wouldn't quit. I regretted that promise more than once."

"Don't push yourself too hard," mom cautioned.

"Mom it's amazing. It's so beautiful up there. Big Kennesaw is connected to this smaller mountain called Little Kennesaw and Micah said that when we're really good, we'll cross the connection and top the smaller mountain as well. Can you imagine? Two mountain tops in one day!"

I told my parents about my plan to improve my time, letting them know I would have to put in some weekend time since I could only go twice during the school week.

"I could take you on weekends," dad offered a little too quickly.

"Great! You could come up with me," I suggested.

"You're not getting me on top of a mountain at my age! I'm just the driver, I'll wait at the bottom while you climb," dad countered.

"But who'll help me if I fall and re-injure my ankle? How will I get down?"

I could see dad considering it, envisioning me alone in the wilderness unable to get back down safely.

"You could take your cell phone," he said, looking pleased with himself.

"Right!" I said as if he were genius incarnate. Then I frowned as if a new problem had suddenly dawned on me. "Of course, reception's not reliable on that mountain. If I do get a call through, I'll have to wait it out alone, fending off wild animals, hoping to be found before it's too late. Still, it's better than nothing."

The 'fending off wild animals' was a little over the top. However, that weekend, Micah accompanied me to Kennesaw Mountain. We debated my plans, trying to figure out the best way to improve my time. Micah seemed eager to help me, offering advice as he guided the jeep into a choice parking spot. He had the soft top down and the sun was doing incredible things to his skin.

After he turned off the jeep, he shifted around to look at me, his extraordinary smile coming into full view. His lips were still sculpted perfection even when he smiled. My heart skipped a beat and I grabbed my water bottle and quickly climbed out. The last time I had wanted a kiss so badly, I ended up stuck on a bus at the bottom of Lake Lanier. Micah grabbed a backpack he'd stashed in back.

"I packed energy bars and drinks," he explained.

We practiced for days, slowly cutting down my time up the mountain. Sometimes we'd workout in silence but more often than not, we talked, covering a variety of topics.

The first time Micah took me off the path, into the woods, I was concerned about leaving the authorized hiking trail. But he was confident in his knowledge of the mountain and selected areas where exploration off the beaten path was allowed. My curiosity overruled my natural caution.

The small secluded clearing he took me to was filled with vivid monochromatic green foliage. I soon lost my reservations and actually looked forward to our ventures into the wild natural splendor.

Micah had discovered yet another stunning secluded spot and spread out a blanket he retrieved from his backpack along with drinks and a couple of energy bars.

It was Friday and we'd made it up Big Kennesaw in record time and I actually stood on top of the boulder. We also topped Little Kennesaw so it was a very good day. I was telling him my parents would be proud of my achievement and how they might even want to celebrate and if so he was definitely invited.

He seemed happy for me but didn't take pride in his own accomplishment. He lay on his back, looking up into the intricate network of tree branches stretching far above.

"Will your parents be proud of you?" I asked.

"Of course," he said distracted. "They just don't make a big deal over the stuff I do."

We were silent a while as I thought of something significant.

"Your parents don't touch you do they?" I asked. "I mean, they don't do the parental hugs and good job pats on the back or congratulatory kisses with you like they do with your brother, Jason, do they?"

He looked at me in surprise and then shrugged casually as if it didn't matter.

"When did they stop touching you?" I inquired.

He waited so long to respond, I thought he'd decided not to answer. He still hadn't revealed his secret to me and I was beginning to think he never would.

"Seven years ago," he finally said.

I was appalled. I knew Micah was seventeen. How could parents stop touching their ten year old child!? That had to be illegal or immoral. Didn't his parents love him? Seven years he'd gone without the warmth of a parent's touch. It was unbelievable, unforgivable!

"Why?" I asked.

He gazed into the canopy of leaves, sheltering us without giving an answer.

"Didn't anybody... comfort you?" My heart ached for him.

I thought of him, a little boy untouched. I couldn't have made it to my teen years without all the life saving hugs and kisses my mom and dad gave me for all the boo-boos, fears, and teasing I'd suffered. I looked at Micah, trying to imagine all those years without a single soothing touch of comfort.

Impulsively, I leaned over and rained down kisses on his cheek. My lips nervously fluttered against the smooth warmth of his skin as I attempted to provide enough kisses to make up for his seven years of drought.

"Hurts never completely heal if there's nobody to kiss them all better," I explained, in a rush, feeling reckless and foolish.

Micah was stunned for a moment, his eyes tense, then he turned his head deliberately as if he wanted me to place a kiss on his lips.

Completely surprised by his reaction, I pretended to misunderstand his intentions and evaded his offering, instead covering his other cheek with kisses.

"Those are for all your future hurts they won't kiss away, either," I said, breathless.

He looked at me, a dazed smile on his face and the most incredible light in his gentle eyes. He moved slowly, still seeking a kiss on the lips.

But at the last second I chickened out again, reaching up to place a kiss on his forehead and felt his lips brush against my neck.

I jumped back, startled by the keen tingling sensation left on my skin just above where my collarbones met.

"Micah, don't. I'm very ticklish," I said. My stomach clenched at the intensity that lit up his brown eyes.

"How's this?" He whispered and tilted his head, leaning in closer, hesitating for just a moment before pressing his sculpted perfection against my lips.

My world burst into a million brilliant sparks, my heart hammering in response to the warm firm pressure. Externally, all seemed calm as we held the kiss but internally everything came unhinged and pulsed wildly.

When he pulled back and looked at me his hazel eyes searching mine, my mind was reeling. I turned away and hugged my knees trying to hold myself together, my joy too great to contain without effort. He was watching me but all my boldness was gone and I couldn't even manage a glance in his direction. We didn't speak for awhile.

I suddenly realized I'd finally gotten my first real kiss, a belated birthday gift. I couldn't believe after all this time, it was over with so quickly. Micah's promise finally fulfilled, late but perfect even without practice.

Micah said that he wouldn't be available over the weekend for our usual mountain hike and he might even have to miss a few days of school the following week but assured me he'd be back. When I asked him why, he said it had something to do with FLEET.

I hadn't anticipated not seeing him for so long. I remembered the time he disappeared without a word and appreciated knowing in advance this time. Still, heading back down the mountain, I couldn't help feeling a cloud had settled over our perfect kiss. I was missing him already.

Micah was gone an entire week, returning on a Monday. He just appeared at his tree one morning when I was on my way to school. I was so excited to see him I stepped off the curb to greet him but then hesitated in the middle of the street, sensing something different about him.

I knew it was the robot who observed me so still from his usual spot but his eyes were more active. They quickly swept over me and then back up the street to his house. I followed his gaze, just in time to see a curtain fall back into place in one of the windows. Were we being watched?

It was strange seeing Micah's eyes so alive in his rigid posture. I waited unsure of what to do. Then to my surprise he stepped out onto the road and joined me in the middle of the street.

It was a total surprise because, though I had crossed to his side of the street on numerous occasions, it was his first time to so much as meet me halfway.

"Hello," he said in his familiar monotone but to my ears it was compelling music filled with wonder. He actually addressed me first! The robot rarely spoke unless spoken to first. He would respond, not initiate.

"Hi… It's good to see you," I understated. I'd been missing him like crazy and his sudden appearance was completely overwhelming.

"It's good to see you too," he said and my own emotional commotion was reflected in his eyes.

"We better go so we won't be late," he suggested with a casualness that belied the intensity of the situation. In unison, we turned and started for school.

I stole a glance back at his house again but it had already disappeared from view. We walked in the middle of the road together in silence. Sensitive Micah remained clearly in the robot's eyes and it was interesting seeing the dual natures present at the same time.

My thoughts drifted to Micah's absence and what he'd been up to, particularly in light of the change in him. I realized I knew very little about FLEET. Micah rarely talked about it.

"So where did you go with FLEET?" I asked.

His answer was surprisingly direct. "I'm not allowed to talk about it with err... outsiders."

His eyes clearly revealed he wasn't comfortable with the restraints placed on him. I didn't pry. Maybe FLEET had something to do with his secret. I talked about what I'd been up to instead.

I had maintained my workout by running in the neighborhood and on the school track but I hadn't been back to the mountain in his absence and I was concerned the week away would hurt my progress. I didn't ask straight out when he would take me back to the mountain again and he didn't say.

It turned out we didn't return to Kennesaw mountain until the following Friday. By that time, things were back to normal. Robot Micah was fully robot again, including the eyes, and sensitive Micah made his rare appearances only when we were alone. And I was still no closer to knowing Micah's secret.

I was pleased to discover my time going up the mountain didn't suffer from my absence. After we crested both mountain tops, Micah led me off the path to a new captivating natural hideaway.

I was nervous, sitting next to him but his relaxed smile and easy conversation alleviated my tension. I was beginning to put the whole kissing episode out of my mind when he turned to me and said, "I had some traumatic experiences as a kid which should entitle me to a lot more kisses." He hesitated but his eyes never left my face. "To make up for the dearth of parental affection... to comfort me."

My heart was in my throat and my stomach seized as his lips found mine. He didn't seem as tense as he did the first time.

He playfully trailed kisses across my face sending my pulse racing. Then he lay still, letting me trace the contours of his face, my fingertips gliding over sculpted perfection, before he drew me close to press our lips together again.

Then he was gone again on one of his FLEET assignments until the following Wednesday! What was going on? It was a bizarre form of torture.

When the dual Micah showed up again at his usual tree, I confronted him.

"Micah, you've got to tell me what's going on with you. I don't understand how you can be so relaxed and open with me but so distant and secretive at the same time. And you keep taking off every time we start to get close. What's happening?"

Once again, we were in the middle of the road, walking to school. He was in robot mode with sensitive eyes and I was beyond frustrated. I'd done everything I could think of to get him to open up to me to no avail. This new dual Micah, the apparent product of our new exquisitely painful game of hide and kiss then disappear, was wrecking me.

Micah placed his hand at the small of my back and gently sent me back to my sidewalk while he walked back to his side of the road. At first I didn't understand why we separated but then the squad car that must have pulled up behind us while I was distracted, slowly glided by. Mr. Alexander's sternly set features didn't turn to look at either of us. He just kept going.

I was stunned. He was blatantly spying on us or trying to intimidate us, maybe both. I stayed on my side of the road the rest of the way to school and Micah stayed on his.

He asked to take me back to the mountain but I refused, holding out for an explanation, but he wouldn't give one. Over the weekend, my resolve weakened but I was still upset as I angrily acquiesced.

With Micah easily striding by my side, I charged up Big Kennesaw and then crossed over and topped Little Kennesaw without a single rest along the way.

When Micah stepped off the authorized trail I hesitated. He reached for my hand and I folded them both under my arms.

"Please, Adisa." It was the sensitive Micah making this simple plea and it shook me. But I held firm.

"Tell me what's going on first," I demanded.

He shook his head. "I can't."

The remorse in his eyes was overwhelming and I knew it was tearing him apart. I couldn't take it.

"At least promise you will some day," I suggested, feeling myself on the verge of capitulating.

I could see the struggle play out across his features before he finally said, "I'll see what I can do." Then he offered his hand again.

When I still wouldn't take it, he hinted, "I have something to give you to remember me by whenever I leave."

My eyes widened in surprise but I tried to play it cool.

"What is it?" I stalled.

"Come and find out," he said mysteriously, his hand still hanging in the air.

I wondered what it could be. Then I realized I didn't even have a picture of Micah. That would be a perfect gift to remember him by.

I sighed then reached out and took his hand.

I sat tense, next to Micah, as bits of sun filtered through the leaves and softly bounced around, illuminating our private space on the side of the mountain.

I felt him brush against the base of my back as he settled in next to me but I refused to turn and face him.

"Adisa, I'm doing the best I can." His voice was on edge.

I didn't respond.

"I'm trying to figure out how we can be together. But there's no precedent. I'm really trying to make things easier for all involved. But it's difficult with you because of the confidentiality," he said and I could hear the indecision in his voice. "I care so much about you but... I have obligations too. Obligations I can't share with you."

I spun around. "It's your dad, isn't it? He hates me!"

He was clearly stunned by my words. "No. It's not like that. He's upset with me. But he doesn't hate you."

"He does too. I can see it every time he looks at me. You said he knows we were in my house alone that time. I know what he's thinking about me. Why shouldn't he? We come to this mountain and hideout so we can...," I turned away again, too embarrassed to go on.

"No, it's not like that. I bring you here because... I can be myself when we're alone. Just being with you... We can talk...,"

"We talk but you never tell me anything important, like your secret. I tell you everything. You're witness to every embarrassing painful detail of my life and I haven't even stepped foot inside your home. Right across the street from where I live!

And that's how it is with your life too. I'm only allowed to know so much and no more. Meanwhile I'm still spilling my guts when I should shut you out like you've shut me out. Just disappear and let you feel some of the Hell I've been going through."

I felt drained after my tirade but it felt good to get it all out.

After awhile, he said, "You're right. It's not fair to you. I thought I was the only one suffering for my choices. I didn't realize..."

Something in me softened at the vulnerability I sensed in him. I slowly turned to him again. He looked so miserable and alone. I touched his arm, trying to reassure him.

His hazel eyes, filled with an intense longing, roamed my face.

"It's not fair of me to ask but please be patient. I shouldn't have even acknowledged a secret existed to begin with. I shouldn't have come... If I could leave you alone, not bother you... but I can't...," His voice trailed off. The regret in his words completely undid me.

"I'm sorry. I didn't mean it. I was just acting like an idiot because I can't have my way. I can really be a spoiled brat when I don't get what I want." I tried smiling to get us back to a lighter mood.

I used my hands to draw the corners of his mouth up and when I removed my hands, the smile held steady on his incredibly handsome face. I was surprised it actually worked.

"Let's see," he said and a lot of the strain had already left his voice, "that's 'idiot' and 'spoiled brat.' Should that be four or six positives you owe me?"

I looked at him puzzled and then it dawned on me. "You're kidding. I'm not doing that negative positive crap now."

"Pay your debts or else," Micah insisted, pulling me down and sliding his fingers threateningly along the exposed skin of my side.

"No fair!" I gasped. "You wouldn't dare!"

But the gleam of laughter in his eyes told me otherwise. I felt a finger flutter against my sensitive skin to emphasize his threat and I quickly caved in.

"Okay! Okay! Just give me a minute to think."

"You don't need time to think when you're throwing around the negatives," he accused.

"Well, I've had a lifetime of practice with that. This positive stuff you keep demanding is completely foreign to me."

"That's been more than obvious. Okay, but hurry. You're on the clock," he said.

I briefly considered before saying, "Here's one, however I can't promise anything miraculous under the circumstances, duress not being one of the conditions I perform well under...,"

His finger wiggled impatiently.

"Okay! Here it is, I'm very... accommodating."

He looked suspicious as if he thought I was trying to cheat him. "That's it?"

"Yeah. I told you I don't perform well under duress. Accommodating, take it or leave it."

"How is that a positive?"

"I wouldn't be in the position I'm in right now if I wasn't accommodating," I suggested.

Micah stopped to think it over. He hovered over me one hand on my shoulder, the other touching my side, his face inches from mine.

He smiled in concession. "It's weak but I'll accept it. That's one. You owe me five more."

"Three not five," I protested.

"I'm counting 'spoiled brat' as two separate negatives," he claimed.

"But I used it as a single insult."

"Tough. Next positive please. Time's tickling, I mean ticking." He laughed, wiggling his fingers again in warning.

I was completely unnerved. "Fine! I'm caring and loyal and won't hurt you too badly for this when I get the opportunity. There, that's three."

He grudgingly accepted all three, even though the last one was a thinly veiled threat, then demanded two more.

"I have great reflexes," I feebly offered.

"You know you can't repeat a positive. You used 'reflexes' that time you tripped on the tree root," he said.

"Oh, yeah. How's this? I'm good at math."

He looked at me, completely thrown for a loop. "Where did that come from?"

"It's an old reliable standby."

"Accepted. One more," he demanded.

I tried to think of something but couldn't. His proximity was devastating my ability to think of anything except the feel of his smooth copper skin as I breathed in his heady scent.

My mind was spinning. "Can I owe you one? I'm drawing a blank here," I finally admitted.

"I'll help you out," he offered, oblivious to my internal commotion.

"Kay," I exhaled, fascinated by the expressions shifting across his fine features.

He hesitated, his eyes lingering on my lips and then I was transfixed by his suddenly shy demeanor.

"What?" I asked, my curiosity piqued.

"You're uh… You… You're a great mathematician."

"I already said I'm good at math. Hey! That's not what you were thinking," I challenged.

He laughed, his eyebrows raised in surprise that I'd caught him.

"What were you going to say?" I asked, dying to know.

"Sorry, I lost my nerve," he said.

"You're not going to tell me?"

"Not now."

"That sounds familiar," I said with heavy sarcasm.

That made him pause for a moment. "I tell you what, I promise I'll tell you some day," he said seriously.

He seemed to be promising something more important.

"Okay," I said, pacified for the moment.

We stayed as we were for a long time, gazing at each other, before Micah finally sat up and pulled a small gift wrapped package out of his backpack.

"This is for you," he said, giving it to me. "I got it for your birthday but put it away after the bus crash."

A secret thrill swiftly passed through me as I sat up. I should've assured him his shelter donation and kiss more than satisfied the gift requirement but my curiosity got the best of me and I quickly ripped off the wrapping paper then opened the lid of the jewelry box.

"It's beautiful," I said breathless.

I lifted the necklace out. Dangling from the delicate chain was a single lustrous black orb. I looked at Micah. Instead of the radiant smile I expected, he wore the broken one that hinted at sadness.

Believing he was reminded of my birthday bus crash, I quickly tried to erase all traces of his sorrow by asserting, "It's the most incredible gift anybody has ever given to me. Thank you."

"Let me put it on you," he offered, taking it from me and reaching around either side of me to grasp the clasps. He fastened then straightened it around my neck, his fingers lightly brushing my skin.

He sat back admiring it. "Stunning. And the pearl's not bad either."

I wasn't even aware black pearls existed. It was such an unexpected gift, not even close to what I'd imagined.

"I thought you were going to give me a picture of yourself," I blurted out before realizing how ungrateful it sounded.

He laughed pulling me into his arms. "Let's hope I'm never that vain. This is a lot better than a picture of me."

I didn't comment, not wanting to insult him further by contradicting him, so I said, "Thank you, Micah. I really appreciate this."

"You're welcome."

His unique gift was all the more special because I knew it must have a special meaning like the thorn-less roses, so I asked, "Why a black pearl?"

"Because it's beautiful dark and rare, just like you. And now, it's my promise that I'll always come back to you."

We sat quietly, both of us admiring the gift.

"I'd better get you back home," he said eventually.

"You're not going to kiss me?" I exclaimed and immediately regretted it.

Micah's sentient smile was mesmerizing. "You want me to kiss you, Adisa?" his velvety voice teased as he cocked an eyebrow.

Shivers were sailing along my spine where his fingers lightly caressed. I twisted away from his piercing eyes completely distressed. "Shut up! I can't believe I said that. I'm so…,"

"Ah ah ahhh, careful," he interrupted, holding me in place and looking completely entertained by his effect on me. "You'll owe me more positives and we both know what a struggle they are for you."

I groaned, completely at a loss for words.

His expression softened then he became more serious. "Adisa, don't be embarrassed. I want to kiss you too but… now that I know it's difficult for you when I'm gone, maybe it's best if we don't, then I won't have to leave," he said.

Now I was really confused. "I don't understand. I thought you said you left because of FLEET? Now you're saying you leave because we kiss?"

"I know it sounds confusing but FLEET…,"

"Wait a minute. Do they get into your personal business like that? Is kissing against their code, something you have to pay penance for by staying away?" I was incredulous.

"Not exactly but something along those lines."

I knew he wanted to tell me more but apparently that was also against FLEET's code.

"So if you play now, you pay later?" I accused, unable to keep the cynicism out of my words. "You could lie to them and deny it."

"I can't tell a lie," he stated, simply.

"Well, you don't have to tell them at all, you know. Just omit it from your report," I said sarcastically.

"Adisa, I've never told anybody what we do in our private time on this mountain. That's why I bring you here, for privacy. How it works with FLEET is… something I can't share with you. Please, understand." His voice portrayed some of his earlier tension.

"I'd understand if you explained it to me," I impatiently pointed out.

He was quietly conflicted.

"So you're never going to kiss me again?" I asked in exasperation. The irony of the situation suddenly struck me. I'd come to the mountain, determined not to kiss Micah and now... I was practically begging for it. How quickly the tables had turned.

Micah touched my face, staring at me intently. "I've always been willing to... pay the penance... the worst part being away from you." He had that familiar broken smile. "But I don't want you to hurt."

He looked at me expectantly, as if it was my decision. I couldn't believe it. What kind of choice was this? Kiss your boyfriend and he disappears or lips off and he stays? It was ridiculous.

"This FLEET group sounds pretty extreme. Have you ever considered quitting?" I asked, tentatively.

I felt Micah tense. "It's something I've been a part of practically my whole life. I couldn't just walk away from it on a whim. Besides, I wouldn't want to disappoint my father. It's been his dream for me since before I was born."

"Are you serious?"

He nodded and even seemed pleased thinking of his dad's approval.

"Micah, is this your dream or your dad's?"

Without hesitation he said, "Both."

I sighed in resignation.

"Well?" he asked.

"Well what?"

"Is it all right if I kiss you?"

In a flash of irritation I thought to myself, my 'begging a boy for a kiss' days are over!

"Do what you like Micah. I don't care," I snapped, glaring at him.

He looked at me considering. I'm sure I didn't look very appealing but like I said, I didn't care. Then his head went into a familiar tilt, and he cautiously placed a lingering kiss on my bottom lip.

It was nice but so strange I had to ask him, "What was that?"

"Well, I was torn. I wanted a kiss but you looked like you might bite. So I thought I'd better play it safe and work my way up to it."

I burst out laughing. The thought of a boy going for a kiss at the risk of being bitten was hilarious. To chance such an injury, either he was extremely desperate or maybe he really did like me after all.

Micah kissed me again, this time fully on the lips. He drew his hands down my arms and up my sides, pleasantly reminding me of our Rumba. Except now, I had no desire to giggle as a flush of warmth spread through my body. There was something intoxicating about the way he kissed me, releasing my inhibitions.

"I love you, Micah," I whispered, the words out before I was aware they were coming.

I felt his warm breath softly fanning my face instantly stop for what seemed like an eternity. He appeared to withdraw, briefly disappearing inside of himself, his eyes completely devoid of feeling and I felt I'd made a big mistake. Then it all came roaring back into his hazel depths. My senses staggered under the full impact of his forceful gaze.

He kissed me, gliding over my cheek and jaw, sliding down my neck, pressing the small round gift into the hollow of my throat. My arms circled him, holding him close and I felt his muscles flex as he adjusted to kiss my face again.

His lips began moving against mine, slowly opening and closing, in an alarmingly curious way. I could feel our hearts racing each other at a dizzying pace. I felt light headed, immersed in my riotous thoughts. For a brief radiant moment, Micah filled all my senses.

Then I felt the back of his hand tremble against my bare skin as his fingertips explored the top edge of my jeans and I instinctively froze, feeling the wild rhythm of his heart. Micah immediately moved away from me, withdrawing his hands. His sharp breathing was peculiar and his eyes refused to meet mine, making me feel I'd done something wrong.

We sat a long time in awkward silence before finally heading back. I tried not to think of him leaving and failing that, I tried to comfort myself with the thought that he would return soon.

Then I resentfully thought about FLEET, the organization that was taking him away from me. It was bad enough when I thought it was just his dad against us. Now, knowing that FLEET was part of it as well, it was even more upsetting. Micah said he'd never told anybody about what we did so I assumed FLEET probably had some type of honor system where you had to submit to your punishment without necessarily admitting your specific transgression.

It reminded me of the time dad took me golfing along with some of his co-workers. We were alone and he was taking a practice swing near where his ball had landed. He accidentally bumped the ball and it rolled just a little ways out of place. Only the two of us saw it.

When he told me he had to call a penalty on himself, I suggested he just put the ball back where it was before. But he said that would be cheating. I hated when he told the group and they teased him loud and long for his mistake. But at the same time, I couldn't help feeling proud of him for not taking advantage. Nobody wants to think of somebody they love as a cheat.

"You still owe me one more positive," Micah said, interrupting my thoughts. I was surprised he was attempting conversation.

I decided that couldn't go unrewarded. "Hello? Did you not hear my heartfelt declaration back there?" I asked with self-deprecating humor.

He stopped abruptly. "That was your positive?" he asked staring at me.

Caught off guard, I answered truthfully. "No. Not really. That just sort of slipped out unplanned. But could it count anyway?"

He thought about it, frowning. "No."

"Why?" I asked, in disbelief, considering that a pretty strong positive.

"Because, I don't want to think of that as something you were forced to say. It's too special."

"Oh," I said, strangely pleased. "Well, give me the positive you chickened out of and we'll use that. You promised you'd tell me some day."

"True but I didn't expect to reveal it so soon."

"It couldn't be any more embarrassing than some of the stuff I've blurted out to you."

"Okay," he agreed. "I was going to say you're a great kisser, which is true, but I didn't want you to think I was trying to pressure you into anything."

What girl could be in a bad mood after hearing a boy say something like that to her!? That coupled with the gentle movement of the pearl against my skin as we continued down the mountain, made me brave enough to take his hand. He held on, tracing patterns all the way down.

When Micah pulled into my driveway, Mr. Alexander was nowhere in sight.

"Hurry back. I'll be waiting," I managed, clinging to my pearl. I felt ridiculous, acting like he was leaving for a few years instead of a few days.

Then Micah leaned over and kissed me, right there in my dad's driveway but it wasn't like our mountain kiss. It was short and sweet.

"You are one brave bizarre boy," I said.

He smiled as he came around to open my door and walk me up my porch stairs. Before he left, he said he didn't know how long it would take but he would be back as soon as he could.

I wondered if it would be the dual Micah who returned or the robot or my favorite, the sensitive one. Maybe he'd come back with a completely new personality I hadn't met yet.

When mom and dad got home, I nervously showed them my gift, explaining it was Micah's belated birthday gift to me. My face burned with shame when dad asked in a very pointed fashion if Micah was expecting anything in return for his gift.

"No, dad! Of course not."

"It's probably just costume jewelry anyway. No seventeen year old boy with a policeman for a father could afford anything too expensive," he grumbled as he walked away.

I considered myself lucky to get off so easy with him.

"What kind of stone is that?" mom asked.

"He said it's a black pearl," I said, worried she would pick up where dad left off.

She just gave me the oddest look but didn't say anything else about it.

I noticed this time Micah's jeep was gone during his absence. His family was still there. I saw them come and go in their normal routine.

When Wednesday came and went with no Micah, I felt my old worry creeping back again. When a week passed and still no word, I mentioned it to mom and dad, hoping they would ask the Alexanders about him. I didn't think my inquiries would be welcomed but I didn't tell mom and dad this.

By the second week of Micah's absence, I'd settled into the familiar and comforting shelter of my anger, preferring it over the mind numbing ache of missing him, fearing he'd never return.

After the third week and still no word from Micah, I put my pearl necklace away. The promise that had once lifted me now felt too much like a lie that weighed me down.

I was being passed around between dance partners in gym just to maintain a decent grade. My blistering Rumba had already immobilized a half dozen unfortunate alternates, when Mr. Winton introduced the Paso Doble to our class. I recognized right away, here was a dance I could get into, as I fervently watched it performed for the first time.

Ms. Becket and Mr. Winton circled each other. He was all proud stance, shoulders back, hips forward making sharp angry movements and she expressive poses of confident feminine fluidity. Their movements matched in intensity.

I couldn't wait to channel my seething emotions into this new dance. But few dared brave the dance with me.

At one point, after watching me dance, Mr. Winton suggested the man was a bullfighter and the woman was his cape. I was nobody's cape! Mr. Winton said I danced the Paso Doble like a man, intimidating my partners. He had me work on the side with Ms. Becket as if she could transfer some of her restrained feminine energy to me in order to curb my forcefulness. I wouldn't be bent to anyone's will.

When she expressed frustration over her inability to help me, I told her I didn't want to be submissive. She said it wasn't submission, it was just a different kind of strength.

When I persisted in my ways, she gave up on me.

I lay in bed perfectly still, immersed in a dark void filled with silver bubbles. I felt Micah press a single kiss on my lips, our bodies buoyed in the black abyss of a yellow school bus. It seemed so real but I knew it wasn't. I'd had enough dreams by then to know the difference between illusions and reality.

The dream was slipping away and I didn't want it to go. He'd been gone for so long and I missed him more than I thought possible. All this time without a single word was devastating. I actually missed the emotional roller coaster, preferring it to this relentless spiral to depths unfamiliar even in my wildest rages. I didn't want him to leave, even if it was only a dream. But he did. I rolled out of bed to start another miserable bottomless day without him.

Mom and dad's early morning departures were never more appreciated. I didn't have the energy to pretend everything was fine particularly with me so worn out from dreaming all night. Dinners weren't as bad because I could use homework and studying to escape to my room early.

On the way to school, I checked his tree out of habit but was greeted with the same empty space every time.

"Ms. Summers, did you bring in any donations today?" Mr. Dunley asked me pointedly.

My homeroom teacher's formal use of our last name grated on my nerves. I looked around and several eyes were watching me expectantly.

Every year, near the holiday season, Talbot conducted a school wide donation drive to give to families in need within the community. Of course, it was a competition between homerooms to see which class collected the most donations.

The only reward was a mention in the school announcements, a picture and write-up in the school newsletter which was also posted in the display box by the front office, and bragging rights in the teachers' lounge, I imagined.

However, every year, Mr. Dunley acted as if his very life depended on winning. Which reduced mornings leading up to the donation deadline, to little more than thinly veiled witch hunts. The witches being those who didn't bring in sufficient donations to satisfy Mr. Dunley's arbitrary demands.

We didn't receive academic grades in homeroom but we did get graded on conduct and Mr. Dunley did not hesitate to let anyone he deemed a slacker know he was perfectly capable of sacrificing a conduct grade for his cause.

"Sorry, Mr. Dunley. I forgot again. I'll try to remember next week," I said, tired of playing his game. My parents did not send me to school to help bolster the ego of my homeroom teacher.

"Ms. Summers, let me remind you that as a member of this class you are part of a team and obligated to support it in any way you can. Last year, you didn't have a bad showing as a donor, placing in the top fifty percentile of the class but right now you're dead last. I wouldn't want your poor performance to be reflected in your conduct grade."

I considered arguing that a grown professional man shouldn't be blackmailing his students over his stupid selfish pride but I didn't have the energy. Besides, Mr. Dunley's ego aside, it was a good cause and I really needed to get my butt in gear and contribute.

Mr. Dunley moved on to Avery.

"Mr. Symmes, you've brought in quite a few things already."

"Actually, I did bring something else in." Avery looked at me guiltily. "My dad gave me twenty coupons redeemable at our restaurant for free pizzas."

Mr. Dunley looked as if he could die of ecstasy on the spot. I almost wished he did.

"Mr. Symmes, that is quite generous of you. The needy families of this community are certainly fortunate to have you in their midst. This will certainly secure your position as the number one donor in this class for the second year in a row. Great job!" he exclaimed as he collected the coupons.

His witch hunt complete, Mr. Dunley closed his attendance book and went back to his desk.

"Adisa, why didn't you let me put your name on that box of donations my mom collected from her Jack and Jill group?" Avery asked defensively when the teacher was gone.

"Because I don't need your charity, to give to charity." I meant for it to be funny but it came out sounding mean.

"You know, I hope Micah shows up soon," he said.

"I thought you didn't like him," I said, surprised at his sudden change of heart.

"I've decided violent nerds are preferable to the ill-tempered walking dead."

In gym, it was Avery's turn to Paso Doble with me. Liz sat in the bleachers while he bravely faced me on the dance floor.

Just before the music started, I reminded him, "What was that you called me... the ill-tempered walking dead?"

During our break Avery meekly requested, "Could you be a little gentler with the flinging me around the dance floor? Unlike your boyfriend, Hercules, I'm fragile."

"Sorry. How are you and Liz doing these days?" I asked.

He looked pleasantly surprised. "Welcome back old friend. It's nice to see you making an effort to lift yourself out of your funk and actually show some interest in somebody else for a change."

I made a face at him.

"Hopefully, you'll be happy to know, that Liz and I are doing better. It was beyond awkward for awhile but I think we've reached a mutual understanding," he declared.

"What kind of understanding?"

He sighed. "It is what it is. All we can do right now is laugh about it."

I was flabbergasted. "Okay. How can you laugh at racism?"

"We've talked about it and she agrees with me that her dad's views are wrong. But he is her dad and she loves him. Me hating her dad won't get me anywhere and it'll only make things worse. So, I make jokes about it. It makes her smile and she doesn't feel so guilty." He shrugged. "Laughing makes us both feel a little less miserable."

"That's pathetic."

Avery sighed, revealing just a hint of frustration. "Maybe it's easier for me because my dad's white."

"Your dad's married to your mom and she's as black as I am. He's not a racist."

"You're right. My dad's not, but his dad is... or was. There was a time my dad couldn't even visit his dad with my mom. But that was before I was born. My dad was stuck in the middle, trying to make the best of a bad situation.

My granddad has always been great to me, reading me bed time stories, taking me fishing with his buddies, letting me come stay with him when the demands of my overachieving parents get to be too much. You know, all that grandparent stuff.

But at the same time, I know he did things in the past that hurt my mom a lot. They're kind of okay now but I know he still has some issues around race. They find ways to laugh at it sometimes and it seems to help. He's working on it but he was already an old man when he started. So, it is what it is."

Break was over and we headed back to the dance floor. I saw Liz watching us. I guess Avery thought she was like his dad, 'stuck in the middle, trying to make the best of a bad situation.' We can't choose our fathers. I was fortunate to have a great one who hated all boys equally regardless of race.

As the music filled the gym and we started to dance, I really did try to take it easier on Avery.

During lunch, I sat on one side of Avery and Liz sat on the other. Liz and I talked to Avery but not each other. I discussed holiday plans. The twins were coming home for Thanksgiving then some of my dad's relatives were coming by for Christmas. Mom's only living relative was her mother so there would be no visitors from her side of the family.

I made it through lunch and the rest of school was the usual mind-numbing exercise in watching the clock.

When I got home, the first thing I did was go through my closet for clothes I could donate and then I hit the pantry and collected some can goods. I didn't have any money to speak of so I called the twins and asked if I could raid their rooms. Mom and dad gave me some things when they returned from work and even dug up some cash. I put everything in a large box and set it by the front door so I wouldn't forget.

Needless to say, Mr. Dunley was in seventh Heaven when I delivered the goods. I tried to keep in mind it was all for a good cause.

I distracted myself outside of school as much as possible so I wouldn't stay up in my room, staring at the empty space where Micah's jeep should be.

Sometimes I went with mom to volunteer at a shelter, helping her prepare food. It was her mission in life to fatten up everybody who came across her path and then track down the rest, to stuff them as well.

I helped dad with many of his projects. We fixed leaky faucets and worked on car maintenance like changing and properly disposing of the oil. He taught me how to change a flat tire, required training for the Summers girls before they would be allowed to drive on their own. We did some yard work but dad refused to let me go out and chop wood for our fireplace. He claimed he didn't want me chopping down the wrong kind of wood and smoking us out of our home. He also pointed out that the few chords of wood we bought yearly was more than sufficient since we only used the fireplace during the holidays.

I even went with mom to visit my grandma one day, not one of my favorite things to do. Visiting Gran always depressed me. She had never been the kind of grandma you read about in books, the kind that sat you on her lap and read stories to you or baked cookies and sent money on your birthdays and graduations.

Ever since I could remember, Gran had lived in a nursing home, existing precariously between reality and nightmare. I always thought of her as a curious mix of scary and sad. She suffered from some sort of perpetual dementia.

I didn't know how mom could stand it, visiting a mother who couldn't even recognize her. Gran had even attacked mom on one occasion but that was several years ago. Mom was still a dutiful daughter, visiting regularly.

Mom would talk to her even though Gran had a far off look that registered nothing, not even the voice of her own daughter, desperate to be heard and seen. Sometimes mom would comb and style Gran's hair or walk with her out in the garden or help her with various craft activities.

Gran didn't seem like a real person except in my mom's memories. She didn't talk about it much but mom could remember a time when Gran behaved like a normal person. I sensed that even during that time, mom and Gran had problems connecting.

Mom never pressured us girls to accompany her on visits to Gran except on mother's day. I thought how sad to have to spend your mother's day like that, honoring a mother who didn't even remember you. But we would all go, and celebrate our mom in the way she chose, in the presence of a mother who looked right through her.

I accompanied mom, desperate for a change to get out of the house and distract myself from my own selfish thoughts. Dad had recently shared a magazine article that claimed one way to make yourself feel better was to help somebody else. I was intent on assisting mom for the selfish purpose of trying to stop feeling sorry for myself.

The home was reputable and affordable and Gran was its longest residing resident. It was located just over an hour from us in a sleepy little community with well manicured lawns and neighbors who regularly socialized with each other.

Mom sometimes complained about the distance but she wouldn't move Gran from the familiar setting, fearing it would so disrupt Gran's world that it could be detrimental to her health. I wondered if Gran would even notice the change but never mentioned it to mom, thinking it would be rude even though I meant well.

Our visit was following its regular pattern. Mom was talking about all the current events in our family as if Gran could really understand. She would occasionally ask a question about how Gran was doing and pause for an answer. Usually it was met with silence or a response that had nothing to do with the question at all.

I quietly sat to the side, speaking only when mom addressed me, attempting to draw me into her one way dialogue with Gran. I was polite but didn't offer anything extra. It hurt seeing mom like this. Her efforts appeared so futile.

Mom silently looked off into the distance, unseeing for awhile then excused herself to go on an errand and I knew it was her usual pretext to go find a secluded place to cry in private because she was overcome by the circumstances.

I tried to engage Gran after mom left, trying to fill the void the absence of mom's chatter had left. But I wasn't as persistent as mom. Eventually Gran and I settled into our usual posture of ignoring each other, lost in our own thoughts.

Gran started talking about her pearls.

"Where's my pearl?" she asked.

"What pearls, Gran?" I didn't remember her having pearls.

"My pearl! I can't find my pearl."

I got up. "I'll help you look. When did you have them last. Mom always says to check there first."

She didn't respond so I started looking on top of her dresser. I made a show of moving things around but there wasn't much there and I could clearly see there were no pearls.

"They're not here Gran. Wait, I'll check your jewelry box." I opened the small decorative box that was sitting in the corner but it was empty. "I can't find them Gran."

She started getting agitated. "If you don't... find pearl... keep looking!" she commanded.

I got nervous wondering if I should go get mom. Then I decided mom needed her break and I could handle things, that was part of the reason for me coming, to help mom.

I pulled open the dresser drawers and started searching around. I worked my way down drawer by drawer. They contained clothing, a few mementos, and an oversized photo album but I didn't see any pearls.

"Gran I don't see them. Are they set in a necklace or a ring or earrings?" I asked, even though I hadn't come across any jewelry at all.

"Everybody says my pearl is so beautiful. You're jealous! You... don't want to find... pearl my...," her voice trailed off in anguish.

"Gran, I really am trying." I went over to her nightstand and checked the drawers there.

"What are you doing, Opal!?" Gran's sharp voice spun me around. She was actually up and out of her chair moving toward me. "You always sneak through my things. What do you want from me?"

"Gran, I'm Adisa, your granddaughter." I stood not knowing what to do.

Gran crowded in on me silently, menacing. I thought about physically restraining her but then remembered the attack on mom and I didn't want to do anything to provoke her further. It would be embarrassing to have mom return to see me tussling on the floor with my own grandmother like she was one of my sisters.

She backed me into the wall and stood glaring at me. I hadn't been that close to her in a long time. She was slightly shorter than I was and her pale skin was a maze of fine creases and a few deep wrinkles. Her thick gray hair was pulled back in a loose ponytail that hung below her shoulders. Her dark eyes inspected me curiously.

"You're not Opal," she said but she didn't move away.

"I'm Adisa, Gran. Opal's daughter. Your granddaughter." I smiled nervously trying to give off calm friendly vibes.

"Adisa?" She looked confused.

"Yes, your granddaughter."

"Shhh!" she insisted and I obeyed.

Mom came in and found us like that.

"Mama! What are you doing?" Mom hurried over to us. She took Gran by the arms and led her back to her seat.

I let out a deep sigh of relief. "It's okay mom. I was just introducing myself to her," I said, turning to humor to relieve the stressful situation.

"Mama, you know Adisa. She's my daughter," mom said, treating my words seriously, as if Gran had committed a social breach that needed correcting.

"No she's not!" Gran said emphatically.

Mom looked as if Gran had slapped her across the face. Then I was surprised to see angry bitterness in her eyes. "Yes she *is*! What have you been saying to her?"

Gran was already sinking back into her vacant stare and didn't respond.

"Mama?" Mom's angry voice failed to reach wherever it was Gran had retreated. "Mama!?"

"Mom, it's okay. I'm fine. She didn't know what she was doing." I'd never heard mom speak to Gran in that tone of voice.

Mom looked at me, startled by my presence, as if she'd forgotten I was in the room.

I thought of mom and Gran's relationship, wondering what I would do if mom slipped into such a state. Would I be able to handle it or would I be too chicken to face her? I hoped I would never have to find out. It scared me to think of her like that.

What was it like for her to see her mom like that when she had memories of a normal mother? Memories like I had of her. I watched mom patiently tend to Gran and felt compassion for her. I wanted to be as strong as she was.

When she attempted to draw me into her one way dialogue, I joined in, actively trying to hold up my end.

We didn't stay long after that. We headed back home in silence.

"Mom do you love Gran?" The question just popped out.

Mom considered carefully before answering. "I've made my peace with her. I appreciate she gave me life. And I try to remember the best things about her." She paused a while to think.

"Even before she became... ill, she wasn't easy to live with. My daddy gave me what she couldn't. He was a saint to stay with her, with us. When he passed she was already showing signs of dementia but we didn't recognize it. I try to honor him through my duty to her. In what I've been given, I've managed to find love for my mother."

It took a lot out of her to work her way to loving Gran.

"I'm sorry we didn't come with you more often. It must really be hard being her only child and having to care for her by yourself."

Mom's eyes quickly met mine for a second. They looked so sad I felt bad for saying what I did. I was trying to show sympathy and I was just making matters worse.

"Mom, Gran was asking for her pearls but I couldn't...,"

The car swerved sharply and we narrowly missed going into a ditch.

"What's wrong?" I asked in alarm, bracing myself as mom struggled to steer us back to our lane.

"There was something... in the road I was trying to avoid," mom explained nervously, adjusting her crooked glasses.

When I looked back, the road was empty. "It must have been an animal. It's gone now."

We drove the rest of the way home, deep in our own thoughts.

Mom had finally run across Mrs. Alexander and asked about Micah. She claimed he was away in Africa on an extended FLEET assignment and had withdrawn from Talbot. When mom delivered this information to me, she was watching me closely.

"That's great," I said. "He told me how important FLEET is to him and his dad. I'm happy for him." I hurried upstairs, hoping it sounded a lot more convincing to her ears than it did to mine.

I took out my pearl necklace. It still looked full of his beautiful promise but when I put it on, the weight of the lie was even heavier. I put it away.

Occasionally, Mr. Alexander's squad car would pass me on my way to school. It felt as if he was taunting me in Micah's absence. I would glare at his retreating vehicle. He must be thrilled, he and FLEET had finally won.

I tried not to think about Micah but often caught myself wondering if I was the reason for his disappearance and what I could have done to drive him away. I was just a girl, what could I do so wrong to cause a person to disappear? I loved Micah and told him so. Was that why he left? Surely it wasn't because of a kiss. The kiss of death, I thought bitterly, that's me. It described me perfectly.

There were times I thought I didn't have anything to do with Micah's disappearance. He had a life and future career through FLEET that had nothing to do with me and it simply had consumed all of his time. He hadn't even said that he loved me so my love for him was no more than a casualty of his career plans. No great mystery there.

At one point, I envisioned filing a missing person report on Micah, to start a manhunt for him. I imagined going to the downtown Atlanta police station and spending hours dictating my report. Then being stunned when I realized it was Mr. Alexander who took such reports. I imagined him ripping up the papers or deleting the files, laughing at my foolishness and claiming as Micah's father he knew what was best for him. And it wasn't me. It was all too hopeless.

The days relentlessly came and went and my hopes of at least getting a phone call or letter of explanation from Micah dwindled. How could he not try to contact me when he knew how much I suffered in his absence? I'd told him how badly it made me feel so I knew he was aware of it. The knowledge that he wasn't coming back left me bitter that I'd ever trusted him.

Avery was still a friend to me even though I wasn't much of one to him or anybody else. I was too consumed with silently obsessing over Micah's disappearance.

We were in gym, taking a class break and Avery had left Liz to come sit by me on the bleachers.

"You and Liz have another falling out?" I asked distracted by my bad mood. When he didn't say anything I added, "What happened? Some of her dad's views starting to rub off. Is she starting to regret that she stole you for her dance partner? Serves you right for ditching me like you did."

I was so wrapped up in my agony over Micah, I couldn't sympathize with him. My anger made it easy to dump on him.

"Now you're stuck with her. Too bad dancing with you is mandatory. I cry myself to sleep every night over it," I said flippantly.

I could tell my words stung him. "You are turning into a real jerk, Adisa. She told me to come over here because she was worried about you."

"Worried about me?" I asked shocked.

"Yeah. You look awful."

"Thanks," I said sarcastically. "Actually, I've never felt better."

Avery shook his head in disbelief. "You never were good at hiding your feelings. Everybody knows you're hurting. You're either dancing like a maniac or sitting over here morose. And we all know it's because Micah's not around so don't think you're fooling anybody."

His voice got real low. "Don't tell anybody I told you this but Liz's mom… is not around because … she's in some mental institution, been there for years. She tried to… hurt herself but she didn't succeed."

When the significance of Avery's word's penetrated my mental fog, I turned on him startled. "Avery, never in a million years would I even consider something like that!"

"I know but it freaked Liz out."

I looked at Liz on the other side of the gym silently looking off to the side, unseeing. She reminded me of mom.

"I gotta go," I told Avery, reluctantly dragging myself off the bleachers.

"Where're you going?"

"Liz."

Avery looked confused and then a look of puppy dog hope came over his face.

I gave him a severe look. "Don't have a nerd-gasm. I'm not promising you a love fest," I angrily threw over my shoulder as I left.

Crossing over to Liz was one of the longest walks of my life.

"Hey," I said.

"Hey."

And then I shut up for awhile because it felt weird talking to her again after I had so perfected ignoring her.

"Avery said you were worried about me. Don't be. I'm fine."

She just nodded. Tension filled silence stretched between us. I impulsively jumped in with both feet.

"Look Liz, I know I've been cold to you lately but I was hurt. When you said you couldn't date Avery because his mom's black that was like you were saying I wasn't good enough because I'm black. It's like you insulted my family and all black people all over the world by saying that.

And you hurt my friend! Avery's a great guy and doesn't deserve that. It just really really sucks what you did." I stopped until I was sure my voice wouldn't tremble. "I couldn't believe you could do something like that. I mean, I know you act a little weird about race but I never thought you'd go that far."

My words ran out and Liz stood silently just taking it all in.

"Adisa, remember last year when I asked to touch your hair?" she finally asked.

I looked at her confused, wondering what she was trying to get at. Was she trying to insult me further? I remembered the shock and hurt I felt at her request. My hair was just as straight as hers then but I knew she asked to feel it because I was black and she was curious about its texture. For some inexplicable reason, instead of exploding in anger, I allowed her to touch it.

I slowly nodded in answer to her question.

"I could tell you were offended but you let me anyway even though we had just met. Why did you do that?" she asked.

I shrugged, still wondering what she was getting at.

"I knew then everything my daddy told me about black people was a lie. I mean I knew it before in my head but with you, I knew it in my heart. You were... gracious. You were gracious and you didn't even know me."

I thought about what she said for awhile. Nobody had ever referred to me as being gracious.

"Well I'm sure in the time since then, I've proven otherwise many times over," I said, thinking of my numerous temperamental outbursts she'd witnessed.

She smiled. "You want to know something else?"

I nodded, truly curious.

"I knew Avery liked me last year."

I looked at her in disbelief because during our freshman year, she'd seemed completely clueless to Avery's feelings.

"I really did," she insisted. "I liked him too but I knew how my dad felt about that kind of thing so I pretended not to know. It was easier that way.

Then, on the first day of school, I heard we would be dancing in gym. I saw Avery and thought it was a way I could get close to him without my dad knowing. And it wasn't like I was actually dating him so I thought it would be okay.

Well, I went over and stood by Avery, hoping he would ask me to be his partner. Imagine my chagrin when you said he had asked you."

I couldn't believe my ears. I remembered how Avery had asked me in a rush. I had been completely immersed in my own selfish thoughts and hadn't even considered that Liz actually liked him. I thought she was just trying to avoid getting a really bad partner like me and Avery were doing.

"I was so jealous of you, even though I knew you didn't like him like that. I wanted him for myself so when he got close, without even thinking about it, I went for him. I was so nervous, thinking he would turn me down. But he didn't. And I was so incredibly happy. Even after that you were gracious."

I remembered clearly the irritation I felt toward them for abandoning me. I'd considered them both traitors when they went dancing off together. But she was right, I didn't blow up then either.

"Then at lunch when I kept acting shocked because Micah picked you over all the other girls, I realized too late that once again I was offending you."

"Yeah. That was pretty low Liz, acting like I was so repulsive you couldn't believe a great looking guy like Micah actually picked somebody like me." I could still feel the sting of my hurt feelings.

"It wasn't about your looks. It's your temper. I see guys looking at you all the time but they don't approach you because you can get really scary when you get mad."

I was thoroughly surprised. "Guys really look at me all the time?" I looked around to see if any of them were looking now.

Liz laughed. "See, you're doing it again. I just implied you're the quintessential angry black woman and you graciously focus on the part that's more complimentary. Yes, Adisa, guys look at you all the time, it's just that temper of yours keeps them away." She hesitated. "You know my mom was like that. Gracious, I mean."

"Really?" I asked, wondering if she was about to confide her mother's attempted suicide and dreading it. But she only nodded.

"Well, I've been pretty mean to you lately and...," I began, trying to work my way up to an apology but she interrupted me.

"I know. But I figured I deserved it. I caused all this and I probably should suffer for it but I feel bad I made you and Avery feel bad too."

"Is that why you've put up with my attitude for so long?" I asked.

"Maybe. At least you didn't curse me out like Sonjia did."

My eyes flew wide open. "Sonjia Jordan cursed you out over Avery!?"

I was shocked because Sonjia didn't care for Avery anymore than she liked me and I knew it was because she thought neither of us acted black enough. I couldn't believe Sonjia of all people would stick up for Avery.

"She was kind enough to at least wait until she caught me alone. It was painful but quick. She called me a few names, told me what she thought of me and my daddy and where we could go, and then she was out," Liz recapped.

"Liz, I have to admit, I couldn't just sit back and take it like you do, even if I thought I deserved it."

"Well, the next time you're rude to me maybe I'll karate kick you in the butt," she said smiling.

"You could try," I demurred. "But I'm a fighter. I have two older sisters I've been honing my skills on since I was in the crib. And I took a self-defense class this past summer and I actually impressed the instructor with my kick."

"Oh really? Well I have three brothers all mad as Hell over the fact that I was lucky enough to be born first but not quite so lucky to be a boy. I've been defending my position for years. Plus, I've been taking a karate class since I was eight."

"For real?" I questioned, looking concerned.

She nodded with pride.

"Well you must not be very good at it, if after all these years you're still taking the same class."

She looked confused for a beat then giggled.

After awhile, I finally said, "You know, I've never been good at apologizing."

"Verbal apologies have been a lifelong struggle for me too. I know I owe you quite a few," she admitted.

We paused, our backs to the wall, side by side, looking out over the gym.

"Well, just as long as we understand each other," I concluded.

"Understood," she agreed.

"Okay, we cool then?" I asked.

"Sure, we're cool."

Then we just stood looking at each other, nodding like a couple of idiots.

Avery came over, a smug smile on his face. "So is the catfight over? I like it when women fight over me but like Rodney King said 'Can't we all just get along?'"

He deserved to be punished for that so I said with exaggerated casualness, "Strawberries. Sweet, juicy, succulent *strawberries*."

I was instantly rewarded. Avery's traumatized eyes froze on me as he turned redder than Liz's hair. There wasn't a trace of a smile on his stricken face. Success!

Later when talking alone with Avery, I admitted. "You were right. She's a very honest person."

Things got better at school after that but I still had to find ways to distract myself when I wasn't at school. I didn't go to Kennesaw Mountain anymore. It was full of too many memories of Micah. I worked out in my neighborhood and ran Talbot's track, now sporting long-sleeved jogging suits to ward off the chill of the changing season. I was determined to make things like they were before he ever came.

I gave menial tasks my utmost concentration, like taking care of the backlog of emails, meticulously cleaning my room and restroom and then expanding to the entire house. I took and passed my driver's license test.

I was in regular attendance with my parents at church and sang in the Youth Choir and concentrated on my homework. I cooked dinner every night during the week over my mom's strong objections.

She started cooking large meals over the weekend so that all I had to do was reheat them. But I wanted the distraction of actually planning and preparing a meal. I appreciated mom's efforts to make things easier on me but I loaded the freezer with her dishes and started my own from scratch.

Thanksgiving came and mom put her foot down. She would not allow me to make the meal all by myself but she did let me help. Kelly and Kylie came home and exclaimed how organized and clean the house was.

We went downtown to help serve a Thanksgiving meal to the homeless and then returned home to share our time together before the twins would have to return to school. Our prayers of thanksgiving were poignant and our familial bonds renewed.

I wouldn't let anybody help me clean up after our meals, possessively throwing myself into the task after chasing everybody away. Kelly let me drive her and Kylie around town, breaking in my new driver's license. I preferred driving Kelly's car over dad's because hers was an automatic. Dad took me to practice a few times on his standard but I hated fighting with the stick shift.

It got to the point where I could go long stretches of time without thinking of Micah. I worked at it diligently. It was the hardest assignment I ever tackled.

School was a great distraction even though I couldn't break the habit of checking his tree every time I passed it. The squad car still cruised by occasionally but I didn't glare at it like I used to.

I was playing Sudoku with dad. It really wasn't a game designed for more than one player but dad was new to it and I was giving him tips and showing him various logical strategies to solving it. It was a numbers puzzle but it really didn't involve math. Since it had numbers and required logic, it was close enough.

It was an early release day and I was back from school and dad had stayed home because he said he didn't feel well and thought the weather was throwing him off his rhythms. Mom said he was coming down with something from the damp dreary weather.

Dad went to the kitchen to get a drink and that's when it happened. I didn't hear a thing. To this day I wonder what made me go running into the kitchen, clutching my heart in fear.

Dad was in the middle of the kitchen floor, his right hand clamped like a vise on his left arm, his face contorted in a horrible mask of pain.

"NO!" I screamed and fell to the floor beside him.

"What's wrong dad?" I kept asking over and over even though I instinctively knew it was his heart. The suffering in his eyes was unbelievable and scared me more than anything had in my life.

I jumped up and dialed 911 keeping my eyes on him as he writhed in pain on the floor. He started making a strangled noise deep in his throat and I knew the pain was worsening. I wanted to call mom but the emergency operator kept asking me questions.

When I heard the sirens getting close, I dropped the phone and ran outside so they could locate the house quicker. Neighbors started gathering outside but I was too distracted to talk to anybody.

The paramedics followed me back to my dad and I explained to them what happened as they took over. I put every hope in their capable hands and they moved with assurance and knowledge of what they were doing. I felt a flood of relief, giving over control to people who were professionally trained to handle emergencies.

They were asking dad questions until he fell unconscious. I called mom, it took me several tries because I kept punching in the wrong numbers while watching them work on dad. I told mom to meet us at Grady Memorial hospital because that's what I heard the paramedics say as they prepared to take dad.

I told mom I would call the twins but she said not to, no need bothering them when there was nothing they could do. But there was something they could do. They could help. They were a lot more capable than I was and there were two of them. But mom insisted, saying it was too close to their finals and they would be home soon anyway.

I rode with dad in the ambulance and knew things weren't going well. At the hospital, I followed the gurney, barely able to keep up, through a maze of hallways but they wouldn't let me through the final doors with him.

Mom and I found each other and held on. I wanted to give her words of comfort but my mind was frozen in fear. She had no words for me either. She just held me and prayed like I never heard her pray before.

How were we going to make it without dad? He was our rock, our center. The doctor came out hours later and told us it wasn't good. Dad had suffered complete heart failure and showed decreased heart function below ten percent capacity.

I mentioned a heart transplant and for the briefest moment I saw the stark truth flash in her eyes. She calmly began explaining the qualifications necessary to be put on a transplant list and how dad's body was too weak to survive the wait let alone the surgery.

Mom fainted and I managed to prevent her from hitting the floor. Nurses rushed over and helped me sit her down and then they pushed me out of the way, working on trying to revive her. I was so scared I was trembling. I was alone. All alone.

I thought of my sisters and began looking for a phone but couldn't find one. I wasted a good twenty minutes before it suddenly dawned on me and I patted my pockets and found my cell phone. I always forgot I had it. A nurse told me not to use it in there so I went outside to make the call. Kelly and Kylie would know what to do.

I hesitated, once I was outside. I had to handle this. My sisters had finals to prepare for and there was nothing they would do that I couldn't do myself. They would be available after they finished their finals and that was just a few days away. Could I really handle things for that long?

I went back inside. Mom had come around but she was still disoriented. Her empty eyes terrified me. I went back out and called information for the number to our church. There was a group of women mom called prayer warriors and Pastor DJ, I knew they would help.

Mr. Alexander walked up just as I got off the phone and he looked truly concerned. Why not, it was me he hated, not my dad. I asked how he found out but he said that was unimportant. I updated him as best I could on dad's condition while we went in together. Mom was coherent enough to be asking for me.

I'm ashamed to say I was glad Mr. Alexander was there as I faced mom. She was like a child, asking me if everything was going to be okay. I was shocked to see her that way. I wanted to be strong enough to send Mr. Alexander away but I was still shaking with fear. I reassured mom as I desperately tried to hold everything together.

Mr. Alexander stayed with mom while the doctor finished updating me on my dad's condition. I listened to her words, the medical terms making no sense to me, feeling hollow inside. Deep down, I heard what she didn't say with words, dad was not going to make it. I felt a gate inside me slam shut and lock.

I had to go down to the billing area because mom couldn't locate her insurance card. I asked Mr. Alexander if he would stay with mom a little longer and he quickly agreed. I couldn't believe I had to deal with a financial issue while in the middle of a medical crisis.

When I returned, Mom didn't want to leave the hospital but there were things that had to be done involving dad's insurance. Mr. Alexander had to leave and I thanked him for his help. He offered to send his wife in his place but I told him I already called people from my church. There was no need for me to take Mrs. Alexander away from Jason. Without Micah there, he'd probably have to go to some sitter he hated.

Only after dad was stabilized and they let us briefly see him, did mom let me take her down to the cafeteria to get something for her to eat. I asked her where they kept the insurance policies while encouraging her to eat. I tried to eat also.

When we went back up, dad still hadn't regained consciousness. The doctors said they didn't expect him to do so any time soon but they would be moving him out of observation and into his own room. I made mom as comfortable as I could in the waiting room, getting a blanket from the nurse and bringing snacks and drinks from the vending machine. I brought over several magazines and placed them next to her snacks.

"Mom, I have to drive home and get some supplies if we're going to stay here over night. I also have to find dad's insurance papers."

"Okay baby," she said but I didn't think she fully understood.

"Mom, I need the keys to the car and I need to know where you parked. I'm going to be gone for awhile so you'll be here by yourself. I left a message at the church but nobody's returned my call yet. Is there anybody else I should call?"

"You need to call your dad's job. He may be a little late for work tomorrow," she said in all seriousness.

I felt tears threaten but managed to smile. "That's a great idea. I'll call his job and yours too."

"Oh, yeah. I may be late too."

I sat with her awhile longer, not wanting to leave her. I knew there was no way I'd be able to persuade her to come with me, not as long as dad was at the hospital.

I dialed information and got the home phone numbers of a couple of the prayer warriors. I left messages with each. It started to dawn on me how isolated my family was. Sure we knew people, but we weren't used to calling on others for help. Dad prided himself on our self-sufficiency and ability to help others. Now that the circumstances had changed, I felt lost, uncomfortable asking outsiders for help.

It was getting late and I wanted to leave so I could get back as soon as possible. I told mom I'd be back as quick as I could and asked if she wanted me to bring her anything. I asked the nurses to keep an eye on her until I got back.

I managed to locate the car in the parking deck despite mom's sketchy directions. Dad had only taken me out in his car a few times so I still wasn't comfortable using the stick shift. The car stalled on me a couple times before I was able to get it going. Once I was on the highway and didn't have to do much shifting, I was okay. But I got turned around a couple times, not quite familiar with the roads.

When I got home I quickly ran through the house collecting supplies and set them by the door. Then I went to the small free standing safe in mom and dad's walk-in closet. I'd never been in it before but mom had told me how to get it open. I knelt down and ran my hand along the back of it. The combination was written in code based on family anniversary dates and taped behind the safe. Since I knew the dates, I quickly decoded the combination and opened the safe.

There was a stack of papers and some cash stored inside. I took all of the papers out and set them on top of the safe. Then I took some of the cash and stuffed it into my pocket.

I took the papers to the family room and spread them out on the coffee table, looking for dad's health insurance. I could hardly focus on the papers, they kept blurring into one another. Finally I just pulled out the papers that were obviously not about his insurance, like graduation certificates and diplomas, birth certificates, the buyer's contract on the house, and a few old family photos. Then I took what remained and added it to the pile of supplies by the door. I'd just go through them at the hospital.

I went through the house making sure everything was closed, locked, and turned off then grabbed my pile of stuff, locked up the house, and headed back to the hospital.

When I reached mom, she was asleep where I'd left her, stretched across several seats. I didn't wake her. The nurse said dad's condition hadn't changed. I sat near mom and started going through the papers. I finally located dad's health insurance and sat back relieved. Whatever else happened, at least this problem was taken care of and wouldn't come back to haunt my family.

The days passed and Dad didn't regain consciousness. The prayer warriors stayed with us in shifts during the day, praying and offering encouraging words and bringing in food. Mr. Alexander came by again but seeing us in their confident hands, he complied when I said it would be less distracting if he didn't return. I told him I'd call him if we needed anything. It was too hard having him around because it made me think of Micah.

Dad's condition slowly deteriorated. Mom still refused to let me call the twins and it was easier for me to obey her wishes once I saw she was back to her old self. She was adamant about not disrupting their finals, stating dad would want them to finish first. I was going to school to take exams and pick up my assignments but then I was excused to leave and be with mom. Avery and Liz offered their support but I told them I had everything under control.

Since she absolutely refused to leave the hospital, mom used the public restroom to take care of her needs and change clothes. I hated staying at the house alone so traveled back and forth for supplies. I went about restocking our provisions and putting mom's used clothes in the laundry room. Then I showered and quickly put on a clean change of clothing.

I collected the papers still on the coffee table to return them to the safe before I returned to the hospital. I was in a hurry and dropped some of the papers as I was cramming them back into the safe.

I retrieved them to put with the others when something caught my eye. It was a birth certificate and it had my name on it. But only my first name, not my last name. The last name was not Summers. It was Valenté.

At first I stared at the document, curiously fascinated that we had somebody else's important papers in our safe and she shared my first name. I'd never come across anybody who had my first name before, and now, under my very own roof, I discover this other person's birth certificate which did.

I read the full name.

First: Adisa

Middle: Musa

Last: Valenté

It wasn't a trick of the light. The name was real.

It seemed my body knew before my mind finally caught up because my hands were trembling as I read the details, still not comprehending. Not only did we share a first name, we shared a birth date and birthplace. However, that's where the similarities ended. The parents listed were Pearl and Cyrus M. Valenté. The paper fell from my hands.

I was still while my mind processed the information. Pearl and Cyrus M. Valenté. I'd never heard of their names before.

I turned back to the safe and dragged out its contents to see what other painful truths it concealed. I found only one. A faded black and white photo of mom as a little girl.

I recognized her because our family photo album contained a few pictures of mom as a little girl. But unlike the pictures in the family photo album, this picture had an exact copy of mom, standing next to her on the playground, smiling exactly the same up into the camera.

It reminded me of a Photoshop trick Kylie did where she put several images of herself in a single photo sharing the same background. But I knew this was no Photoshop trick.

I stared at the picture trying to figure out which of the little girls was really my mom and which was the imitator. I flipped it over but there was nothing written on the back.

I desperately went through all the papers again, studying each closely but there was nothing else incriminating there. I put everything back except for the birth certificate. That was mine. I slammed the safe door shut and scrambled the combination lock. I didn't want to think about all the implications related to the birth certificate. It was easier to focus on the photograph.

So mom had a twin, just like Kelly and Kylie. I remember dad turning up a bit of trivia suggesting that twins commonly ran within the same family. I hadn't believed it at the time, Kelly and

Kylie being the only twins in our family I was aware of. Why had mom never mentioned her twin? Had she died and the memory was too painful for mom?

I piled the supplies in the car, my newly discovered birth certificate on the seat next to me, and pulled out of the driveway. Mr. Alexander was in his yard watching as I drove by and he actually waved. I kept on driving.

I didn't realize where I was going until I was parked. I turned off the engine and sat rocking myself a long time, steeling myself. Where was my rage? I needed it for strength.

A frigid wind whipped at my coat as I stepped out of the car and hurried inside. I detested the cold and it only put me in a foul mood, making it even more difficult to concentrate on what I had to do.

When I made it to Gran's room, an attendant was just leaving. Gran was standing by her window which overlooked a slumbering garden. The bright colors that usually decorated the scene were no longer there, lulled to sleep in winter's cold embrace.

"Hello, Gran. It's me Adisa." My voice sounded like a stranger's.

When she didn't respond, I sat in a chair, overwhelmed with what I was attempting to do. My mind was numb and couldn't pull things together to formulate a plan. How could I get the information I sought from a woman I didn't know how to communicate with?

I was staring at the dresser then got up, going through the drawers, not really understanding why until I came across the photo album.

I flipped through it and found what I was looking for, mom and her replica, little girls in identical jumpsuits. The Photoshop effect, proof that the picture in the safe was not just a fluke. The two really existed.

I continued turning the pages of the album. The girls looked identical through the ages until they reached their teen years. Then they were different, in dress, in expression, and hairstyle. I was able to tell mom from the imitator now, recognizing her straight hair while her twin's hair was cropped in a short afro.

Then it dawned on me. I looked more like the imitator than mom. I gasped as another revelation assailed me. The picture of me and my mom I kept on my dresser... it was the imitator holding me... not mom. I had to take a moment to digest this information. My mind painfully took the name Pearl from my birth certificate and affixed it to the imitator.

For years, the truth had been silently watching over me from a photo on my dresser as I lived my life, blissfully ignorant. I shuddered, shrinking inside of myself, my death grip on the photo album the only thing keeping me from flying apart.

On another page, the imitator was hugged up to and grinning in the face of a tall dark extremely handsome man and I uttered a startled cry. He looked like a masculine version of me! And even though the photo was black and white, I knew that his skin color matched mine. The album trembled in my hands as I turned to face Gran.

She was staring at me as if she was really seeing me and it felt strange. I could feel her eyes passing over my afro. She called me Pearl, and I realized she didn't see me at all. She saw somebody else. Somebody she'd been looking for. Somebody I'd ignorantly searched for in her empty jewelry box.

"Pearl," she said, her voice a raspy accusation. "Where have you been? You didn't have to run off. There's no shame in having a baby. I would've helped you take care of her."

Then she turned away from me, refusing or unable to say anymore.

When I got back to the hospital, mom asked what had taken me so long. I told her I lost track of time. I couldn't tell her the truth, not now with the worry lines deeply creasing her balsa skin, reminding me so much of Gran.

She reached for my hand and I took it in mine. The difference in our skin shades appeared more glaring than ever.

Kelly and Kylie finally finished their finals and arrived. I collapsed in their arms but kept the knowledge of my newly discovered identity to myself. We all wanted to stay at the hospital with dad but mom said that was no good so we set up shifts. Mom also told us to call dad's relatives, they were all out of state.

Dad's parents were deceased but he had a sister and brother. Dad's brother had plenty of kids but had never been married and his sister was married but never had kids, claiming she didn't particularly care for them. Dad wasn't close to his family but they maintained contact and his brother and sister did come but only for a couple of days, both claiming work obligations. I thought I overheard them discussing 'the youngest not really being his' but I was so numb and dazed that my mind may have been playing tricks on my hearing.

Dad hung on for a couple days getting weaker and the doctors told us they didn't think he'd make it to the end of the week. I knew he wasn't my real dad but he was the only one I'd ever known and I didn't want him to leave me. One dad had already left me. I wasn't ready for this one to go.

When I was alone with dad, I curled up on the bed with him to beg God for his life and say my goodbyes, because though I pleaded, I knew it was a miracle too big for me to seriously expect to get.

I cried, prayed, and held dad, his unnatural stillness filling my mind with panic. His skin was papery dry and cool. My own body felt hot in comparison. His heartbeat was a whisper in his chest. I placed my hand on top of it to feel, listening to the irregular beeps of the monitor. I closed my eyes.

It seemed my hand sank inside his chest and in the hollow I could feel the flutter of his heart. All was suddenly calm as my mind emptied and I felt light. I got so hot I could scorch his skin. I recited the twenty-third Psalms, his favorite bible passage.

When I got up, Dad's face was shiny and there were tiny beads of perspiration on his brow but he looked at peace. I kissed his cheek before slipping away.

I was at home for a change of clothes when we got the call. Kelly answered the phone and I knew it was the hospital. I left the room, not wanting to see her face while she spoke because I didn't want to remember what it looked like when she heard our dad had died.

I heard her scream and my heart broke apart and I knew it would never be the same because a part of it would be forever buried in a grave with my dad.

"No! No mom. Disa? Adisa get in here now!"

I didn't want to go but my sister needed me. I went to her and she was crying but wonder of wonders, her face was twisted in a weird mask of joy drenched in tears.

"He's okay Disa," she said, her voice full of the miracle. "He's walking around... and talking... and generally shocking the Hell out of everybody there!"

My hands flew to my face and I crumpled at her feet shaking, unable to believe God would grant a miracle that big. She stooped down and gathered me in her arms, still cradling the phone between her face and shoulder.

I kept shaking my head no, too scared to believe, not wanting to hurt like this all over again when we found out it was all a mistake and he was really dead. But then Kelly was screaming daddy and I knew she was listening to his voice. She held the phone so I could hear too.

"I'm all right," he was saying, his rich baritone enveloping me like a blanket.

We all couldn't stop crying. We could hear mom and Kylie in the background and the doctors and nurses trying to regain control.

Kelly pulled me to my feet and we headed out the door. We were at the hospital in record time. The Summers women huddled together, thanking God for his miracle. Dad was off with the doctors and heart specialists confounding them.

We were laughing, crying, or praying the whole time. Every time we heard the doctors had ordered another test, it set us off again. Pastor DJ came looking all somber and was startled to see us so happy.

When he found out what had transpired, he thanked the Lord and grumbled he wished he'd made it in time to lay hands on dad and pray over him so he could claim the victory. He had us laughing even more if that was possible. He prayed with us and stayed until he had a chance to talk to dad and witness the miracle first hand.

We all stayed close to each other, always touching, like if we didn't have each other to physically support ourselves, we'd fall down. Dad hugged me so tight it hurt but I never complained.

Only then did the locks finally break and the gates fly open. I believed.

"This is the second miracle this family has had this year," Pastor DJ said looking at me and dad.

"I know," mom said. "If Death comes after anybody else in this family, I may just up and leave with him myself because I can't take all this up and down, like a roller coaster."

I laughed so hard with my family that fresh tears came to my eyes. But this time, I didn't know if it was from joy in dad's recovery or from the knowledge of my false identity or from missing Micah.

We lit the fireplace for the holidays. It was the best Christmas we ever had even though we didn't put up a single decoration nor exchange any gifts. We pretty much just sat around talking to one another and appreciating our time together. We celebrated the seven days of Kwanzaa, mama displaying a photograph of Dr. Maulena Karenga in its usual place of honor. We rang in the New Year together lifting our champagne glasses, we three girls drinking sparkling grape juice, poured from a wine styled bottle and mom and dad partaking of the real thing.

I felt split in two. I was deliriously happy but still felt a painful detachment as I watched my family. I thought of Celie in The Color Purple saying, Pa not Pa.

I stood on the porch with my family watching some of the illegal fireworks set off in our neighborhood, decorate the sky. A new year and everything was different. Dad not dad, mom not mom, and sister not sister.

I watched my mom and dad going through the motions of pretending to be my real parents. They were so good at it. No wonder I had been fooled all these years.

I wondered if Kelly and Kylie knew of my true identity. Kelly used to tease me about them finding me in a cabbage patch and how I didn't really belong to them. But I thought she was making it up because she didn't start saying that until after she got a Cabbage Patch doll.

One morning, dad's pursuit of trivia turned up Sir. Francis Bacon's aphorism, 'knowledge is power.' What power did I now possess? I was scared of my knowledge. I tucked the information away and kept it secret. It was too powerful to use on my small family. I feared it would blow us apart and we'd never be able to put ourselves back together again.

That wasn't exactly true. I was scared it would blow me apart and I would never be able to reattach myself to them. I tried to convince myself it wasn't real, just some mistake that could easily be explained away. I couldn't stand another loss.

I tried not to think of Micah but wasn't very successful. I started looping Amy Winehouse's Love is a Losing Game to convince myself it was useless to indulge in such fantasies.

Getting back to normal was hard. Mom and dad had to practically threaten the twins to get them back into Bartlett when the Spring semester started. Dad was doing so well that he returned to work with mom. And I went back to Talbot.

I thought about telling Avery of my true identity but that's as far as it went. I didn't have the courage to give my thoughts words.

Not much had changed at school except for one thing. Everybody was now taking part two of the curriculum but our class schedules remained the same as the previous semester. In computer class, we were moving from web design into graphic illustration to create images for our web sites. In gym, Latin dancing was over and we had moved into group African dancing and I was as relieved as my alternates that we no longer needed dance partners. In math we transitioned to Calculus II.

I was tempted to take the photo of my real mom and dad from Gran's photo album but couldn't bring myself to steal from her. She had so few of her worldly possessions left even if she may not be aware of what they were. That picture was important enough for her to hang onto all those years and I refused to take advantage of her memory loss to satisfy my own selfish needs. Then I remembered that the information desk had a photocopier and I made a copy of the photograph before returning the original to Gran's album.

I had the dream about my family disappearing again, Kelly and Kylie in the kiddie pool and mom and dad in the woods. It was even scarier because now the dream was more like a premonition. I had already lost my family and now, something was waiting out there to tear me apart.

Another night, I dreamed of a tall handsome man whose dark skin gleamed. He was with my mom. They put me in a cabbage patch and left me there. Then the scene turned into a cotton field and I was naked, alone, shivering and scared. A young boy came to me, emerging from the tangle of cotton stalks like a miracle.

He wrapped me in a colorful quilt and sat next to me, holding my hand, speaking words of comfort. My crying became whimpering and then subsided all together. His beautiful copper skin gleamed in the moonlight and he sang to me of a bridge over troubled waters so I wouldn't be afraid.

When I began to squirm, he pulled off my covering and walked me into the shelter of the stalks and averted his eyes. I squatted, still holding his hand, too fearful to let go, and relieved myself. The stream ran in the dirt toward my pudgy foot and I squealed in alarm not wanting it to touch me.

The boy laughed and picked me up, swinging me high and away just in time and it felt like flying. He carried me back to where we were sitting and pulled the quilt back around me, and sang while a golden orb rose in the sky. And then he was gone. The orb turned into a black pearl that still gave off light. It took the form of my mom's face.

I woke up and automatically reached for the photo and stared at the picture I'd kept on my dresser for years. Me and my mom, my real mom. We were pressed cheek to cheek and my miniature afro matched hers. I was careful not to get my tears on the familiar image.

I pulled out Micah's gift. I hadn't looked at it in a long time. I stared at the dark luminous orb in my hand and then I looked at my baby picture with my real mom, in spite of everything my two most treasured possessions. I rolled the black pearl back and forth between my fingers, my eyes still on my real mom... then my black pearl... my mom... my pearl. Something clicked and my world went deathly still. Did Micah know?

I put Micah's gift away and returned my baby picture to its usual place on my dresser. Only after I was sure I was in full control of myself would I emerge from my room to continue living the lie of Adisa Summers and not, in truth, Adisa Musa Valenté.

9 ~ YOU CAN FLY!?

W hen did winter come? I didn't even remember the Fall leave's changing colors adorning my favorite time of season; God's magical explosion of color marching across the thick greenery of Georgia's landscape. Somehow, I had missed the crimsons, golds, and pumpkin gingers decorating the postcard perfect scenery and was suddenly thrust into the dawn of a cold barren gray day.

Micah was back. I hadn't seen him yet but his jeep was parked in his driveway when I woke up. I stood at my window, trying to make sense of what I was looking at. The shiny black jeep was spotless in a sea of brown leaves. I turned from the window and made myself concentrate on preparing for school.

It was quiet as I ate breakfast alone in my empty house. I had my birth certificate in my pocket. I always kept it with me, like I always had my driver's license, forms of identity that I wasn't using. I didn't know what I planned on doing with it. I slipped my hand in my pocket and wrapped my fingers around the folded sheet to make sure it was still there, still real.

I was in no hurry as I left, carefully taking the time to lock the door behind me. When I passed by Micah's tree, I didn't even register surprise when he wasn't there. I was so used to not seeing him there that the mere fact of his jeep materializing in his driveway didn't alter that reality for me.

It felt like something in the woods was watching me pass but that was nothing new, my mind still busy conjuring up images to reassure me that he wasn't gone forever.

I didn't even look back toward his house again to make sure the jeep wasn't an apparition, some figment of my imagination playing tricks on me. I just kept right on walking to school, hugging my thick jacket close against a hateful chilly wind.

School was the same. I stumbled through a group African dance, sat through lunch listening to Avery and Liz try to mask their true feelings with mundane exchanges, and used a graphing calculator to find the values of my calculus problems before walking home.

Micah's jeep hadn't moved from its spot in his driveway.

I let myself in the house, got a snack, and headed upstairs. I carefully closed the blinds and the curtains before starting on my homework.

I had dinner ready when mom and dad got home. When they asked if anything new or interesting had happened, I said no. They weren't the only ones in this family who could keep secrets.

"I saw Micah's car in his driveway. He must be back from that FLEET assignment," dad said a little too casually.

I didn't comment. I didn't even look up. But I still sensed mom and dad exchanging one of their looks. I excused myself from the table and started on the dishes.

I went to school the next day and it was exactly the same as the day before. Except, I did even better, I didn't look to see if the jeep was still there at all. I knew it was without having to visually confirm it.

The following day at the end of school, Ms. Gator called me to her desk and asked me to take a stack of math assignments to Micah Alexander's home, along with assignments from his other classes, because he had to complete them before returning to school on Monday.

"Pardon?" I croaked. I must have miss-heard.

"I've collected assignments from all of Micah Alexander's classes for you to take to his home. He plans on returning to Talbot and he has to complete these assignments before he can be readmitted."

I looked at her like she was a real alligator that had just crawled up onto the chair and sat at the desk casually talking to me, legs crossed in a floral print blouse.

"Pardon?" I repeated, distracted by my gator vision.

"Adisa! For the third time, will you please take these assignments to Micah Alexander?" she said, with impatience.

I stared at her in disbelief and nearly said pardon again but caught myself just in time. "Why me?"

"I guess he asked for you to do it when he called Talbot to get reinstated. Apparently you live right across the street from him," she said as if that simple fact made it unnecessary to explain any further.

"Yes, I do but, I've never stepped a foot inside his home before."

She looked at me as if to say 'What does that have to do with the high price of gas?'

"Adisa, are you all right?" she asked, sounding worried.

"I'm fine Ms. Gator. I'll take them."

She gave me the stack of assignments and I left.

I walked home trying to pretend it was a regular day and nothing out of the ordinary was happening. But the weight of the assignments was distracting. How was Micah ever going to complete all of them? Maybe he wouldn't and then he couldn't get reinstated then I could maintain my tenuous grip on sanity.

As I neared my home, I considered going inside and forgetting the whole thing. I'd tell Ms. Gator winds from one of Georgia's flash storms swooped down and carried off the assignments, disappearing with the fluttering burden as quickly as it had sprung up.

I looked at Micah's house. His jeep still hadn't moved. That's when I felt my first flash of anger and I welcomed it.

Three days! Three days he sat on his lazy behind and didn't drop by or phone to apologize for his unforgivable behavior. Then he calls Ms. Gator, oh apparently his phone is working because he was able to call her, and tells her to tell me to fetch his stinking homework!! Why? Oh get this because it's rich, he plans on coming back to school.

On top of that, he doesn't have a single precious minute to spare to zip down in his shiny black jeep and pick them up himself. But no worries, let Adisa do it. She has no life, just sitting around waiting for him to fall out of the sky into her lap so she can feed him hot fudge and whipped cream on sundaes!

Well he had another think coming if he thought he could just waltz back... oh... and if he thought I was going to be his dance partner again he could forget that! I'd dance with alternates for the duration of my stay at Talbot, even dance with abusive Justin, before I let him touch me again. Then I remembered we had moved on to African group dancing so I didn't have to worry about partnering with him. I held onto my anger anyway.

He wants his assignments. I'll give him his assignments, I'll give them to him right now. And since he was the one who called to command me to bring them, he wasn't getting a courtesy phone call first. I'll just kick his door in and throw it all in his stupid copper face!

I was already stomping up his porch steps grateful my anger, not fear, flared as I got to his door. My arms were full so I couldn't ring the doorbell. I kicked the door three times with my foot so hard I hurt my toe but saw with satisfaction that it left a dent in the door. Unfortunately, it didn't fly open, like I'd imagined, so I couldn't just throw the load in and turn around and leave.

I stood there furious, thinking that if he didn't open the door soon, I was going to drop the assignments where I stood and I didn't care if the wind really did swoop down and carry it all away. I still had my backpack on and the dual burden of it on my back in addition to carrying the load in my arms, left me with no patience under the circumstances.

I was just about to drop the assignments when the door suddenly opened. Mr. Alexander stood there, a severe look on his face.

I lifted my chin a little higher, refusing to be intimidated by him but still hoping he wouldn't notice the dent in his door until after I'd left. I didn't even bother with pleasantries.

"Your son called and asked me to bring this over," I said, indicating the assignments. I sincerely hoped he would pick up on the fact that I hadn't volunteered. I was done chasing after his son.

"Thank you, Adisa. Please, come in. I've been meaning to come over and see your father. How is he doing?"

"Fine, thanks for asking," I said tersely, refusing to let go of my anger, it was the only thing holding me up. Then I thought a gentleman would have relieved me of my burden at the door, not make me carry it inside.

Lazy! Rude! Inconsiderate! Now I saw where his son got it from. I couldn't wait to get out of there.

While I was standing in the entryway, waiting for him to tell me where I could put the assignments, I realized we were not alone.

An extraordinarily beautiful woman was standing just inside a room off the hallway. She had platinum blonde hair and cool gray eyes and flawless pale skin. She stood alert, watching us her face devoid of expression, and I could see she had a great body. The boys in my gym class would have trampled Lucia to get to this woman.

When I heard Mr. Alexander close the door behind me, I realized I was staring.

"This way, Adisa," he said, leading me right into the room with the blonde Amazon. "You can put them there," he said, indicating a desk at the far side of the sparsely furnished room.

I had to walk past the Amazon and I was surprised that she was actually taller than I was by at least two inches. I wasn't used to meeting women who were taller than I was. She was also well built with broad shoulders and her femininely muscular frame was somewhat intimidating.

"Excuse me," I said curtly, showing her I had manners even if she didn't because she hadn't budged the least bit to let me by.

She stiffly stepped aside without uttering a word.

I dropped the load heavily where indicated and turned to leave.

This time Mr. Alexander stepped in my path. "Adisa, I would like to introduce you to Jericho. She works with Micah at FLEET. Jericho, this is Micah's friend Adisa, the one I was telling you about."

She didn't acknowledge the introduction in any way. I extended my hand, again demonstrating a courtesy. "Pleased to meet you, Jericho. If you'll excuse me, I have to go."

I gave her hand a shake and she squeezed too hard but I managed not to wince. When she released me, I headed for the door.

"Adisa, could you stay awhile. I'd like to talk to you...," Mr. Alexander was saying.

"Sorry, I really don't have time right now."

"Adisa wait."

But I was already out the door. I crossed the yard before he reached the porch. I had been fortunate enough not to have run into Micah but I didn't want to push my luck by hanging around any longer.

"Adisa!" Mr. Alexander called but I didn't even slow down.

I crossed the street, hurrying to get to my house but then thought of him following me. I didn't think I could carry my rudeness to the point of not answering the door when he knew I was inside. So I walked around to the back of my house and headed into the woods. Surely, he wouldn't follow me there. Then again, he was part of law enforcement. Could he order me to stop? Would he come after me with weapon drawn?

A lot of the leaves had already fallen but quite a few hardy ones still clung to vines and deciduous trees and bushes, offering enough coverage to hide me soon after I stepped into the woods. The tangle of growth was pretty easy to navigate this time of the season so I kept going.

My heart was beating fast. I couldn't believe how rude I'd been. Regardless of Mr. Alexander's prior treatment of me, he did try to help when dad was in the hospital and there was no excuse for me to act like I did. But there was something about the way he said Jericho's name, like he was proud of her relationship with Micah compared to how he introduced me, 'the one I was telling you about,' like I was some sort of problem. It was obvious he'd been discussing me with her and I was sure he didn't speak of me in glowing terms. The whole situation frustrated me beyond comprehension.

And where had Micah been? As much as I dreaded being in his presence, part of me had been hoping to at least catch a glimpse of him. All I had was a pearl to remember him by. I didn't have a picture of him to satisfy my need to gaze on his features, not that I needed one. I remembered exactly what he looked like. But that didn't lessen my desire to see him in reality instead of just in memory.

Why did Mr. Alexander want to talk to me now, anyway? I was trying to give him what he wanted by staying away but he was making that difficult. All this time he'd driven by in his cruiser without a word and even at the hospital, he wasn't interested in conversation with me, just checked on dad's condition and offered his help.

Now, out of the blue, he wanted to talk. It must have something to do with Micah's return but I didn't see how that concerned me. Maybe he was worried I'd start up with his son again. Well he didn't have to worry about that! I didn't want anything to do with somebody who could just disappear on somebody they were supposed to care about.

Micah did say he cared about me, once, when we were on the mountain. But he didn't say that he loved me. Maybe he didn't. I didn't want to think about the mountain. Thinking about it brought other more painful embarrassing memories. I tried to force the images out of my mind but couldn't. I had kissed him first. It was my fault. I had nobody to blame but myself.

Once the images started coming, I couldn't stop them. It was as if I'd been trying to hold back a wall of water and now that it found a crack through which to escape, it forced itself past my carefully constructed barriers, spilling all of its contents.

Lilac Wine, Micah carefully holding me while we danced, Micah's broken smile, holding my hand under the covers, his beautiful laugh, gentle brown eyes, Micah walking the mountain with me his brilliant skin gleaming, feeling the thunder of his heart as Micah's mouth slowly opened and closed against mine.

I broke out of the woods and stopped in surprise. The shaded confines had been filled with the noisy rustle of leaves beneath my feet, the trees crowding in on me. Now, I was confronted with a quiet expansive view.

There was a rounded clear patch of land in front of me that dropped off suddenly at the far edge but a strip of land free of trees sloped along one side. Spread out beyond the drop off was a beautiful view. It was like I had my own little mountain view practically in my own back yard.

A few tall trees clung to the edge of the drop off, their thick roots clinging in resistance to falling over the side into the thicket below.

I walked to the middle of the clearing and sat down, tired and overwhelmed. It's amazing how you can pass between Heaven and Hell in a heartbeat. Having suffered through the Hell of delivering Micah's assignments, it felt as if I was being rewarded with a little glimpse of Heaven.

I breathed in and out deeply, attempting to expel the aching chaos I'd foolishly thought I had finally mastered by toughing it out through Micah's absence. I didn't want to think any more. I just wanted to feel numb for awhile before I had to go back and face whatever consequences awaited me for my recent burst of temper.

I was tense at first, unable to shake the feeling that I'd been followed and was being watched. But I was sure Mr. Alexander hadn't come after me.

I slid my arms out of my backpack straps, arranging it on the ground so I could lay back, using it as a pillow. It was so peaceful and quiet. I pulled my arms inside of my jacket and held myself.

Storm clouds gathered far off to one side in the distance. The air was dark beneath them and I knew it was the rain that made it look that way. I marveled that I sat dry while watching the rain fall on others, miles away. I couldn't see the raindrops or the people, just the darkness and a few flashes of lightning, the low rumble of thunder following long after.

I stayed there a long time, soaking in the tranquility as my mind idly drifted. I would try to convince Kelly and Kylie to let me go with them to Daytona Beach's Black College Reunion during Spring Break. I was surprised my parents hadn't objected but then realized that since dad's recovery, my parents had seemed a lot more eager for each other's company. When I mentioned this to the twins, they laughed knowingly and said our parents didn't want us underfoot while they tested dad's miraculously healthy new heart.

Summer would come. Since I had my driver's license I would be able to drive myself to the children's shelter to volunteer. Now all I had to do was find a car. Mom and dad would need their's for work and I was sure Kelly wouldn't want to part with hers. Besides, she and Kylie were talking about taking a 'tour of Americana,' their words not mine, to see famous landmarks and monuments like the Grand Canyon, Mount Rushmore, Niagara Falls and places like that.

So I wouldn't be able to use her car for most of the summer anyway. I wondered if they would take me with them. It would be good to get away instead of being stuck for another whole summer with nothing to do except watch the comings and goings of a shiny black jeep.

I let my mind drift like that, avoiding painful memories. I was vaguely aware that my brain was being kindly cooperative for once.

I didn't realize the storm clouds had drifted over me until I heard a muffled clap of thunder. I sat up, pushing my arms back into the sleeves as the first few hesitant drops of rain fell around me. I didn't want to leave. I hadn't found a peace like this in a long time. The wind picked up but still I lingered.

I heard the loud boom and felt the air charged with electricity, even tasted and smelled the burning, all at the same time. It startled me and I fell back cringing in fear.

Everything slowed down and even the fat drops of rain seemed suspended all around me, small clear crystals in slow motion descent to the ground.

I'd learned in science class, that time didn't really slow down, it was the mind that started firing synapses so fast that images and thought processes entered a kind of warp speed, giving the appearance that time stood still.

I was aware lightning had struck nearby and quickly dismissed the idea that I'd been directly hit when I saw the barest wisp of smoke come from one of the tall trees clinging to the edge. It started tilting curiously but it wasn't toward the thicket below, amazingly it was in my direction.

I was already getting up before I reached the end of that thought but I slipped. The rain had already saturated the ground around me, making slick spots in the muddy spaces peeking between the dead patches of grass.

I couldn't tear my eyes from the thick branches of the tall tree swaying in an odd fashion as I scrambled to gain my footing. It appeared to be falling toward me in slow motion.

My feet desperately sought the traction needed to propel me out of the way but I was moving impossibly slow. My mind flashed to Lake Lanier, buoyed in the black abyss of a yellow school bus. This couldn't be happening again!

A movement out of the corner of my eye and I was able to break free of my trance to see Micah moving fast and low over the stretch of land free of trees. I knew he was coming to save me but he wouldn't make it, he was too far away. He was a beautiful shining flash of copper and I wanted to thank him for trying, all was forgiven in that instant.

But something wasn't right. He was coming, but not running. Where were his legs? He was coming, his face contorted in determination... strange, I would have expected the expressionless mask. His arms stretched out to me like a black Superman... I can't believe I'm thinking of superheroes when once again facing death... That's it!!

... a black Superman... Micah was *flying*!

My eyes were showing me the impossible. Micah was flying straight at me. But my mind kept rejecting the image. It froze me in place while it struggled to make sense of the information hurtling toward me.

My inability to accept this reality short circuited my brain and locked on the single impractical vision; Micah was in fact, incredibly, incomprehensibly, impossibly flying to save me. In an instant, I was in his arms.

My body registered the impact, jarring but protectively tucked beneath him, my face looking up at the sky over his shoulder as we flew parallel to the ground. I saw the tree descending fast now, bearing down on us. A fraction of a scream escaped me before he shifted, positioning me completely beneath his body, blocking my view just as the tree exploded against his back in a deafening crescendo of sound.

I felt him shudder with the impact and the air filled with wood chips and sawdust but miraculously, we weren't smashed into the ground. We kept right on flying, the wind rushing around us. His arms were wrapped around me, pinning mine to my sides. He held me tight to his chest and I could feel his sledge hammer heart beating impossibly fast.

I couldn't see where we were going but I sensed we were low in the trees. I turned my head to the side and saw tree trunks blur by at a dizzying speed. He shifted me again as he slowed and now cradled me in his arms while he still flew parallel to the ground.

We landed with hardly any disturbance, smoothly transitioning from air to land and he was running with me in his arms but only for a few strides into an enclosure. It was a sheltered outcrop that mimicked a wide shallow cave. He set me inside on my feet and released me. I nearly fell over and he reached out to steady me but I scrambled away, managing to stay up on my shaky legs without assistance.

I backed away from him and he didn't try to stop me. I could hear my breathing echoing off the rock wall along with his. I felt solid stone press against my back and knew I couldn't go any further in that direction.

"Did I hurt you?" he asked from where he stood.

I could see the rain slanting between the trees just beyond him and hear the storm still raging. I couldn't speak. I just stared at him. He was so beautiful. Small silver droplets shimmered on his dark smooth skin and his wet shirt sculpted his chest and shoulders so solid he appeared to be a statue. Superman transformed into Adonis.

I saw woodchips in the tight black spirals of his close cropped hair. I remembered the air exploding around us and the dizzying rush of wind. The trembling started and I couldn't stop it.

"You can fly?" my voice shook, barely a whisper. Then I felt the familiar comfort of my rage and with more strength, "You can fly!?"

My words loudly filled the small space.

"Adisa, I wanted to tell you but there're confidentiality concerns and the need to maintain anonymity, not to mention...," he exclaimed stepping toward me.

"Don't touch me," I spat out and he immediately halted. I was livid. "You knew I spent years immersed in superhero fantasy and suffered for it. How could you, of all people, question my commitment to safeguarding your true identity?"

I couldn't believe he doubted my ability to keep a secret. The nerve! That hurt almost as much as his abandonment. And how could he fly instead of me? All this time, he had the power of flight and never even told me. Finally his secret was out.

I could feel my heart painfully squeezing in on itself. He didn't trust me. After all my efforts, even declaring my love, and he refused to let me in. In spite of all I had revealed to him, he couldn't bring himself to confide in me.

"You could've trusted me with your secret. You didn't have to run away and leave me," I said.

"I didn't run away. There's so much more going on here and I... Adisa, wait. Where are you going?"

"Home!"

I had stepped out from under the shelter at the far end away from him. I started running, dodging the trees. I was out of control, a hot mess inside and out. Fear, anger, relief, shame, jealousy, simultaneously coursed through my short circuited irrational mind.

I wasn't up to confronting Micah. All I could think about was getting back home. I wanted something familiar and comforting and I instinctively ran for it.

The stinging rain punished the exposed skin on my face and I squinted to protect my eyes. I looked back and saw him coming for me, weaving in and out between the trunks. He was doing it again! Flying!

He scooped me into his arms like I was his new bride, being carried over the threshold. I shoved against his chest as he flew stretched out above the ground, holding me low and close, using his body to shield me from the rain.

"Adisa, stop. You don't know the way and it's dangerous. You could fall off a cliff like you almost did the last time you...,"

He didn't finish but I immediately knew what he was talking about. The last time he had chased me through these same woods.

Had he flown then too? Is that how he miraculously appeared in front of me, pinning me to the ground when only moments before he'd been crashing around far behind me? Was this actually the second time he was saving me? I felt like a fool.

"Put me down, right now! I don't care what happens to me, I don't want you touching me!" After everything he had put me through, all the embarrassing things about me he had witnessed then abandoning me and now I had to suffer the humiliation of him saving me. And even worse, I thought as jealousy twisted painfully in my chest, he could *fly*!

He held me securely while still in flight. "Stop being so hardheaded and let me get you home safe."

He was deftly navigating between the trees, flying, carrying and arguing with me while trying to restrain me all at the same time. As the tree trunks sped by, I suddenly realized how dangerous it was and some of my anger dissipated.

If he was off by even a fraction of an inch, we could smash into a tree. He might survive but I wasn't so sure about me.

"Why don't you fly higher, above the trees? I don't want to crash," I chastised, no longer fighting against him as I realized I actually did care about what happened to me.

"I don't want anybody to see us. It's bad enough that now you know."

I was quiet, resigned to letting him fly me home. Just as quickly as the storm had started, it stopped. We emerged from the woods at the side of my house, Micah now walking with me in his arms. I quickly scrambled to get down and he didn't try to stop me.

I hurried onto my porch, my hands trembling as I unlocked the door then held it open. "Thanks for nothing!" I said before slamming it in his face and locking it.

"Adisa, are you sure you're all right?" I heard his worried voice on the other side of the door.

"I'm fine! Go away!" I called, tearing off my heavy soaked jacket as I stomped upstairs to my room.

I went to my window to watch him cross back over to his house but when I looked, he wasn't headed that way. He was walking around to the side of my house in the direction we had come from. I quietly opened the window all the way and leaned far out to see what he was doing. He disappeared into the woods.

I went in my restroom and slammed the door. My hands fumbled with the faucet fixtures then I repeatedly splashed water onto my face. My brain felt fried and I could feel a tension headache coming on. I wanted to forget all the craziness and give my mind a rest.

I stared at my face in the mirror. Why wasn't I worthy of flight? All those years of ridicule I'd suffered, wanting flight more than any other superpower I'd ever heard of, even more than invisibility or supernatural strength. Why did he have to have it?

After the Hell he put me through, it wasn't fair that he was the one who could fly? Jealousy burned in me making my eyes shine as my mind revealed what I miserably believed to be true. Micah was more deserving than I was. Despite his abandonment, I knew, deep down inside, that he was a better person than I was.

I fought with my sisters, I shunned my own grandma, I offered to invite an abusive jerk to my birthday party to appease his victim, I still felt residual resentment toward Liz even though it wasn't her fault, I was selfish and hateful, and even after all Micah had done I still wanted to touch him in ways that would've permanently stopped my dad's heart. I wasn't a good daughter... I wasn't even a real daughter. My real parents didn't want me.

Suddenly I longed for my brain to just shut down. I didn't want to feel, see, or hear; like it used to be when I slept without dreaming. I focused on that suspended state and finally managed to calm down, gaining better control of myself.

The sound of water made me look down. I quickly turned the faucet off, guiltily thinking of the drought. Just because I was on the verge of a nervous breakdown didn't mean I had a right to squander our precious natural resources.

I opened the door and stepped into my room and froze. Micah was quietly standing by my desk, looking at Kylie's avenging angel drawing. At first I couldn't process it because I knew for a fact I'd locked the door this time.

Then I saw my open window and instantly realized he had flown in! Without permission, without adult supervision, a boy was in my room breaking my promise to almighty God!!!

"I knocked on your front door and rang the doorbell but you didn't answer. I got worried. Oh, and I brought you this. You always manage to leave it behind," he said, gesturing to where he'd put my backpack on the chair. He was even smiling at his clever little joke.

Suddenly my rage was back in a blinding flash of heat. My foot lifted and kicked against and through his chest with the heel in one smooth motion. I saw Micah flip back over my desk and out the window, landing hard on his bottom atop the porch roof. My self defense instructor would've been proud.

I glared at Micah through my window. "No boys allowed without adult supervision!"

He looked at me, clearly in shock but didn't appear to be hurt.

Just to make sure I angrily asked, "You all right?"

He nodded and I slammed my window shut and closed the blinds and curtains. Then I fell across my bed, releasing my hot bitter tears, soaking my pillow.

I twisted my fists in my sheets and pounded them as wave after wave of intense resentment and shame washed over me. No wonder I didn't have superpowers. I didn't deserve them. If I'd had them when I kicked Micah, he could have landed on the moon. God in his infinite wisdom knew better than to give somebody like me superhuman strength.

I was glad nobody was around to witness my outburst. Eventually, I was emotionally exhausted and cried myself to sleep.

I didn't hear mom and dad come home. Mom told me later that I was sleeping so soundly, she actually used a mirror to check and see if I was still breathing. I guess that's what happens when a mother has too many near death episodes concerning her family.

I stayed in the house the whole weekend, fearing I might run into one of the Alexanders. Once my pathetic show of jealousy and self-pity had abated, I began to have questions. Did Micah's parents know about his superpowers? Did his family have superpowers as well? This thought distressed me even more. It was galling to think a glut of superpowers filled the home a mere few feet across the street while I didn't even possess the abilities of a side kick.

Maybe if I was a better person, I would've been blessed with x-ray vision or a little superhuman speed or even the ability to rejuvenate after an injury. Goodness knows I could've used that one after the bus accident. That was one of the most physically painful ordeals of my life.

As Monday approached, I started feeling remorseful for my actions. It dawned on me that Micah had actually saved my life, possibly twice, and I wouldn't even be alive, moping around, if it hadn't been for him. And how did I show my appreciation? I drop kicked him right out of my bedroom window. It didn't matter that he'd entered without permission, in effect, breaking and entering.

Well at least entering, I amended when I remembered I had left the window open so technically he hadn't broken in.

At times Micah acted as if he had no manners or was at least socially inept. How could he think it was okay to just enter somebody's home without their consent?

I knew I was just distracting myself from the fact that I owed Micah a thank you for saving my life and an apology for how I'd treated him. I couldn't believe I had actually physically assaulted him. I usually reserved that only for my sisters. But I'd been taken off guard and reacted without thinking.

Suppose he told his family? They would probably think I was some kind of psycho, entertaining boys unsupervised one moment and then physically attacking them the next. Would Mr. Alexander arrest me for assault when he found out what I'd done?

What was Micah thinking of me? He probably would give up on me now, like Ms. Beckett did when I refused to dance the Paso Doble in a more feminine way. Micah probably thought it was unfeminine of me to kick him like that. Now he wouldn't like me anymore, if he ever really did. Why was I worried about him liking me? Didn't I decide I wouldn't have anything to do with him anymore after the way he treated me?

He abandoned me for weeks without a single word. But then he showed up and saved my life, flying to me just in the nick of time. Why did he have the ability to fly and not me? Maybe if I wasn't so evil and could control my rages, I'd have superpowers. But then the Hulk had superpowers because of his temper so that shouldn't be a deterrent. But the Hulk wasn't real, or was he? I'd probably turn into a villain if I ever got a hold of any super abilities anyway. I truly didn't deserve superpowers. I was nobody special.

On and on my jumbled conflicting thoughts and emotions went. I'd be all prepared to apologize and thank Micah, then I'd feel the heat of jealousy over his flying abilities and resentment for his abandoning me then I'd decide to never speak to him again. But that thought was so disturbing, I'd be off thinking of reasons why that wasn't such a good idea after all.

By the time Monday dawned, my insides were completely knotted. Suppose he was at his tree? Suppose he wasn't? There was no way he could complete all the assignments I'd delivered. Or maybe he had. Since he could fly, there was no telling what other superpowers he had. He certainly had strength. That tree trunk should've crushed us into the ground but it only caused a shudder as it exploded across Micah's back. It made me shudder just thinking what it could have... *would!* have done to me, unprotected by Micah's body. Micah's body so solid and firm and...

I slammed the front door harder than necessary to drive the shameful thought of how closely I'd been pressed against him out of my head. Was I losing my mind!?

My hand trembled as I inserted the key to lock the door. I slowly turned to survey my surroundings. Micah's jeep was still in his driveway and nobody was out. I couldn't see Micah's tree from my porch because the woods surrounding my home restricted my view in either direction of the road. I crossed the street, dreading whatever awaited me.

When I got to the tree, the robot was there. I stood on my sidewalk trying to think of what to say, my emotions a rush of confusion that made my voice shaky.

"Micah... I... Please...," I stuttered indecisively.

He was walking toward me, crossing all the way to my side where I stood frozen to the spot in shame. He embraced then smoothly lifted me in a single motion, carrying me back across the road into the woods, out of view.

I had never actually cried in front of anybody outside of my family since I was in elementary school, except for dad's heart ordeal but that was completely permissible, and I rarely even cried in front of my family. When I realized I wouldn't be able to hold back my tears, I covered my face, too proud to let Micah see me break down in an ugly cry. Micah set me on my feet but held me so I wouldn't turn away.

"Shhhhh.... It's okay. I'm fine. You didn't even hurt me."

I could tell by the sound of his voice alone, that it was the sensitive Micah trying to reassure me.

"Adisa, please, don't cry. I hate it when you cry." He sounded as if this wasn't the first time he'd seen me shed tears. He was gently tugging at my wrists, trying to remove my hands but I wouldn't let him. I knew with his superhuman strength he could have forced them away but he didn't.

Instead, he wrapped his arms around me, hugging me close to his chest, whispering apologies in my ear.

"I'm so sorry. I shouldn't have scared you like that. It's just that I was worried and I'm not used to dealing with social... Please stop crying. I promise, you didn't hurt me at all. The only reason I even fell over was because my shield was down and you caught me off guard. But even so, you shouldn't have been able to... Adisa, baby please, it's okay."

I could feel him caressing my neck in an attempt to calm me and the play of his chest muscles pressing against me was comforting. His words sparked my curiosity, finally turning the tide of my emotions, and I gradually settled down.

Shield? What was a shield? And why was he apologizing? I was the one who resorted to physical violence. I was the one in obvious need of anger management as Kelly had so often pointed out to me.

"Micah... I'm so sorry for... I can't believe I did that after you saved me. I was so scared when I saw that tree falling. Did it hurt your back?" I asked, suddenly concerned.

I hadn't even considered he might have been injured until then. How selfish of me.

"No, I'm fine," he assured.

"Is it okay if I see for myself?" I asked, my voice hitching in my throat.

"Sure," he immediately complied.

He dropped his backpack to the ground and turned, lifting his shirt to expose his back. There wasn't a scratch or even a bruise on his expanse of perfect skin. I ran my hands over it in disbelief, seeking the imperfections that should have covered him but thankfully found none. Then I suddenly realized I had accidentally spread my tears on him.

"Sorry! I'll get it off," I said, distressed. He probably thought I was a complete mess.

I was about to wipe his back with my sleeve but he faced me again before I could, straightening his shirt back into place.

"Don't worry about it. Are you all right now?" he asked, easing my backpack off and taking me in his arms again.

How could he be asking about me at a time like this?

"I'm fine, Micah… just confused. I have so many questions, I don't know where to start. But we don't have time because we'll be late for school. And you probably don't even want to tell me after I acted so stupid. But I'm really sorry about that, it was a dumb thing to do. I think I went temporarily insane because I was so shocked and then the jealousy took me completely by surprise. But I'm better now, really. Oh, and thank you for saving my life. Even though it's probably not worth it because I'm such a…,"

"Hold up, hold up," he interrupted my rambling and he was actually laughing as he placed his fingertips on my lips. Then he quickly removed them but the memory of the warm gentle pressure lingered. "If you keep this up, you're going to owe me a decade's worth of positives before we even get to school.

I knew as soon as I saw you on the sidewalk that you were beating yourself up about this. I bet you did over the whole weekend, didn't you?"

"Well, maybe just a little," I admitted.

"Adisa, what am I going to do with you?" he asked, but he was smiling at me.

"What am I going to do with you?" I responded and even managed a small smile of my own.

We stood, gazing into each other's eyes before he stated, "We'll be late for school if we don't go."

"No," I resisted. "When will we talk about this?"

"Soon."

"How soon?" I challenged. "This is too important to just…,"

"Not now, Adisa," he quickly curtailed my tumbling words. "Not here. We can go to the mountain after school…,"

"No!" I asserted. "My mountain climbing days are over."

"Why?"

I looked at him pointedly, remembering the bottomless days of his abandonment.

"Vertigo," I answered, sarcastically. When he looked as if he still didn't understand I clarified, "I don't want you disappearing on me again."

"I didn't disappear on you. I told you I didn't know how long it would take but I'd be back. And I'm back."

"Well how was I supposed to know you were coming back after you withdrew from school and didn't even call or write to tell me what was going on?" I accused.

His face was solemn now and I could see his temple working.

"I didn't withdraw from school. My father withdrew me without my knowledge." Micah's voice was tight as he spoke. "I didn't find out until after I returned."

It was strange, he sounded as if his dad had no right to organize his son's life as he wished. This was ludicrous because parents could jerk their kids' lives around all they wanted. There was no law against it, in fact, at times, I thought there was a special law mandating it.

"But that's all irrelevant because before I left, I told you I can't tell a lie. That meant when I said I was coming back, I was coming back," he asserted.

"But Micah, I don't understand how...,"

"We really have to go, Adisa. We can't get into this around here. There's no privacy. My father...," he paused searching for words.

"I know. He kept cruising by while you were gone like he was keeping tabs on me or something."

Micah smiled ruefully but didn't comment.

"You could come over to my house," he suggested skeptically.

"I'm not allowed without adult supervision," I said.

"I thought so. Why is it okay for you to go unsupervised outside of homes?" he asked.

"I don't know. Kylie says it's because of the beds. A couple of teenagers, behind closed doors, with a bed, unsupervised... that equals certain disaster in my dad's mind. I guess in public with no beds available, he feels there's a fighting chance," I explained.

Micah smiled. "Interesting. He does realize beds are optional when it comes to that."

I laughed nervously, surprised he spoke so candidly. "Are you an authority on the subject?" I asked, kidding but still curious.

"No, not at all. Why, are you?" His clear eyes stared at me without judgment but I still felt flushed.

"Absolutely not! I just wanted to know exactly what I'm dealing with here," I said, then hesitantly added, "So, you've really never...,"

"Had sex? No. I'd be the first of my kind if I had. Even the way I feel about you is unheard of."

"Why?" I asked, astonished.

Micah looked around. "Not here and not now. We have to find a place we can talk privately."

"We could go to Gladys and Ron's Chicken and Waffles," I suggested, thinking of one of my favorite downtown restaurants. I didn't want him to think I was trying to use him to get a free meal so I quickly added, "You wouldn't have to buy me anything. I can pay my own way and we could talk."

Micah looked at me, slightly amused. "I wouldn't mind spending everything I have, buying you anything you wanted," he assured me. "I thought the Summers girls couldn't date during the week. Your dad let us go to the mountain because it's considered exercise, not a date."

His casual statement of spending everything he had to buy me anything I wanted, so distracted me, I didn't respond right away. Of course, I would never use him like that but it was nice to know he was willing to spend what little money he had, all on me.

"You're right. But it'll be cold on the mountain," I noted, "and I really hate the cold."

"I'll take care of you. Believe me, you won't be cold," he declared.

"No really, Micah, when I say I hate the cold, I mean I *really* hate the cold."

"Trust me, I'll keep you warm," he said. His hazel eyes held mine steady for a moment and I thought I could actually feel myself warming up.

It was getting late so I agreed to go to the mountain with him if my mom said it was okay.

I made it to homeroom just before the tardy bell rang.

"I was beginning to think you weren't coming today," Avery said as I slid into my usual seat next to him.

"Micah's back," I blurted out.

"What?" Avery looked surprised.

"Yeah. I took a load of back assignments over to his house last Friday and he's supposed to find out if they'll reinstate him today," I explained.

"How do you feel about it?"

"I'm okay with it," I answered casually, while avoiding his eyes.

"Well it's good to see you found your smile again. Nice of him to give it back to you," he added with a wink.

Micah had caught up on all of his assignments over the weekend. Incredible! But then again, he was superhuman. He had received an 'I' for Incomplete in all of his courses for the previous semester, pending taking the finals. He was able to schedule early dates to take all of them except for Mr. Winton's class.

"I'm sure you'll do fine on your dance exam, being the best dancer in class, but you'll need time to learn the dance routine since you weren't here during any of the Paso Doble," Mr. Winton explained. "I have the dance on DVD and you can borrow it or you can download it off the school's website but you'll have to practice on your own time. We're on African dances in class now."

After school, Micah walked me home then left to drop off his things and drive his jeep over while I went inside to call my mom for permission. He absolutely refused to give up any information until we were on the mountain. Mom gave her okay but encouraged me to bundle up because even though walking the mountain generated body heat, I was so thin and she knew how much I hated the cold and the last thing she needed was for me to get sick and bring it home to the rest of the family, not that I'd ever been sick a day in my life but there was a first time for everything so I shouldn't think myself immune from life's... and on and on.

T he return to the mountain was done in silence. The jeep's soft top was up and the heater was going. I couldn't believe I was once again sitting in Micah's jeep, making a trip to Kennesaw mountain with him when I'd practically sworn I never would again.

We hiked up but didn't break any records reaching the top. Gone were the summer crowds of stroller pushers, bird watchers, and bikers. The occasional dedicated soul we passed by were there strictly for a workout, not a leisurely stroll. Like us, they were bundled in protective clothing to ward off the frigid temperatures.

After Micah and I finally made it to the top, we crossed to the other peak before leaving the path. It was cold but the physical exertion kept it from being unbearable. I was concerned about how Micah would keep me warm once we stopped moving.

We tramped over the fallen dead leaves, weaving our way between the slumbering trees. The seasonal shedding revealed further into the woodsy depths than usual, requiring us to venture deeper to conceal ourselves from view. We passed by a lone deer and I imagined it was as surprised to see us as we were to see it.

Micah found a secluded spot and removed a folded pile of nylon material from his backpack and tossed it in front of him. While in midair, it instantly popped out into a fully formed tent before quietly bouncing down onto the ground.

He anchored it with stakes and ties but instead of driving the stakes into the frozen ground with a rock, he quickly jammed them in with his hand in one swift motion, smiling sheepishly at me when he looked up and saw me gaping in awe.

When he was done, we went inside and he took off his coat and removed two odd looking stones from his pack, unwrapping the one that had cloth around it. He struck them together and left them nestled against each other in a small wooden bowl. Slowly, they began to glow, releasing heat. In no time at all, the frigid interior of the tent transformed, suffused with wonderful warmth.

He reached for my hands, pulled off my gloves, and began rubbing and blowing on them, sending intense tingling warmth radiating up the full length of my arms. His lips lightly brushed my skin and I shivered more so because of that than from the cold.

"How are your feet?" He asked, while he worked.

"Just fine," I said, quickly tucking them safely beneath me. If he got a hold of my feet, I would literally die laughing because they were extremely ticklish. "I'm wearing three pairs of socks. Won't those rocks burn through that bowl?" I asked, trying to change the subject. I didn't know rocks like that existed. They reminded me of glow sticks but they gave off heat as well as an eerie light.

He shook his head no. "Those are Orion Rocks, also known as O-Rocks. They glow and emit heat but not a flame. You can even touch them and they won't burn you. It's meteorite rock found in an uninhabited part of Africa. Some believe it fell to earth from a star in Orion's Belt. Did you know Afrikaans speakers in South Africa call Orion's Belt 'Drie Konings' which means Three Kings?"

Ahhh, trivia, I thought, *dad would be pleased.*

"Orion's Belt?" I questioned, picking out the one thing that seemed familiar. My mind was so dazed I couldn't quite place the name. I tentatively reached out to test the bright orange glow.

"A constellation of stars. I'll show it to you some night."

My heart raced at the image of me and Micah out together some night as I stared at the red glow penetrating the edges of my fingers enclosing an O-Rock. It reminded me of when I was little and would sneak down at night during Christmas time to hold the fat colorful light bulbs we had strung around the tree in the family room. I would grasp a bulb, my fingers barely able to completely encircle it, and marvel at my closed hand seeming lit from within.

Micah was right, it didn't burn at all. In fact it was only slightly warm even though it heated up the whole tent very nicely. Suddenly the light from the rocks began to fade. Micah took the one from my hand and the one from the bowl and struck them together again and they immediately re-illuminated.

"Once struck, they have to remain touching to generate heat. When separated, they go out," he explained, returning them to the bowl. "Take off your coat," he suggested, watching me as I complied.

I slipped out of my coat, realizing for the first time how warm I was.

He took it from me, managing to casually toss it on top of his own without taking his eyes off of me. I felt nervous under his steady gaze.

"This isn't something you can pick up at your local department store, is it?" I asked, still entranced by the magical stones.

"No. The continent leaders voted unanimously to reserve it for the Sp. world because it's such a limited resource, foreign to earth. Plus we haven't located anymore like it during our Orion explorations. Maybe now that you know about us, you can try to calculate the ancient trajectory path of the meteor and give us space coordinates to locate other pieces that broke off of it before it entered earth's atmosphere."

I stared at him blankly. "Okay, all that you just said, exponentially increases the number of questions I have for you."

I was pretty pleased with myself because I'd managed to cleverly work a math word into the conversation, not 'number,' that's too easy but 'exponentially,' that's a real challenge.

Micah sighed. "There's so much to tell and even I don't have all the answers. It would be like me expecting you to know everything about your entire country or more accurately, all countries, your entire world. Because that's what the Sp. world encompasses plus it extends into outer space as well."

He was quiet for a moment as he contemplated where to begin.

"What's sszzzep?" I asked, unsure of the pronunciation. The word was sharp almost like *zip* but not quite.

"Sp. is a title used for just about anything related to the super culture. Instead of super world it's Sp. world, superbeing becomes Sp. being, superpower is Sp. power. The title is so old that what it actually stands for has been lost; super, superb, special... superior. It's debatable because nobody knows for sure."

"Oh... Well, okay, let's take this slow and not get too technical. Just give me the basics as if you were explaining it to a child," I suggested and he nodded in agreement. "How about starting with your shield, you mentioned it this morning. Is the robot your shield?"

He smiled. "Something like that. It's not a separate thing, we're one and the same. Some Sp. beings have the ability to generate a shield, it's like an alert system that's a protective barrier and it also enhances your powers, enabling you to operate at your maximum capacity."

"So it's something you can turn on and off, like a light switch?"

"Yes. By concentrating, you put it up or down based on your intent. You can still access your Sp. powers whether it's up or down, it just makes the process easier, more efficient."

"Now that was a lot easier to understand," I smiled.

"There's more," he added. "You're more protected when it's up but it affects attitude and perception. When it's up, it suppresses emotion and everything that does not pose a threat, decreases in your awareness."

"That's why you sometimes came across as distant and even rude sometimes," I surmised. Then the floodgates opened. "Do all superbeings have the same powers? Can you all fly? How about your family and if not do they know about your powers or do you have to keep it secret from them like Spiderman and his family? And why…,"

"Hold on," he interrupted. "We're supposed to be taking this slowly. Remember?"

"Oh, right," I averred.

Then he continued. "Before a Sp. being's powers manifest, we say they are asleep. There are a variety of abilities and even I don't know them all. Some can fly, some can't. Some have a mix of powers. I'm the only one in my family with manifested powers. My parents are dormant and Jason is currently asleep until he reaches sixteen when he will either manifest or become dormant."

"So that means you were born with powers… no… did they come later, when you were older?" I was getting confused.

"It's genetic so you're born predisposed but powers don't always manifest. But when they do it's usually around age sixteen and rarely younger. Sometimes they're dormant, meaning they will never manifest. If a generation is dormant then the following generation is even more potent, as if the powers skipped the dormant parents and increased the powers of their child.

Both my parents are dormant. They're past sixteen years so their powers will never manifest. In some rare instances, an individual without Sp. ancestry will spontaneously regenerate and manifest Sp. powers, however, if they do not partner with a genetic Sp. being, they do not produce Sp. offspring."

My mind was reeling as I tried to take it all in without interrupting. My brain bounced around a hundred questions while he spoke and his words generated hundreds more. "So only two genetic superbeings can produce a superbeing baby?"

"No. An earthbound and a Sp. being can produce one as well."

"I take it, earthbounds are people like me and my family," I asserted.

Micah shifted to sit closer to me and my train of thought was immediately disrupted. I closed my eyes to try to regain my composure. Everything in me was attracted to him, making it difficult for me to do the smart thing and get to know all I could about him before getting too close to him. I didn't want to get hurt again.

"Are we called earthbounds because we didn't originate here on earth? Are humans a foreign race from outer space who traveled to earth thousands of years ago?" I asked trying to distract him but also truly curious.

Micah chuckled softly. "No. It's not a destination, it's a condition, bound to the earth. Earth is not the only place Sp. beings reside like it is for earthbounds. It's an ancient word, much older than 'earthling' which earthbounds only started using to distinguish themselves in recent history due to their exploration of outer space."

I stared at him in wide eyed amazement, my wild imagination taking flight into the great mysteries of space.

"Are you hungry?" Micah asked, pulling open his backpack.

"What?" I was thrown off by the unexpected question.

"We've been here awhile and I thought you might want something to eat. I brought a snack and drinks."

"Sure," I said, noting that I actually was hungry.

He turned his back to me as he wrestled with his pack and I used the opportunity to study him closely. His movements were graceful, masking the power contained in his well muscled frame. I watched his back fluidly ripple beneath his shirt and was reminded of when he exposed it to me. At the time, I was too upset to appreciate how extraordinary it was. I certainly didn't have that problem now.

His arms, hidden beneath long sleeves, moved deftly. The strength and gentleness they possessed forever burned into my memory because of the numerous times they'd held me; while we danced, when I could barely walk recuperating from the bus crash, when he flew me to safety, as he kissed me on the mountain ...

How was I ever going to resist him while learning the information I needed to know? I could be stubborn but I certainly wasn't made of stone!

Micah turned around and met my gaze. His eyes were mesmerizing, the dark lashes boldly contrasting his light brown eyes with gold and green flecks encircling the dark pupil.

His flawless skin covered great bone structure giving his face the ideal balance of strength and elegance.

His nose was noble perfection. And his lips, an endless expressive fascination that kept me breathlessly captivated.

All combined, his chiseled good looks gave him the classic superhero look. What did I possess that could possibly attract him?

"Thank you," I said, taking the two thermoses he offered me.

I was surprised to discover one contained hot vegetable soup and the other green tea. I was expecting the energy bars and drinks he used to pack when we hiked the mountain in warmer weather.

"When did you have time to make all this?" I asked.

"I'm a fast worker," he said, reminding me of the mornings he fixed breakfast for me when I was recuperating from my bus crash injuries.

An image of my unrecognizable swollen face flashed in my mind and I cringed.

"What's wrong?" Micah asked, instantly concerned.

"You're so, unbelievably beautiful," I impulsively stated.

Micah looked at me, clearly astounded, then erupted in a fit of laughter. My heart ached at how gorgeous he was.

"You're stealing my lines again. I'm supposed to tell *you* that," he managed to say.

"You've seen me look my absolute worst. After the bus crash, when I was all scraped up and bruised... and my hair." I felt miserable just thinking about it. "I wasn't just beat with the ugly stick, the whole ugly tree fell on me."

Micah suddenly turned serious. "You were the most beautiful sight, I'd ever seen."

"I thought you said you couldn't lie," I reminded him, my voice dry with disbelief.

"I can't." The sober look on his face almost had me believing him.

"I came so close to losing you," he continued. "I tried to visit you in the hospital and again when you were back home. But your father was so protective and wouldn't let anybody see you, least of all me. I felt like I was losing my mind."

He briefly looked away but I still glimpsed the pained expression that passed over his features. He drew a deep unsteady breath as if to rid himself of any lingering barbed memories.

"When he finally let me in and I saw you... you looked so fragile and I knew you were in pain. I was so relieved to finally see you. I wanted to hold you more than anything I've ever wanted in my life.

Then you opened your eyes... and let me hold your hand under the covers... You were the most beautiful sight, I'd ever seen."

I stared into Micah's magnificent face, struggling to understand his attraction to me. I was so plain and ordinary, especially compared to how extraordinary he was.

"What do you see in me?" I asked, bewildered.

Micah's eyebrows rose in surprise and then he frowned. "Are you kidding? Adisa, you're beautiful."

I didn't believe him. I'd seen my reflection often enough. I wasn't perfect like he was. I had blemishes and there was nothing special about my face. My body was too skinny and moved awkwardly and...

Micah was taking my soup and tea away. Then he held me still while he slowly looked me over. I felt uncomfortable face to face with him, knowing my flaws were quite evident under such close scrutiny.

"You're covered in rich dark skin that glows whether you're in the sun or not. And I daydream about touching and caressing you to the point of distraction.

Your eyes are bright with intelligence, blazing when you're mad and sparkling when you're happy. And with those long beautiful lashes, I never get bored staring into them.

Your nose is adorable the way it crinkles when you're not sure of yourself, just like it's doing right now.

And your hair is a lustrous crown, thousands of crinkly coils, soft and springy against my face, an incredibly comforting cushion.

And your lips… are simply… extraordinary."

His beautiful eyes pinned me in place. I couldn't move or protest, not that I wanted to.

"When I look at your mouth, my mind is filled with the wonder of kissing you. That day you asked me to kiss you on your birthday, I thought you had finally read my mind. I'd wanted to kiss you since the very first day of school, when I sat next to you and got a close up view of your fascinating eyes and luscious lips.

I've never met anyone so open and emotionally expressive, incredibly passionate, and physically desirable. Don't you realize, you're absolutely breathtaking?"

I was trembling when he finished. I couldn't believe this stunningly attractive boy thought I was breathtaking. He personified the word.

"And your body," he said, his eyes traveling the length of me and I suddenly realized he wasn't finished. "Even though you keep it covered up extremely well, forcing me to stoop to telling you to take your coat off so I can get a better glimpse, I can still tell it's in great shape, lean, strong, and beautiful. When you're in my arms, there's absolutely no doubt that I'm holding a woman.

I especially appreciated one of the few times I was able to actually see what I've been privileged enough to hold. That two piece white short set…," he recalled, letting his voice trail off as he suggestively cocked an eyebrow.

"Kylie gave that to me," I gasped in shocked remembrance, my mind's eye seeing my mirrored reflection, the outfit hugging curves I didn't know I had in ways I wasn't used to.

Micah's broad smile was wreaking havoc on my senses. "Remind me to thank your sister the next time I see her."

I was experiencing a full body blush so extreme, I thought for sure he could see it this time despite my dark coloring.

I felt his hands tighten on me, pulling me closer and knew he was about to kiss me. I had to say something before he did because once his lips touched mine, I knew I'd completely lose it.

"Micah, I think we should take things a lot slower this time around."

He instantly went still. "Did I do something wrong?" he asked, his gentle eyes full of apprehension.

"No. I just don't want you disappearing on me again."

"That's been resolved. I won't have to stay away anymore."

I was pleasantly surprised but still unsure. "For real?"

"Really. Changes were made that enable me to stay." He smiled his reassurance.

I quickly added, "I also want to learn more about you and the superhero stuff while I'm still in a logical frame of mind and can think rationally. I don't want us to do something we might regret," I said, avoiding his eyes.

It was embarrassing talking to him like that after all the incredible things he'd just said about me. It would've been easier to just give in.

"I went too far the last time didn't I? How slow do you want to go?" he asked and my stomach muscles constricted as he openly stared at my lips, longing clearly evident on his face.

"I thought we could talk awhile, at least several days, before getting physical," I said in a low tentative voice.

"Is it because you're still mad at me?" he asked.

"I'm not mad at you," I insisted, confused.

"You were last Friday. Why were you so angry with me?"

I wanted to disappear. That was the last thing I wanted to be reminded of. I had carefully made a point not to think of that day and had actually hoped the topic would never come up. I didn't know how to put into words everything I'd been feeling.

Micah continued, "I apologize for losing my temper. But you were so angry and I was trying to protect you. I didn't understand why you were fighting me like I was the danger. Of course, your shocked reaction to finding me in your bedroom is understandable but before that, you were already very upset. Why?"

I was surprised to hear him say he'd lost his temper. As I recalled, I was the only one yelling and fighting like a lunatic. "When did you lose your temper?"

He actually looked ashamed of himself as he answered. "I called you hardheaded."

"That's it!? That's you losing your temper?" I almost laughed. I could teach him a thing or two about temper loss.

"I feel really bad about it but I'm not used to all these feelings. Before that first time you took off into the woods, when you scratched up your wrists, I hadn't had my shield down, outside of training, in seven years."

I quickly realized that was the same amount of time he said his parents had gone without touching him. "Why did you keep your shield up for so long?"

"I was in the process of ridding myself of my emotions."

I stared at him in shock. "Why in the world would you want to get rid of your feelings?" I asked, amazed that it was even possible.

He hesitated before saying, "I'm in the FLEET training program to become a Guardian."

There was a long pause. "Okay, I'll bite. What's a Guardian?" I asked.

"It's a very high ranking position within the Sp. side of law enforcement."

"FLEET is a super organization?" I asked in surprise. I hadn't even considered that. "Is the whole Atlanta police force a super organization?"

Micah smiled. "Hardly. We're a small branch of that organization. Not everybody in law enforcement even knows what we do and...,"

Micah went on explaining but I was too dazed to hear what he was saying. A secret organization within the police department, a public organization, just how far did this Sp. thing go?

"Wait a minute, Micah. This really is a lot to take in," I said.

"We should probably go," he suggested, abruptly.

"No! I want to learn more," I said. "I'm not ready to go yet."

"But it'll be dark soon and you seem overwhelmed. You're right, it's best if we take this slowly. We'll just keep coming back until all your questions are answered."

I didn't like having my own words used against me because I couldn't argue against them. So we did what he said, visiting the mountain a couple of times a week. Sometimes we jokingly referred to our meetings as the Sp. education of Adisa Summers, reminiscent of the twins' CD, entitled The Miseducation of Lauryn Hill.

The days blended together and it seemed I only lived for the days we went to the mountain and I learned the truth about a world I'd been fantasizing about my whole life.

Though my education into the super world took place over several weeks, our conversations seemed seamless, blending into one long discourse.

»»»»»» ● «««««««

"I was angry that day of the storm because you abandoned me without a word of explanation," I explained. "Then you showed up, still making no attempt to contact me and explain yourself for three days.

Then you expected me to deliver your school work like I was at your beck and call and the fact that you treated me in such an unforgivable way, abandoning me, didn't seem to matter to you at all.

Plus I was jealous. I couldn't believe you possessed what I'd been wishing and suffering for all my life. And I was humiliated because you saved me and you were the last person I wanted to need anything from. My feelings were hurt, so… I lost it a little bit."

My rant completely stunned Micah. Then he asserted, "I did not abandon you and I certainly didn't wait three days to contact you. I came for you the same day I returned, the day I saved you."

"You did abandon me! What do you call disappearing for over two months and withdrawing from school without contacting the person you know is suffering in your absence? Don't try to deny it because I told you how miserable I was without you just before you disappeared then you up and stayed away longer than you ever have!"

"I know we discussed it. But I promised you I would be back as soon as I could. I even gave you a pearl necklace, to remind you of that promise. Didn't you believe me when I told you I couldn't tell a lie?"

"Micah, everybody lies at one point or another," I wearily exclaimed.

"I'm not everybody and I never lie."

The way he stated it as a fact, not something he was trying to convince me to believe, made me think he may actually be telling the truth.

"I notice you don't wear it," he said. "The pearl necklace, you haven't worn it since I've been back."

I felt pricked by guilt. "You think a necklace can take the place of hearing your voice? If you'd told me that then, I would've given back the necklace and settled for a couple of phone calls. I thought you weren't coming back when you withdrew from Talbot. Why didn't you contact me then and explain things?"

"Because I didn't know anything about withdrawing from Talbot until the day of the storm. Look Adisa, all of this is just a simple misunderstanding, due to my limited earthbound social skills. The buffering effect of my shield is to blame for that plus I've spent very little time in the presence of earthbounds until recently.

Plus you're not aware of how the Sp. world operates. If you knew, you never would have doubted that I would eventually return." He paused, considering how to proceed. "I'll try to explain. Remember when I told you I didn't lie?"

I nodded.

"I meant that. I never ever lie. I can't. I can omit things but I can't knowingly tell a lie. If I say I'll be back, that's guaranteed. When I promised you I'd return, nothing short of death, could keep me from fulfilling that promise. I thought you understood that when I told you I didn't lie."

Now it was time for me to be stunned. However, I persisted with other proof of abandonment, finding it hard to believe what he was saying. "But what about withdrawing from school, what was that about?"

"My father withdrew me without my knowledge. I discovered it when I returned from Africa, only moments before the storm, and not a single day earlier."

"But I saw your jeep…,"

"It was shipped back ahead of me while I finished up my obligations then I… flew back."

I briefly imagined Micah on a plane before I realized he meant 'flew back' as in literally flying his body from Africa to the U.S. I was dazed by the thought.

"Do you mean you literally did the Superman thing across the Atlantic?" I asked.

Micah smiled. "Pretty much."

I still wasn't completely convinced. "Why did you ask me to bring your assignments?"

"That was also my father, not me."

"But why would he do that? I know he hates me but…,"

"He doesn't hate you, Adisa. He's just concerned about my future."

"Why would he make me bring your assignments if he didn't want me around you to begin with?"

Micah sighed his frustration. "He knew I was coming back and I made it clear to him that I was returning to Talbot and maintaining contact with you. At that time, I didn't realize that he'd already withdrawn me from school. I've been too upset to talk to him about it, but I think he wanted to get you to the house to meet Jericho for some reason."

I thought of the blond Amazon with her broad shoulders and felt a pang of jealousy.

"Your dad was probably trying to show me the kind of woman he would prefer seeing you with," I said resentfully.

Micah looked surprised. "My father doesn't want to see me with any woman." Then he gave me a curious look. "Are you jealous, Adisa?"

I was too embarrassed to admit it so I changed the subject. "Micah, why didn't you call me while you were away? Didn't you miss me at all?" I could barely look him in the face.

"I missed you but I was in mandatory training and outside of that, my shield was up and that buffers feelings. I thought hearing from me would make you hurt more because I couldn't come to you. I believed my promise and the necklace were enough in my absence and contacting you was unnecessary since you knew I was coming back. It never crossed my mind that you would ever think otherwise.

I came straight back as soon as I could. That's when I saw Jericho and my father. He was worried about you and told me what had happened. Then the storm moved in and I went looking for you right away. When I think of what would've happened if I'd been even a second later...,"

His temple was working in an oddly familiar way and he was quiet for a long time.

Could it be true? Was it all simply a social misunderstanding, a breech of etiquette due to our ignorance of the other's cultural practices? It seemed too ridiculous to be true.

Micah eventually continued. "My father told me about your father's recovery from a heart attack. I'm sorry I wasn't there to help. That must have been hard on you," he said, carefully.

"It was hard but I got through it," I said. For the briefest moment my mind flashed on discovering the birth certificate containing my true identity. I realized it was in my pocket at that very moment.

I decided not to tell Micah. I was dealing with enough already, trying to handle his confessions. I wasn't up to making any of my own plus I still wondered if the black pearl meant he already knew.

"Did the doctors explain his sudden recovery?" Micah gently probed. "My father had the impression that he wouldn't... that it was unlikely... that things were hopeless."

I flinched at the painful memories his words dredged up. Dad's contorted face, the news of his impending demise, suddenly seeing the miracle of him standing before me in the hospital.

"They can't explain it. The insurance company and the doctors have been battling it out over the bills. Insurance claiming negligence on the doctors' part but the doctors have all the paperwork documenting dad's test results, photographic proof of his severely damaged heart. They say it's a miracle."

"Do you believe that or do you think something else... happened?" He was looking at me as if he expected me to explain how a miracle of God works.

"If the heart specialists are calling it a miracle, that's good enough for me. They're the experts and I can't think of a better explanation. All I do know is that one moment, they were telling me to get his affairs in order and the next, he was giving me a big bear hug, squeezing the life out of me. I prayed for a miracle, we all did. But I didn't, not even for a moment, think it would actually happen. But it did."

Micah was staring at me so intently it made me feel self conscious. He put his arm around me and I wanted to lean into it so badly I ached.

"Why did you have to go all the way to Africa this time?" I asked, trying to distract him as I shifted away. I was still wary of getting too close too fast.

"I... uh... broke a piece of equipment that's necessary as part of my Guardian training. It's mandatory that all Protectors training to be Guardians use it, daily if possible. I had to continue the training but there's only one such apparatus on each continent. Ours was pretty state of the art and the only one more durable is in Africa so I had to go there to continue training. Once the one here was back up and running, I was able to return."

After his explanation, we pulled out the thermoses of soup and tea. The soup was coconut with chicken and the tea was chamomile. I was glad for the break. A lot of the information was really technical and it sometimes felt like I was drowning in a sea of incomprehensible words.

I was excited about finally learning the truth about Micah. It felt good, having him finally open up to me.

»»»»»»» ● «««««««

"What exactly is a Guardian?"

Micah was thoughtful before answering. "A Guardian is like an elite guard or bodyguard for Sp. beings. They also function as sentinels in space outposts."

"How long does it take to become one?"

"It varies but it's years and years of training."

"So you're a Protector now?"

"Yes."

"What's a Protector?"

"Protectors are like Guardian's only not as powerful and they sometimes work with earthbounds. They're more vulnerable in some ways particularly when their shield is down and they're distracted by feelings, like when you kicked me," he said, glancing at me suspiciously to make sure I wasn't about to commit a repeat performance.

"Oh no, not that again! Micah, I'm really *really* sorry about that," I said, the guilt eating me up inside.

Micah smiled. "I'm only teasing. Actually I was impressed. I didn't realize you were that strong or maybe I'm just that weak."

"You seem pretty powerful to me," I asserted, quick to defend him. Then I felt a little awkward because that sounded kind of flirty. So I said in a rush, "Is there anything more powerful than a Guardian."

After giving it serious consideration, he said, "Healers. They can go right through things and withdraw objects, illness, sadness. They can... cure. I don't think there's anything more powerful than that."

In my mind I pictured voodoo doctors doing surgery with their bare hands, reaching into the human body and pulling out bloody diseases. I shuddered and changed the subject.

"That equipment you broke, the one Protectors need to train on in order to become Guardians, what's it called?"

"A Depacitor," he said and then, as if he'd forgotten to mention it, he exclaimed, "If my shield had been up, you could've broken your foot or knocked yourself over when you kicked me."

"What does the Depacitor do?" I asked, inexplicably fascinated.

Micah hesitated and I got the distinct impression that he didn't want to talk about it. He finally answered. "It aids in the removal are deadening of feelings... emotions not sensory."

I looked at him alarmed. "No judgment but that sounds extremely bizarre. How long does it take?"

Micah smiled grimly. "It varies but usually several years."

"Why does this training take longer sometimes than at others?" I asked, recalling how his absences varied in length.

"The more entrenched or deeper the feelings, the longer it takes to remove them. It's important because feelings cloud judgment and the removal of emotions strengthens the shield."

"It seems like too great a sacrifice to make, giving up what in essence makes us who we are," I concluded, thinking of the robot.

"It has its advantages. Wouldn't you rather not suffer from your rages and impulsive actions?" Micah countered. "Your life would be so much easier and better if you didn't have to contend with the chaos your temper creates."

Ouch! I saw some truth in his words but wasn't completely convinced. "True, it might be easier to live but I don't think it would be better, not if I had to give up the way I feel about my family and friends." I neglected to add, 'and you.'

"Besides, why is it so important to strengthen this shield thing anyway?" I continued. "I thought you said you could still use your superpowers even when it's down."

"It's not mandatory for all Sp. beings to remove their feelings. However, the day the shield can no longer be lowered is the day the Protector is a Guardian. This perpetual shield lasts for the duration of a Guardian's life. So you can't be a Guardian unless you perfect your shield. Then you are always in a maximum state of readiness and operate at the peak of your abilities. That's why they are the elite. It's very challenging and there aren't very many. Few are selected, and of those, only a few complete the training."

"Once the shield is up permanently, are they immortal?"

He shook his head. "No superbeing lives forever. We have life spans parallel to earthbounds."

"But they're superhuman so how do they die?"

"Natural causes usually. We aren't indestructible. We can be destroyed."

"How?"

"It depends on the individual and their specific weaknesses."

"I thought superheroes were immortal," I said disappointed.

"We're not heroes and we don't live forever. It's actually easier to kill Sp. beings while they're young before the age of consent when their powers haven't manifested or soon after before they're skilled at using them."

»»»»»»» ● «««««««

"What's the age of consent?"

"In the Sp. world, sixteen is the age of consent. Eighteen is the adult age in the U.S. but it's sixteen in the Sp. world and that's for all over the world because that's usually when powers manifest and decisions affecting the rest of a superbeing's life are made."

"What happens after a person manifests?"

"They enter into a rigorous training program and at some point they're paired with a Sp. being who has similar powers. The learning curb greatly improves then because you don't have to go through trial and error to get acquainted with your powers; your mentor knows first hand about your specific powers and can instruct you on how to maximize them."

"Tell me about the time your powers first manifested," I said, extremely curious.

Micah looked as if I'd caught him off guard.

"What's wrong?" I asked. "Too personal?"

"No. Nothing's wrong," he said. "It's just, I haven't thought about it in years. But I don't mind talking to you about it.

I was very young, only five. It's unusual to be so young when it happens but it sometimes happens to Healers or children with dormant parents.

I was running around outside one night, chasing fireflies. One moment I'm on the ground in my backyard and the next, I was in the air. It scared me to death.

I knew what was happening... I mean I was aware of superpowers and had seen other Sp. beings and their powers. But, it was nothing like I thought it would be.

I was confused and scared because I didn't know how to control it. And I was moving so fast, I thought I would crash. I finally managed to land, about thirty miles from home. It was dark and I didn't know where I was. I was just as scared as any earthbound five year old would be, lost in the dark without parents."

Micah's features had a far off pained expression. "My father found me hours later and he was so excited. He never had superpowers so he didn't understand firsthand how... traumatic it could be. I kept thinking of all that frightening raw power coursing through my body, I was a scared child on the back of a raging bull. It made me feel like a freak. And I was alone out there for so long, with nobody to explain to me what I should do and reassure me that everything would be okay."

I could tell it was difficult for him to share such a painful experience. I felt closer to him because he was able to open up to me.

He sighed. "The loneliness of feeling different and separate from the ones you love, is intense. The shield is a welcome relief from all those bad feelings." he said. "It's a good thing powers usually come later in life when you're more mature and can handle it better. Not to mention all the legal considerations that need addressing."

"Does the super world have its own legal or political system separate from earthbound systems?" I asked, easing into a less emotional topic.

"Yes. There's a whole society of governing bodies producing rules and regulations and also enforcing organizations. It's part of our studies at FLEET but I could study for several lifetimes and still not know everything about it, the same as you and your earthbound governments."

"Is there one super leader for the whole super world?"

"No. Each continent has one leader."

"Seven leaders?"

"Yes. There isn't a single leader who governs over all of the continents. However, Africa is usually deferred to because in addition to being the cradle of civilization, it's the birthplace of the first superbeings. It's also the first continent to organize under one Sp. leader. Are you familiar with the history of Africa, the earthbound history?" he asked.

"Not really," I answered and for some reason felt a little embarrassed by my ignorance.

But Micah only offered encouragement. "Learn your history, not just here in America but on other continents, especially Africa. Knowledge is power and power gives you choices."

»»»»»» ● «««««««

Knowledge is power. Thanks to dad's pursuit of trivia, I knew this simple yet concise expression was attributed to Sir Francis Bacon. What event caused the brain synapse that led to his mental leap, producing the aphorism? The truth of it burdened me. Maybe it would be easier to bear if I shared my power.

"Micah," I began, feeling the weight of my secret as I fingered the familiar folded sheet concealed in my pocket.

But when he turned to me in response, I instantly lost my nerve. If he knew anything about my true identity, he would volunteer it, especially if he really cared about me.

"Micah... did you really go seven years with no physical contact at all? I mean, I Googled it and discovered you should be dead. Seriously, they did some study, probably back in the day when there weren't laws against that kind of thing, where they deprived babies of human touch and they didn't survive. It showed kids without human contact just wasted away. Researchers concluded touch is just as, if not more, important than food."

My rambling made me confront what it would be like if Micah became a Guardian. Would that mean he would be incapable of loving me? I tried to imagine a life with the robot but couldn't. I released the folded sheet in my pocket and withdrew my hand, stiffly pressing my fist into the ground between us so it wouldn't betray me by retrieving my true identity.

"Some touching is permissible," Micah responded, "as long as it's not intimate or familial in nature. A perfunctory task like placing my brother in a car seat is fine. But I'm discouraged from hugging him in comfort when he falls and scrapes his knee. However, treating his injury is fine. Limited contact is practiced but all is performed with the shield up to minimize emotions connected to it. It makes it easier to permanently rid yourself of all emotions sooner. And once that happens, touching is no longer an issue because there are no emotions attached to them."

Micah paused and placed his hand over my still clenched fist. "When we were in the woods and I let my shield down in public for the first time in seven years... it was overwhelming. The slightest touch, even the wind blowing on my skin was such a shock. I can't begin to describe to you what it was like, feeling you without my shield at that moment. A mere caress was ecstasy and agony joined."

His intensity took me by surprise. He drew his thumb over my knuckles, releasing tingling sensations that ran all the way up my arm. We'd managed to share our small tent over several days with little awkwardness, now suddenly our confines seemed crammed to overflowing with tension.

I tried to make things lighter again, slipping my hand from under his and wrapping both my arms around my knees. "Really Micah, if a caress was all that, I hate to think what a kiss was like for you."

I immediately saw my error as the image of me and Micah kissing filled my mind; I knew he was probably imagining the same thing. That certainly wasn't my intent.

I hurriedly tried to cover. "I guess it's good you can go robot whenever your feelings get out of control."

"But even with my shield up, especially our first dance... I feel you stronger than I've ever felt anybody coming through it. When I stopped you from running over that cliff, pinning you down, I could feel you hurting yourself on my shield. I was shocked because I'd never felt anything like that before, usually I'd barely register something like that. All I could think of was letting it down so it wouldn't hurt you."

Micah's eyes were troubled as he said, "Promise you'll never run away from me again. You can't know what it does to me when you do that."

But I did see it, in his eyes. I was speechless, realizing how much it affected him.

He frowned in confusion then suddenly pulled me close. "Adisa, do you plan on running from me again?"

"No... no... I don't," I stuttered, feeling all jittery inside.

"So, you'll promise never to do it again?"

"I promise."

I could feel the tension leave his body as my answer put his mind at ease. I awkwardly reached for his pack putting a little space between us and pretended not to notice his disappointed look as I busily pulled out the thermoses.

"What kind of soup and tea did you bring today?" I asked to distract him.

"An African chicken dish called poulet yassa and green mint tea."

As we ate, Micah explained the complex two day process of making the savory African dish.

»»»»»» ● «««««

"Why didn't you just leave Africa and come back to me sooner?" It took a long time for me to finally ask.

Micah thoughtfully watched me from his side of the tent. I sat opposite him in the small space, choosing this position to keep some distance between us. It was becoming more difficult to resist touching him in our limited confines but I was determined not to be ruled by my emotions.

Maybe that Depacitor thing wasn't such a bad idea after all, I thought sarcastically. It would certainly help me think more clearly if I didn't have to contend with my unruly emotions. I needed to remain logical as I learned about Micah's world and decided how or if I could fit into his life.

Micah finally said, "I considered coming back sooner. But that would have been tantamount to giving up my dream, quitting my FLEET training, something I've worked years for."

His posture revealed how significant it was to him. How could I compete with his dream of becoming a Guardian? I didn't value it but its importance to him was apparent. I couldn't take the place of his first desire. It was vain of me to think that I could. But even if I could, would I want to be responsible for robbing him of his dream?

"It appears you have to make a choice between becoming a Guardian and... being with me." I felt vulnerable putting it out there like that.

"I think I can have both," he said, holding my gaze.

"You really think so?"

He nodded.

"There's a good chance I'll end up getting hurt," I pointed out, hesitantly.

"Yes. But I'm taking that chance too."

"But, you'll get rid of your feelings eventually and stop hurting." I didn't have to take it to the logical conclusion that I wouldn't have the convenience of foregoing the pain of a broken heart. I could tell he already understood.

"If you could skip the hurt, would you take the chance?" he asked.

I shook my head no. "Not if it meant skipping out on all my other emotions as well. Some things are too precious to sacrifice, like your humanity. I'll keep my feelings, thank you very much."

He stared at me a long time after that but I refused to back down and stared right back.

"I'd like to keep you," he said wistfully and I nearly lost it.

"My instinct for self preservation is pretty strong," I countered but I was bluffing. It wouldn't take much for me to give in to him without regard for my own well being.

"I'm really sorry for hurting you when I didn't contact you." His face showed how much it bothered him.

"I survived."

"I'll need your help and understanding to get us through that kind of problem in the future. And I'll try my best to do better."

His words attempted to carve out a chance for us. He'd already decided he wanted to give us another try and was trying to convince me to stop dragging my feet.

I lowered my gaze to the glowing O-Rocks, feeling the weight of the moment. My hand automatically crept inside my pocket, drawing a strange comfort from the birth certificate. It represented truth, no matter how painful.

"Micah, you know how sometimes you hang onto things because they remind you of who you really are?" I asked, unsure of where I was going with my question but sure that I wanted to be as open as he was which meant sharing my secret.

Micah nodded, smiling. "You mean like the necklace I gave you?"

"My necklace?" I repeated, confused.

"I notice you still haven't worn the pearl necklace I gave you."

I immediately felt guilty even though there was no condemnation in his voice.

"Oh! I... uh... I...," I faltered.

"I understand. You thought I'd abandoned you and you were angry. It's okay, I can get you another one if you like."

"Why would you get me another one? I still have the one you gave to me."

"Oh, I thought maybe you trashed it in a fit of rage," he said, matter of factly.

"Micah! I would never...," I stopped when I saw a mischievous grin on his face and I couldn't help smiling in return. "Okay, you got me. I probably am capable of something like that."

"Are you sure you don't have it soaking in a jar of vinegar as we speak?" he asked.

"What do you mean?"

"Vinegar dissolves pearls," he said.

"I didn't know that."

He looked at me suspiciously. "I probably shouldn't be giving you any ideas."

I smiled and shrugged noncommittally.

Micah leaned forward, decreasing the distance between us. "Do you think you'll wear it again? The necklace I gave you," he asked.

"Chances are I will," I began cautiously. "I was wondering, why did you give me a black pearl?"

"What do you mean?"

"Why a black pearl. What's its... meaning?"

"I told you, it's beautiful dark and rare, just like you."

"Is that all?" I asked.

A shade of guilt crossed his features. "I wanted to give you an engagement ring and if you were a citizen of the super world, sixteen being the age of consent, I would have. But I thought it would be more appropriate to abide by earthbound rules and wait until you're eighteen."

"What!?" I exclaimed, completely thunderstruck.

All other thoughts flew out of my mind as I realized Micah was practically proposing to me. Was he seriously saying he wanted to marry me? We were too young to even consider marriage. I was barely old enough to date him.

Then it suddenly dawned on me that in his world, he was already a year into full grown adulthood while I, not much younger than he, was still a child completely dependent for two more years in my world.

"In the Sp. world, we're both adults, old enough to marry," he calmly asserted.

My heart was hammering out of control. It was difficult to comprehend that a superhero actually considered proposing to me. I was too shocked to deal with the topic of marriage head on so I evaded it by hiding behind a joke.

"If you're so grown, why are you still living with your parents?" I kidded.

"I don't. They live with me."

His answer confused me. "What do you mean? Isn't that the same thing?"

"Not quite. It's my house, I bought it. They live with me."

I was dumbstruck. How could a teenager with no visible means of income afford a whole house? Even in this housing slump, they still weren't exactly free. And why did his family choose to live with him?

"Drug dealer, professional athlete, or rap star," I listed. "Those are the only *teens* I can think of who can buy a house. My guess for you would be professional athlete and you keep your family around as your entourage."

Micah laughed out loud then explained. "As a Protector, I've taken a few paid assignments. My family stays with me out of convenience, it attracts less attention than a high school student living on his own in the earthbound world."

"I didn't know superheroes took pay," I said.

"I'm not a superhero, just a superbeing, a Sp. being and it's a job. We often take jobs in law enforcement, the military or private security because it's easier to ply our trade as defenders of the public. You don't begrudge policemen and soldiers their paychecks. It's similar for us sometimes."

"Okay, but I'm guessing they probably don't make as much as you do if you can afford a house on a 'few' assignments."

Micah didn't respond as he casually shifted to sit next to me, stretching his legs out. I was instantly aware of his closeness and the absence of his shield.

"Remember when you saved me from the falling tree?" I asked, searching for a topic to distract my thoughts from his proximity.

"I'll never forget it," he said, his eyes fierce with the memory.

"Well, it seemed like your shield was down. I thought you functioned better with it up."

"I knew I didn't need it in that situation and I didn't want to risk harming you."

"How could it harm me?"

"I was moving pretty fast and the shield could have given you a pretty hard blow. Plus, I didn't want to be desensitized and handle you too roughly. That's a major reason why Guardians work with Sp. beings and not earthbounds, their permanent shield could possibly do more damage than good. I remembered my shield bruised your wrists before and I didn't want to hurt you again."

"Oh. I appreciate your consideration," I said awkwardly. He was really making it hard to resist him.

»»»»»» ● ««««««

"Being with you is teaching me how to be more… considerate," Micah admitted softly.

"Really?"

"I'm learning to think of more than just your safety. I'm more aware of your comfort as well."

His words gave me a strange thought. "Are you 'protecting' me?"

"Yes, it comes naturally to me."

"Why? Am I an assignment!?" Maybe my parents had asked him to be my Protector without my knowledge. It wouldn't be the first secret they'd kept from me.

"No. Nobody assigned me to you."

"Then why are you here?" I asked.

"I just want to be with you and keep you safe."

"Safe from what?"

"Anything dangerous. I patrol the environment to make sure it's safe for you. That's how I knew you were headed for a cliff that time in the woods. I know this neighborhood and the surrounding area in minute detail. I tried to redirect you from the cliff by making noise but you kept turning toward it instead of away from it."

"You were trying to drive me to safety by making all that noise?" I thought about it for a moment. "It makes sense now. You're usually so quiet but that time you were thrashing around on purpose."

"Since you weren't very cooperative, I finally had to give up and cut you off at the pass, so to speak. But I stayed hidden so you couldn't see me fly. If there was anyway I could've saved you from that falling tree without you seeing me fly, I would have."

"Well I'm glad the truth is out. I hate secrets." Then I guiltily thought of the folded sheet in my pocket. "Are there any more secrets you're keeping from me?"

"Well...," he started hesitantly.

I was tense, waiting for his admission. Maybe he was finally ready to reveal what he knew about my true identity.

"I actually saved you another time," he said with a sheepish grin.

"What? When!?" I was completely stunned by his revelation. Surely he hadn't saved me a third time. That had to be some kind of record.

"Your birthday, on the bus, Lake Lanier. I had to rip a seat out to free your foot. I didn't want to be discovered so I stayed out of sight and lifted the bus so they could get to you.

Letting them take you was one of the hardest things I've ever done in my life. I wanted to fly you straight to the hospital myself but I knew there was no way to do so without exposing what I really am to the world.

I knew your injuries weren't life threatening but if they had been, I'd be in a lot of trouble in the Sp. world right now because I would have flown you to help regardless of the consequences."

I shivered at the thought of nearly dying on three separate occasions. Three times I had come close to death and each time, Micah had been there to save me. The cliff, Lake Lanier, and the falling tree. Could something be out there conspiring to kill me?

"Is my life in danger or am I just the unluckiest person in the world?" I asked, attempting to make a joke of it but failing miserably.

"I'd say you're the luckiest because you're still alive. I'll do everything in my power to keep you safe," Micah said and his quiet determination reassured me.

I wanted to be with him but wondered if there could be a happy ending for us. "Micah, what happens to us after this process is complete and you're a full fledged Guardian?"

"I don't know but I'd like to find out."

He reached for my hand and we intertwined fingers. "I'd like to find out too. But with your dad and FLEET against us, I don't see how we'll make it."

"I can handle FLEET."

"What about your dad?"

"It's long and complicated," Micah said, his eyes evasive.

"We've got time."

I waited patiently while he decided whether or not he was going to tell me.

"My father had a Sp. twin," he began, his eyes nervously observing me. I smiled in encouragement and he continued.

"A brother who turned his back on his calling as Guardian and withdrew from the Sp. world altogether. My father believed his twin squandered his abilities and this caused a rift between them.

He was bitter because he wanted to be a Guardian but he wasn't chosen because he was dormant. He took comfort in the knowledge that it was pretty much guaranteed he'd have powerful offspring, Guardian material, if he married another dormant.

So, he married my mother, took a desk job in the Sp. world, and bided his time. He anticipated a son, to compensate for his... inabilities. Now he has me and I was on the fast track to becoming a Guardian. And then you came along and he thinks you could be a hindrance to me."

I realized Micah was out right defying his father to be with me. Mr. Alexander was behaving badly but I didn't want to cause division in his family.

My heart sank. "Micah, I don't want to come between you and your dad."

I tried to withdraw my hand from his but he refused to let it go.

"I think I can have both." His familiar words offered me little comfort.

"We can't have everything we want. Sometimes, we have to make a choice," I said.

Before leaving, Micah separated the O-Rocks as usual and their glow gradually diminished. He carefully rewrapped one in cloth, to prevent them from knocking against each other and restarting the glowing heat. This was a precaution to preserve the life of the stones.

»»»»»» ● «««««««

"But feelings also cause us to be our best self not just our worst. The love a parent has for a child causes that parent to risk life and limb to save them," I argued.

Micah and I had been going back and forth over the pros and cons of emotional feelings.

"But Guardians have to be willing to save more than just their own and fearing for their own safety impedes that. Feelings of jealousy and vengeance can cloud judgment and disrupt the ability to act appropriately. Therefore, feelings are deleted. If there's nothing to feel, there's nothing to fear, and a Guardian will risk all for the mission," Micah reasoned.

"But it leaves you a cold unfeeling robot. Joyless without family or friends or comfort. Is it worth that? It sounds like too great a price. I still say feelings are worth keeping."

I was exasperated because we kept returning to this same argument during our trips to the mountain. Micah was dead set on continuing his training and I feared reviving our relationship because of what the end result of his training would be.

"You're always angry and putting yourself down. Wouldn't it be great if you didn't have to feel embarrassed or unsure, or guilty? Don't you want the peace of feeling nothing?"

"What about love and joy, pride excitement wonder elation passion and courage? You yourself said you admire some of those very same qualities in me. I want peace but I don't want to feel empty inside. I don't want to be dead until my body actually dies.

When you're the robot, even though you're considerate and polite, it's like you don't care about me. I don't want you to save me out of duty. Maybe it's okay for strangers but not for me. I want you to walk through fire for me because you love me, not because you've been ordered to do so. And if it comes down to it, I'd rather you love me than save me. I can save myself," I said defensively.

I watched him in silence, wondering if I was finally getting through to him. I felt vulnerable, pitting myself against a major force in his life but I wanted him to understand how I truly felt.

"What are you feeling now?" I asked. "You don't have to tell me but ask yourself, do you want to lose that forever? I don't. I thought I did when you left. It was awful. Things didn't even taste the same. You probably can't relate because you have your shield to hide behind."

Micah's inscrutable silence was frustrating. After letting me vent uninterrupted, he finally said, "In spite of everything, I'd like you to give us another try."

I was tired of talking, tired of arguing. I wanted to give in but my stubborn resistance had become habitual and was hard to overcome.

When I got home, I put away Amy's mournful musings on love and started looping Corinne Bailey Rae's Like a Star. I meditated on the hopeful innocence in her voice as she sang about how Heaven had been away too long, trying to coax my injured heart into one more try.

My jealousy of Micah's superpowers cooled and I entertained the thought that if I couldn't have superpowers of my own, maybe I could be content to date somebody who did. I would simply have to find a way to save the world with my limited earthbound abilities.

»»»»»» ● ««««««

"When I become a Guardian, my perpetual shield will put me on constant alert, enabling me to function at a superior level."

"So you won't have any feelings for me, right?"

"I'm not sure. When it comes to you, everything is different."

"But you said...,"

"I know and complete eradication of emotions is the norm... for now. But I'm an anomaly. Nobody like me has ever existed before because individuals who develop extreme emotional attachments are naturally deselected by the Depacitor. I have the people at FLEET completely stomped because they've never come across a case like mine. A Guardian in training with a girlfriend is completely unheard of."

Micah smiled as if enjoying the fact that he could confound them before adding, "To be perfectly honest, Guardians have never been capable of love and don't create families. The only things I'm sure about are you and being a Guardian. I'm not ready to let either go. Maybe that's selfish but it's the truth. I just want to keep going until I find a way to have both."

"Maybe you'll be forced to make a choice," I suggested.

"Right now, the choice is up to you," he said, giving me a significant look which put me on the defensive.

"We'll have to also overcome many other differences between our worlds. I don't envy you the task of trying to function in the Sp. world and the earthbound. It must be difficult to juggle the two successfully."

He nodded in agreement. "Just trying to abide by the moral standards is complicated, like knowing what's proper and what isn't. I try to behave appropriately by not going past earthbound boundaries that would be perfectly acceptable to cross in the Sp. world."

I thought it peculiar how he avoided my eyes as he spoke. "Are you talking about the last time you kissed me?" I asked remembering how passionate he'd been before sharply pulling away.

When he didn't respond, I nervously continued. "My sisters say before you date, draw a line you don't want to cross, determining what you will or won't do. That way it's easier to stop when you get to that point and you don't want things to get out of hand. Of course it's a good idea to let the boy know too so he won't be fumbling around clueless."

I smiled and was relieved that Micah did the same as he finally met my gaze. "We didn't discuss anything before hand," he reminded me.

"It's harder to do in practice than in theory. I was so embarrassed I couldn't even think of us like that."

"Well I did, think of us like that," he admitted.

"I am aware," I said shyly.

"I didn't mean to scare you," he said, his eyes worried. "I'm still learning."

"You didn't scare me," I assured. "Surprised me quite a bit. But I knew I could trust you."

"I'm a superbeing, Adisa, not a saint," he said, seriously. "I'm capable of making mistakes. Our cultures are different in significant ways. It's been difficult trying to figure out how to be with you, what's acceptable and what isn't."

"You don't have anybody you trust to talk to about these differences?"

"I mostly use observation and research. I'm private by nature so I don't usually discuss my personal life. It's embarrassing to talk to my mom about these things and my dad's not exactly supportive," he said.

"Why haven't you talked about it with me? I'm sure we could figure it out together."

"Like you said, easier in theory than in practice. In my world, we're adults, and it's difficult to think differently. Imagine reaching nineteen years of age and somebody tells you, the laws have changed and you have to wait another year for adult privileges. It would be difficult to do, especially since you've already spent a year as an adult.

And then there's dealing with Opal and Frederick Summers and getting their permission for... it's an adjustment for me to have to consult them before walking a mountain with you, a *sixteen* year old. "

Micah stretched out next to me, close but not touching and I could sense his frustration. "I've never felt like this before, Adisa. Nobody training to be Guardian has. So be patient with me as I'm breaking new ground in addition to dealing with a culture outside my own. I need you to help me find my way in this unexplored territory."

I felt his hand brush against mine on the tent floor and I didn't move away. I was overwhelmed that a Sp. being was asking me for help.

While my mind was still relatively clear, I needed to clarify things regarding 'breaking new ground' before going any further.

"For the record, I draw the line at kissing. I've just started dating and the kissing thing alone puts me right at my limit." My words were a jumbled rush and I felt heat rising in my cheeks.

Micah gave me a slow easy grin as he stroked my hand reassuringly. "Okay, good to know."

"Where do you draw the line?" I asked, curiously.

"I have no line," he admitted with ease.

I laughed a little, thinking it was funny in a scary sort of way until I realized he wasn't kidding. "You're serious, you don't have any boundaries?" I asked.

"In the Sp. world, the volatile nature of things due to the dangers we face, often leads to the suspension of social pretense and living in the moment is stressed. Certain physical expressions are accepted.

Normally, my Guardian training would preclude me from this possibility. But, as I've explained, I'm different. It makes things more challenging for me. Add your earthbound moral restrictions to the mix and things really start getting complicated. However, I'm perfectly fine with drawing the line at kissing, if you prefer it that way," he said.

I realized we had tentatively agreed to terms giving us another try but I felt self conscious about how to proceed. I felt so green about everything, particularly about the world in general. It wasn't anything like I thought it was.

Micah's hand continued to stroke mine in silence for awhile. "Do you have any more questions?" he eventually asked.

"Not right now," I said, enjoying just being with him in the quiet.

"Good," he said.

Then he sat up and gently tilted my chin up and lightly placed a kiss on my lips. My arms immediately went around him pulling him closer as I kissed him back. I couldn't believe I'd resisted for so long.

Micah gathered me in his arms without breaking our kiss, his hands slowly gliding up and down my back.

After a long while, he pulled back slightly to look at me. "I've wanted to do that ever since I got back from Africa," he breathed, smiling in satisfaction.

I was deep in thought as Micah drove us home. I'd been asleep to a whole existence, completely unaware of what was really going on out in the world beyond the thin veneer of the obvious. Now that veneer was becoming transparent, cracking, and falling away as my knowledge increased.

Several days later, after school, I went home to drop off my backpack and wait for Micah to drive his jeep over to take us to the mountain for more of my Sp. education.

I pulled out my black pearl necklace and quickly slipped it on, for the first time since Micah had returned. I knew he would understand its significance as soon as he saw it so I self consciously tucked it inside my shirt, to reveal when the moment was right. As I headed downstairs to wait for Micah, I heard the phone ringing.

T he muted tone of the ringing phone was in odd contrast to the shrill alarm it raised in my heart. My reaction confused me and I seriously considered not answering just before picking up.

It was Micah calling to cancel because he was called away on urgent business. Not earth shattering but extremely disappointing, nevertheless.

I wanted to ask him all kinds of nosy questions but he didn't have time to go into details over the phone. He promised he'd be back to walk me to school the next morning, no matter what. When I hung up, I realized I didn't doubt in the least that Micah would be waiting for me at his tree the next morning.

I finished all my homework and decided to go for a run before starting dinner. I was in the habit of running in the neighborhood and around the track when Micah and I didn't go to the mountain. I quickly changed and headed out.

As I descended my porch stairs, I automatically checked out Micah's home and saw a man parked out front leaning against his car, observing me.

The vehicle was a nondescript sports car but the owner leaning against it was anything but. His tall frame leisurely rested against the car in a manner that suggested he belonged. His jet black hair was straight and fell to just above his shoulders. His skin was pale white and his prominent cheek bones gave him a noble appearance. His posture suggested a self assurance that emphasized his unflinching gaze, making me feel slightly uneasy.

I waved politely realizing I was staring and he bowed, touching his head with a flourish of his hand, in acknowledgment. A blatant flirt.

I was surprised to see a visitor outside the Alexander home. Except for Jericho, I'd never seen anybody visiting them before. Since the black jeep was gone, I considered telling him nobody would be home for a while knowing that, except for Micah, nobody was usually home until well after six. Then I decided to mind my own business and jogged down to the track.

The weather was finally starting to warm up some but I still wore full body covering to ward off the residual chill in the air. As I finished my run and prepared to leave the track, I was surprised to see the same sports car from earlier parked outside the gate.

I could see the driver was the same man who'd been leisurely leaning against it and to my surprise, Jason was sitting in the backseat behind him.

As I passed, the driver leaned over, lowering the passenger's window then called out, "Adisa? Adisa Summers?"

I was startled hearing my name come from the stranger. On close up observation, I saw he was very handsome in an aloof sort of way. He had beautiful dark glittering eyes that held a hint of coldness.

"Yes," I replied, standing back from the car and couldn't help wondering why Jason was with somebody like him.

"I'm glad I caught you. I'm Victor and I'm watching Jason for the Alexanders. I have to leave and nobody's home yet. Apparently, Micah was called away but I've been told that you're good with children."

"I don't understand," I stammered but did feel more at ease hearing his familiarity with the Alexanders. I tried to remember if Micah had ever mentioned the name Victor to me.

Jason sat quietly in the backseat, watching me. I waved and he returned the gesture.

"Something about working with kids over the summer," Victor continued, sounding impatient.

The thought of the Alexanders discussing my summer activities with this man was unsettling. "Yes I did but I've never...,"

"Please, I'm really in a hurry. Could you grab Jason and watch him until his parents return? It would be a big help."

I couldn't believe the Alexanders would leave their child with this man. Even with their track record of withholding physical affection, I was still under the impression they cared enough to be more selective of who watched over their youngest. This man seemed cold and uncaring, hardly nanny material.

"I wish I could help you but I've never baby-sat for the Alexanders so I don't know if they would be okay with it," I hedged.

"I thought you and Micah were close and since Jason is his brother, I assumed it would be fine," he reasoned.

The way he said 'close' made me feel embarrassed. How could I refuse to care for the brother of the boy I was dating. Something about the situation wasn't right and I had an unreasonable desire to get Jason away from the man.

"Listen, I know this is inconvenient and I'll pay you for your time," Victor said as he withdrew some bills from his wallet and held them out to me.

I couldn't see the exact amount he was offering but I saw at least three twenties among the bills. He was obviously desperate, to throw away that kind of money.

"It's not the money. I'm just not sure the Alexanders would want me watching him since they've never asked me to baby-sit before."

"If you'll feel better, hop in and I can run you home so you can call them and ask if it's okay."

I had no desire to have him drive me anywhere because he was a complete stranger to me.

I impulsively decided to take Jason. What's the worst that could happen? The Alexanders may be upset but at least Jason would be safe and close to home, not getting dragged across the city or who knows where with a man who appeared to be about as nurturing as a snake.

Victor seemed agitated at the hold up and I didn't want to delay him further by asking a bunch of nosy questions, so I finally agreed. "Okay, but keep your money."

"Thanks," he said smiling from ear to ear in apparent relief. But even though he sounded sincere, the smile did not reach his eyes.

I quickly opened the back door and reached across the vacant seat to undo Jason's seatbelt.

"Hi Jason. Remember me? I introduced you to Power Boy."

He nodded while watching me work at the seatbelt.

"I guess you two can get reacquainted while you're staying with me. I can introduce you to some of my other super friends as well." Then I said to Victor, "I can't get this undone."

The seconds stretched out and the buckle still wouldn't release.

"It get's stuck sometimes," Victor said, frustrated. "Give it a good yank."

I climbed in and sat next to Jason to get a better grip and yanked on the belt a couple times but it still wouldn't come undone.

"Here, let me get that for you," Victor offered, and undid his seatbelt to turn around and lean over his seat. But instead of reaching for Jason's seatbelt, he closed the door behind me. Then turned back around in his seat and began driving away.

I was shocked by his impatience. "You really don't have to drive us. We can walk. It's not far and I do it everyday to get to and from school." I tried to keep the irritation out of my voice.

Victor just smiled in the rearview mirror and kept going. When he didn't slow down as my house approached I spoke up.

"My house is right here. I'd rather watch Jason in my own home because I have to get cleaned up from my run and then start dinner for...," my voice trailed off as he passed the Alexanders' home as well. That's when the first twinge of fear set in.

"What are you doing?" I asked, trying to remain calm. I glanced at Jason but he didn't seem worried at all.

Victor's expression didn't change. "You should put your seat belt on. It's safer. Isn't that right Jason?"

"Yes. And yours too Victor," Jason said in a boyish reprimand.

"Oh, yeah. Good looking out Jason," Victor said as he smoothly fastened his seatbelt.

When the car stopped at a light, I tried to open my door, wondering how I could get Jason's buckle undone in time for him to escape with me. But the door would no more budge than Jason's seatbelt.

I quickly lunged across Jason to try his door before the light changed and traffic started moving but it wouldn't open either.

"What are you doing?" Jason asked, and the innocent confusion in his voice only added to the hysteria rising in me. He had no idea we were being kidnapped.

"Adisa, I think it would be best if you put on your seatbelt and kept still. You wouldn't want to upset Jason by doing something dangerous. Would you?"

We made eye contact in the rearview mirror and I debated whether or not to throw a full out fit. But he was right. I didn't want to scare Jason unnecessarily.

"Listen," I tried to reason as I automatically strapped myself in and the car started forward again, "I really don't have time for this. Please, just pull over and let us out. We can make it back home on our own."

I noticed the side and back windows looked darker and was astonished. I clearly remembered seeing through clear glass when I was standing outside the car and had no trouble seeing Victor and Jason inside before Victor rolled down the window. The windows continued to darken until I couldn't see outside anymore. With a sinking feeling, I realized I wouldn't be able to signal anybody outside of the car.

I could still see through the front window and tried to spot familiar landmarks so I would know where I was. I caught the driver's glittering eyes in the rearview mirror again and a cold smile spread across his face.

"I regret to inform you that this magnificent Georgia view will be temporarily unavailable to you," he said as a completely opaque partition went up, dividing the back from the front. Now, I couldn't see outside the car at all and anybody outside couldn't see me. The interior was softly illuminated by light from the ceiling and door panels.

I tried not to panic for Jason's sake but being completely enclosed in the small space without a clue as to what was going on had my nerves stretched to the limit. Everything had happened so impossibly fast and with an ease that sickened me at my own gullibility.

"Are you okay Jason?" I asked, wondering if the stranger had somehow threatened the boy to be complicit in the abduction.

"Yeah. You look weird."

"I'm just a little concerned because... I don't understand what's going on. Do you?"

"Yes. Victor says it's a surprise," Jason exclaimed, his face brightening in anticipation.

"Really? What kind of surprise?"

"I don't know. But Victor always has great surprises."

"He does?" I briefly wondered if this really could be some kind of surprise. Could Micah somehow be in on it? I seriously doubted it. Micah was not the type to unnecessarily frighten people. Envisioning his calm and steady expression helped me settle down and think.

"How long have you known Victor?" I asked.

"For a really really really really really long time."

"Wow, that's a... really long time. Who is he?"

"He's Victor."

"I know he's Victor but is he a friend of your family or does he work for you guys? Where did you meet him?"

"He's Micah's brother," Jason said then looked away guiltily as if he'd revealed something he wasn't supposed to.

"What do you mean? Victor doesn't look like either of you," I said, thinking the white man driving the car couldn't possibly be a blood relative of the Alexanders.

"You don't look like your sisters but you all are sisters," Jason pointed out defensively as if I'd accused him of lying.

"That's different," I said, before remembering my true identity. "I mean, your family never mentioned you have another brother when they had dinner with us," I reasoned.

"Victor's not my brother. He's Micah's brother," Jason said with slow emphasis as if he was explaining it to a child.

"How can he be your brother's brother without being your brother too?" I was getting confused and frustrated. Jason was talking nonsense and even though he was just a first grader, I expected him to have better sense than that.

"Is Victor adopted?" I asked. That would certainly explain the complete difference in race.

Jason shook his head no.

Suddenly Victor's frigid voice filled the back of the car, "Adisa, interrogating a child? I expected more from you. Leave Jason alone. I'll explain things to you during our stay together."

"How long do you plan on keeping us hostage?" I asked, angry he was eavesdropping and even angrier with myself for not suspecting that he would.

"Not long but I consider you my guest, not a hostage."

"I can't be classified as a guest because I don't consent to any of this!"

"Well, I believe you'll change your mind soon enough." His words sounded like a veiled threat.

"Don't bet on it. Do you think my parents will be happy about this?"

But he didn't answer.

"Mr. Alexander works with the police department so don't think you'll get away with this!"

He still didn't respond.

"Why are you being mean to Victor?" Jason asked.

I sat back, trying to calm down. "I'm upset with him for not letting me go home. I have a lot of obligations and I don't have time for... surprises!"

Jason didn't comment and I decided not to upset him further by impressing upon him the illegal actions of his brother's brother. I determined a better use of my time was to discover as much as I could about my kidnapper.

"Victor has different parents from you and Micah. Right?"

Jason nodded.

"So how can he be Micah's brother? Are they play brothers?"

"No. They're real brothers. They're twins."

I was stunned. How could they be twins? The age difference alone would have been too great. Micah was a young boy and this was a grown man. Then I had an uneasy thought. When Micah had spoken of his dad's super twin, I naturally assumed it had the same meaning as in the earthbound world, babies who share the same womb and birth date. Could the word twin have a different meaning in the Sp. world?

"Are they... *super* twins?" Even though Micah said his family was aware of his superpowers, I still felt as if I was betraying his secret by saying it out loud.

"Yes!" Jason said and appeared pleased. "Micah told you about all that? We usually have to keep it secret. I can't believe he told you."

"Well he didn't really tell me. I saw him fly. Then we talked about it and I found out not only can he fly but he's very strong and fast and he said he didn't lie. Is that true, he can't lie?" I asked, still somewhat doubtful.

Jason nodded. "He can't ever tell a lie. But his best thing is flying. Did he take you flying? That's a lot of fun. He takes me in the woods sometimes so nobody sees and he flies me all over the place. But only if I behave in school.

The first time he took me was after we had dinner at your house. He wanted to know what we did when you took me up to your room but I wouldn't tell him. But he kept asking so I made him promise to take me flying before I told him. I guess he really wanted to find out about you because that never worked before. He didn't used to ever let me fly with him until then."

Jason's words spilled out as if relieved to finally be free to share the long held secrets. I listened to his chatter unable to make complete sense of his words but hoping they held some clue to how we could escape.

"I like him more since we moved here, too," Jason babbled on, glad to have somebody he could talk to unguarded. "He's different, in a good kind of way. Now he's more like a real brother is supposed to be, like Victor is. Victor always played with me even before we moved here but not Micah. But now Micah plays with me too. And it's even more fun than playing with Victor."

"Thanks a lot kid!" Victor voiced sarcastically.

Jason laughed. "Well I can't help it if you can't fly. Flying's the best."

If I wasn't in a state of shock, I would've agreed with him. It dawned on me that Micah had never offered to take me on a flight just for fun. I couldn't believe in all the time we spent during my Sp. education, I'd never even considered asking him to take me. I sat mute, listening to the playful exchange between Jason and our captor.

"Since flying is so great, I guess I won't take you sledding, skiing, or skating anymore," the voice coolly threatened.

"Okay! Okay. I like playing with you both. Victor, I'm hungry. Are we almost there?"

"Not yet. I could pull into a drive through and get something for you. Any specific requests?"

I straightened up thinking I might get the opportunity to attract somebody's attention at a fast food restaurant. Maybe yell out or bang on something.

"I want a cheeseburger without all the lettuce and tomato stuff and some French fries with ketchup."

"One cheeseburger plain and French fries but no ketchup. I don't want you messing up my seat back there. How about you Adisa, are you hungry?"

The way he said hungry sent chills up my spine. I didn't respond, still busy formulating what I could do to let somebody know I was being held against my will.

"I guess it's just as well. Nothing for you. Oh, and Adisa, don't go getting any ideas. It's soundproof back there once I turn the intercom off. So behave because you don't want me to take my belt off and come back there." I could hear him laughing suggestively and my stomach twisted at the threat concealed in his words.

"Are you really going to spank Adisa?" Jason asked in innocent laughter. "Don't spank her, I like her."

"If she's naughty, I may have to punish her."

"I won't let you," Jason came to my defense.

"Oh, really. Well, we'll see about that," Victor's icy voice jeered playfully.

"I'll give you a Power Boy punch in the eye," Jason giggled, gesturing the motion as he spoke.

"I'd like to see you try," the voice challenged.

"You won't see it because my fist will be in your eye and your eye will be swelled up shut." Jason was laughing so hard he probably would've fallen off his seat if he hadn't been belted in.

I felt nervous listening too them and was disoriented because the blackout windows concealed the direction we were traveling in.

We drove for a long time before I felt the car finally slow down and come to a stop. I listened intently, trying to determine if we were in a drive through lane but I couldn't hear anything beyond the backseat enclosure.

I considered screaming, weighing the chances of my success against the amount of trauma it would cause Jason.

"Jason, I bet you can't yell louder than I can," I said, nervously.

"Nobody screams louder than me."

"Yeah, right. I bet you scream like a girl," I accused.

Jason's only response was an ear-splitting scream that took me completely by surprise.

"Now let's hear you," he challenged after he was done.

The shrill scream that ripped past my vocal chords stunned even me. Surely the whole of Georgia could hear me.

Jason looked at me with newfound respect in his wide eyes, clearly impressed. He felt he had to take another turn, claiming it was too close to call. He strained so hard trying to outdo my efforts, I thought he might actually hurt himself.

Then I had another go at it, attempting to give as much as Jason had. And then he took another turn and I joined in. We screamed in unison to see which of us drowned out the other.

When I felt the car start moving again, I stopped to try and hear what was going on outside our confines. Jason kept right on yelling.

After he stopped, the familiar icy voice declared, "Adisa wins on pure volume but you Jason, are the champion based on endurance."

"Ha ha, I'm the champion," Jason crowed with pride as my hope dwindled to nothing.

The partition came down and through the front window it appeared we were in the middle of nowhere on a dark country road.

I avoided Victor's eyes in the rearview mirror as he tossed a fast food bag to Jason and passed a drink to him as well. The food smelled delicious but mixed with my fear, it curdled my stomach. The darkness prevented me from seeing much but even if I could, I was sure I wouldn't recognize my surroundings. I worried what my parents must be thinking because they were home by now.

Jason was happily munching on his burger as Victor finished off his own sandwich. With the partition down, I could see the car's headlights reflecting off of trees on either side of the road.

We drove in silence after Jason finished his meal. It wasn't long before I felt him slump against me in sleep.

"Did you put something in his food?" I asked in alarm at how quickly the boy dropped off.

Victor's eyes registered surprise and then settled into their usual cold disdain. "Would you rather he be awake to see what I have in store for you?" A malicious smile twisted his handsome features in vulgar suggestion.

I put my arms protectively around Jason, seeking to console myself more than offer his oblivious form comfort. The partition went back up and I was relieved not to have to look at Victor's sinister face.

We drove a long time before coming to a final stop. The whole way, I'd been left to wonder about the Alexanders' relationship with Victor. Jason appeared to be completely unafraid of him and spoke as if he'd known Victor all of his life. The knowledge that Victor was Micah's Sp. twin was especially shocking. Why had Micah kept this from me?

How could the Alexanders allow such a dangerous person easy access to their sons, regardless of the Sp. twin relationship? And since he was apparently part of the super world, why wasn't Victor exhibiting the rigid emotionless posturing Micah had when his shield was up?

Maybe he didn't have superpowers. Maybe he was dormant. I sincerely hoped that he was because the thought of this dangerous individual possessing superhuman abilities frightened me. I didn't want to believe that I was actually in the presence of a super villain. It was beyond comprehension. How could I, a mere earthbound, fight against such a being?

The door next to Jason suddenly opened and Victor was reaching in, unclasping both our buckles with ease. He started to pick Jason up but I gripped the tiny form defensively.

"I'll do it!" I whispered insistently, trying not to wake Jason.

Victor's steely gaze never left my face as he backed off. I gathered Jason onto my lap and eased out of the car, careful not to bump him as I stood up. He wasn't very heavy so I managed okay.

We were inside a garage that resembled a giant cement box. The walls, ceiling, and floor were all made of the same gray solid material. The cold quickly penetrated my lightweight running outfit. Victor opened a sliding door, which was made of the same gray substance, and stood aside to allow me to pass.

I stepped into a larger cement box. The only comforts were a large bed, two folding chairs and a folding table, and a flat screen television. There was a small kitchen to one side of the room. To my utter amazement, there wasn't a single window anywhere.

There were two other doors, the same as the one to the garage. One was open, revealing its interior. I could see it was a small restroom without any windows. I wondered what the other door concealed.

"Put him on the bed," Victor instructed.

He pulled back the covers and I placed Jason on the bed, quickly slipping off his tennis shoes. Then Victor pulled the blanket up around him.

I backed away, hugging Jason's shoes close to my chest. Victor gave me the briefest glance and then hopped over Jason onto the bed and stretched out placing his hands behind his head. The jostling didn't disturb Jason's sleep.

"Your room is through there," Victor said nodding at the closed door.

I stood frozen to my spot, not knowing whether I should be relieved or not.

Seeing my hesitation, Victor grinned evilly. "Of course, you're welcome to share our bed if you like. But we must take care not to disturb Jason." He patted the space next to him, opposite from Jason.

There was something cold and calculating about his extraordinary eyes that pinned me in place. He waited for me to make a choice and I sensed his growing impatience.

"I'm sorry to frighten you this way but I assure you, it's for a good cause," he said as he slid off the bed.

He reached out and lightly stroked the line of my jaw with his cold fingers. I cringed just out of reach. "Micah has incredible taste but I must admit, you are a big surprise, nothing like I imagined. I've always wondered about Micah's fascination in you over the years but I never thought of you as having any real significance until...," He abruptly stopped himself as if realizing he was about to say too much.

My head ached in confusion. What did he mean by 'over the years?' Had he and Micah known me before the school year started? No, he was just trying to mess with my head. But why?

"You will be my guest for seven days," Victor said briskly, startling me with his revelation.

"Why?"

He smiled cruelly. "Because I want to feed you, Adisa."

When he saw my shocked expression, he seemed pleased and continued. "I certainly don't enjoy cooking but I have an ingredient that will make my food... irresistible.

Regardless, you should be familiar with the practice since your mother is very adamant about feeding strangers. So if it makes things easier for you, think of me as your mother."

Nothing about this stranger reminded me of my mom. Had he been watching us and knew about her volunteer work in the shelter's kitchen? I felt chilled to my heart thinking of him watching my family, watching me.

"So, tell me, what will it be, our bed here or door number one?" he asked.

Without further delay, I walked over to the door, deciding that it would be better if I stayed as far away from Victor as I possibly could. The room might even have a way to escape.

The smooth solid door had no doorknob and I transferred Jason's shoes to one hand so I could use my other one to search for a way to open it.

"Allow me," Victor's voice, right in my ear, startled me and I quickly moved aside. One thing he had in common with Micah was how quietly he moved.

The door glided open but I didn't see how he had done it.

"How did you do that?" I asked.

He held his hand out to me in invitation. "I'll show you."

The last thing I wanted was for him to touch me but I needed to know how to operate the doors if I wanted to escape. I placed my hand in his and gasped at how cold it was. He firmly gripped it, before I could withdraw, and pulled me closer to him.

"Pay close attention," his silky voice commanded and I couldn't help staring at him in hypnotic fascination. He was so close I could feel his breath on my face like a cool breeze. I could see now that he was only a young boy, easily the same age as Micah.

His dark eyes appeared bottomless and slowly moved over my face in humorous curiosity. I felt him sliding my hand inside his pocket and I briefly felt something solid before snatching my hand away in alarm.

I instinctively backed inside through the open door to get away from him, prepared to fight if I had to. I quickly looked past him to see if Jason had seen and was relieved to see his still form hadn't shifted from his original position on the bed.

Victor chuckled softly and reached into his pocket and withdrew a remote.

"Adisa," he said with wide eyed innocence, "whatever were you thinking?"

He laughed softly at his cruel joke just before he pressed a button on the remote and the door slid closed between us. I stood where I was, shivering for a long time before I could bring myself to investigate my new surroundings. A single light bulb in the middle of the ceiling lit the small space. The walls, ceiling, and floor were made of the same hard cold gray material. And still, not a single window in sight.

How could a house not have any windows? It was like a giant coffin. Was this where I would die and if so, what form would my death take? I shivered, wrapping my arms around myself and realized I still had Jason's shoes. For some reason, this brought tears to my eyes and I cradled them close as I explored the room.

A cot with a neatly folded blanket took up one corner and another knob-less door was in the center of one of the walls. I wondered if it led outdoors but doubted it. I dropped Jason's shoes and ran my hands over the entire surface of the door but it wouldn't budge.

Suddenly I felt claustrophobic and the thought of defenseless Jason, sharing a bed with that coldhearted monster sent me running back to the door I'd entered through. I tried knocking on it but it hurt my knuckles and didn't make much sound.

"Victor," I called and the door slid open almost immediately.

The sound of the television leaped out at me. Victor was back on the bed, watching a news program. I realized my room was soundproof because I hadn't heard the television until the door opened.

"What do you want?" Victor asked without looking at me.

"Is it okay if Jason stayed with me?" I asked haltingly.

He gave me a brief sneer before turning back to the news. "That cot's barely big enough for you. However, the invitation to share our bed out here is still open."

I cringed in dissent. "What do you want from me?" I asked, changing the subject.

"I already told you."

"How long do you plan on," I hesitated significantly, "feeding me?"

He looked directly at me. "Like I said before, seven days."

I shuddered, wondering how I would be able to endure it. "How do I know you're telling me the truth?"

"I don't lie."

A surge of hope went through me. If he was incapable of lying and I could get him to promise to free us unharmed… maybe I could save us.

"So, you're like Micah. You can't tell a lie."

"No. Micah can't tell a lie. I choose not to lie. Which do you think is more noble?" he asked in a surprisingly conversational tone.

I didn't want to participate in any games comparing Micah and Victor because hands down, Micah would win and I feared Victor's reaction.

"Is it okay if I use your restroom?" I asked, dodging his question as I realized I had a real need to go.

He was off the bed and at my side in a single smooth motion, sending me stumbling back into my small room. He reached into his pocket and the door slid closed behind him.

I felt trapped with him in the small space and was alert, prepared to defend myself by any means necessary. Maybe he restrained himself from harming me in Jason's presence but now that wasn't a problem. I was tense, wondering if Victor was about to make a move and I mentally ran through defensive moves I could use to protect myself.

Victor walked over to the door in the center of the wall and it slid open revealing an even smaller restroom than the one in the outer room. It held a sink, toilette, cabinet, and shower stall with a clear shower curtain.

I eased around Victor and stepped inside the cramped space and waited for the door to slide close behind me. When it didn't, I turned around in confusion. Victor was leaning against a wall watching me. I felt sick to my stomach as I realized what he planned on doing.

"Are you going to watch?" my voice squeaked, incredulous.

His face held no expression. "I can't chance you escaping."

"And how would I do that?" I said, turning around in place, emphasizing I had no means of escape. "Through the drain?"

Victor laughed in surprise but didn't elaborate.

"I'm not Houdini you know!" I flung out in frustration.

"There are towels in the cabinet you can use to cover up as you relieve yourself and the shower curtain is clear but it distorts so I can't see details."

I was completely stunned. He really expected me to carry out my most private restroom activities with him watching. I wouldn't allow my own family to do that, let alone a complete stranger.

"There's also clothing and toiletries in the cabinet," he said with finality.

Suddenly I felt small and defenseless as I realized how much time it must have taken for him to plan everything. This was no spur of the moment kidnapping. Whatever his intentions, he was serious and I had little hope of escaping.

"Victor, please," I pleaded.

His mouth went into a firm line and his eyes turned cold. "This isn't a negotiation, Adisa. Hurry up before your restroom privileges come to an end. Because once they do, I put you to bed and all the doors close and I'm not getting up again until morning."

I felt sticky and gritty from my run and I really had to go. So I set out towels and a change of clothing, which to my embarrassed surprise included underwear.

Then in resignation, I fumbled around with the largest towel, trying to figure out how best to conceal myself with one hand while attending to my needs with the other. Finally in frustration, I pleaded with Victor one last time.

"This isn't going to work. I can't even change in front of other girls for gym. There's no way I'll be able to go with you watching." I hated hearing my voice shake, knowing I was on the verge of tears.

Victor snorted with real impatience before abruptly saying, "I'll give you ten minutes but I'll have to make it freezing in there."

"Okay. Anything, just as long as I have privacy," I gushed in relief.

I expected him to go adjust the temperature controls but he remained where he was and the temperature suddenly plummeted.

"Oh!" I expelled as if I'd taken a physical blow to the stomach.

I was instantly doubled over and my arms defensively wrapped around me to ward off the assaulting cold. I looked at Victor in confusion. His lips were barely parted and it appeared he was blowing out but it was so subtle I couldn't be certain.

"Ten minutes then it's open sesame," he said, then the door quickly slid shut.

I was shivering violently and didn't want to move. He wasn't kidding about making it freezing. I could barely breathe and was momentarily transfixed by the wispy cloud of my breath.

I remembered his ten minute warning and began fumbling with my clothes, my fingers stiff and sore from the cold. I kept a large towel within hand's reach in case the door flew open unexpectedly.

I tried not to think of Victor standing just outside the door as I finally relieved myself. My teeth chattered so sharply the noisy staccato reminded me of the clickety clack raised on typewriters by secretaries in old black and white movies.

I pulled off my clothes and stepped behind the shower curtain. I could see blurred shapes through it but as Victor had stated, I couldn't see any details.

My hands trembled as I adjusted the water flow, keeping it at a trickle, so as not to get drenched while washing myself, fearing if I did, I'd freeze solid.

The water never got anywhere close to hot. I quickly lathered up then gingerly rinsed before roughly drying off. Then I stiffly pulled on a change of clothing while still standing in the shower. The clothes he'd provided were very loose, the oversized top fell to my knees over the baggy pants.

I felt the contents of my jogging pants pocket as I gathered them up and nearly fell out of the stall as I realized my cell phone had been there all along. Unbelievable! Even after having it for so long, I still forgot I had one.

I debated whether or not I had enough time remaining to try and make a call before Victor opened the door. My nerves got the best of me and I put the cell phone along with the birth certificate I always kept with me in the large pocket of my loose fitting garment.

I finally stepped out of the shower as the door sprung open. Victor didn't look the least bit ashamed of himself and I mentally berated myself for hoping that he would. I tried not to think of how close he'd come to catching me with my cell.

I wondered what to do with my dirty clothing as I stood shivering. Then put them on a bottom empty shelf in the cabinet. Victor allowed me to brush my teeth but it was without benefit of a mirror because there wasn't one available.

He closed the restroom door after I came out then closed the bedroom door too after he left without a word. I released a huge sigh of relief that I wouldn't have to fight him off as I had imagined.

The slight chill of the room was a relief after the unnatural freezing temperature in the restroom. My stomach growled but there was no way I was going to call Victor back and ask for something to eat. With my luck, he'd probably encase it in a block of ice.

I pulled my phone out of my pocket and turned it on. I could see it roaming for a signal before the message that one didn't exist popped up. I moved around my confines trying to find a signal but couldn't get one. I put my phone away in defeat.

The cot looked small and uninviting. I considered turning off the light but then decided against it. I wondered what my parents were doing. They must be out of their minds with worry by now.

I picked up Jason's shoes and curled up on the cot with them, pulling the blanket over me to block out my scary predicament. But my nightmare followed me into my dreams. Something was chasing me and I couldn't get away from it. It pursued me for hours. Then Micah was there, scattering all my fears in a rain of kisses.

"Everything will be all right, Adisa. Stay strong," he commanded.

I had the distinct impression that someone had just called my name. I drowsily floated in darkness while my ears pursued in what direction the sound of my name had come from. I wasn't alone.

I bolted up on the cot, realizing I was living the same nightmare from the day before. Victor sat on one of the folding chairs and indicated I should take the other one on the opposite side of the table.

The door behind him was open and I could see Jason wearing headphones, the old fashioned kind that completely covered his ears and holding a remote that allowed him to play a game on the flat screen TV. He didn't look hurt or traumatized in any way.

"So he won't disturb us," Victor explained kindly and I was shocked by the change in his personality. He'd seemed so menacing the day before. Now, he appeared to be genuinely nice. It was disconcerting in my drowsy state.

I picked up the scent of something delicious and was up off the cot without thinking. Jason's shoes fell to the floor unheeded as I hurried over to see what smelled so wonderful.

Victor smiled at me and I realized he was incredibly good looking and really closer to Micah's age than I'd initially thought, not like the man I saw last night. His straight black hair and dark glittering eyes contrasted against his pale skin, giving his handsome features a dramatic look.

I quickly lowered my eyes to the food on the table when I realized I was staring. It was soup. What was up with Sp. beings and soup? Micah's offerings on the mountain had always been delicious and smelled wonderful. But the soup on the table smelled even more amazing and I was sure it would taste even better. I felt a small pang of guilt for thinking that Victor's soup could possibly be better than Micah's.

"Good evening, Adisa," he said.

Evening! Was it really that late?

"Have a seat. You must be starving since you missed dinner last night and both breakfast and lunch today. I thought it best to wake you for dinner so you wouldn't waste away to nothing while in my care. You're already so thin."

"You sound like my mom," I grumbled, momentarily lulled by his good mood as I slid onto the chair. Then I became suspicious. Did Victor really just want to feed me? Why? Maybe he put something in the food.

I felt disoriented as it dawned on me how late it was. Was it really evening or was Victor simply playing mind games? Then I remembered he said he didn't lie and I mentally started working on a plan to keep me and Jason safe and hopefully get us free.

"So, you know about our Sp. world." It was a statement, not a question so I didn't respond. "Well, that'll make things a lot easier on me, now that I don't have to deal with the code of silence. Exactly how much do you know about us?"

I refused to answer as I tried to figure out how best to negotiate a quick release. But it was hard to concentrate due to the distracting aroma of the soup which was the only thing cutting through the grogginess of my thoughts.

Victor became impatient. His eyes narrowed and his voice took on a threatening tone. "You know Adisa, I'm aware that threatening you with violence probably wouldn't get me very far. However, if Jason was the object of my anger... I would hate to prove to you that I'm willing to do whatever is necessary to get what I want."

I was surprised by his swift mood change and quickly explained what I knew. "I don't know a whole lot, just that you have an organized society with its own rules and regulations. Superbeings sometimes marry into the earthbound world. And your life span is like ours and you have a variety of powers. And...," but I couldn't think of anything else.

"Now that wasn't so hard was it? And nobody had to get hurt." He sounded as if he was already back to his good mood. "Did you sleep well last night?"

"Yes, thank you," I answered automatically.

"Good. I've prepared something for you to eat. Are you hungry?"

"I want to make a deal with you," I blurted out, wanting to take advantage of his good mood.

He looked at me curiously.

"I'll do anything you want, if you promise to let Jason and me go unharmed after it's over," I said in a rush.

"Anything I want?" he asked with suggestive emphasis.

I nodded, intentionally not repeating the 'unharmed' part. I hoped his focus on the 'anything' part would cause him to agree and then I would hold him to his word, reminding him at that time of the 'unharmed' part.

Victor stared at me in silence before quietly stating, "I can't promise that you won't be harmed."

I quickly understood that I would most likely suffer and that worried me. But he didn't try to bluff me with a lie! He could've lied and gotten what he wanted from me without a fight, all the while intending to hurt me in the end. Maybe it was true. Maybe he really didn't lie.

"Can you at least promise to let Jason go unharmed?" I asked as I quickly glanced at Jason, innocently playing his game, oblivious to the danger we were in.

"Agreed, if you do anything I ask." Victor smiled as if enjoying a private joke but I put my trust in him anyway because I had no other choice. I sought comfort in knowing that I had at least saved Jason.

I felt trapped and alone. "Would it be okay if we could spend some time together, me and Jason. I think it will make things easier for all of us."

"Sure," Victor quickly consented, surprising me.

Then his tone and manner completely changed and I was filled with dread as he announced in an icy voice devoid of even a fraction of warmth, "Now, no more stalling. It's time to get down to business."

These are the seven days of my captivity.

Day 1: chicken noodle soup

"To ward off the chill in the air," Victor explained as he slowly pushed the steaming bowl toward me. The mouth watering fragrance rising off the soup's surface filled me with a deep craving. "It also gives a sense of familial love but...," he paused dramatically, "is that love altered if the family is false?"

My heart skipped a beat as the implication of his words seeped in. False families, families that were not true. Did Victor know my secret?

"What's your name?" Victor asked.

"You know my name. It's Adisa Summers." I tried to sound calm but every fiber of my being felt electrified with the knowledge that Victor knew my secret.

"He hasn't told you who you really are?" he said, his eyes never leaving my face.

"Who?" I asked in a hoarse whisper.

"Micah."

Hadn't I suspected Micah knew? If he did know, why hadn't he told me after all this time. But if I suspected, why didn't I have the courage to confront him about it?

Victor's sinister voice cut through my chaotic thoughts. "You don't even know who you really are, Adisa. Strange thing families, not always what they appear to be."

Victor casually stirred the soup, releasing more of the incredible aroma. I'd never smelled anything more delicious in my life and that was saying something considering what a superior cook mom was.

I had to jam my hands into my lap under the table to prevent myself from snatching the soup from Victor and drinking it straight from the bowl. I tried to concentrate on his words to distract myself.

"You've heard of the cuckoo bird I'm sure. Well, some of them have a curious habit." Victor maintained an icy calm tone as he disclosed his story. "The mama cuckoo does not make a nest. She lays her eggs in the nest of another bird. And the unsuspecting bird then raises the baby cuckoo as its own."

I felt as if he'd thrown a bucket of ice water in my face. Not only was he revealing that the Summers were not my true family, he was calling my real mom crazy! How could he speak so callously about my family. I wanted to hurt him like he was hurting me.

"Look at you and look at the Summers," Victor mused. "Do you really think you came from them, Adisa?"

In that moment, Victor was pure evil to me. After everything he'd already done, now he was heartlessly passing on this shocking information and probably enjoying it. He was trying to take my family away from me emotionally as well as physically. How dare he know more about me than I knew about myself.

Well I had a shock for him. I already knew! Propelled by an angry desire to wipe the superior gloating look off his face, I snatched out the contents of my pocket and threw it in his face.

I was so angry, I didn't realize I had grabbed my cell phone along with my birth certificate until I saw it bounce off his jaw. Victor didn't even flinch.

"I already know they're not my real family. So take your squawking bird stories out of here and let me see Jason like you promised!" I shouted vehemently.

I saw Jason snatch off his headphones. "What's wrong?"

"Everything's fine Jason," Victor quickly smoothed over. "Remember our agreement."

Jason hesitated and then put his headphones back on and turned back to his game again.

Victor gave me an icy smile. "I'm sure you've already discovered that you can't place a call from inside these walls. I built this place specifically to keep you from getting out but fortunately for me, the material in these walls also blocks cell phone transmissions."

Victor reached into his pocket and the door behind him slid shut, blocking us from Jason's view. "It appears I've underestimated you, Adisa. I'll do my best to never make that mistake again."

He was up in the blink of an eye and had me in his arms, his cold hands authoritatively roaming my body. They paused briefly when he discovered my pearl and his mouth twisted into an ironic smile. I shoved against him alarmed but couldn't break free. His hands continued to search until they were satisfied I wasn't concealing anymore surprises before finally releasing me.

Then he quickly searched the entire room which took no time at all since it only had a cot, blanket, two chairs and the table. He even checked the inside of Jason's tennis shoes. He scooped up my phone and birth certificate, depositing the certificate in his pocket. He held the phone in his hand and it seemed to frost over. Then he squeezed it and it shattered in his hand.

Then he quickly searched the restroom, shaking out my clothes, feeling inside my shoes, and moving things around to look inside, under or behind them.

After his search was complete, he closed the restroom door and sat back down. "Sit!" he hissed, as his hand impatiently raked his dark hair back from his eyes.

But I was still too shaken by his abrupt and intrusive handling of me to obey his command. I stood in a corner with my arms wrapped around me, hugging myself as I shuddered with revulsion.

Victor swore under his breath and was up again in an instant. My first instinct was to fight back. I thought of kicking him but he was already too close for it to be effective. So I prepared to grab him to use as a counterbalance as I drove my knee into his sensitive area and then shove the heel of my hand up into his nose.

My hesitation gave him the advantage as he easily side stepped my efforts and twisted me around, lifting me with ease then placed me in my chair with more care than I had expected and held me in place.

"You nearly got me, Adisa. Better luck next time," he whispered harshly in my ear before releasing me. I was too stunned to move, realizing how easily he could have destroyed me. The soup's intoxicating aroma engulfed me and all the fight drained from me as I sat awaiting my fate.

Victor sat down again and observed me with something akin to admiration. "Eat!"

This time, I automatically did as he ordered, lifting a spoon full of the hot soup without hesitation. The delicious flavor filled my mouth with wonder and I quickly took another spoon full even though I wasn't completely finished with the first.

I mentally tried to make myself slow down. I was so taken by the dish that I forgot to be self conscious about Victor watching me as I continued to ravenously consume the chicken and noodle ambrosia.

"I apologize," Victor said as I continued to gulp down the soup. "I lost my temper for a moment but it was over my own carelessness. You're full of surprises, Adisa. I can see why Micah is so... intrigued."

By the time he finished his apology, the bowl was empty. A sharp sense of regret filled me as I scraped my spoon across the bottom of the empty bowl in disbelief that something so magnificent had come to such a swift end.

"May I have some more, please?" I asked, trembling with the intensity of my need.

Victor leaned forward, his glittering eyes staring at me expectantly. "There isn't any more. How do you feel?"

His question filled me with uneasiness, curbing my disappointment over none being left. "Fine," I said in a small voice, cringing away to put more distance between us.

He continued to watch me for awhile longer.

The time lengthened and I finally grew impatient with the wait. "Is it okay if Jason came in now?" I asked, realizing I had completed his request.

Victor sat back in resignation. Then impatiently stood and quickly cleaned up the cell phone debris. His hand went into his pocket and the door slid open.

Jason was still playing his game.

"Jason. Come and see Adisa," Victor called out.

Jason instantly took off his headphones and came into the room. My arms reached for him and he let me hug him.

"Are you all right?" I asked, feeling uneasy.

"Sure," he answered as if it was a stupid thing to ask. "I'm playing a great game Victor bought for me. Do you want to play?"

"No. Adisa has to stay in here," Victor interjected.

"Ahhh come on, Vic. Why can't she...," Jason's voice ceased its whining at Victor's severe look.

I clutched Jason to me tightly, glad to have him with me and pleased beyond belief that he was okay.

"Adisa. You're squeezing too hard," he protested, squirming in my grip.

"Sorry," I said, loosening my hold but refusing to release him. "After this is all over with, you'll get to go back home. Victor promised."

Jason gave me a curious look and I thought he didn't believe me. "Didn't you promise Victor?" I asked so he could confirm it.

"Of course," Victor said without hesitation.

Relieved at his easy admission, I began questioning Jason. "Are you hungry? Did you get anything to eat?"

"I'm stuffed. Victor made pancakes for breakfast and then we had Chili cheese dogs for lunch and spaghetti and meatballs for dinner and chocolate cake for dessert."

So I really had slept a whole day. Satisfied that Jason was okay, my thoughts turned to my own family.

"Victor," I began tentatively, "my family must be worried to death...,"

"Jason, go back to your game," Victor ordered abruptly.

"No! Not yet. He just got here," I quickly objected.

"Let him go, Adisa. We have things to discuss in private." His steely voice left no room to equivocate.

I reluctantly released Jason and watched him as he happily returned to his game.

Victor said in a low voice, "You must behave yourself, Adisa or I won't let you see Jason at all."

"But you promised and you can't lie," I reminded him in desperation.

"I choose not to lie," he corrected. "But I assumed you would prefer not to see him at all rather than have him spend time with you while you're bound and gagged."

My jaw dropped in disbelief. "You wouldn't dare." But the cold look in his eyes told me otherwise. "Okay, I'll behave."

"Good, no more alluding to your kidnapping around Jason. As for your parents... the less they know, the better. I'll give you a restroom break now then you get some rest. I'll feed you again, tomorrow."

After we were done, Victor collected the folding chairs and table and left. I stared at the closed door that separated us, feeling completely defeated.

The floor was cold so I curled up on my cot with the blanket wrapped around me. I was sinking into despair and had to mentally give myself a shake. I'll fight him again! It was hard to think about fighting when Victor was actually present but I had managed it, even though my efforts were completely futile. I had no doubt Victor would easily win again but I'd rather fight than give up without trying.

Then I remembered Victor's promise. Jason would be safe. I didn't want to jeopardize that. I thought of my family and Micah and school and church. All the people who would miss me if I never returned. I'd already survived one day, only six more to go and I might be reunited with them.

Why was Victor doing this? Was it some kind of revenge on Micah or the Alexanders? Did it have anything to do with my true identity?

I drifted off to sleep. Micah and Victor were fighting. Each had one of my arms and was pulling.

Micah's grip was warm and comforting while Victor's was cold and more insistent. I could feel myself slipping from Micah's grip.

"Hold me tighter," I pleaded with him.

I could see the panic in Micah's eyes as he struggled to maintain his hold without harming me.

"Too late brother," Victor's voice taunted. "She's mine now."

Then they morphed into my sisters, Kelly pulling me one way and Kylie pulling me another.

"You're putting too much smoke on her eyes, Kel! She can't see."

"What do you care, Ky? She's not even our real sister," Kelly retorted.

Then Mr. Winton was there. "That's no way to treat your dance partner. Watch me," he insisted. Then he danced off, angrily twirling Ms. Becket along with him.

"I can't keep up," I sobbed, stumbling as Avery danced me around the gym.

"You could if you wanted to," he accused.

"I can't," I insisted.

"You can! You just don't want to forgive Liz."

"No Avery. It's not true. I forgave her."

"You forgave Victor?" Micah asked, as he held me gently but firmly, guiding me with the utmost care around the floor.

"No! I'll never forgive Victor," I swore.

"But you have to. He's my brother."

"I don't care. I'm never forgiving him for what he's done to me."

"Please, Adisa, for me."

"I can't. I won't."

Then I felt the warm pressure of his lips on mine and I hugged him tight so I wouldn't lose him again.

"I love you so much," I breathed against his lips, closing my eyes as I kissed him back.

His lips became more insistent and then turned cold.

I pulled away and to my horror discovered it was Victor. "Please, Adisa, forgive me," he pleaded in desperation.

Day 2: bread

"What!?" I asked in shocked confusion.

"I said, let's forgive each other by breaking bread together."

I struggled to a seated position on my cot, groggily surveying my room.

Victor was once again seated at the folding table, a small loaf of fresh baked bread sitting in front of him.

"Oh, goodness, that smells incredible," I said, scurrying off my cot and over to the table.

A wisp of steam rose from the loaf and dissipated in the chilled air.

Victor smiled pleasantly. "Thank you, Adisa. Have a seat."

I quickly sat down, barely able to wait for him to invite me to eat.

"You know, Jesus and his disciples broke bread together. We do it to strengthen family ties and form bonds of friendship. So, let's break bread, Adisa. Be my friend," he said as he offered me a piece of bread.

I snatched it from his hands, wishing he would shut up so I could eat in peace. My senses felt overwhelmed and my hands shook as I crammed the bread into my mouth. Delicious explosions of warm buttery flavors coursed through my body and I had to briefly put my head down on the table to stop my world from spinning.

Victor watched me eat, offering me one piece after another, as if it gave him greater pleasure to feed me than I took in eating. "Tell me, Adisa, do you ever wonder who your real parents are?"

I stopped eating. What was he up to this time?

When I didn't answer, he continued. "Who has your family broken bread with recently?"

I decided to play along to see what I could find out. "It's hard to say because my mom's mission in life is to quite literally feed the world."

He smiled, "Yes, but who are the most recent newcomers you've entertained in your home, broken bread with at your very own table."

I nervously accepted another piece of bread from him before asking, "Does cornbread count?"

He laughed. "Of course."

"Then, that would be the Alexanders but I'm sure you already knew that."

His dark eyes danced delightedly. "Maybe you'll find the answers to your true parentage lies with the Alexanders."

I swallowed the last of the bread as he said this, wondering uneasily if I was related to the Alexanders. Could I be a long lost sister of Micah's, and that's why Mr. Alexander objected to our association, fearing it would turn romantic? My stomach churned as I tried to shove the frightening thought away. *I'm mahogany not copper!* I mentally chanted over and over to console myself.

When Victor finally allowed Jason in to visit with me, I looked the boy over closely, still wondering. It couldn't be true. Victor was just playing mind games with me. Micah said he had no boundaries but he would never...

I clutched Jason close as I listened to his enthusiastic description of his most recent game. Five more days and then he would be safe. I thought of Micah. There was no way he'd be able to find me. How could he? He had saved my life three times, three strikes and he was finally out. I would try to repay him by saving the life of his little brother. I could do it. It wasn't difficult... yet.

Day 3: vegetables

"Have you heard of Veggie Tales, Adisa? I actually learned about them through Jason. An interesting concept, Veggie Tales; children's Bible stories told using animated vegetables as the characters. The idea being, the tales of the Bible are good for us, like vegetables are good for us, but since we don't like vegetables, we need to make them more appealing.

So, the lessons of the Bible are transformed into entertaining animated stories starring vegetables. However, this concept implies we are resistant to that which is good for us and therefore need it to be forced or tricked upon us.

I've steamed these vegetables especially for you, Adisa. I've added something special to make them even more palatable. It makes my dishes irresistible. Eat up, they're good for you."

I didn't need a second invitation. The earthy aroma of the colorful dish was a feast in and of itself. I tried not to eat too fast so I could enjoy it longer. The distinct taste of each vegetable flavor stood out. Rather than compete against each other, the carrots, broccoli, onions, peppers, squash, and tomatoes enhanced the flavor of each beyond what it could attain on its own.

"Did Micah cook for you, Adisa?"

I nodded suspiciously. It seemed that every time I was in the middle of enjoying my meal, he interrupted with something upsetting. It was as if he was intentionally trying to ruin my enjoyment of the food.

"Do you know if he ever put anything in your food?"

My fork clattered noisily against the empty bowl. What was he hinting at? He always spoke in code. Then it dawned on me. He wasn't talking about Micah. He was talking about himself.

He was putting something in my food! I had suspected it in the beginning but had become hypnotized by the incredible flavors. Now his words reawakened my paranoia. What was it, poison? How could anything poisonous taste so good?

Victor sat quietly with me for awhile, as he always did after I finished eating. I wanted to ask him so many questions but fear and pride kept my tongue in check.

"No. I don't think he put anything in your food. He considers himself too noble to stoop so low," Victor answered his own question.

"Unlike you," I accused.

Victor's dark eyes never wavered from mine. His voice was low, frostily emphasizing each word. "Sometimes, my dear, nobility can be a very selfish quality."

"I think that being noble is a quality we should all strive for," I stated defiantly. "It's obvious you're jealous of Micah because he has managed to attain it and you apparently have not."

Victor clutched his chest in a mocking gesture. "You wound me deeply."

"I doubt it."

"Which is more noble, the saint who is not tempted by sin and easily resists it or the sinner, who chooses not to sin and struggles to do so successfully, every waking hour?"

"You think the one who struggles is more noble, don't you?" I accused.

"Yes!" he snarled and his eyes flashed with deep seated pain, born from years of resentment. "To go unrecognized in the presence of one who has not earned his adulation but was born to it, jealousy is a word too frail to describe what I feel. It's not expansive enough to capture the depths of my emotions when it comes to Micah."

"Why do you hate him? It's not his fault if people prefer him over you."

"I don't hate Micah. Quite the contrary. I'm trying to save him."

"By destroying me!" I retorted, thinking of Micah's lifelong struggle to become a Guardian and how I complicated things. I laughed bitterly as I thought of FLEET and Mr. Alexander. Now I could add Victor to the list.

"Because he doesn't have the guts to do what's necessary to get what he wants," Victor retorted.

"If you're so jealous of Micah, why are you helping him?" I asked.

"It's far more complicated than mere jealousy. He's my Sp. twin. If you had been raised as a Sp. being, that alone would explain everything."

When Jason was finally allowed in, I sat on my cot holding him, taking comfort in his chatter. I was happy he was able to keep his spirits up. I didn't think I would've been able to cheer him up had he needed it.

Day 4: oatmeal

"Have you heard the story of the three little bears? Of course, they used porridge, which is actually oatmeal. I assure you, Adisa, this is neither too hot nor too cold. It's just right.

Would you like to sit on my lap while I tell you a story? No? Well, have it your way," he smiled wickedly as I fidgeted in my seat, trying to ignore the innuendo in his words.

Victor stirred the oatmeal slowly before spooning a portion up and offering it to me. I hesitated, imagining the suffering poison could inflict. But the irresistible aroma won out and I opened my mouth.

I shuddered as the warm moist delicious flavor of oats filled my senses and brought tears to my eyes. Surely nothing so incredibly luscious could ever harm me.

I considered asking Victor straight out about the poison since he wouldn't lie. But when he offered another spoon full and there was no hesitation on my part to take it, I decided I would rather not know for sure.

What difference would it make? I'd still eat to save Jason even if I didn't find the food so irresistible. I accepted another spoon full and Victor began telling his story.

"Once upon a time there were three little bears, the mama bear, we'll call her Kylie, the papa bear, Kelly of course, and the baby bear. Can you guess the name of the baby bear?" he asked.

"Adisa?"

"Such a bright child," he proclaimed as he deposited another spoonful of creamy hot oats in my mouth. "The mama and papa bears were always too extreme, too hot or cold, too soft or hard. However, the baby bear was always just right. Perfect."

Ironically, I miscalculated the next spoon full and got some oatmeal on the side of my mouth. Before I could wipe it away, Victor used the spoon to scoop it off and successfully deposit it in my mouth. I felt like a big baby but didn't protest because I didn't want to interrupt the flow of hot oatmeal.

"Are you perfect Adisa or have you been ruined?"

I looked at him suspiciously. "Are you trying to insult me?"

"Why in the world would I do that?" he asked innocently.

"Because you're evil and take pleasure in upsetting me!"

Victor burst out laughing which took me by surprise. The sound filled the room as he rocked back in his chair. His eyes were shiny when he finally settled down.

"You keep that up, Adisa, and I just might fall in love with you myself," he said, grasping my hand and pressing it against his chest for emphasis.

I savagely ripped my hand away, almost falling over backwards. Victor's quick reflexes steadied me then he offered me another spoon full of steaming oats.

"Now eat!" he commanded in a hard voice.

When the bowl was empty, we sat in our usual expectant silence. He looked frustrated as he finally called Jason in. He watched us, brooding from his chair, as we sat huddled on the cot.

Jason wasn't as animated as he usually was. I thought that maybe he was finally starting to get bored with the DVD games Victor had stocked piled and perhaps he was beginning to miss his parents and brother.

"Cat got your tongue today?" I teased, trying to coax him into a better mood.

He quickly glanced at Victor who appeared to be deep in thought. Then he turned to me and whispered, "I think he's putting something in your food."

I felt as if the wind had been knocked out of me. So it was true. Victor was poisoning me. Why was it taking so long? Was he inept or conflicted? Why didn't he give me a dose that would end it once and for all?

Then I felt guilty for selfishly thinking of myself. Jason had witnessed somebody he apparently cared about, trying to poison me and it scared him.

"No way," I denied, avoiding his eyes. "It was probably just some seasoning," I whispered and then thought hopefully maybe it actually was.

"When I asked him about it he wouldn't answer me."

My heart sank as I realized Victor was omitting in order not to lie.

Jason stared earnestly into my face. "Is he hurting you, Adisa?"

I was touched by his concern. "No. He hasn't hurt me," I tried to reassure him.

"Jason!"

We both jumped at the explosive sound.

"What are you two whispering about?" Victor's frigid tone made me shiver.

Jason stared defiantly at Victor but didn't respond.

"It's nothing," I dismissed, fearing a rift between them would not go well for Jason.

"Visiting hours are over. Back to your games kid," Victor practically growled at the boy.

Jason didn't budge and I had to walk him to the door to get him moving. He clung to my hand and I didn't want to let go either but I knew his safety was in the balance. So I gave his hand a final squeeze then pulled mine away. Jason slowly went and sat on the bed but he didn't resume playing his game.

Victor stood, glowering coldly at me. "What are you up to?"

"Nothing!" I insisted, backing away before hurrying to the safety of my cot. I hated him for making me feel like a coward.

Day 5: cake

I awoke to the sound of singing.

Victor entered singing Happy Birthday while carrying a miniature cake with a lit candle in the center of it. His voice wasn't half bad and gave a festive flair to the song.

He walked over and knelt beside my cot as he said, "My apologies for this belated birthday celebration but I didn't get an invitation to your sweet sixteen."

His hand went in his pocket and the door slid shut before I could see what Jason was up to. "But then, we hadn't been properly introduced at that time," he continued.

I scrambled to a seated position, feeling vulnerable lying down while he was so close. I was immediately drawn to the delicious smell of the cake. Whatever he was putting in my food was transforming it into an exquisite assault on my senses.

"Do you remember your first kiss with Micah?" Victor asked abruptly. He did enjoy shocking me and it irritated me that he was so good at it.

I showed my defiance by not responding. I wasn't about to share my intimate business with him.

"Do you?" he repeated icily.

I capitulated, staring at the beautiful cake he held inches from my face. "Yes, on Kennesaw Mountain," I confessed in a low voice, unable to meet his eyes.

I remembered how I had initiated it, covering Micah's cheeks in kisses, being startled by his kiss on my neck before finally having the courage to kiss his lips. But of course, I didn't share all the details with Victor.

Victor looked surprised. "Au contraire, mon cheri. Your first time wasn't on top of Kennesaw Mountain. It was at the bottom of Lake Lanier."

Impossible, I thought. I'd never been to the bottom of Lake… Then I remembered the bus crash. Micah had saved me but he never mentioned kissing me. My mind dredged up an old dream, being kissed in the black abyss of a yellow school bus. But that couldn't be! It was only a dream.

Victor smiled while watching my expression. "How ironic. Your first time didn't take place at the height of a mountain, but rather in the depths of a lake."

I shivered, my eyes lowered to the cake. Was there nothing true between me and Micah? It appeared that Victor had revealed more truth in a week than Micah ever had in all the months we'd known each other. I felt a great sadness for us. All the time we'd spent together felt full of deception.

"Do you think that's a bad omen for you two love birds?" Victor persisted as if he wanted me to feel as miserable and low as possible in the presence of the delicate cake overpowering my senses.

His mention of birds, reminded me of the cuckoo, foisting her offspring on unsuspecting birds. Was my real mom crazy like Gran? Was I? My eyes were full of unshed tears and Victor smiled in satisfaction.

"You can blow out your candle now and make a wish."

I hesitated, too numb and tired to cooperate in spite of the incredible temptation of the cake. Things were different now that I knew for sure it was poisoned.

"Blow it out," Victor ordered coldly and I thought of Jason as I complied.

Victor pulled out the single candle. "Let me guess, you wished for a birthday kiss. Shall I give you a birthday kiss Adisa?"

Something deep inside of me sparked back to life in the face of his insolent cruelty. I felt the warm comfort of my anger envelope me.

I vigorously shook my head no and snatched up the cake, jamming the delicious moist confection in my mouth so nothing else could occupy it. When I was done, I took great care to lick my fingers clean.

Jason was subdued during our brief visit and we didn't get to discuss anything in private because of Victor's vigilant watch.

Day 6: hot chocolate

"Chocolate is the ambrosia of the Gods, the food of lovers," Victor mused over an extraordinarily large steaming cup of hot cocoa, sitting on the table between us. "Are you going to be my lover Adisa? Will you love me today? No, still no attraction? You heart breaker."

Victor gave a self deprecating smile. I was not amused. I was glad the door was closed and Jason couldn't see us. Victor seemed especially moody and I was sure it was because I had only one day of captivity remaining.

"Try this," he said, sliding the dark drink closer to me.

The steamy chocolaty aroma battled my resistance. I had to use both hands to lift the heavy cup. Victor watched me take my first tentative sip before beginning his story.

"Proverbs 31:10, 'Who can find a virtuous woman? For her price is far above rubies.' But in your case perhaps pearls or opals would be more fitting than rubies."

My hands trembled at the mention of my mothers' names and I nearly spilled some of the hot chocolate.

"Careful," Victor cautioned. "Are you a virtuous woman, Adisa? I imagine Micah would only want a virtuous woman. But once he got a hold of her, I'm not so sure she would remain so."

I tried not to listen to him as the warm liquid filled my mouth with a delicious flavor that left my knees shaking uncontrollably. I pressed them together in an effort to quell their knocking.

"Has he taken your virtue, Adisa?"

I set the hot chocolate down abruptly, choking on his boldness. Then glared at him refusing, to answer. I silently berated myself for still allowing him to shock me after all the horrible acts he'd already committed. I wanted to be like stone in his presence.

"No, it's still intact," he affirmed, casually reaching out to stroke the back of my hand. He laughed as I snatched it away.

"Drink, Adisa. Now!"

I picked up my cup with trembling hands and did as I was told. Now I was sure he was deliberately trying to provoke me while he fed me. What was the purpose of his actions? What was he trying to accomplish?

"You are a virtuous woman, Adisa. I can see it in your frightened eyes." He looked away before I could confirm a flicker of guilt in the black depths of his own.

He was quiet for a long time, his face haggard. "Did you know he burns for you, Adisa?" His voice was so soft, at first I thought I'd imagined it. "Burns for you, his virtuous woman... literally, not figuratively."

Then he looked directly at me. "Everyday, without crying out, stoically bearing the pain, willingly, gladly... burns... just for you." His eyes slowly drifted over me in wonder. "Every touch, every caress, every kiss laid bare for all to see."

He abruptly straightened up as if suddenly coming back to himself and his eyes glittered coldly again. "Would you like to know how old he was when he first burned for you? Five. Five years old and even then he wouldn't cry out though he suffered so they thought he would lose his hand. Don't stop drinking now!"

He didn't continue until I brought the cup back to my lips. "In that moment, they knew he was Guardian material with the potential to be the best there ever was." His brooding dark eyes turned bitter. "He was... extraordinary in his suffering... all for you.

What did you do to his hand, Adisa? What could a three year old do to a five year old's hand to cause it to burn so bright, it lit up the entire Portacle?"

Victor's eyes chilled me to the core as he leaned in closer. "Did you kiss it? Or did he use it to take your virtue?"

My temper finally roared to life, cutting through my fear. "I didn't even know Micah until I was fifteen. What are you thinking in that twisted mind of yours?"

"Drink!" he hissed.

I angrily complied, trembling with fury. The cup seemed bottomless with an endless flow of the sweet chocolaty nectar. I was drowning in it.

"Forgive me, Adisa, but we're running out of time and...," He stopped short, refusing to explain further, and observed me in silent resignation.

"The first time you two met, was in a cotton field. He was five and you were three. After that, he has returned over the years to watch over you because... he couldn't resist the flame," Victor surmised, callously laughing under his breath before continuing.

"The first time I met... no... saw you, was while he was still in Africa, weeks before he returned to save you from that falling tree."

I nearly choked on the chocolate as I remembered the constant feeling of something watching me from the woods. Even the day of the falling tree, I had sensed something watching me.

"Oh, yes. I was there. Micah didn't have his shield up. If he had, he might have sensed my presence but he was too intent on you."

"You mean you would have let me die?" I asked. There was absolutely no bottom to the depths he could sink to.

Victor gave me a frigid smile. "I mean, I knew I wouldn't even have to try. He always saves you just in the nick of time."

He waited for me to begin drinking again before he continued. "I must admit, I was confused that he would choose you. Now your sisters, I could understand him burning for one of them. But you... the manic little fire ball, the dark natural beauty."

I gulped down the drink, trying to block out his words and avoid thinking of Victor secretly watching my family. It was beyond creepy.

"But now I think I understand," he professed. "All that innocent passion." Victor placed his hand on my thigh and I steeled myself from reacting to his intentional provocation and focused on finishing the drink as quickly as I could.

"It must be addictive," he persisted. "How do you love Micah, Adisa? Is there room in that raging little heart of yours to love another? Love me Adisa! Show me how much you can love me too."

I shoved his hand away. "Please, the chocolate's all gone, see." I turned the cup upside down to prove it was empty. "Now let me see the boy!" I insisted but Victor was relentless.

"Do you feel anything for *me*, Adisa?" he persisted, grabbing my arm and causing the cup to shatter on the floor. "Anything at all?"

His eyes contained the same look of desperation from my dream. I turned away, not wanting to see. "Send in Jason! You promised!" I screamed as I resisted him. How could I feel sympathy for a man who was slowly poisoning me to death for his own morbid pleasure?

Victor slowly released me then picked up all the pieces of the cup. He gave me a final cold brooding look before opening the door and allowing Jason to come to me.

Day 7: apple

"This is our last day, Adisa. Our time together is finally coming to an end. Let's hope the seventh time is actually the charm."

We sat at the table facing each other. I couldn't believe I'd made it. I felt completely worn out as if I'd been in the fight of my life.

"I must admit, I have enjoyed our time together and truly hate to see it end. Micah is a lucky man, but then, he always has been. And that is precisely why we're in the predicament we are in today."

He paused to briefly assess me then held up a shiny red apple. "What story shall I tell today, Adam and Eve or Snow White?"

He pulled out a small clear vial of white powder and placed it on the table. Then he carefully sliced the apple into sections.

"I guess since you're such an incredible black beauty yourself, by default there's no need to dredge up Snow White... unless we're speaking of your virtue again." He paused to give me a wicked smile but I proudly refused to react.

"Oh, well. Due to the legends of our origins, I've always been partial to Biblical stories. Did you know, the legends say we Sp. beings are descended from celestial beings?" he asked.

My curiosity was piqued but I still remained silent.

"Forgive me, I digress. Adam and Eve, where it all began. The tree of knowledge, truth," he said, sprinkling the white powder on the apple sections, completely abandoning all pretense.

I shivered in fear as an irresistible aroma of fresh crushed apples converged on my senses as soon as the powder lightly dusted the first slice. Involuntarily, I inhaled deeply.

"The snake, in essence the devil... played by yours truly," he said as an aside, "offers Eve," he handed me a slice of apple and I accepted with trembling hands, "the forbidden fruit."

He paused his story and I began to eat. "It's a wonder we even eat the things at all today after all the trouble they've caused. But I must admit, they've always been a favorite of mine."

He handed me another slice and continued talking. "Do you know why the serpent did what he did?"

I shook my head, tired of his stories, wanting this to finally end. Apple flavor burst inside my mouth as I bit into a slice, my tongue dazzled by the surge my senses experienced with each and every bite.

"No clue?" He leaned forward dramatically and whispered, "Jealousy."

He passed another slice to me as he continued. "Jealous of God's love for man. The same sin you believe drives my relationship with Micah. Will you love me instead of him, just for today? It's our last chance, Adisa, our last day."

I felt like Eve, eating the forbidden fruit, and my head was swimming with the knowledge of Victor's stories.

His eyes appraised me as he gave me another slice of apple. "You've impressed me with how well you've held up during this entire week. Please indulge me, one last story. Are you familiar with Cain and Able?"

"Yes, they were brothers," I replied, holding my hand out for another slice of apple.

"Very good my little acolyte," he smiled in cruel anticipation, caressing my palm as he placed a slice in my waiting hands. "You're probably wondering, what does Cain and Able have to do with us. Well, in the case of me and Micah, allow me to re-introduce myself."

He stood up majestically, towering over me and in a harsh voice emphasizing each word, he announced, "I am Cain."

He watched intently as confusion played across my face. In a heartbeat, I froze in comprehension. If Victor was Cain, that meant Micah was Able.

Cain killed Able!

"Are you going to kill Micah!?" I asked in horror.

He smiled as if pleased that I figured it out so quickly. He placed both hands on the table between us, leaning in real close to my face.

"Mi amor...," his voice was ragged with emotion, "...ya tengo."

I was shocked. Was it true, had he already killed Micah? But when? Had he left during the night? I didn't want to believe it.

Victor burst into a laugh so horrible and loathsome, it chilled me to the bone. It was a classic villain's laugh and I knew in that moment, he spoke the truth.

"You are the Healer, Adisa. You must love me because he loves you. Can you do it Adisa? Can you save Abel and redeem Cain?"

I was tired of his stories. He had gone too far. In a rage I snatched up the final slice of apple.

"Stop!" Victor ordered but I crammed it in my mouth and swallowed it whole. It hurt going down as I choked on it.

Victor's eyes immediately widened in alarm. "Adisa NO!" he bellowed, lunging while knocking the table aside, both of us falling to the ground.

I futilely fought against him, noticing his eyes were no longer icy but ablaze. He grabbed my jaw tightly with one hand and the pain of his brutal grip forced my clenched teeth apart. Then he jammed the fingers of his other hand down my throat gagging me more.

I bit down hard and it was like biting on fleshy ice. He swore in pain as he jerked his hands away. I wiped his blood off my mouth, coughing to dislodge the apple still stuck in my throat.

The emotions charging across his face were indescribable. Suddenly his eyes glazed over and his face went blank as an invisible barrier went up between us. He held me down using the painful jaw hold again, forcing my mouth open then pinched my nose closed with his other hand as he covered my mouth completely with his own.

Would I now have to endure a fate worse than death in addition to death!? I fought like something wild but I couldn't budge him. I felt him suck in and a great pressure built up around the apple lodged in my throat before it suddenly popped free like a cork propelled out of a wine bottle.

The apple was swept up and out by his inhale. He removed his mouth and turned his head to the side and spat the apple out then stared at me while I was still pinned down by his weight.

I took in deep ragged breaths of air, gasping at the sudden access it had to my lungs. I repeatedly filled and expelled them in great physical relief.

There was no inflection in Victor's voice as he said, "That temper of yours might get you killed some day. Do you know what you almost did?"

But I didn't have time to answer because the door exploded open and the room filled with Atlanta's finest.

Micah was the first across the room, snatching Victor off of me, murderous rage in his eyes. Victor struggled but could not break free as Micah dragged him across the floor.

The strangest sense of déjà vu spread over me as I watched Micah's copper hands slam Victor against the wall.

He was alive! Micah was alive. Victor had lied.

It was noisy and confusing but I distinctly heard somebody say, "He'll kill him!" The words of the anonymous speaker cut through my happy haze.

Micah's hands were around Victor's throat squeezing. I knew the strength he possessed, strength that withstood the force of a crashing tree and lifted a school bus out of water.

Victor's neck should have snapped in two but it was still intact thanks to his shield. However, his expressionless face had turned a scary shade of blue. It was Micah's contorted hate-filled face that spurred me to speak.

"Micah, no!" I yelled. As much as I hated Victor, I knew I couldn't let Micah kill his own brother. That would destroy what was good in him, what I loved most about him.

"Micah please!" I pleaded in desperation as I struggled to my feet.

Micah abruptly released him and stepped back. "Fine! Go to him," his voice rasped with raw emotion.

He turned away from me and his defensive stance and angry words confused me. I was hurt by his obvious rejection of me.

When I didn't respond, he turned and glared at me. "It's what you want, isn't it?"

The pain and anger that filled his brown eyes broke my heart. What had I done wrong?

I felt faint. "I don't want to go to him. I want to be with you." My voice was weak and I could barely stay on my feet.

Micah's expression changed to shocked disbelief. Then he was finally moving toward me, gathering me in his strong embrace. I leaned against him in relief and exhaustion.

"Adisa, did he hurt you?" he asked in a strained voice.

"No. I'm all right."

The relief that spread across his face filled my heart. He crushed me to his chest and I breathed in his familiar scent. He felt like a dream.

"Son, we've got to leave now. The Presider is convening a special session to hear this case," Mr. Alexander said, appearing out of nowhere. He was holding Jason who was asleep in his arms.

Micah nodded. "She'll need a change of clothes and shoes," he suggested indicating my loose fitting clothes and bare feet.

"I'll have somebody take care of it at the Portacle," Mr. Alexander said.

Micah lifted me in his arms and carried me out. I saw broad shouldered men and women handling Victor. I was surprised at how small he looked in their midst.

The outside was lit up like the fourth of July with all the flashing red, white, and blue lights of the police cars. I couldn't believe all this commotion was over me.

Micah placed me in the back of his dad's squad car and climbed in after me. Jason was handed in to him before Mr. Alexander slid behind the wheel and we tore off, sirens blaring.

Micah sat in the middle, supporting both me and Jason. I rested my head on his shoulder, something only moments before I thought I'd never be able to do again. It felt so good to hold him.

"Adisa," Mr. Alexander called, breaking into my reverie. "I wish we had time to speak alone but we're pressed for time and there are procedures we are required to follow."

"Not now. Can't you see she's exhausted," Micah intervened.

"I can see that," Mr. Alexander snapped. "But we need to take advantage of the little time we have alone. You should put your shield up Micah to control your emotions."

Micah pointedly ignored the suggestion and I hugged him tighter, grateful to feel his firm yielding muscles rather than the rough rigid shield.

Mr. Alexander addressed me again. "Adisa, did Victor tell you why he took you?"

"My parents. I have to tell my parents I'm okay," I said.

"That's been taken care of but now you must concentrate…,"

"I want to see them now. Please, I want my mom and dad." I was upset that Mr. Alexander didn't realize the real urgency behind my desire to see my parents. Didn't he understand that earthbound kids needed the touch and comfort of their parents, especially after a long scary ordeal?

"I know you do, honey," he said and I was shocked to hear genuine tenderness break through his tough official shell, for me of all people. "But you have to wait a little longer. Can you do that?"

"It's okay, you're safe now and you'll be back home with them tonight," Micah promised.

"Adisa, please. We need your help," Mr. Alexander implored.

"Okay," I nodded, still clinging to Micah for support.

"Now can you tell me why Victor took you?" Mr. Alexander asked.

"He said he wanted to... feed me."

I felt Micah's muscles tense beneath me and saw him exchange a look in the rearview mirror with his dad.

"So, he did feed you?" Mr. Alexander asked.

"Yes."

"Did you eat it?" he asked.

I nodded feeling guilty at the memory of enjoying the incredibly delicious food so much. "It smelled so good, I couldn't resist and he would've hurt Jason if I didn't eat."

"It's okay," Micah reassured. "You didn't do anything wrong."

"Do you know if he put anything in your food?" Mr. Alexander continued.

We were already turning into the parking lot of the downtown police station and I suddenly realized all those hours of riding with Victor when he kidnapped me must have been in circles just to confuse me. The man was certifiably diabolical.

"Yes, he did. I don't know what it was but it looked like baby powder and made the food taste unbelievable."

"Did you change Adisa?" Mr. Alexander demanded in a rush and we almost went off the road.

"What do you mean?" I asked.

"Did you feel different? Did anything peculiar...," his voice faltered as he met my confused eyes in the rear view mirror and a look of defeat came over him.

Mr. Alexander's grip on the steering wheel tightened and he glared straight ahead. "It doesn't matter. What he did was wrong, regardless of the outcome. If he thinks he'll get away with this just because he's your Sp. twin Micah, he's in for the surprise of his life! This time, he's really gone too far," he said angrily

As we pulled into a parking spot, our car was surrounded by plain clothed people as well as those in uniform.

"Once we leave this car, I'll do all the talking," Mr. Alexander informed us. He lifted Jason out of the car and Micah carried me.

We were escorted into the police station.

"Is the girl cleared for Portacle entry?" one of our escorts asked Mr. Alexander.

His mouth set in a firm line as he dismissively nodded and I knew he wasn't pleased with the fact that I was.

"Did she manifest, sir?" a young officer asked, pushing past the escort while looking at me in awe.

Mr. Alexander glared at him but ignored the question.

The escort shoved the officer aside and resumed his position. "The Complainant is already inside but the proceedings haven't begun yet."

"He's the Complainant!" Mr. Alexander nearly shouted. "He comes to my continent, in my jurisdiction and abducts an earthbound practically in my own backyard...,"

"He's prepared to challenge her earthbound status, sir," the escort interrupted.

Mr. Alexander halted abruptly, bringing our whole group to a stop. "On what grounds?"

"Her true lineage," the escort said in a low voice, obviously trying to prevent me from hearing by turning away from me.

Mr. Alexander briefly glanced at me before we resumed walking. "That's never been officially established. And it still doesn't give him the right to commit a forced manifestation in my jurisdiction without my knowledge and certainly without my consent!"

"Sir, I believe he thought that since he was doing it on behalf of your son you would be more... sympathetic."

"Well he thought wrong," Mr. Alexander exploded, before lowering his voice again as Jason shifted in his arms. "Son or not, nobody gave him clearance to do what he did, least of all me. Make sure she gets some regular clothes to change into and shoes too."

"Yes, sir. I took the liberty of listing Micah as a Supporter...," the escort informed and continued updating Mr. Alexander but I found it hard to concentrate on his words.

Micah carried me effortlessly in his arms and I tried to stay conscious, hardly believing that we were together again. I drowsily wondered when we'd have the opportunity to be alone. There was so much I wanted to discuss with him and I didn't want to do it in a crowd of strangers and certainly not with Mr. Alexander present.

But there was one thing I had to confirm with Micah right away and I did when we were briefly left standing alone while somebody went to retrieve shoes for me so I could walk on my own.

"Micah, did you really kiss me on the bus in Lake Lanier?"

His face was close enough that I could clearly see he was surprised by my question. Then he was smiling. "Yes," he admitted, unashamed.

"Not very appropriate under the circumstances... at the bottom of a lake... me on the verge of drowning."

"But you insisted. You were delirious and refused to be still unless I did. I didn't think you'd stay put on the back of that seat if I didn't. Besides, I keep my promises."

It felt good knowing I'd gotten my birthday kiss after all, even if I only remembered it in a dream.

I pulled my necklace out and let it dangle outside my top. "When the time is right, you'll tell me the whole truth about this?"

"I will," he said. "I promise."

M icah guided me through the police station behind his dad who was still carrying Jason. I was wearing a pair of tennis shoes with the promise of a full change of clothes before I went home. We all entered an elevator with several other people and the doors closed behind us.

Mr. Alexander did a quick visual check and then withdrew a remote and held it toward the control panel while pushing a series of buttons.

A voice asked for a verbal verification and Mr. Alexander gave his full name three times at different pitches. The voice thanked him and the elevator began to descend which shocked me because we were on the ground floor and the elevator panel did not have a button for any floors lower than ground.

Everybody turned to the back wall of the elevator and Micah turned me as well.

"We're about to enter the Portacle, a secure underground area that holds the Sp. branch of the law department," he explained quietly.

When the elevator came to a stop, the back wall slid open and we all exited. The first person I saw standing at the end of the hall was Victor. I gasped in surprise and stepped back.

Micah held me closer. "Don't be afraid. He won't hurt you." His voice was grim as he glared at Victor.

"What's he doing here?" I asked.

"This trial is about him and what he did. He has to be present."

"A trial? Don't we need time to talk to lawyers and prepare our case?"

"In the Sp. world, lawyers are rare because the majority of us don't lie. However, those who are able to lie have the option of retaining a lawyer if the Presider feels one is necessary. During trial proceedings, we meet, speak the truth, and a Presider makes a decision."

We stopped a few feet away from Victor. Mr. Alexander told us he would return after locating Mrs. Alexander. Then he hurried off with Jason still asleep in his arms, without saying anything to Victor. Micah and I ignored him as well and Victor made no effort to speak to us either.

"It may take awhile before we're called so you might want to sit down," Micah suggested.

"No. I'd rather stay like this." I felt secure in his arms, my feet barely touching the ground with him supporting most of my weight, and I certainly didn't want to let go of him. "But if you're tired of propping me up, I'll sit."

Micah's eyes were warm on my face. "Are you kidding? I don't want to let you go."

I leaned against him, watching people going about their business as if it wasn't the least bit strange to be working for a subterranean law department in the super world.

Some of the people appeared normal and had the mannerisms of earthbounds. But there were some who carried themselves exactly like Micah did when his shield was up. And then there were a few formidable looking ones who were broad shouldered and taller than everybody else.

One of the broad shouldered individuals passed by wheeling a cart loaded down with food. I should have been hungry but the thought of Victor feeding me drove all thoughts of hunger from my mind. Then I remembered Victor asking me if Micah had ever put anything in me food. I thought of the soup Micah prepared for our winter mountain hikes during my Sp. education.

I looked at Victor and was startled to find him staring at me. I suddenly had an uneasy thought.

"Micah," I said nervously. "The soup you made... did you ever put anything extra in it?"

I felt Micah's arms tighten protectively. "No."

I wanted desperately to believe him. If I couldn't trust him in the midst of where I was, who could I turn to?

"But why did you make soup for me?" I asked, unsure of what to believe.

Micah shifted to look in my face. "Adisa, it's me. You can trust me."

"But there are so many things you didn't tell me. Like Victor being your super twin and...," I thought of how Victor had alluded to Micah knowing about my true parentage but I couldn't bring myself to say that out loud.

Micah studied my face intently. "Sometimes I withhold information I think may hurt you. I don't want to do anything that would intentionally harm you in anyway. My relationship with Victor is complicated. Talking about him would lead to topics that would bring you pain."

I said nothing and Micah pulled me back into his arms. After a while, his voice quietly informed, "Your mother said you loved soup and it was cold on the mountain. I made it to nourish you and help keep you warm."

I closed my eyes as my tension eased. "You were thinking of my comfort as well as my safety."

"Exactly," he said, his voice rough with emotion.

When Mr. Alexander returned, Jason was missing.   "Your mother's in my office with him," he explained.

Micah nodded and we all stood silently together. After awhile Mr. Alexander began shifting from one foot to the other, looking more and more uncomfortable before finally saying under his breath, "You may want to put your shield up. They'll be calling us in soon."

Micah shook his head no and I distinctly heard a derisive laugh from Victor. Mr. Alexander's jaw clinched and I knew he'd heard it too. He gave Micah a stern look of disapproval.

"It comforts her," Micah said defensively and Mr. Alexander looked away, saying nothing more about it.

They finally called us in and we filed into a room that didn't have a stick of furniture. Everybody stood in designated areas.

There was a man who stood at one end of the room and everybody faced him. Victor took a spot at the front facing the man and Micah led me to the front as well and we stood not far from Victor. Micah considerately placed himself between me and Victor. Mr. Alexander stood a couple feet behind us along with a small group of what I assumed were spectators.

Most of the people stood in rigid posture with their arms straight down by their sides. Mr. Alexander, Micah, Victor, and I were among the few who obviously didn't have a shield up.

The man at the front didn't appear to have one up either. He began speaking once everybody was in place.

"As the premier Presider of the North American courts, I conduct my trials in strict compliance with the SCCC. I assume you, Victor, as a Protector, are familiar with the SCCC?"

"Yes Presider, the Sp. Code of Court Conduct," Victor readily responded.

"Then why are you presenting in my court with your shield down?" the Presider asked in a clipped tone that expressed his annoyance over the violation.

"I didn't think it necessary."

"And what led you to that conclusion?" the Presider asked, giving Victor a stern look.

"The Objector's support does not have his up even after he was asked to do so by an officer of the Portacle."

The Presider turned to observe Micah and me. He looked slightly uncomfortable as if facing a situation he was not used to dealing with.

He waved his hand in our direction as he said, "Micah, you are aware that this... your actions will cause you suff...,"

"I'm well aware of the consequences, Presider, and I'm fully prepared to face them as usual," Micah interrupted him.

A rippling murmur spread through the spectators but quickly quelled when the Presider passed a baleful eye over the gathering.

I thought he would be upset over Micah's abruptness but he did not react. Then he sighed heavily as if he regretted having to bring up such a trivial matter. "Micah, do you have an explanation for having your shield down?"

Micah didn't acknowledge Victor as he answered. "After all the suffering the Complainant has caused the Objector, I hardly think it fair of him to take away what small comfort my shield being down gives her. She's already exhausted from a failed attempt of forced manifestation, now she has to stand through the rigors of this trial. And she's a minor who has yet to be reunited with her earthbound parents, after suffering this seven day ordeal."

I heard some low rumbling conversations from the crowd and the Presider warned, testily, "Those of you without shields will be asked to leave if you cannot control your emotions and keep silent in my court."

Then he quietly observed the two of us in each other's arms as if giving the matter serious consideration. I began to feel self conscious as it dawned on me that Micah's shield being down was a serious violation of their court proceedings.

"Micah," I whispered, "maybe it would be better if you put your shield up."

"It's okay," he said reassuringly.

The Presider finally reached a decision. "Since Micah is here as a supporter and not presenting, I will allow him to remain as he is, in deference to the Objector's condition. However, you Victor, as the Complainant, are presenting so put your shield up now."

Victor's face clearly showed what he thought of the Presider's decision. Then he looked directly at me as if to emphasize the preferential treatment Micah was receiving. His shield went up and he assumed the rigid expressionless posture expected.

"Now, there is one more issue to clear up before we can proceed with this trial. I did not see Adisa Summers listed in our contact data banks at all and I don't know what her clearance status is. So how can this earthbound be cleared to present in my court?"

Mr. Alexander stepped forward and requested to be recognized.

"You're recognized George," the Presider said. I found it strange that he used first names in such formal circumstances.

"She has not been added to the data banks yet because I've only recently discovered that she has knowledge of the Sp. world."

"Please rectify that at your earliest convenience. You may step back. I will allow Adisa Summers to present as Objector. Now, we can start these proceedings."

It took about five minutes to go through the official ritual of opening the trial and then Victor, as the Complainant was allowed to present his complaint first.

"I discovered evidence in Africa that the Objector, Adisa Summers, is a Healer. In light of my Sp. twin's imminent demise, and since the Objector is already the age of consent, I deemed it critical to try to... help her manifest. So I took emergency steps to do so.

I would like to make it clear that I did make misleading statements to carry out my plan. However, I never stated an outright lie. I also induced an atmosphere of fear and confusion but it was done to increase the chances of a successful manifestation.

According to the World Agreement signed by all seven continent leaders, all Healers, regardless of birth origin, are Sp. citizens of Africa and fall under that continent's rule. Therefore, as a fellow Sp. citizen of Africa, I have a claim on Adisa Summers and demand that she be given over to me immediately."

I couldn't believe my ears. Could I really be handed over to Victor, the villain? Didn't I have a say? I felt Micah's hold on me tighten as I began to tremble.

I couldn't believe Victor was being allowed to make such outlandish statements in a court of law. I wasn't a Healer and Micah wasn't dying. Why were they allowing Victor to lie?

The Presider responded, "Victor, I have several issues with your complaint, a major one being that your twin's *imminent demise* is due solely to your gross negligence! And now you seek to ruin another life in an effort to reverse a wrong you are responsible for. Are you familiar with the earthbound saying 'two wrongs don't make a right?'"

"That's assuming my recent actions were wrong," Victor interjected. "It's my understanding that hasn't been decided yet and in fact, that's why we're here now."

The Presider gave Victor a warning look. "These 'emergency steps' you mentioned, how long were you in this continent planning them?"

"Several weeks."

"And in all that time, did you have an opportunity to officially share your intentions with the proper authorities so that you could get clearance and save us all the aggravation we're experiencing tonight?"

"I suspected my efforts would be obstructed."

"Why?"

"Because the people I would report to are personally involved and cannot be objective," Victor stated.

"The same could be said about you. I find it interesting that even though you claim to be acting on Micah's behalf, he appears to be, based on his apparent alignment with the Objector, one of your biggest obstacles."

"And I get the impression you've already decided this trial and I'm wasting my time," Victor retorted. It was strange to hear such defiant words devoid of any emotion.

"Don't provoke me Victor. Did you think we, the Sp. citizens of the North American continent would just sit back and let you do whatever you pleased simply because of your African affiliations?"

"My position is based on law inherent in the World Agreement, not feelings of superiority."

"Your complaint is weak at best. But I'll allow it to go forward in the interest of public awareness. I believe all the continents should be made aware of Africa's covert actions against foreign citizenry on their own continents. It will all be on record and hopefully benefit future generations by preparing them to better address these issues.

Before we hear the Objector present, please pass forward the 'evidence' you spoke of finding in Africa that precipitated your actions."

"I don't have the evidence with me but I will put in a request to the griot and have copies sent to you."

"Do you have any additional evidence to present?" the Presider asked impatiently.

"Yes. Medical records showing the Objector's father, Frederick Summers, recently experienced an Episode. He was clearly on the verge of death from complete heart failure and made a full miraculous recovery."

I wanted to object as Victor calmly handed over copies of what I assumed were my dad's private medical reports. Whatever happened to doctor patient confidentiality?

"The before x-rays clearly shows his heart was more than fifty percent destroyed and the after shows a complete restoration. The heart is perfectly healed with no defects whatsoever."

Was Victor trying to prove that I was responsible for my dad's miracle? Surely nobody would believe such a wild claim.

The Presider finished collecting the documents and then turned to me and I felt completely unprepared.

"Don't worry. I'm here to help you," Micah whispered his support, still holding me close.

"Okay, Adisa Summers, as the Objector, it's now your turn to present."

My mind went blank. I had absolutely no idea about how to proceed or what to say. I turned to Micah.

"First, request a copy of all evidence. You're entitled to that."

"I would like to request a copy of the evidence please," I stated in a shaky voice.

"Granted," the Presider allowed, briskly.

I turned to Micah again. "Just tell the truth about what happened, what Victor did to you."

I thought back to the day Victor took me. It seemed so long ago. What was happening that day, before I climbed into Victor's car?

"I would like to tell the court what happened," I said.

"Proceed."

"I was home alone and decided to go for a run in my neighborhood when I saw Victor for the first time a week ago. He was outside the Alexander home. After my run, Victor drove up with Jason, Micah's brother, and asked me to watch him until his parents returned home.

When I got in the car to get Jason, Victor closed the door and I couldn't get out. I told him to let us go but he refused. Then he took us to a building made entirely of what looked like cement and it didn't have any windows. He said it was specially built to keep me from getting out. When I asked why he brought me there, he said he wanted to feed me.

He made me use the restroom in freezing temperatures which I endured because the alternative was to have him watch." I felt ashamed just remembering how humiliating it was.

"You didn't at least have the decency to build a self contained pod so that wouldn't be necessary?" Micah suddenly spoke out, angrily addressing Victor directly for the first time.

"I didn't get the proper purifying equipment for a self sustaining unit in time so I had to tap directly into the city pipes," Victor explained offhand. "Because the pod's plumbing and water access were linked directly to the outside, I had to watch her or freeze her whenever she was in the restroom in case she manifested unexpectedly.

I didn't want her to end up lost in the public sewer system. Believe me, my main objective wasn't to ogle your girlfriend." He made girlfriend sound like a dirty word even though his voice made no inflection.

"Micah, you can't speak out like that. You're here as a supporter," the Presider reprimanded but not unkindly. "And you, Victor, do not address him," he said harshly.

"Micah, put your shield up if you can't control your emotions," Mr. Alexander said under his breath.

I could feel Micah trembling with the effort to control himself as he turned away from Victor. But he left his shield down, holding onto me protectively.

"You may continue, Adisa," the Presider informed me.

"I tried to use my cell phone to call for help but I couldn't get a signal. When Victor found out, he got mad and... body searched me."

I felt Micah tense up, holding me tighter. I quickly glanced at his face to make sure he was okay. His expression was hard as he stared straight ahead.

"Victor threatened to hurt Jason if I didn't cooperate," I continued. "So I did what he wanted, seven meals in seven days. With all the meals he would tell me stories to upset me, each story would be worse than the last one. They were pretty shocking and some were even vulgar.

Sometimes he let me feed myself and then other times he would actually feed me like I was a helpless child. I remember everything he gave me tasted incredibly delicious," I admitted, guiltily.

"The first day he gave me chicken noodle soup. The second day I had bread. The third day was steamed vegetables. The fourth was birthday cake... no... it was oatmeal. I remember because that's the day Jason told me he saw Victor put something in my food and I realized Victor was poisoning me. The fifth day was birthday cake. The sixth day wasn't food, it was hot chocolate. And the seventh day was an apple. I saw him actually sprinkle the poison on it after he sliced...,"

"He gave it to you raw!?" Micah's enraged voice savagely tore through the courtroom, startling everybody especially me. His eyes were wild with shock.

I was too stunned to speak.

"Guardians!" the Presider called out.

Micah turned to his dad and simply said, "Please," as he handed me off. I was surprised to see Mrs. Alexander and Jason standing beside him.

The next thing I knew, I was in Mr. Alexander's arms and Micah was no longer beside me. I saw people moving so fast it was a blur.

"*Baseborn!*" Micah's voice raged brutally. "After everything that's passed between us, you do this!? You could've killed her!"

I saw him straining toward Victor but two of the formidable broad shouldered men were struggling to hold him back. Another, this one a woman, had already single handedly slammed into Victor, lifting and moving him out of Micah's reach. Then she stood protectively in front of Victor, her expressionless eyes observing her fellow Guardians' conflict.

"Let me go!" Micah demanded, his hostile face contorted in defiance. He violently fought to get to Victor, wildly struggling to free himself as ferocious sounds escaped him. His rigorous efforts didn't stop the two powerful men, slowly moving him back with obvious difficulty.

"The both of you together can't subdue one Protector?" the Presider decried.

On that, the two Guardians actually lifted Micah off the ground but somehow he still managed to maintain a forceful opposition that they had to exert themselves against to reach the exit.

Micah yelled out, "Don't let him near her or I'll...," One of the Guardian's clamped a hand over Micah's mouth before he could finish but Micah managed to twist free. "Victor, you are no longer my twin. You are not my brother!"

I saw Jason's eyes wide with fear as I extricated myself from Mr. Alexander's hold.

"Adisa!" Micah cried out and it wrenched my heart because it was full of regret acknowledging his defeat.

I stepped toward Micah and Mr. Alexander quickly drew me back, explaining that I couldn't follow.

"Take him to a holding room and put a third Guardian in with him," the Presider ordered.

The courtroom seemed unnaturally silent once Micah was removed and the doors closed.

The Presider looked at Mr. Alexander shaking his head in disbelief. "He's still getting stronger in spite of his involvement with the girl...," he stopped abruptly and glanced at me then quickly looked away.

In the absence of Micah's physical support, I felt myself sway as I stood facing the Presider alone.

"Permission to interrupt," Mr. Alexander's voice spoke out behind me.

"Proceed," the Presider said.

"May I bring a chair for the Objector. Her ordeal has exhausted her and Micah was holding her up."

"Of course," the Presider consented.

I started to refuse the chair, not wanting to appear weak by being the only one sitting among so many strangers but my vision became blurry and my swaying had become more precarious.

Out of the corner of my eye I saw Victor move toward me as the floor tilted up beneath my feet. My mind screamed *no don't touch me* but the words never actually made it out.

Somebody must have heard me because he came to my defense. Jason straddled me protectively, yelling as enormous balls of fire exploded from his hands which he hurled successively at Victor. I felt waves of heat rolling off his small body as I cowered beneath him.

"Micah said stay away! Leave her alone!" he yelled furiously and he didn't resemble the guileless boy I'd spent the past seven days trying to save. He was now defending me.

The massive fire balls flew at Victor who had halted and was calmly blowing them like dandelions that exploded in a shower of sparks and then disappeared. I felt his frigid breath in spite of the intense heat Jason was giving off.

I saw Mrs. Alexander reach out for Jason but Mr. Alexander pulled her back.

"No Harriet. He's manifested, it's too dangerous," and despite his concern, I could clearly see the pride in his eyes.

A Guardian lifted Jason, pinning his hands to his sides. The fireballs immediately ceased.

"I hate you Victor! You tricked me," Jason sobbed, looking like a little boy again, sad and upset.

I managed to stand up but still didn't feel very steady.

"Is this his first time manifesting?" the surprised Presider asked the Alexanders.

They nodded in unison, clearly overwhelmed by the event.

"It's probably due to the stress of the forced manifestation. And since Victor was preparing both of their meals, the Elysian powder probably cross contaminated and Jason got some in his food," Mr. Alexander suggested.

"Very well. You're dismissed to look after him."

The Guardian carried Jason out and the Alexanders followed but then Mrs. Alexander sent her husband back to stay with me, claiming it was what Micah would want.

"I'm going to suspend this trial and enter a temporary verdict before we have any more outbursts," the Presider stated wearily. "As you all know, we are not here to assign fault. Our courts and all affiliated including Complainants and Objectors work together for the sole purpose of discovering the truth. And the truth is you, Victorio Guillermo Carazo, did initiate and complete seven days of a forced manifestation without prior approval. You acted recklessly endangering life, liberty, and property.

Even if, as you claim, you did not tell an outright lie, you intentionally deceived the Objector. Due to the duplicitous nature of your words and actions and the unnecessary terror and suffering they caused, you are hereby banned from the North American continent for a span of one year.

You will be returned to your Sp. citizen continent of Africa and from there you will be allowed to travel to any continent at will, barring this North American continent. Do you have anything to say before I end these proceedings?"

"Yes. I was within my rights to do what I did and I reaffirm that it was necessary. I did not violate the code of silence our society is bound to. I did not tell a direct lie. And I stayed well within the bounds of allowed practices and procedures regulating forced manifestations.

In any event, as you can see, no harm has been done. The girl is perfectly fine. I did not succeed in my endeavors and Micah, my Sp. twin, is the only one who will be harmed in the end. I did this for his sake, not mine. By allowing this court to be swayed by Micah's pristine and good nature, you are condemning him to an early death. Because he would never have the guts to do what I did, even though his very life depends on it."

Victor's words revealed a hatred of Micah that belied his claim of altruism. He was obviously a liar of consummate skill and I hoped the court wouldn't fall for his deception.

"Punishing me is neither fair nor just and you will be hearing from the African council on this matter," Victor warned.

The Presider dismissed everyone and Victor was escorted out. I quickly requested to see Micah and was immediately granted permission. I heard Mr. Alexander tell the Presider he would check on Jason before returning me to my parents then he requested that Micah be released to assist with Jason since he and his wife were both dormant and not prepared to properly restrain...

The rest of the exchange faded behind me as I followed a Guardian through the maze-like hallway of the Portacle, unable to see around her because her broad shoulders completely blocked my view.

She stopped at a door and entered, without having to unlock it. Micah sat rigidly on a chair, palms down on his thighs with three Guardians standing around him all in the same wooden posture, hands firmly down by their sides. He stood when we entered but kept his shield up.

My escort left with the three Guardians without saying a word. The door closed behind them and I felt awkward finally being alone with Micah, unsure of how to proceed.

"What was that?" I asked, slowly walking toward him. "Your rages make mine look like temper tantrums." I gave a tremulous smile and Micah's only response was to let down his shield.

"Then after you left, things really got crazy. Jason started hurling fireballs at Victor who blew them out like candles on a cake. I have to admit I'm feeling really... really...,"

"Scared?" Micah offered.

"No. Jealous," I corrected.

An incredulous smile spread on Micah's face. "You never cease to amaze me," he asserted as I stood directly in front of him. "Is Jason all right?" he asked.

"Your mom and dad are with him. May I use your chair?" I asked, barely able to stay on my feet.

"Of course."

Micah helped me to sit down then knelt beside me.

"I'm sorry for causing you all this trouble, Micah."

"You didn't do anything wrong," he insisted.

"You kept your shield down for me and lost control of your emotions."

"That's not your fault. I wanted it down for selfish reasons as well as to comfort you," he admitted.

"Why?"

He smiled. "I like holding you... especially when there's nothing between us," he said. I hugged him and he wrapped his arms around me.

"Why am I so exhausted? I haven't done anything for a week except lay around and eat and listen to stories," I said, my words muffled against his shoulder.

"It's the Elysian powder Victor put in your food. It breaks down defenses and depletes strength. It's used to force superpowers to manifest. The more stressful the forced manifestation, the more likely it will succeed. Some have been brutal... a few even resulted in death."

I shuddered involuntarily and had to reassure Micah I was fine before he would continue.

"The powder has an additional side effect, causing the recipient to bond strongly with a person near them while taking it.

That's why I thought you were screaming to save Victor when we finally found you. I thought you wanted to be with him."

I shook my head in denial as I touched Micah's face, hoping to relieve some of the tension the memory brought him. His features softened again.

"I was worried about *you*," I clarified. "I knew you wouldn't be able to live with yourself if you killed your brother in cold blood. Why did Victor want me to bond with him, anyway? And why does he think I have superpowers?"

"Because of an African prophecy he discovered that states...,"

"Never mind. I don't even have the energy to deal with another story or any new information."

"I'm really sorry you had to go through all of this. I never thought Victor would... go this far." He looked hurt and angry. "I don't think I can ever forgive him for this. Not this. I know he must have been frustrated when it wasn't working but to feed you a full raw dose... that's insanity."

"What's wrong with taking it raw?"

"Elysian powder, in its natural raw state, is a deadly poison if a full dose is ingested."

I felt Micah's strength. I had nothing to fear, I was safe with him. He seemed invincible. But Victor's words haunted me.

"Micah, are you dying?"

Micah held me so that he could look into my eyes. "You don't have to worry about that Adisa. What's important is that you're safe now and we're together."

He stared at me, his eyes roaming my face curiously. Then his expression was replaced with shocked disbelief then barely contained fury as he slowly turned my face up to view the underside of my jaw.

"He did hurt you!" he ground out.

"No he didn't," I quickly denied, fearing he would lose control again and get into more trouble.

"Then how did these bruises get on your face?" he asked as he gingerly probed my jaw.

I winced when he found a tender spot. Victor must have bruised me during his efforts to extract the apple but my dark coloring had camouflaged the marks until now.

I quickly explained how Victor fed all the apple slices to me except for the last one which I snatched up against his warning and ate despite his protest. I told of how Victor saved my life by extracting the apple I was choking on, apparently bruising my jaw in the process. Then I remembered how I'd bitten him in anger and told Micah about that as well.

"You really bit him?" he asked, smiling in admiration but still clearly upset. "I bet he wasn't expecting that."

"Well, he shouldn't go around sticking his fingers in people's mouths. It's not sanitary!" I stated, indignant.

That made Micah laugh out loud and it felt good to hear it. Then his head tilted as he moved in closer but he stopped short, unsure. "I'm sorry. You're tired and hurt...,"

I closed the distance and hesitantly began moving my lips on his, trying to imitate the way he kissed.

He was stunned for a moment as if he'd forgotten how. Then our mouths were slowly moving together, performing a dance in perfect unison. It sent vibrations through my entire body and I melted in the warmth of his strong embrace.

I was thinking I wanted to stay like that forever when suddenly...

"MICAH!!!" a voice bellowed, so distorted by outrage it was unrecognizable.

Micah and I jumped apart, startled, then scrambled to our feet to face Mr. Alexander.

"Don't tell me you're still *comforting* her!" he said in derision as he glared at Micah.

I felt so ashamed, I actually stood a little behind Micah who didn't seem the least bit intimidated. He faced his dad as if they were equals. Superpowers or not, there was no way I could ever face my dad the way he did in that moment.

"No," Micah replied laconically, "comforting me."

I nearly fainted on the spot. Here we were, totally busted, after all our efforts to keep our relationship private, and Micah was being flippant. Unbelievable!

Mr. Alexander was not amused in the least. "Micah, go home to your brother. His powers manifested and he's very unsettled," Mr. Alexander commanded.

Micah looked as if he was going to defy his dad but I spoke up. "Please go Micah. Remember what it was like for you the first time you manifested? You don't want Jason to go through the same thing, do you?"

Micah looked torn. "Are you sure you're okay?" he asked in concern.

"Never been better." It was a lie but I certainly wasn't going to have Jason endure what Micah experienced when I had something to say about it. The poor boy had already suffered enough on my account.

"I'll go but I'll walk you to school tomorrow morning," Micah said and I got the impression it was more for his dad to hear rather than me. "Since I'm headed home, I can drop you off," he offered.

"No," his dad interjected. "The Presider has a few more questions that need answers."

"She has a right to Sp. counsel if she's going to be interrogated and I'd like to be present as one of her witnesses as well," Micah challenged.

"It's not an interrogation, just a few details that need to be clarified and we need to fill her in on the quarantine excuse," Mr. Alexander said.

"Adisa, you can stop their questioning at any time by claiming suppress," Micah informed me.

"Don't you mean duress?" I asked.

He smiled. "No. It's suppress. You claim it when there's any information you don't want to share. You don't have to give a reason, either."

"She's not part of the Sp. world so she doesn't have access to the rights and privileges that cover its citizens," his dad asserted, clearly irritated.

"Then she doesn't have to cooperate at all!"

Mr. Alexander said nothing and Micah turned back to me.

"At anytime, Adisa, you can request to leave and they have to abide by that law. Do you understand?"

I nodded. Micah reluctantly left and I allowed Mr. Alexander to escort me to the Presider's office and I was relieved to see though it was sparse, it was actually furnished. I gratefully sank into the nearest chair .

The Presider started right away as Mr. Alexander took a seat next to me. "George and I thought it would be best if we went over your explanation for your absence before returning you to your parents. We also wanted to make sure you understood what you just went through and answer any questions you may have. By the way, I'm Gaerd, pleased to finally have this opportunity to meet you."

I shook his hand, confused as he bowed deeply over my hand, displaying a complete change in demeanor.

Mr. Alexander looked uncomfortable during our exchange.

"I hope your ordeal with Victor wasn't too harrowing. Believe it or not, he didn't start out intending to harm you in anyway," Gaerd said.

It sounded as if he was now defending Victor's actions, a direct contrast to his courtroom position.

"It was a nightmare and if there's anyway I can help get him locked up, I'll cooperate," I said.

Gaerd casually reclined in his chair looking from me to Mr. Alexander and then back to me again. "Really? I'm surprised because it's my understanding you stopped Micah from killing him right after he stopped Victor from attacking you. Why the change of heart?"

"I didn't have a change of heart and Victor wasn't attacking me. I don't want him killed, just punished. Plus he shouldn't be free to terrorize other innocent people."

Mr. Alexander finally looked up in surprise. "What do you mean he wasn't attacking you? I was there. I saw him on top of you holding you down."

"He saved me from choking on a piece of apple."

"What?" both men said in unison with the same shocked expression.

"He was feeding apple slices to me but he left out the last one and just kept telling his mean crazy stories. I lost my temper and grabbed the last one. He told me to stop but I ate it anyway and ended up choking on it. He pushed me down and had just extracted the apple slice when you all broke in."

A look of utter relief came over Mr. Alexander as he slumped back in his seat and started laughing.

Gaerd chuckled quietly to himself. "Well I'll be."

I looked at the two men suspiciously. "What's so funny?" I asked confused by their reactions.

"It appears, young lady, that you have brought us some wonderful news. We were under the impression that Victor had gone villain. But your story assures us that isn't the case. In fact, it proves he's potentially redeemable," Gaerd explained. "If we can just get past this latest rift."

"Can you believe, he didn't even bring up the apple scenario in court to hide behind?" Mr. Alexander asked, incredulous.

"Probably because it would've revealed he's warm hearted," Gaerd suggested.

Both men laughed loud and long over that. I found their behavior very unprofessional.

"Okay, granted, he saved me from choking but let's not forget, I wouldn't have been in that position if he hadn't kidnapped me in the first place," I insisted.

"That's true, Adisa. But you don't know the whole story," Mr. Alexander asserted.

"Then tell me. I've heard enough stories the past week to last me a life time but I'm willing to listen to that one."

Mr. Alexander looked at Gaerd who shrugged. "It's your family, George."

Mr. Alexander looked at me as if he were trying to make up his mind about something. "Adisa, there is so much you don't know." He stopped in consideration and it felt like it did when Micah first started with my Sp. education on top of the mountain.

"You know Micah and Victor are Sp. twins, *super* twins. Well, they used to be extremely close but then... they had a falling out. But they worked through it and now... Victor feels responsible for Micah. He acted irresponsibly, thinking he could help Micah."

I was confused. Mr. Alexander appeared to be explaining the situation but at the same time, holding something back. "I don't understand. Isn't Micah's life in danger because of Victor?"

"How do you know that?" Mr. Alexander asked.

"Gaerd said so in court. Plus Victor told me he killed Micah or was going to. So if you locked Victor up some place where he couldn't hurt anybody then Micah would be safe."

Mr. Alexander suddenly looked as worn out as I felt. "Adisa, I'm afraid it's more complicated than that. Victor wasn't lying when he told you he killed Micah."

"It was obviously a lie," I adamantly protested. "We've all seen Micah alive and well walking around just fine. So whatever lie Victor told you for needing to kidnap me was just that, a lie," I was feeling delirious and couldn't understand why they couldn't see the truth staring them in the face.

"Adisa, you don't understand…"

"George, it's late and she's clearly exhausted. It's a wonder she's as coherent as she is. Plus she still needs to be brought up to speed on the quarantine story before being released to the Summers. We can resolve this Victor situation another time," Gaerd suggested.

Mr. Alexander briefly studied me before finally agreeing, "You're right, Gaerd."

"Of course I'm right. I'll go let the others know we won't be pursuing charges against Victor while you wrap things up with her. You'll see she gets home?"

Mr. Alexander nodded.

I wanted to object but things were moving fast and I was tired, confused, and didn't want to delay seeing my parents any longer. Gaerd rose and shook my hand goodbye, bowing deeply again, then headed out. Mr. Alexander located a change of clothes for me and I went to the restroom and quickly changed into them.

He filled me in on the 'quarantine' story while he drove me home. He told me how my parents had been informed that I had been quarantined for coming into contact with an individual suspected of carrying a highly contagious disease, perhaps SARS or a rare form of TB or something that had flu-like symptoms. Through testing and investigation, it was found to be a hoax and he was personally delivering me home as a neighborly courtesy.

He seemed distracted as he relayed the story. "We kept the details hazy and mind benders assisted to ensure they wouldn't reject the story plus my department is the one your parents contact for information so we're able to control what we want them to know."

"What are mind benders?" I asked. My head was throbbing after receiving the quarantine information on top of everything else and I couldn't believe I was being coached to lie to my parents by a law enforcement agent. Now, it sounded like my parents were given some kind of mind altering drugs.

Mr. Alexander looked startled and I realized he'd revealed more than he intended.

"That's not important. There's something else you should be concerned about. Look, we'll be at your home soon so I'll make this quick. In light of everything you've been through and because of things you still know nothing about, I think it would be best if you didn't see Micah anymore. Things would be so much... easier if you let him go.

I've tried to talk to Micah about this but he's being irrational. So I'm pleading with you to make the right decision. You're experiencing first hand how complicated and dangerous this can be. This... relationship isn't worth ruining his dreams over or yours for that matter."

I couldn't believe he just dumped it on me all at once. We pulled into my driveway and I could see the lights on inside and knew my parents were up. I wanted to jump out of the car and run into their welcoming arms but I remained and thought carefully before responding to Mr. Alexander.

"I want you to know, I love your son. I don't do it for spite, I can't help it. Micah is a good person and he helped me to see that I'm a good person too. I do have a temper and a negative attitude at times. Sometimes I have trouble forgiving others. But I'm working on all that. And I know you're worried about the FLEET thing but Micah says he thinks he can have both. So if you would just give us a chance because we're trying really hard here. And... Anyway, you may not think much of me but know this, I would never hurt your son."

He watched me with a blank expression and I couldn't tell what he was thinking. *Well, I tried* I thought in exhaustion. I opened my door and got out. I was surprised that he got out too and followed me.

Mom and dad both answered the door and I was immediately immersed in their hugs and kisses as they drew me inside. I kept my face out of any direct light so they wouldn't see my bruises. Mr. Alexander stayed awhile and was helpful because of the questions my parents asked. He handled them all smoothly. He certainly had no trouble lying. I shuddered to think how things would've gone if Micah brought me home with his inability to lie.

When the subject of school came up and I told my parents I planned on returning to school the next day, they objected. But I insisted and to my surprise, Mr. Alexander supported my decision. Surely he knew I was eager to go because I wanted to see Micah.

Just before Mr. Alexander left, my parents thanked him profusely for all his help, especially for the lawyer he referred to help them wade through all the quarantine bureaucracy.

Mr. Alexander asked them to contact the school in the morning to leave a blank permission slip allowing him to personally escort me from the premises at any time for any testing or questioning that may be necessary in the future, stating that such arrangements usually worked out best for all involved.

Apparently my parents, believing Mr. Alexander a saint with our best interests at heart, were as gullible as I was because they instantly assured him they would contact the school as soon as it opened. It all seemed too easy to me. Even my dad, a naturally suspicious man, accepted my seven day quarantine as completely logical.

We were all too exhausted to stay up late so we went to bed soon after Mr. Alexander left. I slept deeply as strange shadows plagued my dreams. When I tried to wake up, strong hands firmly held me back, refusing to allow me escape from my nightmares.

I woke up in a fog, my mind fighting to surface and awaken. I felt drained and surprised to be in my own bed instead of a strange cot. My mind suddenly cleared as I realized Micah would be waiting for me. To my utter amazement, my parents had already left for work as usual as if my seven day absence amounted to nothing. I found a message from them taped to my restroom mirror, reminding me that I didn't have to go to school if I wasn't up to it. I ripped it down and quickly got ready for school and then headed out.

Micah was there, as expected, and I could hardly contain myself as we entered the woods. It became darker once we left the light from the street lamps but Micah had no problem negotiating a path through the woods.

Even though I couldn't see them, I knew there were buds on the trees and new grass sprouts sprinkled the ground. The harsh cold was over and the air held a cool chill that didn't penetrate my jacket. When we found a nice clear space beneath a large tree, Micah pulled out the familiar O-Rocks, for light more so than warmth.

We shed our backpacks and Micah sat on the dry ground with a tree against his back then pulled me down onto his lap. I rested my head on his right shoulder as his arms went around me.

"Finally," I whispered and he seemed to understand as his arms protectively tightened in response.

We sat quietly together, in silent appreciation.

"How's Jason?" I asked.

"He's doing fine. We talked for a long time and I think he's dealing with things a lot better than I did. We were still up when my father came in. I wanted to come to you but it was late and it wouldn't have been appropriate. Plus, your parents deserved time with you, undisturbed."

I smiled imagining my parents' reaction to finding Micah on their doorstep expecting to come in for a visit that late at night.

"How's your... evil twin? And while we're on the subject, what makes him your super twin? You can't be blood related to that villain," I said.

Quiet laughter rumbled low in Micah's chest. "He's in Africa. We won't have to worry about him for awhile. When Sp. beings share a birthday, even though they are not blood related, they usually develop a sibling bond because they train together. Sometimes, when that bond is broken and they are at odds, one of them will 'go villain' and they can become arch-enemies. I think everybody's worried that may happen if Victor and I don't patch things up."

"Victor may be a villain already," I ventured. "He could be the monster who lives at the bottom of the pool, pulling people under."

Micah looked at me, puzzled. "You're safe now. Try not to think about it." Then he changed the subject. "How was the ride home with my father? As brutal as you thought it would be?"

"No, not really. You know what I'd like?" I asked, not liking that subject either.

"What?"

"I'd like you to take me flying. If it's not too much to ask."

Micah smiled. "Are you with me only because I can fly?" he joked.

"I admit, it's a pretty strong selling point. But you have so many other qualities that would more than suffice in the absence of your ability to fly."

He laughed and the vibrations were pleasant against the side of my face.

"All right," he said. "When do you want me to take you up?"

"Now," I said hopefully, trying not to sound too eager.

"Okay, but let's wait until it's a little lighter. I wouldn't have any problem seeing but you might enjoy it more if you could see too."

While we waited for the sun to illuminate things, Micah kissed me, gentle teasing kisses that left me tingling all over.

When it was light enough, he put away the O-Rocks and we left our backpacks behind. Micah lifted me in his arms and ran a few steps before smoothly leaving his feet in flight.

I clutched him convulsively as we rose, completely unprepared for my visceral reaction to suddenly leaving the familiar safety of earth's gravity in such an unusual way.

"It's okay. I won't drop you," Micah reassured, unable to completely conceal his amusement.

I replied in a shaky voice, "You better not. My dad would be very angry with you and you don't want to get my dad angry. He may seem mild mannered but like the Incredible Hulk, he'll kick your behind and if you resist, he'll just keep getting stronger and stronger until he succeeds."

Micah laughed but slowed his flight down to humor me. At first I was too scared to look around but then my natural curiosity took over and I timidly turned to see. Instead of whizzing by, the trees floated past dreamily. I saw the feint blush of green buds and the sparse carpet of new grass sprouts spread out before us.

We weaved around trunks, bushes, and vines, sliding through monochromatic browns and grays tinged with newly blossoming verdant shades. We skimmed the tree tops, not going much higher for fear of being seen and it looked like a river of sticks and limbs.

When I asked to fly out over a stream, he obliged, putting up his shield to be more alert since it was an open area. He felt more solid beneath me and I felt safe as we sped along just above the water.

When the sun hit the water just right, I could actually see the shadowy figures of fish darting about just beneath the surface. I trailed my fingers in the water sending up silver splashes, transformed into a glittering spray of jewels by the sun's rays.

At the end of our flight, I commented on how boring it must have been for him to crawl at a snail's pace all over the mountain with me when he could fly like he did. He said the one great positive about me was that I definitely was *not* boring.

We collected our backpacks and hurried off to school, surprised at how quickly time had passed. Once we made it there, it seemed time actually crawled until gym when I could legitimately be in Micah's arms again.

Mr. Winton, probably due to a touch of Spring fever, allowed us a free day of dancing. We could pick the music and dance with anybody or nobody, which ever we chose.

So instead of participating in African group dancing, Micah and I danced slowly in each other's arms while all around us, our classmates were shaking, twisting, and jumping around to the latest pop songs. My head rested on Micah's right shoulder as we made slow turns around the floor, somehow avoiding the animated efforts of fellow dancers. My right hand rested in his and I felt familiar patterns being traced onto my palm.

After class, Micah left as usual for his FLEET training and I was on my way to my next class when I was surprised to see Mr. Alexander coming down the hallway. My parents, true to their word, had given the school blank permission to release me to his care.

My brow instinctively raised in question when he guided me to an unmarked sedan. "What, no squad car with lights flashing and siren blaring?"

"I only use the squad car for special assignments," he said briskly.

"Like when you want to intimidate your son and his girlfriend?" I accused.

I could tell my words hit the mark by the stern look that flashed across his features.

Initially, we drove in silence but after we were on the highway, he tried giving a limited explanation of what he was up to.

"Adisa, I know you're wondering what this is all about. I believe you have a right to know what's going on and I can show you far better than I can tell you. I've tried talking but apparently, I'm not a very persuasive speaker. Since, seeing is believing, I'm sure that once you've seen, you'll come around to my way of thinking."

His eyes nervously darted around the traffic and he seemed indecisive. Then his hands gripped the steering wheel as a fierce determination settled over him. I shifted uncomfortably in my seat next to him but remained silent.

"I know Micah wouldn't approve of what I'm about to show you but he leaves me no other choice," Mr. Alexander resumed. "He refuses to listen to reason. And you are just as determined as he is. Though I admire your youthful... tenacity... I believe it's misguided. So I hope this will once and for all, put a stop to these juvenile games."

He looked at me, trying to gauge my reaction. "You're very quiet. What do you have to say about this?"

"With all due respect," I answered truthfully, "you're rambling, just using a whole lot of words to say absolutely nothing. And I should know, I'm the queen of rambling. Plus, I'm not one hundred percent behind all this misleading of my parents.

I know as a teen, I'm supposed to be going through this rebellious stage where I carve out a life for myself apart from them but the lengths you're willing to go, especially considering you're part of law enforcement, it's more than a little disturbing.

And I'm aware we're facing extraordinary circumstances here with the whole *Sp.* world thing and everything that goes along with that. But I was totally freaked out with how smoothly you laid out the *quarantine* lie to my parents. And I bet that lawyer you recommended is working on your behalf, not ours. And I'm not too thrilled with myself for just going along with it all like I don't have a mind of my own.

And what the Hell are mind benders? Are you drugging my parents? You're in law enforcement for...,"

"I'm not drugging your parents. Mindbenders are a type of Sp. being, not a drug," Mr. Alexander interjected, seeing how worked up I was getting. "They can put visions or ideas in a person's mind. We used them to make your parents' minds more receptive to the quarantine... explanation. We couldn't risk them running around traumatized, drawing attention to a situation only we were capable of addressing. Trust me, they weren't harmed in any way."

I was furious. He'd subjected my parents to some kind of super mind control and acted as if he'd done them a big favor. "I don't trust you, Mr. Alexander. I don't think you have our best interests at heart, not when it comes to my parents, me or Micah. Whatever you're about to show me is for your own selfish reasons, not because you're doing what's best for all involved."

My reproach didn't faze Mr. Alexander in the least as he parked his car and we headed inside the police station. We descended to the Portacle and Mr. Alexander warned me not to make a sound no matter what I saw.

We entered a completely different area from the night before. We stepped inside a small alcove which had a window revealing a large dark empty round room with a spacious central area recessed into the floor. There wasn't a stick of furniture anywhere which reminded me of the trial room where everybody stood. What was the Sp. world's aversion to creature comforts? Was it some kind of Sp. macho thing?

Mr. Alexander reminded me not to make a sound regardless of what I saw. He said a barrier around the recessed center would prevent us from being easily detected but we had to be as quiet and still as possible in order not to distract the proceedings.

After awhile, a circle of light filled the central area, beaming straight up from the floor to the ceiling. Its brightness did not penetrate the shadows that hid us. Micah and about twenty other people all dressed in the same simple white loose fitting tunic emerged in the light through an entrance that opened in the center of the floor. They quietly took up positions equally distant from each other, ten to a row. Micah was in a row by himself. I felt a thrill deep inside me at the sight of him but I contained myself as I stood, concealed in the darkness next to his dad.

Seven people wearing sleek casual business attire and carrying handheld computers entered behind the group. Mr. Alexander whispered to me that the seven were monitors and all the others were Protectors. There was one monitor for each row of ten Protectors, but Micah had five monitors. I quickly did the math. Enough monitors for fifty Protectors were set to observe only Micah. A sense of disquiet began to sink in as a whisper of apprehension slowly settled in my mind.

The Protectors had their shields up which was evident in their wooden posture. The light in the center of the room dimmed and a quiet soothing voice that could've been either male or female stated that shields could now be lowered.

The suddenly relaxed postures clearly indicated they had done so except for one woman. Her body overall was taller and more developed in musculature than the others. She tensed with the effort to lower her shield then released back into a rigid state and then tensed again. Suddenly, her body relaxed.

"You're close," the monitor of her row informed. "More than likely, next time, your shield will be permanent. We'll start preparations for your Guardian ceremony."

He smiled as he punched buttons on a handheld computer but the woman had no reaction at all to his words.

I looked at Micah's relaxed face, desperately wanting to go to him but there was no door into the room, only the one door leading back out into the hall.

I felt the humming before I heard the sound, a low rumbling that was foreign to my ears but familiar to something deep and primal inside of me. I was startled as red flames suddenly flashed into life and flickered steadily on all of the protectors.

Their flimsy tunics quickly went up in flames and they all stood completely naked. Alarmed, I instinctively stepped toward Micah but Mr. Alexander's strong hands drew me back immediately, prepared for my reaction. I averted my eyes from their nudity.

"It's painful but they're not harmed physically. Look at their skin, it's not actually burning," Mr. Alexander quickly explained.

I looked again and he was right. Their skin appeared to be untouched even though real flames of red fire danced across the surface. I couldn't believe what I was seeing. They were burning, really on fire, yet their flesh looked unharmed. The white tunics were small piles of ashes at their feet. They all stood, naked as the day they were born, men and women together. But nobody seemed the least bit distressed about any of it.

The sight of them burning was a bigger shock than their lack of clothing and after my initial surprise, I didn't take note of their nudity again. My heart raced as I saw the subtle changes coming over the Protectors as they reacted to the burning.

There was hardly any change in a few whose flames flickered weakly while others showed slight discomfort and a couple actually cried out, according to the amount of dull red and orange flames lighting their body.

The intensity of the hum barely grew yet the change in some of the Protectors was very pronounced. Many now had postures of agony and actually cried out in obvious pain as the orange flames sometimes showed a few flashes of yellow leaping out and then quickly disappearing. The eerie flames danced lightly across their skin, engulfing the writhing figures.

My eyes stayed glued on Micah. He was the only one with a completely solid patch of yellow flame. It burned on his right shoulder and pulsed down the length of his body to just above his knees, disappearing again into the reddish orange flames that covered most of his body. There were also flashes of yellow on his face and his mouth seemed to be lit from within by flashes of white light. His face was contorted in pain but he never cried out.

I subconsciously moved toward him again but Mr. Alexander's arms were still restraining me. My mouth flew open in protest but his hand covered it before sound could escape.

"Be still and learn!" he whispered harshly against my ear.

I wanted to shut my eyes to block out the suffering I was witnessing but couldn't. I had to see what was happening to Micah. I went still and did as Mr. Alexander insisted.

The humming sound subtly shifted again but there were no changes in the Protectors, except for Micah. He was completely ablaze. All of the colorful light intensified in brightness, exploding in bursts off of his body. The yellow circle on his right shoulder turned white hot and his lips now glowed with intense heat waves.

Micah's face was horribly contorted now, reminding me of dad's face during his heart attack. Low moans and groans escaped from him but he still would not cry out like the others. I was terrified and screamed for him but it was muffled by his dad's strong hand still firmly clamped over my mouth.

"Micah, step away if it's too much," one of his five monitors suggested, standing back from the flames.

I silently cried out for him to step away, surprised and elated he could end his suffering at any moment. But Micah didn't respond. My brief relief ricocheted back to terror as he remained where he was, suffering. Why did he refuse to save himself?

Some of the other Protectors were suffering less as the flames diminished and their bodies slowly relaxed again. A few others continued to suffer but none as severely as Micah yet he still refused to cry out. The intensity of his suffering caused him to alternately shudder and strain against it, his muscles and tendons so tense they stood out clearly defined. His hand hovered over his chest as if it was too painful to actually touch.

The single monitors walked up and down their row of ten, observing then feeding information into their handheld computers. The other five monitors moved around Micah a safe distance from his blazing body, conferring with each other as they pointed out different areas of his anatomy.

"Micah, step out! You should spread this over several days instead of taking it all in one shot," another monitor urged, as she studied the heat waves coming off of his lips. But still, Micah refused to save himself.

I suddenly had a shocking realization. The reddish orange areas on Micah's body were areas I had briefly touched or brushed up against and the yellow and white flames outlined areas I'd rested against him, my head on his right shoulder as we danced and as he embraced me in the woods. The heat waves coming off of his mouth indicated where I'd recently kissed him. Had our tender kisses caused all this suffering? Was I the reason Micah was burning?

I felt sick as I wrenched away from Mr. Alexander but he quickly recaptured me and dragged me out of the room and back into the hallway before releasing me. The bright lights hurt my eyes and my stomach heaved as my hands flew to my mouth.

Mr. Alexander understood and quickly escorted me to a restroom. I stumbled to the toilette bowl just in time as my entire body strained to turn itself inside out. When I realized Mr. Alexander was still holding me in support so I wouldn't completely collapse into the toilette, I didn't have the strength to shove him away.

When my body stopped its retching, he calmly said, "I'm sorry. I should have warned you about what you were about to see. But you needed to be shocked. Hopefully shocked to your senses so you'll end this… attachment you have to my son, now that you know what it's doing to him."

He helped me over to the sink and I rinsed my mouth and splashed my face. I couldn't look in the mirror, not wanting to see my guilty selfish reflection mocking me.

"Let's go up to my office. There are some questions I need to ask you," Mr. Alexander said as he pressed paper towels into my hands.

His office was located in the earthbound section of the police station. It was small and cluttered but private with a door that was currently closed. I sat staring out the window, my mind numb.

Mr. Alexander distractedly rearranged papers on his desk, pulling out some written notes, then cleared his throat, in obvious agitation. "Before we start, do you need anything to drink?"

"What were they doing to him?" I quietly demanded, ignoring his question.

"It's not them. It's you," he quickly retorted.

I flinched. "Why didn't anybody help him? They were all just watching him suffer."

"He's the first of his kind. Nobody has ever been strong enough to endure what he's going through. All other Protectors have broken down long before reaching the level of purging he's at." A strange look of pride briefly crossed Mr. Alexander's face.

Then his attention returned to me. "Before we get into this, are you sure you don't need something to eat or drink?"

I cringed at the thought of food.

"Can it kill him?" I asked nervously.

"We don't think so. But I'm sure there've been times he wished it did."

I couldn't think of anything else to ask after that, so I finally answered his question.

"Hot tea please." I barely recognized my voice. I wasn't the same person. Everything had changed and I looked out at Mr. Alexander through new eyes.

He stepped outside his office and soon came back with a cup of hot tea and a couple of sugar packets.

I sipped the tea straight and the heat settled my stomach and calmed my nerves.

Mr. Alexander cleared his throat a final time before beginning. "Reading you your Miranda Rights isn't necessary because you aren't being charged with a crime. Besides, this is a Sp. matter, not an earthbound one, and different laws apply. But let me be clear, that your cooperation can be forced. However, I would hate to go to those lengths…,"

"You can skip the tough cop speech. I want to cooperate… if it will help Micah. So go ahead, interrogate me. I'll tell you anything you want to know."

Mr. Alexander was clearly surprised but didn't waste any time. "I realize this sounds unorthodox and may cause you some… embarrassment. But I need to ask you detailed questions about your relationship with my son. We're studying him because his situation is an aberration. Micah is exhibiting some unexpected side effects that we're trying to find answers to.

But first, do you have any questions about what you just witnessed down in the Portacle?"

He paused but when I didn't respond, he continued. "That was an EP, extraction process, the trainees were undergoing. They were in a Depacitor, undergoing a cleansing burn that's not physically damaging but as you clearly witnessed, is extremely painful. Some Sp. beings go through this process to rid themselves of emotions, making them better at doing their jobs.

The process works in progressively deepening levels to dissipate emotions. The first level is crimson, then there's golden, next lightning, and finally a recently discovered level that we didn't even have a name for. We've dubbed it nuclear for now." Mr. Alexander looked at me steadily as if to impress upon me the significance of his words but I sat in silent confusion.

"Well, let's start with Micah's first day of school at Talbot Academy. After his first two classes, computer and gym, he came here for his FLEET training and we immediately noticed a difference during his extraction.

He started off as usual entering the crimson stage and showing flashes of golden. But then he sustained the golden stage, something we'd never witnessed on this continent. The flame pattern on his body indicated he might have been embracing somebody. We've concluded, it was due to his dancing with you. Is this true?"

My hands trembled with guilt as I cradled the cup of tea. "I don't know what it's due to," I said defensively. "I'm sure he touches lots of other people besides me."

"Micah burns for nobody but you," Mr. Alexander said.

"Why?"

"We haven't figured that out yet," he said. "He was ahead of schedule, his shield nearly perfected. His flames were minimal even after coming into contact with us. At such a young age, his shield was on the verge of permanence. Then he went to school with you and it was like he was at square one again."

"Are you positive?" I asked, not wanting to believe him.

"We've touch tested him. He still has a minimal reaction to everybody's touch, except yours. We still maintain the imposed physical distance as part of his training." Mr. Alexander's eyes softened as he took in my expression.

Then he sighed deeply. "So, where were we? Oh yes. Did you two dance together on the first day of school?"

"Yes, we did. Didn't you ask Micah about this?" I asked.

"Yes but he refused to cooperate. I believe my reaction to his choices caused him to make decisions he thought would protect his relationship with you. Our research has been very difficult because he's been extremely uncooperative."

Mr. Alexander's piercing eyes turned to me for answers.

"Yes, we danced. I'm the culprit," I stated flatly. Micah had been burning since our first dance. I didn't want to believe it. Why would he volunteer for something so insane? No wonder Mr. Alexander had been working so diligently to break us up.

"Was that the first time you recall ever physically touching Micah in anyway?"

"Yes," I said, staring down into my tea as if I could find answers there that would make sense to me.

"Do you know whether or not he had his shield up during that dance? You do know what a shield is, don't you?"

"Yes, I know. And yes, it was up."

Mr. Alexander looked incredulous. "For the entire dance?"

"Yes. Micah's shield is always up when we dance." Then I remembered one night, dancing with Micah with no adult supervision. Shame kept my tongue still as I decided I'd cross that bridge when Mr. Alexander got around to crossing it. I wasn't about to voluntarily give up shameful information on myself.

Mr. Alexander's mouth went into a firm line as he entered information on his desk computer. The monitor was turned away from me so I had no idea what he was typing.

"Is something wrong?" I asked.

"It's just unusual that anybody would reach and sustain the golden stage unless their shield had been down at some point during contact."

"At that time, Micah hadn't had his shield down since he was ten. Except, I imagine, for the extraction process. So it was definitely up the whole time," I assured.

"How do you know about him keeping his shield up for all those years?"

"He told me, months later, after I found out he could fly."

Mr. Alexander continued typing a while before proceeding.

"The next significant event occurred about five days later when you left with your parents to…..," he consulted his written notes, "… I have here 'take your sisters to Bartlett.'" He looked up at me and I nodded in confirmation as I remembered delivering the twins to college at the end of my first week of school.

"Did anything significant happen that day between you and Micah before you left?"

At first I drew a blank, unable to remember anything before being on Bartlett's campus. Then I remembered the car ride with my sisters, rocking the car down the highway, singing about me being ready. Then I recalled why I was ready, why I'd changed my mind about going to Bartlett in the first place.

My first time in the woods with Micah, running in fear from the unknown thing crashing through the trees behind me, only to discover it was Micah. A different sensitive Micah who's eyes filled with his emotions.

I realized Mr. Alexander was watching me intently and guilt washed over me. How could I possibly explain?

"I… We… It was the first time he let his shield down in my presence," I finally admitted.

"What made him do that?"

"Pardon?" I asked, stalling for time, hoping an easy explanation would come to mind.

Mr. Alexander exhaled in exasperation before asking in a raised voice, "Why, within a week's time of attending school with you, would my son, suddenly lower his shield in public for the first time in seven years?"

I didn't want to aggravate him further so I hurried into my explanation.

"He didn't want to hurt me. I nearly ran off of a cliff. I was hysterical and he was holding me down and I was bruising myself on his shield. So, he put it down so I wouldn't hurt myself."

Mr. Alexander was typing as I spoke.

I was scared to ask but I had to know. "What happened in the Depacitor?"

Mr. Alexander's eyes darkened at the memory. "Micah's hands lit up like Roman torches and he had flashes of a stage many have only read about, the lightning stage."

My stomach turned as I remembered Micah's stone shackle hands turning warm and smooth as he restrained my wrists; for this they burned.

"Is the lightning stage the white flames?" I asked in a subdued voice.

Mr. Alexander nodded grimly then asked, "Did you two dance out there, with his shield down?"

"Not then," I answered, still guiltily delaying the inevitable. "Why?"

"The pattern indicated he was holding you close." Mr. Alexander looked at me, waiting for an explanation.

My mind flashed on Micah struggling to restrain me on the ground. His shield had been down for only a moment before he released me. My eyes went to my fidgeting fingers as I explained. When I finished, I quickly glanced at Mr. Alexander to gauge his reaction.

He was staring at me in open mouthed disbelief. Then he asked in a strained voice, "Are you trying to tell me, my son struggled with you, on the ground, prone on top of you, with his shield down?"

"It was only for a few seconds," I rushed to defend. "And he rolled off as soon as I calmed down."

"As soon as you calmed down," he repeated sarcastically, each word a sharp jab of accusation. "And for this, he burned at the lightning stage... the *lightning* stage." He seemed barely able to contain his fury. He was frowning in frustration as he impatiently resumed striking the keyboard.

This was a nightmare come true, explaining in intimate detail my physical interaction with a boy to his dad. The only thing that could make it worse was if my dad came walking through the door and joined us. I suddenly thought of all the times Micah and I had kissed. There was no way Mr. Alexander would be able to live through those descriptions.

"Maybe it would be best if you sent somebody else in to finish taking this report," I suggested. "Aren't you a little too close to the case... too personally involved, to be objective?"

"My son is my responsibility. I'm taking this report... nobody else. Me!"

After he finished typing, Mr. Alexander perused his written notes again. "After you returned from Bartlett, I understand my son visited with you in your home and your parents were not there."

Oh no, the inevitable had arrived.

I remembered Micah pinning Avery to the wall. Then Avery left and I was alone with Micah.

I took a deep breath and imagined I was ripping off a Band-Aid to get it over with as quickly as possible, reciting all in one breath, "I know you think Micah and I were up to something with no parental supervision but all we did was dance with his shield down and we didn't even have any music on. That's all that happened. Then he left."

Mr. Alexander looked unconvinced. "Are you sure that was all."

I nodded. "Why? What happened?" I asked, my voice almost inaudible.

"He didn't just flash the lightning stage, he sustained it. Do you know how incredible that is? I find it hard to believe that lightning stage was sustained because you just danced. Are you sure that's all that happened?"

Shame washed over me at his insinuation but I defiantly looked him straight in the eyes. "Yes, I'm sure. We danced and talked. Oh, and I sang a song to him." Surely that wasn't a crime.

"You sang to him while you were dancing, with his shield down?"

I nodded, "Yes."

"What did you sing?"

"Alicia Keys, Diary." It sounded harmlessly innocent in my ears but the look Mr. Alexander gave me made me feel like the biggest fool to ever walk the earth.

He'd never heard the song so to convince him it wasn't all vampy and suggestive, I told him to pull it up on YouTube so he could hear it for himself.

He did and we both sat listening. As Alicia's words flowed from the computer, I couldn't help feeling exposed. I remembered the song being sweet and safe, an innocent attempt to get Micah to open up to me.

But now it came across as manipulative and seductive. My face burned in embarrassment. The interrogation was going from bad to worse and I hadn't even reached the salacious parts yet. How was this going to help Micah?

After the song ended Mr. Alexander didn't even look at me as he started typing. "So, you were trying to seduce my son into revealing his superpowers."

"No! Well... I thought about it but I failed miserably and I didn't know his secret had anything to do with superpowers. I just tried to tell him what was in my heart, that I cared about him and he could trust me."

Mr. Alexander snorted in derision.

"You know, Mr. Alexander, this would go a lot easier if you didn't freak out over every little revelation. Your psycho cop impersonation isn't the way you want to go here."

"What makes you think it's an impersonation?" he asked harshly, his fingers jabbing at the keys.

I was scared but I wasn't about to let him know it. "Maybe we should stop now because things get a lot more tender and I'm not so sure I can be totally open about it if I'm in constant fear of police brutality."

"Tender?" he barked, stopping in mid-type.

"You know, sweet. Intimate. Physical. Like kissing hugging touching; the usual teenage romantic wrestling routine."

"Are you trying to tell me you two had sex!?"

"NO! Are you crazy? I know you don't think much of me but have a little faith in your son." Then I remembered Micah saying he had no boundaries. "Look, it's too strange talking to you about this when I know you hate me so could I just write something out and turn it in?"

Mr. Alexander chuckled bitterly. "This isn't a class assignment you hand in for a grade, Adisa. And I don't hate you."

"Yeah right! You forget I was an eyewitness to your Academy Award performance in 'Quarantined' with my parents last night. So I'm aware of how well you lie. Your hatred of me is super apparent as evidenced by your numerous glaring drive bys especially when Micah was in Africa."

"Micah told me to check on you, to make sure you were okay. And as I recall, you were the one doing all the glaring."

He was right. But had he really been looking out for me instead of mocking me? I found it hard to believe.

"I don't want to fight with you, Adisa. Believe it or not, we're on the same side, we both want what's best for Micah. But we differ on what we think that is. I'll try to turn down the dial on concerned parent so things won't get overheated. Okay?"

I nodded in relief. "Okay."

"Good. Now, about your mountain time together."

He was really in for it now.

"In the beginning of your mountain excursions, everything pretty much returned to normal for Micah, for well over a month. But then one day…," Mr. Alexander looked at me expectantly.

"Exactly what day would that be?" I hedged. "We spent a lot of time on the mountain so you have to be a little more specific." My delaying tactic didn't fool Mr. Alexander for one second.

"If you expect me to keep my temper in check, you need to stop playing games. You know exactly what day I'm referring to." His nostrils flared but he managed to keep his voice level.

"Oh yeah, that day. I remember now. Well, Micah mentioned that you and Mrs. Alexander didn't give him physical affection. And I thought that was wrong for parents to treat their own child that way."

I gave Mr. Alexander a defiant look but he didn't even blink. "So I tried to remedy it by... uhm... by... kissing him to make up for it."

I squirmed as the silence stretched between us. Mr. Alexander stared at me for a long time, before calmly stating, "My boy's whole face went nuclear. We thought it would never stop burning."

My head bowed in disgrace. I sank lower in my seat, thinking Micah burned for a whole week because I covered his face in a deluge of kisses. I was beyond horrified.

"Sorry," I mumbled.

Mr. Alexander typed.

"Would you like to know why he had to leave for Africa?" he asked without looking at me, his fingers angrily stabbing each key.

"He said he broke the Depacitor," I offered in a hoarse voice.

Mr. Alexander slowly said in a tight voice, "All Hell broke loose. The whole thing exploded and the place caught on fire. Fortunately for us the Portacle is filled with Guardians so nobody was seriously injured. Would you kindly tell me exactly what happened between you and my son that time?"

Tears slowly filled my eyes as I remembered feeling the back of Micah's hand tremble against my bare skin as his fingertips explored the top edge of my jeans.

It was just as Victor had told me, 'Every touch, every caress, every kiss laid bare for all to see.' Nothing was private, all was revealed and Micah was the one suffering for it all.

Try as I might, I couldn't escape the ultimate truth. Micah, my superhero, the last person I would ever want to hurt, was burning and it was completely my fault. Why did somebody as good as Micah choose to suffer over somebody like me?

Mr. Alexander and I went on for a long time, back and forth. He asked questions, I made sordid revelations and then he would reveal the atrocious consequences Micah had suffered. It effectively converted me to total body abstinence. I recoiled from the very thought of ever touching Micah again.

After we were done, Mr. Alexander drove me home in blessed silence. School had already been out for a long time. I mechanically went through the motions of making dinner. The phone rang but I ignored it, not even checking caller I.D. to see who was calling.

A fiery nightmare was replaying constantly in my mind all evening. Mom and dad attributed my somber mood to weariness for over doing it so soon after my quarantine and sent me up to bed early. I didn't mention Mr. Alexander had pulled me out of school. I wasn't capable of coming up with a good lie.

I lay in bed, staring at my ceiling. Every time I closed my eyes, I saw Micah's tortured contorted face, silently suffering. I tossed and turned, unable to sleep. But that was fine with me because it meant I wouldn't have any nightmares which were invariably worse than anything my waking mind could conjure up.

After mom and dad went to work, I got ready for school early because I wanted to straighten things out before going back to Talbot.

I walked over to the Alexander home and rang the doorbell, ignoring the voice in my head chiding me for not calling first; under the circumstances, I reasoned an unannounced visit was justified. I dully observed that the dent I'd made the last time I was there was missing but now, I had no desire to create another. I'd done enough damage to last a lifetime.

Mr. Alexander let me in and indicated the same room where I met the Amazon. I walked inside as he closed the front door.

Micah was there and I had the distinct impression that I'd interrupted their conversation. His shield was up but he lowered it immediately when he saw me.

"Adisa," he said, a warm smile on his face but his eyes grew concerned as he came toward me. "You didn't go to math yesterday and I...,"

I backed up so quickly, I nearly ran right over Mr. Alexander who had followed behind me.

Micah froze in mid-stride. "What's wrong?"

I stepped behind Mr. Alexander as I answered him. "I saw you, in that Depacitor thing. And you were burning and it's all my fault." My voice sounded shrill, on the verge of hysteria.

Micah was instantly plunged into shock and confusion. "What? How... When?"

"Yesterday," Mr. Alexander supplied. "I brought her to the Portacle just before your EP.

"You saw!?" Micah exclaimed, his eyes meeting mine in horrified disbelief. Then he turned to his dad. It was evident he felt deeply betrayed by him. "Why?"

"Because you wouldn't listen to reason. She had a right to know what was going on, what your actions were resulting in."

"Your dad's right, Micah," I interjected. "Why didn't you tell me what was happening to you? Why would you put yourself through something like that?"

"I'm used to it. I can handle it," he defended, harshly.

"It's a horror show!" I practically screamed. "I saw it, Micah. No more. It's over."

"But Adisa...," he said, taking another step toward me but I kept Mr. Alexander firmly in between us.

"Don't you dare touch me. You can't ever touch me again. I'm not participating in your burning!"

The look on Micah's face broke my heart. He looked back and forth from me to his dad, as if we were co-conspirators.

"Are you happy now?" he said in a dead voice to his dad. "You've finally gotten what you wanted." His shield went up and he left the room.

I left soon after, completely defeated by Mr. Alexander's encouraging words that I was doing the right thing and how I'd look back some day and appreciate the decision I'd made and how grateful he was that I had the good sense to blah blah blah until I thought my head would explode.

I felt empty as I walked to school. Micah was by his tree. I ignored him even though he called my name. I actually choked up hearing the emotion in his voice and I feared I might weaken and give in.

I pushed forward, hugging myself, willing my legs to carry me to school instead of across the street into Micah's arms. I couldn't let him burn because I wasn't strong enough to comfort myself.

I deflected Avery's concerned questions in homeroom. Computer class was torture, sitting so close to Micah, trying to ignore him.

"Adisa, you've got to talk to me," he said quietly.

"Why should I? You don't lie but you omit and that's just as bad as lying."

"I was waiting until you knew more about my world. When the time was right, I was going to tell you."

"Why do you get to decide? Because you're a *super*being and I'm just an earthbound? Just because you're super doesn't make you superior!"

"Adisa Summers! Is there a problem?"

I realized my voice had risen above the angry whispers I was trying to maintain. "No, Ms. Fulton."

"Micah, how about you. Problem?" she asked.

"I apologize for being disruptive," his expressionless voice answered.

Gym was tolerable because I danced in the girl group while Micah danced with the guys which was how all of the African dances we were learning were set up.

Micah doing Latin dance was very impressive. Micah doing African dance was a jaw-dropping heart-stopping eye-popping marvel, making it extremely difficult for me to keep my eyes off of him.

He was unapologetically masculine and moved with an unearthly graceful power. I felt like Justin must have felt when he would watch Lucia after I completely wrecked their partnership.

My body moved mechanically to the drums and chants, performing the dance steps from memory. I danced but my every thought was focused on Micah the whole time.

"That boy looks absolutely delicious," a lilting voice practically sang in my ear.

I turned to find Lucia looking at Micah in a way that made me want to blind her.

After class finally ended, Micah left, as usual, for his FLEET training, for the Depacitor. I took a measure of comfort in the knowledge that he wouldn't be suffering on my account because I had avoided all physical contact with him. I found it ironic that now, the absence of his touch caused me physical as well as emotional pain.

I anxiously waited for his return in math class and felt immensely relieved when he appeared, looking normal. I studiously ignored him so he wouldn't be aware of my feelings. He didn't try to talk to me until after school.

"Be reasonable, Adisa," he said from his side of the street. "The mature thing to do is to at least discuss it."

"The mature thing to do would've been for you to tell me about it instead of treating me like a child and letting me hear it from your dad and getting the biggest shock of my life. Do you know how humiliating that was? And then describing to him in detail every intimate exchange between us. That was off the charts."

"Why didn't you claim suppress? You didn't have to tell them anything," he argued.

"You were suffering, Micah. I wanted to help."

"I didn't need your help," he said, heatedly.

His angry words painfully crashed down on me. "And I don't need you," I fumed.

That shut him up for a while. He followed me up onto my porch.

"You know the rules, Micah," I said when I realized he was behind me.

"Let's go to the mountain so we can talk in private," he coaxed, his voice low and tempting and I trembled as I felt myself responding to it.

"Forget it!"

"You're not being fair, Adisa."

"It's too much, Micah. I thought I could handle the whole *super* thing but I can't. It makes everything so one-sided. I don't like being in the dark about things you should've told me about and then having it dumped on me by people who are after their on selfish interests, not caring at all how much they hurt others."

I yanked on the uncooperative doorknob but the door wouldn't open as I continued my tirade.

"I feel as if Victor and your dad, though brutal, have both been more open and honest with me than you have. Amazing, since you're the one who can't lie. How do you think that makes me feel?"

"I'm sorry about that, really. But shutting me out isn't the answer," Micah reasoned.

"I'm not shutting you out. I'm shutting us down. After everything I've learned, we just don't make sense together."

The door finally opened. "Bye, Micah," I said before disappearing inside.

It was hard walking away from him but thinking of his contorted face when he was in the Depacitor gave me the strength to close the door and lock it. Then my legs buckled and I slid to the floor as weak as a newborn for several minutes before my strength returned and I got up again.

Micah continued to show up at his tree every morning and at first he tried to get me to talk about renewing our relationship but I held firm. I could tell he was growing frustrated with me.

One day out of the blue, he was suddenly crossing the street, a look of determination in his eyes as he slipped his arms out of his backpack and I wanted to just let him take me wherever he wanted to go.

Completely taken off guard and terrified of my reaction, I panicked, "Micah, I'm not playing with you, one more step and I'll scream my head off!" I stood facing him in defiance, ready to fight him off if necessary.

He pulled up short, completely shocked. Something in my eyes must have told him I wasn't kidding. He turned and stalked back to his side of the street, his body going rigid as his arms extended down by his sides, his backpack still dangling from his tightly clenched fist.

I kept my eye on him after that until I was safely seated in homeroom, only then realizing the absolute futility of me fighting him. I was so shaken by the encounter, I came close to confiding in Avery.

He cornered me after homeroom, insisting I tell him what was bothering me. I couldn't even think of a lie.

"I can't tell you, Avery. I just can't," I declared, trying to avoid him but he blocked my way.

"I hate seeing you like this, Adisa. I've been worried about you practically since the first day of school. You're having such a rough year and I want to help. But I can't help if you don't talk to me."

He put his arm around me and I leaned in accepting his comfort, internally debating how I could tell him without revealing too much. I was on the verge of confiding in him but the thought of exposing Micah stopped me.

"Really, Avery, if I could tell anybody, you know it would be you. But I just can't talk to anybody about it. But I'll be okay. Really. I just need some time alone."

"Are you sure?" he asked, unconvinced.

I nodded in misery.

"I don't like it, but okay," he said, his hand sliding up and down my back in a soothing motion. "I'll give you time. You can talk to me any time, day or night, seriously.

But I'm warning you, if I don't see a change for the better soon, I'm showing up on your doorsteps to talk to Frederick and Opal; see if we can't straighten you out."

I looked at him sideways. "Since when have you been on a first name basis with my parents?"

"Oh, we're close," Avery said, grinning into my eyes as he continued to rub my back.

"Really?" I asked, skeptical.

"Really. We have long drawn out conversations about when we should have you committed before you end up killing somebody."

"If you don't watch yourself, Avery Symmes, you'll be the first one I take out," I threatened, feeling a little like my old self again.

"Stronger ones have tried and failed but none meaner," Avery assured.

I couldn't help smiling.

"Finally! I haven't seen that in days. I thought Micah had taken it for good this time," Avery said in relief, as he pulled me in for a quick hug. I awkwardly returned it.

Avery was well aware of my aversion to touchy feely public displays so he must have really been concerned about me to reach out to me the way he did. I appreciated his consideration.

As I turned to walk away, I saw Micah watching us with his expressionless eyes. He didn't try to speak to me at all in school for the rest of the day. As I headed home afterward, I didn't see him. I miserably contemplated where he could be and wondered if he had finally given up and deserted me.

"I can't touch you but you allow Avery Symmes to put his hands all over you?" Micah's angry voice accused.

I spun around to confront him. The wounded look in his eyes surprised me. I'd been so careful to stay far away from him that his sudden nearness overwhelmed me for a moment.

"He did not have his hands all over me. He was being kind because you upset me with your psychotic bum rush this morning."

We stood facing each other, neither one about to back down. His eyes were hollow and I couldn't believe how tired he looked. Regardless, I still felt myself drawn to him.

It was a warm Spring day, bright and beautiful and I thought of spending it with him on the mountain in a secluded area. I subconsciously swayed toward him before abruptly catching myself.

"Micah, there are so many other things you could be. Why a Guardian?"

"I'm not quitting," he stubbornly persisted.

"You have to choose." I didn't want to be the reason for anybody's dream getting deferred but I didn't want to be the reason for them burning either.

"I choose both," he stated, emphatically.

"How do you expect me to enjoy being with you when I know you'll burn for it? I'm not that heartless. You burn, even if we accidentally brush against each other."

I looked at him in hopeless desperation. "Is there any way we can touch and you not suffer for it?"

He didn't answer. He slowly reached out for me.

"Micah, I can't," I said stepping back and he stepped forward.

"This is insane. I feel like I'm in some kind of freak show," I said as I watched his hand slowly reach out again.

"I want to be with you, Micah, but I can't have you. I don't know why it's like this but it is. Maybe I'm just not good enough."

"Negative and positive rules still apply," he said, softly. "You owe me. I've been keeping track."

He smiled at me and I felt a desire to touch him so intense it made me catch my breath. Then his smile twisted into a mask of pain in my mind's eye and his hand lit up like a Roman torch.

I stumbled back, snatching my hand away just before he could touch it. Then I turned and walked away.

I forced myself to do other activities to demonstrate to myself that there was more to life than kissing Micah.

As the days passed, Micah retreated behind his shield and spoke less and less. I could tell he was thoroughly miserable, masquerading as the hollow man but he wouldn't go away.

I was surprised by how much I missed him, not just our physical contact, but sharing our thoughts and experiences. I missed his smile and our laughter, our talks on the mountain. I felt myself closing inside and tried not to concentrate on the pain that was settling permanently in my chest.

Mr. Winton ended our African dancing early one day and called me over to where he was standing with Micah.

"Adisa, it's time for Micah's dance exam from last semester. I figured I'd better get it in before this semester is over. You two go ahead and get ready for your Paso Doble."

"Why me?" I cut my eyes at Micah but he showed no reaction.

"Because you were his dance partner," Mr. Winton explained dismissively.

"I forgot the steps. It's been a long time." It was a lie but the best I could do on such short notice.

"I'll dance with him!" Lucia chimed in. I gritted my teeth against the flaming jealousy that instantly flared, catching me by surprise.

"Thank you Lucia but I'd feel more comfortable with my old dance partner and nobody else," Micah smoothly declined.

I felt equal measures of shock, relief, irritation, and dread.

"Adisa, this final is worth fifty percent of Micah's semester grade. So, since you were his dance partner, I have to insist," Mr. Winton stated.

My classmates were spread out on the bleachers and against the walls, lounging around talking in small groups as they enjoyed their unexpected break.

Micah and I walked to the middle of the floor and I reluctantly allowed him to take me into his arms.

"Put your shield up!" I insisted under my breath when I realized he had it down. I knew right away because our embrace felt too intimate, he was much too close.

"Put it up!" I hissed after he ignored me.

"No!" His eyes glared back into mine.

My hand trembled in his as the warmth of his long absent hand traveled up the length of my arm. It had been so long since I felt him it was like a welcome shock bringing me back to life. I started to walk off the floor but he pulled me back, firmly holding me in the start position.

"You don't want to be responsible for me getting a failing grade. Do you?" he asked. As if he really cared about that.

"Better than being responsible for your suffering," I said as I tried to disengage myself from his hold.

"The damage is already done," he said, referring to our current physical contact.

The music began and I felt self conscious as heads turned to watch us standing in the middle of the gym. I would have to make a scene to be free of him.

I felt trapped and I snapped as my frustration angrily boiled over. "Fine then. Burn!"

We began the dance on cue. My movements, infused with the fury and dissatisfaction of suppressed desire, were an angry invitation that he met with equal passion.

Our Paso Doble was my most dangerous dance yet. I connected to it on a deep level, channeling my rage into the dramatic steps. The pulsing music surged, driving us to the very limits. The looks I threw at Micah could melt steel and shatter diamonds. They would have destroyed a weaker man but he matched me step for step.

We circled each other, the brooding stalker and seductive challenger. We were a terror of enticement. I spun around him, dragging fire down his back and hips then blazed a trail of flames up his legs and arms. He offered himself up never flinching, guiding me into a more daring dance with his proud provocative gestures. If he was the bullfighter and I the cape, I draped myself around him, burning him mercilessly.

When the music ended, Mr. Winton's eyes were bright with unabashed admiration as he led the cheering. "Bravo!" The applause was thunderous. I realized everybody had stopped and gathered around to watch.

I looked at Micah and saw the rise and fall of his chest and the intense look on his face. It brought me back to my senses. He would pay dearly for my recklessness. My eyes pleaded with him and he finally assented. All signs of his breathing vanished and his face went blank.

I watched him leave, knowing he was going to endure the Depacitor. And thanks to me, he would burn. My head began to swim as our dance replayed in my mind. There wasn't much of Micah I had left untouched. I was disgusted with myself and felt sick to my stomach.

I ran to the girls' restroom and found myself once again hanging over a toilette bowl but this time I was alone. Images of Micah's suffering vividly exploded in my mind. I braced myself, prepared to have my insides turned out. I felt an arm go around my waist and heard a concerned voice reassure me.

"You're okay. I've got you," Liz assured and she didn't even recoil as I began to heave. "That's good. Let it all out, Adisa, you'll feel better."

After I was done, she stayed with me while I washed up.

"Adisa, are you in trouble?" she asked tentatively.

"What do you mean?"

"Are you pregnant?"

My shocked eyes met her worried ones in the mirror. I laughed so hard my sides hurt.

"No," I said, gasping for breath. "I'm definitely not pregnant."

When I finally regained control of myself, I said, "Thanks for helping me."

"No problem," she replied.

"You must have a stomach of steel."

She gave me a rueful smile. "I have a daddy who's been drinking too much ever since my mama went away. The stuff I've cleaned up behind him has made me impervious to anything that comes out of the human body. This was nothing, at least it wasn't coming out of *both* ends of you."

"Eww, TMI! I might get sick again," I said, playfully screwing up my face.

"No way. After all that you put out, there's nothing left," she assured me, grinning.

"I guess you would know, you're the expert."

She nodded. "You wouldn't believe the mess I cleaned up behind him after his binge on her birthday."

The far away look in Liz's eyes erased all traces of humor. I felt sad and worried for my friend.

"Birthdays can be extremely traumatic," I said sympathetically.

"Tell me about it," she said, bitterly.

I wanted to do something nice for her. Something to make at least one birthday less traumatic.

"When's your birthday," I asked.

She looked at me and laughed. "Same day as yours."

"You're kidding! Why didn't you say?"

"At the time, I didn't think you really wanted to hear it."

"Oh, yeah," I said, guiltily.

"We'd better go. We're already late for class," she said.

When we came out, Avery was waiting.

"You okay?" he asked anxiously.

"Why Avery, I didn't know you cared," I teased, uncomfortable with all the attention. "Between you and Liz, it's like I have my very own pubescent parents. Gee dad, mom already asked if I was preggers. Are you gonna grill me about drugs?"

Avery's features twisted in suspicion. "Well you must be high on something, the way you were dancing with Micah. I thought you two were going to kill each other."

"Yeah," Liz agreed, enthusiastically. "You guys looked incredible together."

I became light headed again just thinking about it. "Thanks. I'm going to lie down in the nurse's office. I'm still not feeling one hundred percent."

I didn't leave the nurse's office until my math class started. But Micah wasn't there. I wanted the floor to open up and swallow me whole.

After school, he was waiting for me on his side of the street.

"Are you all right?" I asked, crossing over.

"Yes."

"I'm so sorry, Micah."

"I'm not. You were hot," he said. Then he gave me a slow suggestive smile and a wicked wink.

I shook my head in utter disbelief. "Why, Micah? Why are you putting yourself through this?"

The smile left his face and his eyes became serious. "I'd rather burn than feel nothing," he said quietly.

Those six words changed my world. "Okay. We'll talk."

It took us several days of arguing back and forth to set up the ground rules. No more mountain trips until we got everything figured out. What needed to be figured out was what degree of touching would be permissible because we both agreed we were miserable without each other.

Because Micah had no boundaries, the degree of touching would have to be balanced against what I found tolerable regarding his suffering. I was shooting for crimson with a minimum of gold flashes. We would conduct a series of tests to see what kind of touching produced the desired effects.

Micah had to allow me to view his extractions during our testing period. We argued back and forth about this for days but due to his tendency to omit, I wouldn't budge. I had to see it for myself.

At one point, I suggested that he let me try out the Depacitor personally to see what it actually felt like. He refused so vehemently I didn't try to bring it up again.

He finally relented to allowing me to view his extractions after a long standoff that was getting us nowhere.

The final ground rule was that all testing would be conducted on my front porch. Micah nearly fell over in shock.

In defense of my reasoning, I firmly asserted, "There's no way I'm going back up to Kennesaw and rolling around on that mountain with you while we're doing this."

"On your front porch for the whole world to see? Can we at least do it on your back patio?" he countered.

"No. You burn for the whole Sp. world to see," I accused. "So what's the difference?"

"I don't want to make it easy for my father to make another front row surprise appearance while I'm kissing my girlfriend," he said, referring to the time we were busted by Mr. Alexander.

"Good. It'll keep you in check," I retorted. But honestly, for days afterwards, the 'kissing my girlfriend' part had my heart fluttering like crazy whenever I thought about it.

Micah looked at me, clearly insulted. "You can trust me."

"I know I can, Micah. Look, it's no big deal. Your house is the only one that can see mine so anybody else would have to be directly in front of my house to see. And this is serious testing.

You said your dad told you based on my interrogation, it's the intensity of the emotion you're feeling at the time of physical contact that causes the greatest agony. I figure, conducting our tests right here on my front porch will fix that."

He didn't respond.

"Take it or leave it Micah. Open buffet is closed. Now, I'm a one trip salad bar and it's only one item per trip," I said, impatiently.

He laughed then and after thinking about it awhile longer, he finally agreed.

Our first day of testing was awkward but went relatively smoothly. We sat on the porch swing discussing which of my body parts to begin with. Despite his reservations around being on the front porch, Micah wanted to go straight for the kiss but I would have to work my way up to that bold act.

We finally agreed on my hands. So Micah and I silently held hands for a few moments. To ensure emotions wouldn't interfere, there was no talking during contact. Then he immediately drove us to the Portacle, careful not to touch each other.

He deposited me in what I discovered was one of many alcoves around the outer wall of the Depacitor auditorium. It was like a medical theater designed for people to inconspicuously slip in and out of the alcove rooms to observe.

When the humming began, I was so focused on our trial I didn't even notice the nudity as the tunics went up in a burst of flames. Micah's hand was the only thing that lit up. It was red with bursts of gold and never got worse as the humming progressively increased.

I smiled in the dark. Hand holding had passed the test; just barely. I would have to revise my acceptable levels or hand holding would be the only thing that passed. I could tell Micah was intentionally not showing discomfort to hide any physical signs of pain and I confronted him about it afterwards. He argued that since I was going by fire hue and not grimaces, it didn't make any difference.

We moved on to my forearms, then upper arms, then shoulders, and so on, carefully testing only a single body part a day then observing the results. When it was my turn to see what parts of Micah I could touch, we quickly discovered, I couldn't touch him anywhere at all. Anything my hands came into contact with, went nuclear except for his hands. So after our first tentative efforts it was decided I couldn't touch him at all except to hold his hands.

Through trial and error, we came to an agreement based on our testing. All things being equal (meaning if nothing was done to heighten Micah's sensitivity during contact – translation, I couldn't do anything stupid like telling him I loved him while we touched), this is the contract we negotiated.

THE CONTRACT

Level 1: Crimson
(Forelegs and forearms)
My safest parts, not so bad

Level 2: Gold
(Hands and upper arms)
I expected these to only be crimson but surprisingly, boys are a lot more excitable than I realized or at least Micah is.

Level 3: Lightning
(Shoulders, neck, face, ears, stomach, back, and – strange as it may sound but he insisted on testing them – feet)
These were my most ticklish parts to test so it was torture for me but delightfully amusing for Micah. Apparently he's a sadist as well as a masochist. Grudgingly allowed with strict restrictions.

Level 4: Nuclear
(Lips)
Tried once and never again! Micah was really upset my lips didn't make the list but I was adamant after I saw deadly looking heat waves rolling off of him like I'd seen coming off hot Georgia pavement, as if the very air was melting in the fiery heat. It just wasn't worth it, all that suffering for a little kiss. Ridiculous!

Level 1 & 2: Wrists, elbows, and knees could go either way

Level 2 & 3: Ankles could go either way

Absolutely <u>NO</u>:
Full body hugging
Kissing (except on rare occasions Micah could but only on my hands or forehead or cheek)

Micah could only use his hands. Very rarely his lips but only on my hands or forehead or cheek.

I positively absolutely could not touch or kiss Micah but it was okay to hold his hands.

Everything else was strictly off limits and we didn't even attempt it!

Once our testing period was over, I recaptured a certain level of sanity as we finished hammering out our agreement. We were able to be together again and our hostilities ceased as we now worked together. Micah was actually happy and smiling again and the hollowness left his eyes. He stood firm on barring me from the Depacitor auditorium once our trials were over but reluctantly agreed to turn over our research findings to his monitoring team.

We had an uneasy truce with Mr. Alexander. I felt like a selfish beast in his presence. But to his credit, he didn't go ballistic when he found out what we were doing. He simply accepted it in grim resignation. I believe even he had been alarmed by Micah's hollow man appearance and appreciated our efforts to rid Micah of that scary character. And though Micah still burned, he was no longer a raging inferno thanks to the contract.

Micah and I started hiking the mountain again, our front porch peep show days transitioning back to keeping it on the down low.

We'd argue over what day it was saying 'this is a leg day' or 'neck day.' Then, in seclusion, I would expose whatever body part we agreed on to his hand then lay perfectly still for his touch.

Many days I felt like a chicken being served up in parts. But quite often Micah would choose to simply hold my hand and I found I preferred this as well. If we wanted to feel especially close, he would stroke my face or kiss my cheek.

It wasn't ideal, however it allowed us to be close physically while causing Micah a minimum of suffering. Micah wouldn't give up on me nor his training obligations so my goal was to keep him from burning or at least burn as little as possible.

When I thought of the free reign he had before I was aware he burned, especially the kisses, I'd grit my teeth in angry agony, thinking of what he must have endured.

I remembered how he said he was willing to pay the penance, the worst part being away from me. How about Hell fire raging through your body, that didn't count as the worst of it? But I didn't mention this to Micah. I was tired of fighting with him.

Of course, Micah wasn't thrilled about going from an all you could eat buffet to a strict diet of controlled portions but it was better than the starvation diet he'd been on when I first discovered how he suffered.

My carefree days of blissfully singing I was ready from the backseat of Kelly's car were now nostalgia. I'd done everything I could to keep Micah's suffering to a minimum. We now walked the fine line of ecstasy and agony together. To his credit, he never took advantage and stayed within the strict boundaries of our contract.

However, he did ask if it would be okay if we kissed each other on graduation day. At first I said absolutely not but then reconsidered, carefully thinking it over. After all, it was a special occasion. And what was one little kiss, a kiss Micah was willing to burn for.

15 ~ THE QUILT

The end of school was drawing near and the lazy hot Georgia days hinted at the long tranquil summer awaiting us. We spent restless days, anticipating the final bell releasing us for good until the following school year. The sun streamed through the kitchen patio window, revealing suspended motes floating in and out of its path.

My sisters had already retreated upstairs to their rooms, refusing to sample the dinner I'd prepared. Before leaving, they did mercifully warn Micah not to eat the meatloaf if he valued his life.

Micah sat in our breakfast nook with the plate he'd defiantly taken from the shelf sitting in front of him on the table.

"You don't have to eat it," I conceded, in defeat. "It'll probably make you sick."

He quietly began dipping up a serving.

"Really, Micah. You don't have to. They're right, it's suicide." I stood up to clear the table of the revolting dishes.

Micah held up his hand to halt me, careful not to actually touch me, this being his rare kissing day he didn't want to accidentally forfeit it. I sat back down.

He continued to fill his plate. First the meatloaf then the yams and finally the green beans.

"You don't have to prove anything to me," I assured him. "This isn't bravery, it's insanity."

He finished serving himself and picked up his fork prepared to eat.

I quickly said grace on his behalf and he smiled as he bravely went straight for the meatloaf.

"I can't watch," I said but I couldn't take my eyes off of him as he slowly began to eat. I'd expected him to work his way up to the meatloaf, first going for the yams and green beans. They at least looked like yams and green beans were supposed to look. The meatloaf was a hot nasty mess.

Micah worked his way around the plate, his face not hinting in the least at the horror show playing inside his mouth.

"Your days of stoically enduring the Depacitor are paying off," I commented glumly.

A short burst of laughter escaped him but he quickly recomposed himself and continued eating.

"You can at least put your shield up to help minimize the taste," I suggested. He just kept going as if he hadn't heard me.

When he was almost finished, in a flash of madness, I grabbed his fork from the plate and speared the last bite of meatloaf then popped it in my mouth before I changed my mind.

Oh! It was too nasty!

I suppressed the urge to spit it right back out. My eyes watered and I squeezed them tight, quickly fanning myself with my hands, as I chewed, releasing gross explosions inside my mouth. How could he stand it? Only a superbeing could survive such torture.

I shuddered as I gulped down his icy drink, for once grateful for the searing cold that washed down all traces of the vile taste. Micah laughed as he gallantly handed me his napkin to wipe my tears away. I knew he wanted to wipe them for me but he wasn't going to do anything that jeopardized his kissing day.

"Why did you do that?" he asked.

"I couldn't bear to watch you suffer alone," I said, setting down his cold sweet tea.

With a deliberateness that sent shivers of anticipation through me, he placed both his hands behind his back. Then he leaned over and kissed my cheek, slowly drawing his lips back and forth across the surface before carefully stopping just short of my lips.

Pleasant warmth spread from my cheek and suffused my entire face. His light heady scent drifted between us. I closed my eyes feeling all jittery inside.

"All better?" he whispered and I nodded.

We were sitting at the breakfast table, with my dad watching television in the family room right next to the kitchen.

"Thanks for cooking for me," Micah murmured politely before pulling back. "I really appreciate your efforts."

"I appreciate you coming up with something both positive and true after eating that," I said, sincerely.

Dad walked by the kitchen without looking in. He had refined his glaring patrols, settling into unobtrusive glide bys, which allowed him to covertly take in the scene via his peripheral vision.

"Opal, are you ready? I'm hungry," he called from the bottom of the stairs.

"Mom's not up here, dad," Kelly returned.

"I think she's out back in her garden," I said.

I heard him go out.

"They'll be heading out soon and we'll have to clear the premises before they leave," I informed Micah.

"Kelly and Kylie don't count as adults?" he asked.

"Not when it comes to supervising boys. Dad considers them co-conspirators."

We had cleared off the table by the time dad came back with mom in tow.

"We're going to grab something to eat before checking on Gran. You two still going to the movies?" dad asked pointedly.

At least mom had the grace to look a little guilty with the full meal I'd prepared carefully stored in stacked containers still sitting on the stove, untouched by all except for Micah and me.

But they had suffered through my cooking for much of the school year so I really couldn't begrudge them their weekend reprieve.

"Yes. We were just heading out," I said.

"Good," dad said and then just stood there, watching us.

Micah got the hint. "Nice to see you again Mrs. Summers, Mr. Summers."

"Kelly, Kylie. We're heading out," I called.

They soon appeared, ready to go. Micah and I were giving them a lift to Greenbriar mall before we went to the movies at Atlantic Station. Kelly's car had been giving her trouble and they were home for the weekend so dad's mechanic could check it out.

"I'm glad I can still count you amongst the living, Micah. I thought Disa's meatloaf would put you six feet under for sure," Kelly teased.

"Give it time to work its way through his system," Kylie chimed in. "Disa's proteins usually self destruct in the intestines."

I considered rescinding the invitation to drop them at the mall but I didn't want to reveal my evil side in Micah's presence.

The jeep's top was down and the ride down the highway was blustery, preventing any real conversation. When we got to the mall, the twins' hair had that just stepped out of the clothes dryer windblown look.

Their long straight hair was twisted in disarray around their heads. They used their fingers to try to comb it out of their faces and back into some semblance of a style.

My afro had grown out quite a bit and had withstood the battering of the wind very well. A decorative scarf held the thick tight curls away from my face and I didn't have a strand out of place.

Kylie told me their friend would give them a ride home and thanked us for dropping them off. Kelly grumbled something about Micah putting the top up when he had female passengers.

"Why?" Micah asked, looking all innocent. "Adisa likes the top down."

He winked at me behind Kelly's back and if I didn't know better, I would say a partner in crime was lurking in the depths of his gentle brown eyes.

I stifled a giggle as Kelly stalked off, still raking at her head to repair the ravages of her windblown look.

We drove to Atlantic Station and parked underground. We decided to walk around until the movie started. Micah seemed agitated as we walked side by side, not touching.

"Adisa, there's something I've been meaning to tell you. Victor was able to overturn the ruling and he can travel to this continent…,"

I froze. I was shocked to hear the subject brought up so unexpectedly. I had carefully avoided the topic because I preferred not to relive those seven terror-filled days.

"I know how you feel but there's nothing to be afraid of. He won't hurt you," Micah tried to reassure me.

"Does he have the right to take me away?" I asked in a panic.

"No. The ban was lifted on his travel but that's all. He can't force you to do anything or take you away." Then he hesitated before adding. "He'll be here before school is out."

"Micah, that's only three weeks away," I exclaimed in alarm.

"I know. If it will make you feel any better, I'll tell him to stay inside the house during his visit so you won't run into him in the neighborhood."

"He's staying at your home?" I asked, the thought hadn't even crossed my mind until his comment.

"Yes."

"Why?"

"He usually stays with us when he visits. Since I renounced him, my parents are trying to get us to reconcile because it's not good for Sp. twins to stay in contention."

"So you've forgiven him?" I asked, desperately wanting him to deny it.

"We still have issues to discuss. But I've forgiven him other transgressions in the past."

Transgressions! Worse than my kidnapping? What could be worse than that?

"How can you trust anything he says, Micah? He's a liar...,"

"But he chooses not to lie. He can mislead with the truth but he doesn't lie."

"A person who can take the truth and twist it around to make you think something false is worse than a liar," I claimed. "He kidnapped me, Micah. Maybe that's acceptable in the Sp. world but in the earthbound world, that's pretty serious.

And the victim's boyfriend doesn't blindside her by announcing the criminal is visiting his home, which happens to be conveniently located right across the street from...,"

"I'll tell him he can't stay," Micah interjected. "I'm sorry, I didn't realize... I'll tell him he can't stay."

I was crushed we were really so far apart in our thinking that I actually had to break it down to him like that.

"You really don't understand how traumatic it was for me. You superbeings may have realized Victor didn't want to hurt me but I didn't know that. Aren't you even upset that he kidnapped Jason?" I asked in exasperation.

"Technically, that wasn't a kidnapping. It was prearranged that Jason would be staying with him, as he's done numerous times in the past.

Victor started building a pod... a special shelter to contain you, long before that, while I was still in Africa, and he finally had it completed. When he saw his chance to take you, he sent me on a bogus mission and then went after you. He never intended to actually hurt you."

I stared at Micah in wordless wonder.

"Don't look at me like that, Adisa," he said, guilt clearly etched into his features. "If I'd known in time what he was up to, I would've stopped it."

"I didn't know if I'd live to see you or my family ever again," I tried to explain. "I thought I was going to die."

Micah's expression was pained. "He was desperate, Adisa. I'm not excusing what he did. But haven't you ever done something out of desperation that you regretted later?"

"I don't think Victor regrets what he did to me," I challenged and then dejectedly added, "I feel as if I've been the object of the worst practical joke. I'm on one side alone, and the Sp. world is on the other, giving Victor a wink and a nod for what he did to me."

"Nobody's laughing over what Victor did to you, least of all me. Everyone knows how dangerous it was. My mistake, was not talking to you to find out how you feel."

Micah was polite enough not to fault me for discouraging the topic in the past but I still regretted my decision to keep my head stuck in the sand for so long.

We walked along in tense silence before I could continue, deciding now was the point of no return.

"All pride aside, why should I forgive Victor? Is there really a reason that justifies his actions toward me?" I took a deep breath and finally asked the question I'd been avoiding since the trial.

"Are you really dying, Micah?" Then, suddenly afraid of the answer, I rushed on. "If so, what can we do to stop it? If we can't stop it, how long do you have? And... is Victor really responsible? I need to know the truth."

Micah was quiet. We walked around the square behind Rosa Mexicano, past Copeland's Cheesecake Bistro then headed for the Fox Sports Grill. We passed by the Cold Stone Creamery and I shuddered, watching the customers enjoy their frozen treats. We took the road by Dillards and Micah finally opened up once we were on 17th Street headed for the arch.

"It's true, I hold things back, omit, because I want to protect you. But if it will help you understand Victor better, I'll answer your questions. Ask them again, one at a time. But please understand, this is very difficult for me."

Brand new townhomes lined the street in an orderly fashion and I envied the carefree independence the young professionals who inhabited them possessed.

"Are you really dying?" I asked, then held my breath, praying for the best but expecting the worst.

Micah's expression briefly twisted in anxiety then his clear eyes held mine steady. "Yes."

My heart sank in horror as I realized just how desperately I expected the answer to be no. Micah appeared so healthy and strong, there wasn't a hint of death about him anywhere.

Even though I knew he spoke the truth, I couldn't help expressing doubt. "But you look so healthy."

"I'm asymptomatic. But the closer I get to death, I'll most likely show signs then."

"What can we do to stop it?" I asked, my voice softened by fear.

His face looked strained. "Victor has already done the only thing that might have saved me and it failed."

Tears welled up in my eyes. "You're referring to my kidnapping."

Micah nodded.

"How long do you have?" I asked, sadly.

The familiar broken smile ghosted across his features. "A few years. Three or four if I'm lucky, no more than five at best."

We passed under the arch then took the stairs down to the lake. We were surprised to discover a museum tucked down there, beneath the arch. We walked around to the bridge, and stood next to each other, staring into the calm water.

"Is Victor really responsible?" I asked.

"Yes," Micah admitted quietly, without a trace of rancor.

It was surreal, such an idyllic setting in which to finally confront Micah's imminent death.

I was immediately consumed by my own selfish guilt. Micah had forgiven his brother for this ultimate sin. And here I was, whining and giving him grief over a few days of my own personal discomfort while he was facing death.

"We were just kids," Micah began explaining, "ten years old, when it happened. It was an accident. Victor's powers had just manifested. I'd had mine since I was five so I had better control over them. We were training, one on one combat. I had my shield down to go a little easier on him. Even so, I was easily winning, getting the best of him time after time.

He was so excited about his new powers, at first it didn't matter to him. But then, I don't know exactly at what point, it did begin to matter.

I didn't realize how humiliating it was for him. I thought it was understood, this was just to test his limits, not a true contest. A true contest wouldn't have been fair, like a veteran... a professional against a novice."

Micah's head bowed with the weight of his memories. He drew in a long deep breath before continuing.

"In desperation, he flung a shard at me, freezing it in midair just before it touched me. But he didn't account for my momentum which carried my forward, burying the shard in my heart."

Micah tensed as if he was being pierced anew. I instinctively reached for him, stopping when I realized he would burn for it. I hugged myself instead, digging my nails into my sides to distract me from Micah's pain. He looked drained as he continued.

"It's still lodged there and can't be removed. I would have died instantly but for Victor's freezing it first. Like I said, he didn't have full control at the time and he blasted the thing strong enough to keep it frozen for years. It's slowly thawing now and at the rate it's going... well, that's how we know about how long I have."

I didn't want to believe it. But Micah was saying it, so it had to be true.

"What the Hell is a shard?" I asked, angrily envisioning the mysterious object silently melting in Micah's chest, threatening his life.

"A fragment... sliver of lightning collected by some superbeings for weapons. There aren't many weapons in the Sp. world because powers are usually stronger so the weapons that do exist are extremely deadly. Victor admired the shard and took it... stole it, planning on returning it. But then...," Micah's voice trailed off.

"Why doesn't Victor just go away and disappear for ever?" I asked, bitterly. "Everything he touches, he ruins."

Micah's eyes were agonized as they met my unforgiving gaze. "He wants to make things right, Adisa. Superbeings seek forgiveness, just like earthbounds. They want to be absolved of their sins, some even pray, like everybody else."

My mouth dropped open in shock. "You're kidding!"

"No—even Sp. beings want to go to Heaven." He managed to smile at my incredulous expression. "Victor was crushed. He hated himself and couldn't face what he'd done. He changed his Sp. citizenship to Africa to get away from me. We spent a few years apart because he was too ashamed to face me.

Finally, with the help of professionals from both of our continents, we reunited. Jason was about three or four by then and the two of them bonded immediately after meeting for the first time. It was as if Victor was trying to make up for what he did by doing everything he could for Jason because he knew there was nothing he could do to save me. That is until...," Micah paused significantly, staring at me before continuing.

"Until he discovered an ancient African prophecy that told of a Healer I would fall in love with. And my life would be spared if this Healer forgave and learned to love Victor. Victor believed you were the Healer but still asleep. So he tried to force you to manifest, become the Healer, forgive him, love him... all to save me."

Confronted with the whole crazy story, I found myself concentrating on one vain thought. Outside of Micah's almost marriage proposal, this was the closest he'd ever come to actually saying he loved me.

I forced my mind to release this selfish thought and deal with what I was desperately trying to avoid, Micah's death. Victor's forced manifestation had failed. Did that mean Micah would die?

Did it mean he was supposed to love somebody else, whoever this Healer was? I was no Sp. being. I didn't have the parentage. Or did I?

"Micah, I'm not a superbeing. How could I be unless… my parents…," I held my breath, unable to go any further. Would this be enough to finally get him to tell me the truth about my true identity? I could see him struggling with the decision.

Micah finally nodded confirmation and my skin became prickly, anticipating a final admission. But his answer was still ambiguous. He hadn't stated that the Summers were not my true parents.

"Which one?" I pressed for specifics.

He was indecisive again but eventually answered. "Your father."

My mind staggered under the truth of my real father as a superbeing. But Micah's response was still ambiguous, implying Frederick when I knew it was Cyrus.

"It's best you didn't discuss this with Mr. Summers," Micah said. "You're not supposed to know."

Micah hadn't lied but he still hadn't told me the whole truth either. I decided to stop pressuring him. This was about him, not me. My issues could be dealt with later. I nodded my assent to his suggestion and Micah looked relieved.

"Where did Victor get the prophecy from anyway?" I asked.

"They're handed down through the generations by griots, African storytellers who verbally preserve history through stories and song."

"And that's allowed in your courts as evidence, some random person's say so?" I asked in contempt.

"It's been proven that their oral histories are more accurate than many western written histories," Micah stated sagely, disregarding my rude tone.

I felt rightfully chastised for my disrespect. "I'm sorry. I didn't mean… I never did get a copy of that evidence, the African prophecy," I tried to amend.

"It came. You have to go to the Portacle in person to request it. I didn't mention it before because you said you weren't ready to rehash that experience."

It was true, I'd said exactly that once when Micah tried to bring it up during one of our mountain hikes. At the time, I just wanted to put it behind me and forget about the whole traumatic experience.

I sighed in resignation. "I guess I have to be ready now. I don't have a choice. Can you take me to get it sometime?"

"Sure. But I've already seen it and have it memorized. It says,

> *Twin brothers not of blood will*
> *rise up both warriors*
> *One will be accepted the other*
> *rejected will steal the shard,*
> *The accepted warrior's heart will*
> *be pierced*
> *He will surely die lest the healer*
> *save him.*
> *The healer, one he loves not of blood,*
> *must forgive the guilty with love."*

After Micah finished reciting the prophecy, I ventured, "Micah, I don't mean to offend you but it's so hard to believe. Do superbeings really believe prophecies come true?"

"Yes and this one is pretty clear, hard to misinterpret. I thought you were the Healer too," he continued, openly. "We all did. But when Victor's forced manifestation didn't work, we realized it wasn't true. You're already sixteen with no concrete evidence of any superpowers."

"Then why are you still with me? You should be out looking for this Healer and falling in love with her so you can be saved. Maybe that's why things always go bad between us. Maybe we're not supposed to be together." My heart wrenched in my chest at the thought of giving him up. But I certainly couldn't stand around, doing nothing, and watch him die.

"Healer or not, I'm committed to you, Adisa. I'll never leave you." He leaned over and slowly drew his lips across my cheek, warming my face with his breath.

I wanted to stay with him too but I wanted to save him more. "Could I be the Healer, and not know it, never manifest, and still save you?" I asked, hopefully as I pulled away from him.

Micah's unfathomable eyes carefully considered me before he answered. "Forced manifestations have a one hundred percent success rate. Those who don't manifest during the process, never do. That means, you're dormant. You're not a Healer. And you can't save me."

It was so hopeless. Micah's time with me was being wasted. I needed to release him so he could save himself. But how could I?

"I don't want you to die, Micah. I need you to live, even if I can't have you." A dry sob racked my body.

I saw him tense as he resisted the urge to take me in his arms. "I will live, with you, for how ever long I have."

I felt his lips on my cheek again, lightly skimming the surface with a soothing back and forth motion.

"But you have to fall in love with a Healer so you'll stay alive longer," I stubbornly insisted though unable to move away again.

"I'd rather have a few years with you, than a lifetime without you," he spoke against my cheek.

The heat of his kiss was melting away my reserve and my heart rejoiced, hearing his declaration. But at the same time, I felt a crushing selfishness that would not let me rest easy.

We went to the movies. I didn't want to but Micah insisted, claiming he wanted things to be the same between us. But how could they be? How could they ever be the same when I possessed the power of life or death over him?

There was only one thing I could think to do, since he refused to try to save himself. I would have to pick up Victor's cause and try to save Micah myself. I would find the Healer and bring her to Micah.

I didn't have a clue as to how I would do this, but I would. It would break my heart but at least he would live. I loved Micah too much to let him die.

The movie we saw was a romantic comedy. Micah seemed to enjoy it but I couldn't laugh even though I knew everything would work out in the end.

One evening, I sat on our back patio with mom, shelling peas we'd picked up at the farmer's market. We were shaded from the glaring rays of the sun under the shelter of the portable awning dad had put up for us.

Mom had been discussing the end of year party she was giving for me since my birthday party had never taken place. I'd already received several RSVPs confirming attendance and we were discussing the logistics of accommodating a crowd in our home.

"Your dad will move all the furniture against the walls so there'll be room for dancing. But I don't want him doing it all by himself and I don't want you girls straining yourselves either. Ask Micah if he'll come over and help."

"Sure mom."

"Kelly and Kylie will be done with their finals so they'll be able to help out. I can't believe my babies are completing their first year of college." Mama's smile spread in pure satisfaction and I could see her eyes tearing up.

"Mom, don't get all sentimental, you'll be soaking the peas in your tears."

"I wish Gran were well enough to come," she said out of the blue. "I sure hate we didn't raise you girls around family more. That is my one great regret."

I thought about the meaning of family. Then I thought of how difficult it was for Micah to tell me the truth, not wanting to hurt me. He might not ever be able to. It was like the Sterling roses he'd given me after the bus crash. They had no thorns. He was so protective of me, he couldn't even give me roses with thorns. Suddenly, I had a pressing need to know, regardless of the thorns. I needed somebody to confirm it for me besides Victor.

"Mom, I didn't want to bring it up at the time but while dad was in the hospital and I had to take care of things, I came across some papers."

I stopped shelling and wiped my hands on a towel then fished a photocopy out of my pocket. Victor still had my birth certificate but I still had the photocopy of my real mom and dad.

"I got this from Gran," I said, passing the paper to her. "And I found a birth certificate for Adisa Musa Valenté in our safe."

She stared at the photo for a long time. After her initial shock, tears silently rolled down her face. I took her bowl of peas.

"Well, imagine that." She spoke softly, caressing the face of her sister.

"She always did have all the luck with the good looking guys. And I'm not slighting Frederick in the least by admitting that."

Mom looked at me then, the truth clear as day in her eyes. And I knew she would tell me.

"I promised myself, from the beginning, that if you ever came to me and asked, I would tell you the truth." She took in a deep breath and let it out slowly. "I'm sorry you had to carry this alone for so long. Especially during a time when family matters most."

I didn't say anything. I sat still, afraid any reaction on my part would stop her.

"This is Pearl, my twin sister… your real mother."

There, it was out. Simple and clear. Lightning didn't strike and the earth didn't stop spinning. I really was Adisa Valenté. There was no Adisa Summers. She had never existed.

Mom reached for my hand as if to ease the blow of her words but I jerked back, a natural reflex that I immediately regretted. I reached out and took her hand.

"Tell me about her." I squeezed her hand in encouragement.

The corners of mom's mouth turned up at my request. "She was beautiful. Everybody adored her, including me… for the most part. And my mama, Gran, favored her."

Mom was smiling but I could tell the memory pained her.

"Gran spoiled her while being hard on me. I never knew why. I was jealous of her, I'm ashamed to say. My own baby sister. And I was hard on her too, like Kelly is on you sometimes.

You're surprised. You didn't think I paid attention to that. Well, parents know a whole lot more than they let on." Mom patted my hand for emphasis.

"I was hard on Pearl out of jealousy but out of worry too. Nothing but heartache awaits a pampered and sheltered black woman. Only white women can afford the luxury of being spoiled."

Mom's racially tinged words took me by surprise. I'd never heard her talk like that before. She returned from whatever far off place she'd gone and looked at me.

"Kelly's trying to make you strong for what life has in store for you, the same as I tried to do for your mama. But I didn't succeed with Pearl. And maybe I spoil you a little out of guilt.

You're like Pearl, an innocent free spirit. You worried me half to death with your head in the clouds over all that superhero foolishness, living in a world of make believe because you couldn't handle this one. It reminded me so much of Pearl. But I've been more lenient on you to make up for how hard I was on her."

Her hands anchored me to the moment. I felt I could go spinning out of control but she was holding me in place. "Tell me about him, my real... Cyrus."

Mom's smile broadened but managed to look sad at the same time. "Cyrus. Your daddy was the most gorgeous man I ever met in my life. Flawless beautiful midnight skin and dark eyes that could see clear through to the depths of you. A smile a mile long full of great white perfect teeth. You have his smile. He was the kind of man who made you feel special when he was in your presence. He was like a king, more than... more than a king... the first of men, a true African.

And he was crazy about your mama, genuinely in love. I never saw a man so far gone over a woman. Pearl loved him right back. A woman would have to be out of her mind not to. Daddy had already passed and it was just the three of us women, holding each other up. That's why when Frederick went down with that heart attack... it just reminded me of that bad time in my life.

Well, when Cyrus showed up, your mama was ready to be saved. We were both suffering under mama's possessiveness in daddy's absence. Mama tried to keep us so close, she was suffocating us. Cyrus represented freedom for your mama. But she was only sixteen and Gran wouldn't let her go.

Cyrus didn't seem to understand. He treated Pearl like she was a grown woman. But even she wasn't strong enough to disobey Gran for long. So Cyrus went away, hurt."

Mama shook her head in sympathy.

"We grew up, I met Frederick and got married and left home, leaving Pearl with mama. I was glad to be gone and rarely visited. Gran's pampering made Pearl needy and dependent so she stayed, even after she was grown and could live on her own. It must have been horrible for her to have to deal with our mama all by herself with nobody to turn to.

Eventually, I had Kelly and Kylie. Then the next thing I know, Gran was calling me, saying Cyrus had returned. She was scared he'd take Pearl away from her. Then she called claiming Pearl was pregnant. After that, Pearl disappeared before having the baby. I think that's what pushed Gran over the edge and it's like she just gave in to her dementia more and more until I eventually had to put her in a home."

Mom's hands repeatedly twisted and untwisted her apron, as if trying to wring out her guilt.

"Pearl sent a few letters saying she was doing fine and she even included a few pictures. But she never gave a return address. Then after the urgent message to come and get you, I never heard from her again."

"What urgent message?" I asked.

Mom looked at me guiltily. "The urgent message to go find you in a cotton field. I didn't believe it at first but Pearl had included your birth certificate. So we all piled in the car to go check it out. I don't know why they left you out there all alone. And Lord knows how you survived the night all by yourself with just that quilt and not a stitch of clothing on your back. We haven't heard from your parents since. I honestly don't know if they're dead or alive.

I still have that quilt stored away, so it wouldn't bring back any bad memories. But safely preserved, just in case you ever want it back. After all, it is the only thing you have from your parents."

I immediately wanted the quilt, a link to my real parents. Mom would probably feel hurt, interpreting my desire for it as a rejection of her. So I said nothing and let her continue telling her story.

"I didn't want you to know the pain of being abandoned by your own parents plus the message they sent suggested that your life may be in danger so we decided to hide your real identity.

We made up the story of accidentally leaving you behind to explain away any memories you or the twins had about that day.

Frederick was able to get new documents on you and we just started acting like you were our own natural child. There was nobody close enough to us to know any different so it wasn't too difficult to pass you off as one of our own."

Mom and I talked until dad came back home. She promised to tell him and the twins. I didn't want to do it and I didn't even want to be present when she told them. I knew I was being a coward but I was mentally fried. I didn't need another emotional upheaval before the end of school. I was reserving that for Victor's visit.

M icah answered his door before I had a chance to ring the doorbell. I knew right away his shield was down. He looked devastatingly handsome in a black shirt and faded blue jeans. I felt rather plain in my simple white halter dress but the twins assured me I looked quite stunning. I wore strappy sandals that had a daring heel, to dress up my outfit, and I still had to look up to meet Micah's eyes.

"Hi. Come in," he said, stepping aside.

I felt self conscious as I entered. I'd been to his home twice before but both times I was so upset I didn't really pay attention to my surroundings.

I now saw that Micah's home was as sparsely furnished as the Portacle. But it was done in a tasteful minimalist style. I saw equipment in one corner that seemed out of place.

"They're treating the whole house to make it fireproof," Micah explained. "Jason is going through a highly combustible stage right now and we're trying to make everything as fire retardant as possible."

Even though his words were completely freaking me out on the inside, I wanted to appear unfazed.

"I can relate," I said, casually. "The twins went through a stage, playing with matches. But we didn't have to treat the house. They got over it after dad lit up their backsides."

Micah gave me one of his gorgeous smiles. "Well, we have different methods here."

"How's my little hero?" I greeted Jason as he joined us in the family room.

Jason looked at me shyly, not quite sure whether or not he approved of my nickname for him. He was wearing some unusual looking gloves and hid his hands behind his back when he saw me looking at them so I didn't comment.

"What are you doing here?" he asked.

"Your brother's taking me to the High museum for the Luvre exhibit."

"That's in Paris," he said.

"Jason, I'm impressed. How'd you know that?"

"I've been."

"Of course you have. Don't I feel foolish." That's what I get for condescending to a first grader. "Anyway, you're right. The Luvre is in Paris but they've loaned some art pieces to Atlanta."

"Cool. Can I come too?"

"No. Maybe next time," Micah interjected, reaching around and shaking one of Jason's gloved hands significantly. "When you have better control."

Jason snatched his hand away.

"Jason, how'd you like to come over to my house and see Power Boy again and some of his friends too?" I asked, trying to smooth things over as I put my arm around his shoulders. But he pulled away from me too.

"Power Boy sucks!" he declared, backing away. "And Micah needs to get a running start to fly. He can't even blast off from standing like Hancock.

He just jumps in the air and stalls like a car out of gas. Then falls back to earth like any old regular earthbound." He flung the last part out as if it was the biggest insult he could think of then ran from the room.

I was surprised by how much his words hurt, after all, he was only a kid and probably didn't really mean it. Surely he didn't really believe that Power Boy sucked.

"Don't listen to him. He's experiencing a kind of superpower hormonal thing. Plus he's self conscious about the gloves so I guess it was kind of insensitive of me to do that," Micah explained.

"What was that about Hancock?" I asked.

Micah looked chagrined. "He thinks it's cool the way Will Smith's character in Hancock can just rocket up into the sky from a stand still. I haven't mastered that yet."

"Oh, it's a guy thing. What are the gloves for?" I asked, changing the subject, not wanting to bruise any fragile egos any further. Boys! Always trying to be so macho.

"They're sort of like training wheels. They help him adjust to his powers without burning himself or anyone or anything."

"I thought I heard a visitor," Mrs. Alexander said as she entered. "Welcome Adisa. We so rarely receive visitors. I'm sure you can guess why."

I smiled in understanding.

"Do you two plan on hanging around here today?" she asked and she sounded as if she genuinely wanted us to.

"No, mother. We're going to the museum today but I wanted to show Adisa my room first."

Mrs. Alexander looked surprised but not displeased. "Well, maybe next time you'll be able to stay awhile and visit with us."

"I'd like that," I said and meant it. She was vastly different from her husband.

As Micah and I went upstairs, I suppressed my guilty thoughts. There was an adult in the house so I hadn't broken that rule. They did have a different rule about guests going upstairs to private bedrooms but, I rationalized, when in Rome.

Then I remembered Micah was a grown man and actually owned the house. So he probably didn't have any rules that he had to abide by. No pressure.

Micah's room was spacious and sparingly decorated in muted blue and silver tones, a big contrast to the earth tones and bursts of color in my own cluttered space. He had a bed, a desk with a chair, and a large storage unit. Each piece looked like a beautiful work of art with superior craftsmanship and all of it was exceptionally sturdy looking. The bed was particularly imposing.

"I'm sometimes a little rough on furniture," Micah explained with a shrug of his shoulders. "One of the drawbacks of having my Sp. powers."

"Oh, please. Cry me a river, will you," I said, feeling more than a little envious. I still longed for superpowers of my own.

The colossal bed commanded attention, clearly the centerpiece of the room. I did my level best to pretend it wasn't there. But I found it very difficult, almost impossible to prevent myself from envisioning Micah lying there.

I felt self conscious standing right next to Micah with that big luxurious bed staring us in the face. Maybe dad actually had a valid point.

I moved over to the window. Micah's desk was there the same as in my room. Next to his computer, there was a framed picture. I was surprised to see it was of me.

I picked it up astonished. It wasn't a glossy photograph. It was a newspaper print, cut out from the bus crash article that ran in the paper. Talbot must have provided my freshman school picture because my hair was long and straight.

"Don't you have pictures of your family?" I asked.

He came over and pulled out the desk drawer and withdrew a small photo album. He gave it to me and I flipped through it. It had pictures of his mom, dad, Jason, and one of him with Victor. They were young boys in the photo and looked like any other two friends posing in the traditional buddy style with their arms casually draped around each other, grinning from ear to ear. There was also a family shot of them all together, including Victor.

On the last page of the album, my birthday invitation was preserved. My finger lightly traced the pen and ink profile as my breath unexpectedly caught in my chest. I had an overwhelming desire to kiss Micah.

I closed the album and handed it back. Micah put it away. I looked out the window and could clearly see my bedroom window.

"I didn't know you had such a great view of my room. I hope you've never seen me in any compromising situations," I kidded.

I laughed at my own joke but Micah didn't.

"Micah? What did you see?" I asked horrified. My frenzied mind conjured up embarrassing images of me, some of which had never even happened.

Micah avoided my eyes.

"Oh no you don't. None of that omit stuff. Tell me." I cornered him.

"Promise you won't be embarrassed."

"I promise," I quickly agreed, anything just to get him talking.

"Remember the time, after I told you about Lilac Wine, I disappeared for a couple days? It was dark when I returned,s we drove into our driveway. My parents carried Jason inside and I was about to follow but then I turned to look at your window."

I nodded in relieved remembrance as I recalled sitting on my desk top wearing an oversized cotton nightgown, nothing clinging to my curves or skimpily revealing.

"You had the light on…,"

"Yes?" I answered, not comprehending his hesitation over a modest nightgown that completely covered me.

"You were… backlit and I could see right through…,"

My mind suddenly flooded with the image. "You've got to be kidding me," I wailed thoroughly embarrassed as I slumped against his desk.

"You promised you wouldn't be embarrassed," he reminded me.

"I lied. Besides, I'm not so much embarrassed as mortified."

"Don't be. You were beautiful, a sculpted work of art. Like Rodin's lovers in The Kiss."

"Yeah, and just as nude!" I exclaimed. Then I looked at him suspiciously. "Okay, Micah, you can stop staring at my lips now. They're not in the contract so back off. Besides, today is a handholding day and I'm not changing it. I've been daydreaming all day about strolling hand in hand with you around all that French art."

"Can you blame me for trying?" he grinned, good-naturedly.

"I can and I do."

I began to feel awkward being so close to him.

"You never did explain Lilac Wine to me," I quickly accused, leaning further back onto his desk to allow a little more space between us.

"It tells our story. Listen to it again with that in mind," he suggested and left it at that.

As we left his room, I impulsively asked, "What room would Victor have if he stayed here?"

Micah took my hand and led the way.

"It's toward the back of the house, where it's shady. Victor prefers it cool."

I kept my comments to myself because mom always said, if you can't say something nice, don't say anything at all.

The room was painted in dark cool colors and there was only a bed and a chair. It was the barest room yet.

"What, no massive storage unit?" I asked.

"Everything he brings usually fits in the closet."

"Oh." I fidgeted while trying to decide exactly how to word what I wanted to say. "Micah, I've been thinking. Victor's your twin and he obviously means a lot to you and your family. So when he comes... you can go ahead and let him stay here."

"Are you sure? I want you to feel safe and we've already arranged for him to stay somewhere else."

I was grateful for his words and it made my decision easier for me. "It's your home and I wouldn't feel right coming between family. And I hate making you choose. But thanks for choosing me."

"What Victor did was way out of line. My parents are bringing in professional counsel to see if we can patch things up. It's not good for Sp. twins to be enemies but I'm having a more difficult time dealing with what he did to you than I did with what he did to me."

"Well believe this, I'll kick Victor's behind black and blue if he comes anywhere near me. I was holding back the last time because I feared for Jason's safety. So no joke, I will set it off if he steps out of line."

Micah squeezed my hand reassuringly. "That won't be necessary. I've already told him to stay away from you or he'll have a problem with me. Thanks a lot, Adisa. We have a lot to work through with him and it's a lot easier to have him here."

I could tell by Micah's face that he was thinking of that day, in the courthouse, when he tried to attack Victor.

"Micah, there's something I've been meaning to ask you. What's baseborn?"

Micah looked as if I'd knocked the wind out of him. His eyes locked with mine and in that instant, I saw wounds centuries old that still plagued him, then he looked away.

"It's something I never should have said, something meant to hurt Victor as much as he'd hurt me," he said. His face was so pained I couldn't bring myself to pursue the matter any further so I let it go.

Micah and I had a nice day together, walking through the exhibit and then walking around the arts district and talking. I told him about Kelly and Kylie completing their finals and returning home for summer break.

I didn't tell him I was avoiding my own home because mom was telling them about my true parentage. I just held his hand and listened to him talk and tried not to obsess over how much his hand would burn.

I made sure we got back late, hoping I wouldn't have to face the twins. I was surprised mom and dad had actually gone to bed. They usually stayed up until I returned safely from my date. The lights were on under the twin's doors.

I was in bed under the covers pretending to be asleep when they came into my room. Harsh light penetrated my eyelids.

"No Kel. That's too bright."

The brightness went away and I heard somebody flip the switch in my restroom.

"You can stop pretending," Kelly said.

I rolled over, incapable of keeping up the pretense.

Kylie sat next to me and took my hand.

"Tell me the truth, did you guys know?" I asked.

Kylie quickly shook her head no. Her face was all screwed up like she'd been crying and was on the verge of doing it again.

"We didn't know, Disa," Kelly said. "I remember going to the field that day. And how I always thought you were a big baby who could walk. But I thought it was just childish memories."

Kylie found her voice. "Mom said dad still hasn't come to talk to you about it. Is that true?"

I nodded, holding back my tears, not daring to make a sound.

"I'm sorry, Disa. It'll be okay," Kylie consoled.

They lay down with me, one in front and one in back of me. Kelly whispered fiercely from behind me in the darkness, "No matter what, we're *all* still sisters."

Then I felt something wet on my neck and I was surprised. Kelly never cried. I felt this gave me permission to release my own. I fell asleep with them holding me and the nightmares stayed away.

Mr. Alexander unexpectedly came to pick me up after gym class one day. I seriously considered refusing to go with him but changed my mind, thinking of the valuable information I learned the last time he took me out of school.

"What horror do you have waiting for me this time?" I asked. "It must be something Micah wouldn't approve of since you're sneaking in after he's left again."

"Please, keep an open mind and give me at least five minutes of your time," he said looking nervous. "And I would appreciate it if you kept this from Micah."

That's all he had time to say before he was pulling into his driveway. For some reason, this worried me more than going to the police station would have. At least that was a public setting with witnesses.

Mr. Alexander escorted me into the same room I'd met the blond Amazon in. It appeared to be a home office. He excused himself but soon returned and my heart stopped when I saw who followed him.

Victor!

He still possessed the same pale dramatic good looks and entered the room as if he owned it. Facing Victor and Mr. Alexander alone, I momentarily thought they had joined forces to do away with me once and for all. All my bravado about kicking Victor's behind flew right out the window.

"Victor has something he wants to say to you," Mr. Alexander said.

I couldn't believe it. Hadn't he said enough? I didn't want to hear anymore of his sick stories.

Victor's cold eyes glittered like jewels as he watched my every move.

"For taking you against your will and intentionally misleading you with the intent to escalate your emotions and elicit superpowers during a forced manifestation, I offer you my most heartfelt apology. I deprived you of your freedom and terrorized you.

I thought I could save my brother without harming you unduly. I now believe, you are not the Healer so you don't have to be afraid of me."

Talk about a jaw dropper. What was this, some kind of twelve step superhero recovery process? I didn't know what to say. Victor waited, silently, still observing me with his cold eyes. I shook my head to clear it.

"This is why you pulled me out of school?" I asked Mr. Alexander. "What do you two expect me to do? Forgive and forget? For everything you did to me, the worry you put my family through, a simple apology won't cover it. Not even close."

"I told you, you were wasting your time," Victor said to Mr. Alexander. It sounded like a sneer in my ears and my temper flashed.

"You're right. And it's a waste of mine too. Do you think you're better than I am just because you have some special abilities? You think you can treat people anyway you feel like and not suffer any consequences for it?" I accused in disgust.

"I was trying to save my brother," he stated as if that absolved him of everything.

"He renounced you. Remember? He's not your brother!" I flung out, trying to hurt him. "This is my life! You should have asked me first."

"Your consent would have diminished the effort and I seriously doubt you would have given it," he scoffed.

"Then you don't know me very well because I'd give my life for Micah. He's good and noble and you know it because he forgave you for committing the unforgivable you disgusting piece of...

Even now, Micah still cares about you and hopes you two will be able to repair your relationship. And he wants to be a Guardian, dedicating his life to helping others which is more than I can say for you. He's going to do great things in this world. And he's worth more than a hundred of you, me or you too Mr. Alexander. I'm out of here. You can keep your tired apologies."

I started for the door.

"Adisa, please. I was only trying to help," Mr. Alexander said.

"I know and I really appreciate the effort," I said, my voice dripping with sarcasm. "But don't take me out of school again without telling me what it's about first. I don't want to waste anymore of anybody's time, especially mine."

"At least let me drive you," he offered.

"No thanks. The walk will give me time to forget about all this craziness and get back to a normal frame of mind."

I felt better once I was outside and on my way. I was deep in thought when I registered somebody standing under Micah's tree.

"Victor! How did you... I don't even want to know. I thought you told Micah you'd stay away from me you liar."

Victor smiled wryly. "Actually I didn't. But Micah did threaten me if I didn't stay away from you. So I guess my fate is in your hands." His dark eyes quietly questioned me.

"I don't want to see Micah suffer for destroying you. You're not worth it," I assured. "Did you follow me because you were scared I would tell Micah, you stinking coward?" I asked, detesting him with an intensity I could barely contain.

I saw anger flash in his eyes before he answered. "No. Based on our limited time together in the pod, I was pretty sure you wouldn't tell him. You were the one who convinced him not to kill me. Remember?"

He paused as if he was genuinely intrigued by me. "I want to make up for what I did to you. I really am sorry for what I put you through," he said roughly, sounding surprisingly sincere.

"I don't want anything from you, Victor," I scornfully exclaimed as I turned away from him.

"No? Not even the story about how a little girl named Adisa Valenté came to live with the Summers family?"

That stopped me in my tracks. He still had the power to shock me.

"You haven't told anybody about this yet, not even Micah. Have you?" he asked, handing over a familiar folded sheet.

My hand shook as I took my birth certificate from him.

"Why haven't you asked them about it? Did you tell the Summers that you know? It's a burden you shouldn't have to carry by yourself, Adisa," he said gently.

Then that cold hearted fool actually tried to hug me!

"I really don't need your pity," I protested, stepping away. But I didn't leave. His offer to tell me about myself was too tempting.

When Victor saw my indecision he suggested, "Perhaps we should step into the woods for privacy. Isn't that how you and Micah usually do it?"

Heated embarrassment flashed through me.

"No thanks," I declined in a low controlled voice. "I prefer dealing with you out in the open." I shoved my certificate in my pocket.

"Fair enough. Are you ready?" he challenged.

I nodded decisively, my hands dangling uselessly at my sides. I felt completely defenseless as I waited for his words.

"Micah and I were both told by his father not to search for you. He received word you were alone in a field and your new family wouldn't be there to pick you up until the following day.

I was the rebellious one. Normally, it would have been me disobeying and going after you. But I was still asleep, waiting on my powers to manifest. So I couldn't go.

Micah had recently manifested and only he could make it in time. I gave Micah a quilt to wrap you in. It was the only thing I had from my mother and I gave it to him, for you. I know what it's like to be left out in the cold."

A self deprecating smile briefly twisted his features. I refused to feel sorry for him and remained silent.

"I sometimes wonder, how things would have turned out if I had my powers at that time and I, not Micah, found you out in that field. I can't help thinking you were supposed to be mine! You and I make more sense than you and Micah. I wasn't chosen so I don't have to endure the Depacitor.

Never in history has any Guardian fallen in love and started a family. The extraction of their emotions prevents it. Do you really think you and Micah are going to have a 'happily ever after?'" he demanded but didn't wait for my response.

"If I had found you instead of Micah, everything would be different. I wouldn't have done what I did and Micah wouldn't be dying," he concluded.

I couldn't believe my ears. Had he actually deluded himself into thinking he really had feelings for me?

"You don't care about me, Victor. You just want me because Micah wants me. You need to let go of your fixation on him, it's not healthy," I said.

I could feel a frosty chill spread from Victor's body, enveloping me. He was standing too close.

"You and I belong together, Adisa, for more reasons than you know. Someday, you'll come to realize that, like I have. When that day comes, I'll be waiting for you."

I shivered and took a couple steps back, seeking the natural warmth the day provided. My mind completely rejected his words as impossible. I would always love Micah.

Victor smiled and I hated the way it conveyed that he knew way more about me than I knew about myself. "One more thing Adisa. Aren't you wondering why Micah's father was notified in the first place?"

I swallowed hard, bracing myself for what he would say next, well aware at this advanced stage of his penchant for shocking me.

"Your father, Cyrus, is George Alexander's Sp. twin."

I actually staggered back a step. Victor paused, alert, but I stood firm after my initial faltering step.

"That's why I thought there was a possibility you were a superbeing," Victor resumed. "You are descended from a very powerful Mindbender, the strongest in modern times. It's truly a shame you're dormant. You would have had the makings for something truly great."

I had to concentrate on breathing in and out to keep me on my feet. My real father and Mr. Alexander were *super* twins. I tried to digest the information but it wouldn't go down easy.

Was Victor trying to mislead me again?

If what he said was true, that meant my real dad was the one who withdrew from the super world. The one Micah spoke of when he told me how his father was bitter when his super twin squandered his abilities by turning his back on his calling to be a Guardian and withdrawing from the super world altogether.

I hated that once again, it was Victor revealing a truth to me that Micah should have disclosed. But Micah couldn't bring himself to hurt me, even if it was the truth. He would only give me Sterling roses. I couldn't dwell on it. Instead I focused on what had gotten me into all this mess to begin with, saving Micah.

"Victor, I hate your guts for what you did to Micah. But, for his sake, I'm… I'm desperate. The prophecy says that Micah needs to fall in love with a Healer. I'm going to find her but I don't know anything about hunting one down. I thought maybe you could help me."

Victor observed me with his cool dark eyes. "You'd really give him up to somebody else?"

"This is Micah's life we're talking about here. Of course I'd give him up. He's too good to die. The world needs him... it's a mess. My happiness is insignificant compared to that."

"Have you told Micah about your plan to find a Healer?" he asked.

"Well, not exactly. And I'd appreciate it if you didn't tell him. I don't think he'd be very cooperative."

"Tell me about it," Victor said with dour humor. "I'd love to help you, Adisa. But I can't."

I couldn't believe he refused to help me. "Why not? I thought you wanted to save him you gutless selfish...,"

"Because there isn't one," he declared, his voice rising above mine. "That's why I tried to conduct a forced manifestation on you."

"What do you mean there isn't one?" I asked in alarm. There had to be one.

"One does not currently exist. There are always other Sp. beings who possess my powers and Micah's, even Jason's and your father's. But a Healer, is very rare. If one existed, believe me, I'd know. And I would've tracked her down a long time ago."

I was crushed. My plans had failed before I'd even started on them. I looked at Victor's brooding face and couldn't take it anymore. I had to get away.

"I guess, I don't have anything else to say to you then. Thanks for telling me about myself." I hesitated but then added, in a rush, "Sorry about biting your hand and thanks for the quilt."

I turned my back on him and left. How ironic that it would be cold blooded Victor who gave up something to keep me warm all those years ago. How galling that the quilt came from him, not my real parents. That meant my parents abandoned me with absolutely nothing.

When I got back to school, lunch time was already over. But I wasn't hungry anyway.

Micah was back when I went to math class but I didn't tell him about seeing Victor. He'd threatened Victor and I knew he would keep his word. I certainly didn't want to be responsible for that.

The morning of my party, I woke up, my dream still vivid. I could hear the little boy singing, feel the security of his hand in mine, the sensation of the soft warm quilt wrapped around me.

The little boy was Micah and he had defied his dad so I wouldn't spend the night alone in a cold cotton field.

I pulled out the new cell phone dad had given me after I told him my other one had been confiscated and lost during my 'quarantine.' The lie had come easily to me.

I knew it was early to be making social calls but I wanted to do it before I lost my nerve. After I got off the phone with Micah, I felt good about what I'd done. Micah had assured me he would bring Victor along when he and his family came to my party.

Just about everybody I invited came; the Alexanders and Victor, Avery and Liz, Fran and Dee, Lucia, and even Sonjia. There was also Beverly, and Kylie's date, Ryan. Fabian was about two boyfriends ago and now she was with Ryan.

There were no decorations this time, just good music, good food, and great times. I made up my mind, for tonight, I would try not to dwell on Micah's imminent death. Besides, anything could happen in those few short years.

"You never did answer my question about our graduation kiss," Micah reminded me when he had me cornered in the kitchen alone.

"Hold that thought. I'm supposed to rendezvous with your brother upstairs in my bedroom now."

"Victor?" He asked, working his features into a realistic mask of shocked jealousy. "I thought that wasn't allowed."

I laughed. "Very funny."

Micah's features softened into an easy smile. "Thanks for inviting him."

"No problem. I figured he could distract the ladies and give them something different to drool over besides you. I must admit, he's a lot more responsive to their advances than you've been. And the ladies seem to appreciate that quite a bit."

"Victor always has been quite the ladies man. Women are extremely attracted to him and he has no problem getting whatever he wants from them. Present company excluded of course."

I smiled. "That's because I have better taste in men."

Micah's hands went behind his back and he leaned in slowly. I shifted, to make it easier for him to avoid touching me unnecessarily and tilted my head as I closed my eyes, fully prepared to actually participate in this kiss. I'd been anticipating it as much as he had.

"Adisa! What's taking you so long?" Jason's indignant voice interrupted, calling from upstairs.

"I'm on my way," I sprang back guiltily, stepping around Micah and making a hasty retreat.

Once in my room, I pulled out Power Boy.

"Before he got his powers," I began, "Power Boy thought being a superhero was the greatest thing on earth. But when it happened to him, it was scary and confusing and hard. Things were strange and unpredictable and he wanted his powers to go away. For a time Power Boy even thought he was a freak."

Jason stood before me, silently hanging on my every word.

"But over time, he learned how to use his powers for good. And he saw how it made his life and the lives of those he cared about better. He learned to like himself.

Since then, I believe he's dedicated himself to helping others through their difficulties. I know he's helped me through a lot of hard times in my life. But I think I've learned all that I can from him. It's time for him to move on and help somebody else. The trouble is finding him a new home where he'll be cared for and appreciated. I was hoping that was you. But if you still think he sucks…,"

"I don't think that anymore," Jason earnestly assured me with wide eyes.

"Okay. Then he's yours," I said and without hesitation, I handed him over. It didn't hurt nearly as much as I thought it would.

Jason cradled him in his gloved hands. "Thanks Adisa. Wow. Thank you, thank you, thank you."

We headed back down together to rejoin the party.

"Come on. Let's show them what we learned in gym class this year," Sonjia suggested as she dragged Victor to the middle of the family room. He followed looking more than a little appreciatively at her ample curves. Everybody was crowded inside the family room.

"Let's Jive," Liz quickly agreed.

"Frances, do you believe this girl?" Dee interjected. "Compound fractures and lawsuit."

Fran followed up with, "She must be out of her mind, Delaney Rose. I cannot believe she would make that suggestion after we all witnessed the abuse Adisa perpetrated on Micah with that dance. In this small space, she could seriously injure her partner and innocent bystanders as well. Since I'm not trying to get kicked to death up in here, somebody needs to suggest a different dance cause I'll sue in a heart beat."

"Exactly what I was trying to say, compound fractures and lawsuit," Dee wrapped up.

"We can Rumba. I like to Rumba," Lucia suggested, looking hopefully at Ryan. She couldn't resist the opportunity to dance with a college boy and Beverly seemed permanently attached to Kelly's side. Since there was a shortage of guys, Kylie allowed her date to be used as an alternate.

"My personal favorite is the Paso Doble," Micah actually smirked. I couldn't even get mad at him. It was a special night and I was having too much fun.

Mom found some appropriate music and put it on. Micah and I had our moves down and Liz and Avery were pretty good too but the other girls had to walk their partners through the unfamiliar steps. Sonjia had Victor and Lucia had snagged Ryan. Beverly reluctantly partnered with Dee while Fran energetically instructed a shy Jason who vehemently refused to put down Power Boy or take off his gloves as she had asked.

While dancing, I tried to touch Micah as little as possible, aware that he still had a standing appointment with the Depacitor. I glanced over at dad to see how he was handling the sight of me in Micah's arms.

His eyes were sad, like they'd been since mom had the talk with him. An invisible wall had sprung up between us.

There wasn't a hint of anger in his posture. There was a time he would've dragged us both off the floor right in front of everybody and thrown Micah out. Now, he only looked sad and defeated.

I excused myself from Micah and walked over to dad.

"May I have this dance?" I asked, extending my hand.

Dad didn't budge. "I don't know how, String Bean."

"I'll show you... *dad*." Emotion suddenly welled up in my voice, infusing the word with all the love I'd experienced growing up in his home.

He smiled then, confidently taking my hand. I walked him through the motions. And I'm proud to say, I didn't hurt him at all.

Mr. and Mrs. Alexander surprised us with a very respectable Paso Doble of their own. Then Kelly and Kylie partnered and did a hilarious dance not even close to being a Paso Doble but definitely more entertaining.

The next song started and mom came and claimed dad for a dance. I watched them gazing into each other's eyes, their movements perfectly synchronized from years of a dedicated partnership.

I was lost in my thoughts about how much they loved each other when I heard Micah's voice whisper in my ear to meet him on the front porch swing.

When I made my way out, he was already there, casually swinging himself. I sat next to him, careful not to touch him.

He reached out his hand but I shook my head no.

"D.A.D.," he said in hushed tones even though nobody else was out.

"What does my dad have to do with it?" I asked.

"No. D.A.D.; damage already done," he emphasized. "We danced," he said to further clarify.

"Right," I said, remembering our brief Paso Doble in which we'd captured and released hands several times. I put my hand in his and we sat swinging in contentment.

"It doesn't forfeit our kiss, does it?" he asked.

But I didn't get a chance to answer him.

"I thought I'd find you two love birds out here," Victor said.

I instinctively froze at the mention of birds, thinking of the cuckoo. I certainly didn't want him bringing up my true parentage in front of Micah.

I withdrew my hand from Micah's and tensely watched as Victor casually walked over to the porch railing and sat down in front of us.

"Nice party," he said conversationally.

"Would you be more comfortable if we went back inside?" Micah offered, considerately.

And I almost said yes but then I thought defiantly, this is my house. I'm not running in my own home.

"Thank you, Victor," I answered, refusing to cower. "I'm glad you're enjoying yourself." When I tried, I had impeccable manners.

Victor smiled congenially as if recognizing my posturing for what it was, pure bravado.

"And such a perfect night for a party," he continued. "Reminds me of that time we were on assignment in D.C. for the Senator's family. Remember, Micah?"

Micah didn't answer, just stared at his twin without emotion.

"Oh that's right," Victor continued, unperturbed. "You don't like to discuss your assignments, unnecessarily. Pity, I'm sure Adisa would be extremely impressed. I bet there are a lot of things you haven't told her, no doubt out of some grand notion of not hurting her. You should open up more, brother. You'd be surprised by how strong she is and how much she already knows."

"What Senator?" I interjected, trying to cover Victor's obvious efforts to blab my secret to Micah. But I was also truly amazed that they, mere teenagers, would be assigned to someone as prestigious as a Senator.

"The Senator of Illinois," Victor said with a cryptic smile.

It took me only a few seconds to put it together.

"Barack Obama!?" I asked Micah in astonishment. But he still said nothing.

I turned to Victor. He had always been willing to tell me the truth, no matter how much it hurt or how sensitive the information.

He did not disappoint. "Yes," he said. Then, to astound me even more, he added offhand, "He's dormant you know."

I was much quicker this time.

"He's one of you!?" I asked, practically falling off the edge of my seat. Victor still had the power to shock me but I was beyond caring.

"True blood, straight from the motherland. His father was from Kenya," he said, smiling broadly at my reaction.

I marveled at the very idea. Then a significant thought occurred to me and I turned to Micah to ask. But seeing his nobly set and completely closed features, I swung back around to Victor. I didn't even need to ask out loud.

He nodded, "Yes, she's dormant too."

My excitement actually lifted me off the swing. "That means their children, the two girls, they're just like you and Jason," I said to Micah, hardly able to contain myself with this unbelievable information. How could he not have told me?

"Have they manifested?" I asked Victor, not even bothering to address Micah this time.

Victor was about to answer but Micah smoothly stood up between us.

"I think you've said enough for tonight, Victorio," he said as he practically lifted me to steer me back inside.

"Be careful of that one, brother, she bites," I heard Victor say before the door closed between us.

Micah refused to say any more on the subject as we rejoined my party. It went late into the night and the energetic music we danced to earlier, transitioned to slow rhythmic tunes that better suited the nostalgic mood that now permeated the atmosphere.

My classmates and I reminisced about the past school year and made predictions about the future one. Soon people were leaving and we were promising each other we'd stay in touch over the summer break.

The Alexanders left, taking Victor, who'd been a hit with the ladies, with them. I could see him and Micah walking together, talking as they lagged behind. I felt a twinge of regret that I hadn't gotten my graduation kiss.

Mom went to bed, worn out from all the preparations and dad stayed up to keep an eye on my sisters and their dates, who were the only guests left.

I considered going to bed, even though I wasn't the least bit tired, but didn't because I just couldn't pass up the opportunity to watch dad give the twins' dates the evil eye. It was a lot more entertaining when it wasn't Micah on the receiving end of it.

Micah returned as Kelly was setting up so we could watch some home movies. When he asked to speak to me privately out on the front porch, dad gruffly invited him to sit down and watch the home movies with us instead.

Micah sat next to me on the loveseat and it looked as if dad was seriously considering squeezing in between us even though there was no room for him. He finally chose the oversized recliner opposite the loveseat so he'd have the best vantage point to openly spy on us. The twins were on the sofa with their dates as the movie began.

The large screen TV suddenly filled with the image of me and my sisters jumping on the bed singing along with Alicia Key's Superwoman. We watched, laughing and arguing over which one of us looked the coolest in our towel.

The TV Kelly was swishing her long towel hair from side to side like she was Cher and we teased Beverly, calling him Sonny. Kylie's persona, was making dramatic eyes at the camera and the black towel on her head gave her a mysterious Egyptian look. If Ryan was crazy about her before, he was completely gone now as his eyes bulged out of the sockets in obvious admiration. He was looking back and forth between the girl sitting next to him and the one dancing and singing on TV as if he couldn't believe his good fortune. Then he practically pulled Kylie onto his lap and all three of us girls quickly looked over at dad in alarm. But like a guard who's fallen asleep at his post, dad was peacefully dozing in full recline. When the bed broke on screen and the three of us fell, we all tried not to wake dad with our laughter.

Then my sisters started roasting me, calling out flashes of my most memorable moments from the past year, starting with last summer; how I butchered my hair and what a shame there was no photographic evidence, my double date with Kelly and Beverly and what happened to that guy I treated like a leper anyway, nearly putting out Bartlett Avery's eye when he tried to kiss me at the Student Union dance and how close Micah had come to losing me to a college boy, me in the bus crash finally becoming a hero but sucking down drought-stricken Lake Lanier's water level by two more feet in the process, how I finally converted my sisters to superheroes on my birthday and we simultaneously started singing three superheroes jumping on the bed one fell out and bumped her head, how I really grew up when dad had his heart attack and what a tough break for me to find my birthcert... but Kelly nudged Kylie who guiltily changed the subject to the way I danced the Paso Doble with Micah nearly setting our house on fire, and climbing the mountain with Micah all those times must have brought us closer to more than just nature, and why didn't I run in the kitchen and whip up some of my famous meatloaf or chicken spinach and rice dish because it would've been a party hit, and that time Micah and I drove the twins to the mall in the jeep and they had that windblown look more like Hurricane Katrina look but my Jill Scott fro didn't have a hair out of place.

We had another whole year of memories to laugh it up, fuss about, and shed tears over around the dinner table.

Soon Kelly and Kylie drifted out onto the front porch with Beverly and Ryan, extending their good byes.

Micah and I went to the wall at the back of the hallway, to talk privately.

"You've been avoiding me all evening," he accused.

"I wonder why, Mr. 'My personal favorite is the Paso Doble,'" I mimicked his deep voice.

Micah dazzled me with his gorgeous smile. "Guilty," he admitted. Then he turned very serious. "I have something important to ask you."

I was ready. I'd already made up my mind to give him his graduation kiss. He'd agreed to my Birthday kiss and turnabout was fair play. I nervously licked my lips in anticipation.

"Adisa, will you marry me?"

I was on the verge of automatically saying yes when his real question registered. I stood, mouth agape, completely floored.

"I want us to be a family," he rushed on in explanation. "I can leave FLEET and spend all the time I have left with you."

It was like a dream, too good to be true. "When did you decide all this?" I asked, unable to wrap my mind around what was happening. A superhero had just asked me to marry him. Surely the sight of me leaping on the bed, my towel cape flapping in the wind didn't bring this about.

"I don't want you to be alone anymore. I want to be there for you and keep you safe."

"Micah, I'm not alone. I have my family...," then it dawned on me... family. Micah found out something about my family recently, sometime between when he left my party and now, causing him to return to talk to me privately.

I remembered him leaving my party with his family, lagging behind with Victor, talking. Victor! He must have finally told. Now Micah knew I was aware of my true identity and had been keeping it a secret all this time. Did he pity me? Was this some form of charity? One wildly delirious voice at the back of my mind was shouting *Who cares!*

I decided to listen to the more cautious one that asked *Why would Micah want to give up becoming a Guardian to marry me?* He had repeatedly made it clear that he wanted both.

"Why, all of a sudden, are you willing to leave FLEET?" I asked, cautiously.

He shrugged dismissively. "I want to marry you and FLEET is standing between us. As a married man, I'm going to want to go way beyond our contract. And I believe you'll have objections unless I stop burning. I'll have to quit my training for Guardian to do that."

My heart was pounding a mile a minute. "Is that all?" I asked, because I could tell he was still omitting.

"You're an extraordinary person, brave, warmhearted, smart, a great dancer and an incredible kisser. Why wouldn't I want to marry you?" He smiled at me with his gentle brown eyes but I could see he was still leaving something out; still offering only Sterling roses.

"You can lie by omission," I blurted out. "If you're going to stand there and tell me who I am, then tell me who I really am. I can take it so don't omit. Tell me, Micah! Who am I?"

He didn't want to hurt me, I could see that in his hesitation. He reached for me and I instinctively drew back. I needed to hear him say it. He had to tell me now.

"You're Adisa," he said and for a long while, that's all he could manage.

"You're the girl… I've loved since I was five and found you in a dark cotton field all alone. The girl who's parents left her there, out of love, so she would be safe. The girl who held my hand as I wrapped her in a quilt. The girl I sang to, who slept peacefully in my lap until morning." He paused remembering and I could see it too. It was no longer a dream but a memory, clear and immediate.

"The girl I watched ride away with a new family and couldn't bear to see her go. So I followed, to make sure she was okay. The girl I've visited over the years to make sure she stayed safe."

His eyes filled with admiration. "The girl I saw terrorized by her sisters but instead of curling up and taking it, gave it right back as good as she got." He smiled at me then, in remembrance and I smiled, remembering too.

"You're a fighter, your anger doesn't make you a bad person. It protects you. So don't worry, you'll learn to control it.

You're my lilac wine, sweet and intoxicating, making me do things I shouldn't… You help me be what I really want to be, a better man."

He touched the black pearl dangling around my neck for emphasis then finally said it, out loud.

"You're Adisa Summers… Valenté, first born of Pearl and Cyrus. You're the woman I want to spend the rest of my life with.

I love you, Adisa. Will you marry me?"

I went to him then, reaching for him without fear or anger. The fact that I wasn't a Healer didn't stop me. We were supposed to be together so I let him hold me. In that moment, I made up my mind, if I couldn't be a superbeing, I'd settle for the love of one.

"How long have you known?" Micah asked, his words muffled in my hair.

"About my parents, since my dad was in the hospital. I found my real birth certificate. But I only recently found out about you finding me in a cotton field and falling in love with me when you were five. What's up with that?"

He laughed at me and squeezed me tighter. It felt wonderful to be in his arms again.

"I watched you grow and the whole time, I just felt protective of you. But on the first day of school when I saw you in class... it was different. I've never felt this way about anybody in my life," he murmured, as he slowly started kissing me. I automatically tensed.

"No more burning," he whispered, reminding me of his offer to leave FLEET.

I felt a twinge of guilt as I thought of my real father, squandering his abilities. And then I thought of Mr. Alexander, facing the same thing again but this time it was his son instead of his brother rejecting his role as Guardian. But he still had Jason, who definitely wasn't dormant, to pin all his hopes on now. *What kind of married life can Micah and I have if he continues as a Guardian trainee and especially once he becomes a Guardian* I thought selfishly. He could take another position that wouldn't require him to burn or lose his love for me.

"Never run from me again, Adisa, and I promise, no more burning," Micah vowed, his voice full of emotion.

He gently reclaimed my lips, stiff with resistance, but his rhythmic motion reassured me, coaxing me to relax.

Release came slowly, freeing me to kiss him back without the horrible images of him burning terrorizing me. He wouldn't burn for this, at least not in this lifetime. My hands shyly moved over him, getting reacquainted after the long absence of touch.

His kisses were exhilarating as they deepened and changed into something more intimate. We held onto each other and I felt safe and cared for. He had finally confided in me, telling me everything. He loved me and I loved him. We would be a true family.

His breathing was coming faster and I felt dizzy from the rush of sensations coursing through me. I saw bright lights behind my closed eyelids and my heart beat so fast it hurt. I held my breath, overwhelmed and awed by my racing emotions.

Vivid images and flashing thoughts not my own assailed my mind, filling it to overflowing; the stronger ones boldly forward and the others swirling in jumbled confusion just beneath.

I could feel Micah's passionate emotions and felt his sorrow for my loneliness and disconnectedness. How did he know? I felt his regret for not telling me sooner about my Valenté roots and he agonized that I found out alone, too scared to confide in him. He was giving up his Guardian dream for me. I felt his anguish over this decision pushed aside by his determination to restore family to me and take me away from all the loneliness and pain I'd experienced.

Then I was suffocating in the woodsy smell of timber and tasted cottony insulation and felt cool smooth steel and plastic then rough grating bricks slide against me, so fast it felt like I was slipping through them. A wrenching noise engulfed me, tearing me from my world. My eyes flew open in shock when I hit the ground.

A great black blanket, full of twinkling stars stretched high above me. I immediately recognized what it was but it took a moment for my mind to adjust and accept it as the sky. I felt the itchy grass beneath me. How did I end up outside?

Micah! He must have been too rough, letting his emotions get away from him. His passion must have pushed me right through the wall!

I sat up ready to flip out on him for letting his emotions get out of control. How would we explain a gaping hole in the side of the house to my parents?

But there was no hole.

I placed my hand against the solid panels and brick to prove my eyes weren't playing tricks on me in the dark. That's when I felt a breeze on parts of my body that weren't supposed to be exposed to the elements.

I looked down and to my utter astonishment, discovered I didn't have a stitch of clothing on. I gasped in horror, hunching protectively over my nakedness while I quickly scanned our yard to see if anybody had seen me. What was going on?

I felt vulnerable; naked, alone, shivering and scared. I stayed crouched trying to conceal myself, as I looked around for a safe place to hide. I was at the back of the house and I would have to run across the open lawn, well lit by the bright full moon, to get to the woods. I could hear conversation drifting on the air from the twins and their dates, still engaged in the long good bye on the front porch and unaware of my predicament.

Then I thought of Micah and in the same instant, I distinctly remembered him saying, *Healers. They can go right through things...*

My whole body jolted with the realization. I passed through a wall. I was a Healer. I wasn't dormant. I could save Micah! My excitement was snuffed out before it could fully ignite when I heard somebody trying to unlock the patio door not far away.

Micah! He was looking for me. Oh no! I didn't care if I had to claw my way to the deepest recesses of Hell, I was NOT going to be lying out buck naked for all the world to see when Micah rounded that corner! He would not be witness to *that* humiliation.

Running across the yard for the sheltering trees was out of the question, Micah had a clear view of it. And the only thing worse than him finding me stretched out naked on the lawn, was him watching me bouncing in the breeze for several yards while I ran to conceal myself in the woods.

But I couldn't go around to the front door either. The twins would be merciless and there were boys there too. I could hear Micah finally unlocking the patio door and I panicked.

All I could focus on was getting back on the other side of that wall. But how? It was solid now. I'd knock myself out if I tried to run through it.

I heard the patio door sliding open and I held my breath, pressing myself firmly against the rough wall in desperation. My heart was hammering and my ears were ringing with the blood coursing in them.

I tried to become one with the wall, the bricks scratching my exposed skin. As I heard Micah step out, my mind desperately prayed *Please! Please! Please!*

I felt dizzy from lack of oxygen before I felt myself falling through. Again, I sensed the brick, steel, insulation, and timber as I fell. I hit the floor and opened my eyes.

I did it! I was back inside. I didn't know how I'd done it but I didn't waste time trying to figure it out. My clothes lay on the floor beneath me and I quickly scooped them up as I scrambled to my feet and ran up the stairs taking them two and three at a time. I dropped something but kept on going.

I had to make it to the safety of my room before anybody spotted me. Once inside, I slammed and locked my door. I hopped around my room, trying to contain my excitement, as I shoved my limbs back into my clothes, banging my leg on the nightstand in my frantic haste. *How in the world could I twice go through a brick wall and then get taken out by a little nightstand,* I thought rubbing my sore shin.

I didn't feel safe until my trembling fingers finally did up the last button of my outfit. I pulled on one of my shoes but couldn't find the other one so I collapsed on the floor, needing to compose myself before I went out to face Micah again.

My jumbled thoughts instantly converged on the kiss. Was that what put me through the wall? I more than felt the wall as I fell through, I could taste and smell it, sense its properties.

That must be how I knew and felt Micah's emotions, I fell through him, through his arms, holding me tight as we kissed. It was as if for a brief moment, I became one with whatever I was falling through.

While I was falling through Micah, I must have sensed his thoughts, a multitude of them and images too. But four thoughts stood out significantly; his shining wonder over our love, his sadness for giving up his Guardian dream, his dread of disappointing his father, and his pain for me discovering I was living a lie. His final decision to give up being a Guardian to become family with me for the few years he had left was a gift of sacrifice.

But now things were different. I went through a solid wall. I was a Healer. I could save him.

But how? Could I really learn to forgive and love Victor to save Micah? Or would I simply have to reach in and pull out the shard lodged in Micah's heart? Where would I fit in the super world? Would I now have to join FLEET to learn about my new life as a superbeing? Or would Micah and I follow the path my real father took and withdraw from the super world all together? And what about my real parents, were they still alive? Why did they abandon me all those years ago? Would I ever get to meet them in person?

I felt swamped by a multitude of questions. But I wasn't going to find the answers sitting on my bedroom floor.

I got up and left my room in search of Micah. He was at the bottom of the stairs patiently waiting for me, my missing shoe dangling in his hand.

I saw the glow of hope and love in his gentle eyes. I hesitated, overcome by what I could now offer him.

I'd been asleep for sixteen years. But no more. With my newfound power, I would try to do better, be better. I had to live up to the impossible gift I'd been given. I drew strength from Micah, knowing he would be by my side, helping me negotiate the new hurdles I now faced.

I started down the stairs more confident. There was an endless list of things I needed to do. I had to answer Micah's marriage proposal, get started on saving his life, and learn more about my real parents like why they left me naked and alone wandering out in a cotton field. I needed to find somebody to help me learn how to use my new powers and figure out how to keep my clothes on when going through things.

I forced my mind to stop its rambling and concentrated on Micah, the boy I loved, the superbeing I would save.

A single thrilling thought filled me as I finally reached Micah.

I'm awake now, so bring on the bad guys, I'm ready to save the world!

Author's Note

Many thanks to my daughter, KJ, for her dedicated efforts to make this story shine and to my husband, Kerry, for his encouragement and support.

The Atlanta Children's Shelter (where Adisa volunteered) is a real shelter that provides a variety of services to homeless children for free. You can learn more about this organization and make a donation at http://www.atlantachildrensshelter.com Tell them, Adisa sent you ☺

The Wesley Child Care Center in Cincinnati, Ohio is an organization dedicated to caring for children (I supported when GIANT SLAYERS was first released). Visit their web site at http://www.wesleychildcarecenter.com

ASLEEP is Book I of a trilogy.
AWAKE, Book II of the trilogy, will be available soon. For a Readers' Guide to ASLEEP and to learn more about Adisa and Micah's story, please visit my website at: www.wendyravenmcnair.com

Wendy Raven McNair

Sequel to *ASLEEP*

Awake

Book II of III

(PREVIEW)

Wendy Raven McNair

Seed of Betrayal

MY boyfriend's supposed to fly in today but not like you're probably thinking, safely tucked in a seat on a commercial airplane. No. Micah is literally flying, Superman style, from a paid assignment—the details of which are confidential. I know the assignment is extremely dangerous because when I asked Micah, he talked all around the subject but never answered it directly. That's what he does, omits, because he can't tell a lie.

My boyfriend is a superbeing.

Since he can't tell a lie, I made him promise to be back for the first day of school and that's tomorrow. I'm on my porch swing, the heat just this side of bearable, staring at his black jeep parked in his driveway, debating whether or not to cross the street to his house but I don't have the nerve. I'm not welcome there.

When Micah gave up training to become a Guardian, a prized position in the super world he's been groomed for since birth, his dad, Mr. Alexander, blamed me and now treats me like a pariah. He's done everything to break me and Micah up short of having me kidnapped and disposed of.

I decide to go for a jog through the neighborhood to distract me from the wait. As I pass Micah's house, I crane my neck to see if I can catch a glimpse of him. I'm being ridiculous because I know he would come find me right away if he was back.

Kelly and Kylie, my older twin sisters, are already back at Bartlett since their school started before mine this semester. I teased them about being mere sophomores since I'm a junior now but they're quick to point out that college sophomore tops high school junior and I can't argue with that.

At the end of my run I pass the Alexander home again and see Jason out front playing with a couple of other boys. I'm surprised because the Alexanders rarely have visitors.

"Hi Jason. Is your brother home?" I ask, jogging in place while using my T-shirt sleeve to wipe my sweaty face.

Jason and his friends look up startled as if they're up to something they're not supposed to be doing.

"Run for it!" one of the boys yell and all three take off for the back of the house.

I jog over to the bush they were standing near, thinking it's too hot for this foolishness. Singed leaves trailing down to a burned patch on the ground are still smoking. Those idiots were playing with fire! I take off after them then stop, deciding it would be better to let the Alexanders know what their seven year old son is up to.

I hurry onto the porch and ring the bell then wait impatiently. After the third ring with no answer, I head on around back. I spot the safety gloves Jason has been wearing all summer carelessly tossed on the ground and I'm instantly charged with fear. Jason isn't supposed to ever take them off in public. The two boys with him could get seriously hurt. I start running.

Jason is at the back of his yard and the two boys stand aside watching, clearly impressed as Jason spins a fiery ball on the tip of his finger. It looks like a flaming basketball and the heat is so intense, I can feel it even though I'm a few yards away.

"Jason!" an enraged voice bellows from behind me and I spin around to find Mr. Alexander standing in the back door. His furious expression shifts to a sickening look of horror.

To my shocked surprise I see why reflected in the large glass window. The fireball Jason was spinning is now hurtling straight toward me.

My breath catches as I duck and cover my head but I feel the burning blow of the fireball as I'm engulfed in flames. The taste of sulfur and smoke chokes me. I must be dreaming! This can't be happening to me but it is.

I'm on fire. Suddenly, I feel a chilly blast of water and I scream because the icy stream is far more painful than the fireball was. I roll on the ground trying to get away from the freezing water.

"Jason, put your gloves back on and put that fire out! And you two, get inside and wait in the game room until I get there. Move!" Mr. Alexander barks his orders and I hear feet instantly spring into action.

I lower my arms and see Mr. Alexander standing over me with a water hose that's only dripping now.

"You can get up now," he states calmly. "You're not hurt."

But I'm not so sure. I look at myself. My clothes are burned but I'm not even singed. I look at Mr. Alexander in surprised relief.

"It must have gone right through me…," I begin before I remember my promise to Micah. I said I wouldn't tell anyone.

But it's too late. Mr. Alexander heard and he understands. He drops the water hose and yanks me to my feet. In the process, my burned clothes reveal more than he expected and he quickly releases me as I gather the shreds of my top and try to keep myself covered. How would I explain this to my parents?

Mr. Alexander pulls off his shirt over his head and hands it to me, turning his eyes away as I take it with trembling hands.

"Thank you," automatically pops out, my good manners coming out even under these extraordinary circumstances.

I turn away and quickly pull on the oversized top. I'm barely done when I feel Mr. Alexander's vise grip on my arm and he's dragging me inside the house.

I see the large glass window is shattered and Jason has just finished using a fire extinguisher to put out the flames inside the kitchen. The counter is completely destroyed. Jason has a pained expression on his face as he tries not to look directly at me. I realize he must have had lots of training to be so efficient at putting out a fire.

"Good job son," Mr. Alexander says and he doesn't sound as upset anymore. "Go on up to your room and we'll talk later."

"It was an accident…," Jason's anxious voice begins to explain as his now glove clad hands set the extuinguisher on the floor but his dad cuts him off.

"I know, I startled you. You didn't do it on purpose. Now go on upstairs."

Jason glances guiltily at me and I want to assure him that I'm okay but he's gone, heading for the stairs in a flash.

I don't have time to worry about him as Mr. Alexander pulls me along. We pass through the game room, his grip still firm, and the two boys are seated on a bench looking equal parts awed and scared. The room is filled with oversized game machines the likes I've never seen before.

"When my wife gets back, I'll have her run you two back home. In the mean time, stay in this room and you're welcome to play any of the games you want," he tells them.

"Are you going to arrest us?" one of the boys asks but they are both staring at me.

"Not this time. But you have to promise me something, you never mention this to anybody; not a word about it, *ever*."

They quickly agree then Mr. Alexander takes me to a room at the front of the house that I'm familiar with, his home office.

He closes the door before finally releasing me. I rub my arm wondering how a fireball could pass right through me but I couldn't slip through his painful grip. Micah told me his dad is dormant, no superpowers, so I should at least be able to defeat him. However, it's obvious that even though I possess a superpower, in my untrained state, I'm not a real challenge to him.

"I believe hot tea is your preference, straight, if memory serves," he says as he retrieves a fresh shirt from a closet and puts it on.

I decline his offer and he sits behind his desk. "Suit yourself. Have a seat."

The office is sparsely furnished so there's only one other place to sit. I apprehensively ease into the vacant chair and the backs of my thighs feel sticky against the surface.

"So, how long have you known that you're a Healer?" he asks harshly, coming right out with it.

I consider feigning ignorance but we've been in this position before. The last time was in his office at the police station where he interrogated me about my relationship with Micah. Thanks to me, he knew far more than a father should about his grown son's intimate business. But that seems like ages ago. This is the first time he's spoken to me since Micah informed him he was quitting FLEET, a secret organization that was training Micah to become a Guardian before he dropped out to be with me.

"Was it when you healed your father?" Mr. Alexander asks impatiently when I don't respond.

I shake my head no, recalling my dad's miraculous recovery from a heart attack. At the time, I didn't realize I was the one who'd cured him. I still found it hard to believe especially in light of my recent failures with Micah.

I think of Micah's passionate kiss during my graduation party and all the sensations I felt as I fell through his arms. I feel as if I'm right back in Mr. Alexander's police office, revealing embarrassing details about my relationship with his son. I decide to leave out the kissing part this time.

"During my graduation party, I accidentally went through a wall," I admit.

"You've known all summer," he asks in disbelief and I guiltily nod once.

"Does Micah know?"

I nod again.

Mr. Alexander's face is grim. "Why didn't either of you tell me?"

I look at him without a word. He already knows why, probably better than I do. Micah doesn't trust him.

He sits back in resignation. "I guess it's my fault, the way I've handled everything. But surely you understand, Adisa. You've always seemed the more reasonable one."

I look down at my hands, busy worrying the hem of his oversized shirt.

"My son is dying!" he exclaims and I jump, his harsh words revealing the depths of his anxiety. "And you have the power to save him. What kind of game are you two playing?"

"We're not playing around. I've been trying to heal him but... it's not working. Micah says we have time...,"

"Not much," Mr. Alexander interjects. "Do you want him to die, Adisa?"

"No. I don't," I say as I shake my head for emphasis.

"Then why haven't you come to me or somebody at FLEET who can help?"

As a super organization, FLEET, the Future Law Enforcers Elite Team, would be the most knowledgeable place to turn to for help but Micah stubbornly refuses whenever I bring it up.

When I don't respond, Mr. Alexander continues, "I don't want to watch my son die... so I'm willing to help, but we have to do it my way."

I look at him then and he sees my desperation. All summer, since I found out I had the superpowers of a Healer, I've been trying to remove a deadly shard from Micah's heart. According to an African prophecy over a thousand years old, a Healer would cure Micah and I'm the only Healer in existence, so it was up to me to save him.

But something was wrong. All summer long, I've tried to penetrate Micah, pass my hand into his body, to remove the shard only to fail repeatedly.

In spite of Micah's confidence that we'll figure it out eventually, I'm beginning to have my doubts.

"What does your way involve?" I ask, fearing my words will lead me down a path I'll end up regretting.

Mr. Alexander smiles, he knows I'm desperately in love with his son and will do anything to save him. Something bitter takes root in me, a seed sending down its first tender shoots to lay claim on the barren ground of my attempts.

"I'll have to arrange things first," he says, cautiously, "and fill you in on the details later. For now, you can*not* say anything about this to anybody, especially Micah."

In resignation, I agree.

When Mr. Alexander asks, I can't think of an excuse to tell my parents about why my top is burned half off my body. He orders me to throw the burned material in his trashcan and tell my parents I dropped by his house to ask about Micah and ruined my top when Jason spilled spaghetti sauce on it so I borrowed his shirt. He always was good at coming up with lies to keep my parents in the dark about the super world.

I return home and fortunately, my parents don't see me so I don't have to lie to them. I go straight to my room and yank Mr. Alexander's shirt off.

I stare at my face in my restroom mirror, to see if I look different since I've formed a secret alliance with Mr. Alexander, carefully searching for physical evidence of my internal change. But I still have the same dark mahogany skin and thick afro now gathered in an oversized elastic band low on the back of my head. Was that a shadow of guilty accusation in my dark eyes, my full lips diminished by suppressed tension? I turn away unsettled.

I sit on the edge of my tub thinking about what just happened. Only a couple hours ago, I was anxiously yet happily anticipating Micah's return. Now I'm twisted inside, still wanting to see him but dreading it at the same time. I feel as if I've made a deal with the devil to save my boyfriend.

I fill the tub with hot water and completely submerge myself, seeking to rid myself of the sweaty grime from my run.

Micah calls later in the day. I'm thrilled to hear his voice, remembering a time he didn't understand the importance of calling somebody you cared about during a long absence. In his world, such courtesies aren't practiced and this cultural difference led to misunderstandings and heartache between us in the past. He once told me that they don't even practice the courtesy of greeting each other, explaining that since they usually sense the presence of others before actually seeing them, it isn't necessary.

"It's so good to hear your voice," I say into the cordless. I've brought it up to my room for privacy.

"I'm sorry I won't make it back tonight, they're adamant about me staying, but I'll be there to walk you to school tomorrow," the warm vibrations of his voice reassure me.

He can't lie so I know worst case, I'll be in his arms before school starts.

"Anything exciting happen today?" he asks when there's silence on my end.

"No." Unlike him, I *can* lie. Not all superbeings are burdened with that particular trait.

I try to envision where he's at but since he won't give me any details, my mind can only conjure up gray space around him.

"Have you been moping like this the whole time I've been gone?" he asks, well aware of my negative tendencies.

"I've kept myself busy. I finished my school shopping. Dad even let me take the car on my own after we dropped the twins off at Bartlett last weekend."

"Oh no, the twins didn't drag you off to a wild college party did they?"

I laugh at the mock jealousy in his voice. My beautiful sisters and their exploits with the opposite sex are legendary.

Unfortunately I don't possess their talents so Micah has nothing to worry about.

"No. Beverly transferred to Bartlett to be with Kelly and his presence has curbed her recklessness and Kylie is still with Ryan, a record for her, so things were pretty tame."

I listen to his breathing.

"I miss you so much," he says and I'm quiet, feeling the ache of our separation as deeply as he does.

When I'm finally in bed, drifting off, I pray for the dreamless sleep I used to have before I ever met Micah. But tonight I'm not so lucky and the nightmare comes.

Dead bodies are strewn all around me and I rush from one to the other, trying in vain to revive them. I try not to look at their faces because I don't want to see the accusation in their lifeless eyes. As usual, in the end, I can't resist... I look... and my heart swells in my throat, choking off my scream as I stare at the innocent faces forever asleep. The last body I turn over releases my pent up scream, to my horror it's Micah.

I surface from my nightmare the next morning, restless. I quickly get ready for school. Mom and dad are already gone to work, as usual, but they left a note for me wishing me well on my first day back to Talbot. I fold their message and put it in my pocket as I glance across the street at Micah's home. His jeep is still parked in the driveway. I walk along the sidewalk headed for Talbot. Micah isn't beside the tree where he used to wait for me when I was a sophomore.

I stand under his tree. He can't lie. He will come.

I start to get concerned when I remember he once said nothing short of *death*, could keep him from fulfilling a promise.

Suddenly, I am lifted from behind and I'm speeding through the air. Copper arms cradle me as the ground beneath me falls away and we turn into the dense woods.

"Micah!" I fume but I can't hide my joy.

We rocket past the trees, over around and between natural obstacles. Micah, unapologetic, flashes his gorgeous grin at me.

"Somebody could've seen you," I reprimand halfheartedly.

"Nobody's out," he counters.

Flying in his arms like this is like riding a rollercoaster. The dense greenery of the woods flash by on either side of us as he deftly makes hairpin turns, miraculously finding a path through the wall of foliage.

"Where are you taking me?" I ask breathless.

"We're here."

Micah gently lands on a wide ledge. I spot his backpack propped against a boulder as he puts me down.

"How long have you been here?" I ask as he leads me away from the edge.

"Not long."

He looks at me and I feel the usual rush of heat at the intense look in his eyes and expectant tilt of his head.

As he slowly moves in closer, I quickly press a kiss on his lips and then stand back.

"Take your shirt off," I demand in a hurry as I drop my backpack.

There's a mischievous gleam in his eyes. "Shouldn't we get a room first, preferably with one of those beds your father's so afraid we'll discover?"

"*Micah*, quit playing. We'll be late for school," I say, blushing at the mental image his words create.

He smiles as he unbuttons his shirt and slips it off.

I ignore the rapid beat of my pulse at the sight of his perfect bare chest and pull him to the ground with me. We face each other on our knees and Micah waits patiently as I vigorously rub my hands together.

"You know, when this actually works I won't *need* to take my shirt off," he says. "Not that I'm complaining."

I ignore his words and reach out, placing my hands over his heart, and close my eyes so I won't be distracted by his beautiful copper skin. I feel the rise and fall of his chest, his heart pumps out a healthy strong rhythm. It's hard to believe there's really something there, cutting his life short.

His hands, strong and sure, slowly slide up my arms and I shiver involuntarily from the trail of heat he traces up to my shoulders.

"Micah, stop. I'm trying to concentrate. You should be too."

"All right," he says as his hands reluctantly fall away.

I press on his chest, trying to remember what I was thinking and feeling when the fireball went through me. I frown in concentration seeing the fiery ball hurtling toward me in slow motion, I feel the flames, taste the smoke, breathe the sulfur... nothing.

So far, I've only been able to go through things *in*voluntarily. I've never intentionally permeated anything yet. Then I remember going back through the wall a second time when I first discovered my supernatural ability. I had to find the common thread between those permeations to figure out how to penetrate things at will.

I feel Micah's eyes on me, waiting. Mine are closed tight as I direct all my energy into my hands. I don't have a clue about what I'm doing or how this is supposed to work. No other Healer exists so there's nobody I can consult.

"Did you get to do some more research on Healers?" I ask Micah without opening my eyes.

"Yes but I didn't find anything new," he admits.

How can he be so calm and patient, like he doesn't care if he lives or dies? I press harder on his chest, leaning in with all my weight and he doesn't even budge.

"Aiieeerrhh," I scream in frustration as I shove away from him. My anger is a sickening heat at the pit of my stomach.

"Adisa don't," he says and he's reaching for me.

I let him take me in his arms and I wrap mine around him and bury my face in his chest.

"I thought it would work this time. I *really* thought it would work," my words are muffled.

"Why? Did something happen while I was gone?" he asks.

I consider telling him, almost do, but my fresh failure silences me. Mr. Alexander has connections in the super world. He might be able to help us and I don't want Micah to fight against it just because they are at odds.

"Micah, maybe we should tell somebody at FLEET," I manage to suggest.

I feel his body instantly tense up. He still doesn't trust them. In the past, at the urging of his dad, they opposed our relationship.

"You don't know how they operate, Adisa. They could end up separating us. I believe we can do this on our own. I'll keep researching, I'm bound to come across something soon."

"But it's taking so long and if we run out of time you'll...,"

"Shhh. Don't think about that. We have time." His soothing voice and the warm gentle pressure of his hands rubbing my back temporarily calm my fears.

He carefully lifts my face to his and the warmth in his hazel eyes is breathtaking.

"Now may I please get a proper welcome back," he teases and I can't help smiling.

My kiss is hesitant at first and I feel like Judas. Then the pressure of his lips on mine is more intent, and we're sliding and settling against each other in a familiar way. I hold onto him, trying to commit this moment to memory. My resolve is now strengthened; I won't let him slip away.

I used to dream of saving the world, now all I want is to save Micah.